*S*he vowed never to give her heart again—
until the barbarian laid siege to her land...
and claimed her as his pagan bride.

"IF EVER I WED, 'TWILL BE SOLELY
FOR MY DESIRE AND CONVENIENCE."

"How like a man," she whispered, "to wed solely to sate his lust."

"How like you to twist all I say into what 'tis not."

Eglantine arched a brow, inviting him to explain.

"If ever I wed, my lady Eglantine, 'twill be to a woman without whom I cannot draw a breath, a woman who has laid claim to my heart, a woman from whom I cannot bear to be parted."

Her lips quirked. "And you shall cast her over your shoulder in good barbarian fashion."

"I shall woo her until there is naught in her heart but me."

Eglantine swallowed visibly as she stared up at him. "Then woo Alienor," she suggested, her voice catching on the words.

Duncan let his gaze drift to her lips as he drew her closer. She caught her breath, her lips parting, and he knew with sudden clarity what he did want. "Nay, Eglantine," he whispered, his lips a finger's breadth from her own. "I cannot woo Alienor. 'Twould be far too simple to live without her presence."

Eglantine almost laughed. "You and your whimsy. Tell me where you will find a bride of finer birthright, of more noble lineage, of more beauty than Alienor?"

Duncan smiled, the word rising to his lips with such ease that he knew 'twas the truth. "Here."

The
Countess

Claire Delacroix

A Dell Book

Published by
Dell Publishing
a division of
Random House, Inc.
1540 Broadway
New York, New York 10036

Front Cover art by Alan Ayers
Insert art by Pino Daeni
Copyright © 2000 by Claire Delacroix, Inc.

ISBN: 0-440-23634-7

Printed in the United States of America

Published simultaneously in Canada

August 2000

10   9   8   7   6   5   4   3   2   1
OPM

In memory of Carol Backus—
collector of Scottish lore,
author,
and friend.

Blessed be.

Prologue

EGLANTINE HAD BEEN CERTAIN THEOBALD'S FUNERAL would be the worst of it, but she was wrong.

When she first awoke to the gray slant of rain, she had feared that she would not provide the example expected by the villeins of this small manor or—worse—that she would fail to mask her own feelings before her children.

Eglantine had managed both, though only barely, and she laid the credit before her brother's wife, Brigid. That sweet woman was so heavy with child, so sympathetic to Eglantine's loss, so obviously missing Guillaume, that it had been easy to be strong in her presence.

To be strong was Eglantine's gift, after all.

Eglantine's mother had arrived from the manor of Crevy-sur-Seine with Brigid, though nursing a cold. That woman's illness seemed to prompt her to keep her usually shrewd observations to herself.

'Twas a blessing.

For the first time in her life, Eglantine was glad that her brother had been called to the royal court, for she could not have faced him this day. She knew well enough that her husband Theobald had betrayed Guillaume's trust, a trust Guillaume had bestowed to ensure his sole sister's comfort. Eglantine chided herself silently, for she was glad to be spared Guillaume's discovery of how poorly Arnelaine had fared beneath Theobald's hand.

If only for the moment. The storm would undoubtedly come, but she would not have to face it this day.

'Twas not until all the mourners were departed that the true challenge assailed her. Louis, Arnelaine's châtelain, stepped out of the shadows of the silent hall. Without a word, he summoned Eglantine, something in his manner making her heart stop, then race anew.

She understood in that moment that matters were even worse than she imagined. How badly *had* Theobald managed Arnelaine? Eglantine was not certain she wanted to know.

'Twas unlike her to be a coward, though, so she followed Louis to the chamber where the manor's books were kept, acting as if naught were amiss.

'Twas strange to be ushered to the lord's place at the table. She ran her hands across the smooth wood, painfully aware that she sat in the place of her spouse—in his chair, at his table, with his papers arrayed before her—while Louis reviewed matters he should have discussed only with a man.

'Twas then that Eglantine realized she would never hear Theobald de Mayneris roar for more wine again.

Her unexpected grief surprised her with its intensity. She blinked back tears, unwilling to admit that she would miss in any way the man who had so carelessly cast her heart aside.

Though she had once loved Theobald, his behavior had made it clear that he had not loved her. Wed once for duty and once for what she believed was love, Eglantine had learned that marriage held no promise for her. At least—at twenty-eight summers of age and twice widowed—she would not have to embark on that fool's journey again.

Encouraged by such small mercies, Eglantine listened to the châtelain and realized she had missed much of what he had said. "I beg your pardon, Louis. I did not heed your inventory of the estate."

The older man glanced up, his gaze sharp. "There is no inventory, my lady."

Eglantine straightened at this odd news, knowing that Louis had always kept impeccable records. "How can that be?"

The châtelain looked discomfited. "Because the estate was not held by your spouse upon his demise."

Eglantine frowned. "Louis, Theobald was invested with the estate at my brother's behest. Has Guillaume retrieved the manor, as is his right, due to some disagreement?"

Louis shook his head. "Nay, Lord Guillaume has done naught."

"This is a poor jest, Louis." Eglantine spoke firmly. "We both know that a vassal has no right to relieve himself of a holding held in trust for his overlord."

"'Tis no jest, my lady." Louis's tone was equally firm. "There is no inventory because there are no books, and there are no books because there is no seal."

"What nonsense is this?"

"The books of the manor are no longer in my possession." Louis held Eglantine's astonished gaze as his voice dropped. "My lord Theobald may not have had the right, but he had the seal of this manor in his hand. I regret to inform you, my lady, that he wagered it and he lost."

Eglantine blinked, her composure slipping a fraction. "But that cannot be."

"Nonetheless, 'tis."

"But there must be an error, Louis. Theobald would not have been so foolish." Even as the words crossed her lips, Eglantine knew very well he could have been.

'Twas why her heart hammered so.

Louis said naught more so Eglantine leaned forward to argue on her dead spouse's behalf.

"Theobald would not have left Esmeraude with naught! Our daughter was his pride and joy, her future his sole concern!" 'Twas as if she would convince herself. "Esmeraude's dowry must be bought and all our bellies must be filled. There is *my* dowry held in trust, which is mine alone! Theobald would not be so remiss in his responsibilities as this!"

The châtelain rubbed his chin as he surveyed her, the gleam of sympathy in his eyes telling Eglantine more than she wanted to know. 'Twas clear Theobald would have done as much.

Because he had.

Eglantine dropped back into her chair and fought against her rising anger.

When Louis finally spoke, his words did little to reassure her. "He would not have been so rash when he was sober, certainly."

'Twas true enough and not a welcome reminder.

Eglantine pushed away from the table, rising to stare blindly out the narrow window. She rubbed her temples with her fingertips. The rain beat coldly against the stone, a trickle of it running into the chamber, the weather reflecting her glum mood.

The seal was gone.

Her brother Guillaume would have to pay the debts left by his vassal and brother by marriage, or lose this part of his holding. Eglantine knew that Guillaume would never suffer the loss of so much as a blade of grass of the family holding. Crevy-sur-Seine was his pride and joy, a close second only to his blushing bride.

Eglantine ached at the price her own folly would bring to her family. Why, oh why, had she been so smitten with Theobald? And why had she begged her brother to grant Theobald some small holding so that they might make a match?

Oh, she had cost her family dearly, there was no mistake of

that. And for what? A man who drank and gambled and cost her all.

And left her penniless to raise his child.

Eglantine heaved a sigh and turned back to the patient châtelain who had served her family all his life. "We have lost it all, Louis?"

The older man nodded his head, no more happy with the truth than she. "Every *denier*, child, every last cursed *denier*." For the first time in her recollection, Louis's words were heated. "Do not imagine that I did not try to stop him."

Eglantine summoned her composure, though 'twas more of a challenge than usual to act as expected. But she still was the daughter of Crevy, the lady of Arnelaine, the one to whom all would turn for answers, at least in the short term.

"I am certain that you did, Louis. Your loyalty to Crevy and my family is beyond reproach."

The châtelain bowed slightly. "I thank you, my lady."

"I shall ensure that Guillaume understands your efforts in this. 'Twas not your error, and I shall do my best to see that you do not pay for Theobald's folly."

"Again, I thank you. You have always been most gracious." Louis met her gaze steadily and his voice dropped lower, as if he feared he might step too far. "I would dare to suggest, my lady, that 'twas not your error either."

Eglantine was not so certain of that. She took her seat again, choosing not to reprimand Louis for his familiarity. "But I shall bear the price of it, you may be certain."

"If I may be so bold as to ask, my lady, what will you do?"

There was no point in artifice, Eglantine realized, for she trusted this man. She let her mask of confidence slip. "I do not know, Louis. Esmeraude will need a dowry, and . . ." Her voice faded, for she could not even think of the betrothal of her elder daughter, Jacqueline, without becoming angry.

No coin meant no ability to fight that marriage contract with Reynaud de Charmonte.

Eglantine frowned at the desk, deliberately speaking of her stepdaughter instead. "And I cannot turn away Alienor, even though she is not my own blood." She would be hard-pressed to salvage this situation, and she could not imagine where to begin.

Neither apparently could the châtelain, for he said naught.

Curse Theobald! At the very least, matters could not be worse. Whatever she did could only improve the situation.

They shared a moment's silence, then Louis offered a piece of parchment with a slight clearing of his throat. "This missive came from Charmonte this morn. 'Tis addressed to you."

"Charmonte?" Eglantine recoiled. "Already?"

"I am afraid so, my lady." Louis grimaced slightly, his manner reflecting Eglantine's thoughts. "Sadly, the betrothal agreement for your daughter Jacqueline is not missing from the former Lord d'Arnelaine's papers."

"That would have been against my current run of fortune."

They exchanged a quick wry smile as Eglantine reached across the desk. There was no point in avoiding the truth, though she was disturbed that word had come so quickly.

Reynaud de Charmonte was an old comrade of Eglantine's first spouse, Robert de Leyrossire. On the birth of Eglantine and Robert's daughter, a betrothal agreement with Reynaud had been negotiated. The arrangement had been too painfully familiar to her own circumstances for Eglantine to find it acceptable.

Robert, three decades older than Eglantine, had not been interested in her view.

Eglantine turned the missive in her hands, remembering all too well how miserable she had been in that match. She hated that she would be compelled to condemn her beloved daughter to the same unhappiness she had known.

But what choice did she have?

Eglantine now had no coin of her own.

Eglantine could not ask Guillaume to buy out the arrangement, especially not now that 'twas clear Theobald had served him so poorly.

Eglantine had no champion of her own with Theobald dead, not that he had been much of one while he still drew breath. Even her stepson by Robert had shown that he had no compassion for women. That, after all, was why Robert's daughter Alienor had come to Eglantine, seeking shelter when her own blood cast her out.

Eglantine heaved a sigh and placed Reynaud's missive on the desk, delaying the inevitable. "Grant me some consolation, Louis. Tell me that the holder of Arnelaine's seal is a compassionate man, one who will grant me the opportunity to set matters to rights."

"The tale, my lady, is not mine to tell." Sympathy gleamed in Louis's eyes and he conjured another document from his ledger. 'Twas tucked into the end paper and written upon fine vellum. Eglantine's heart skipped a beat when she spied her name scrawled across it in Theobald's familiar hand.

"Your lord left you naught but a letter, my lady." Louis handed it to her, then stood and bowed. "I hope it will explain matters more satisfactorily than I ever could."

Naught but a letter, its seal unbroken. Eglantine was not certain she wanted to open it either. 'Twas no less than Theobald's last words to her.

She did not trust him not to cast yet another shadow on her circumstances.

Ever-tactful Louis left her alone, closing the door behind himself. Eglantine crossed to the narrow window again, taking a deep breath of the cool breeze as she turned the letter in her hands.

She could smell Arnelaine's fields, the rich scent of the soil turned with manure before the winter. That mingled with the smell of the fires in the village nestled against the château walls and the sound of the river splashing in the wheel of the mill. The bell rang out from the chapel, a mournfully slow clang, reminding her all too well that the lord of the manor had passed from this earth and been laid to his rest this day.

But Theobald had not been lord of Arnelaine of late, though she had not known of it.

He had deceived her.

Eglantine tore open her spouse's letter, surprised at the heat of her anger. Theobald had betrayed not only her but her daughter, her stepdaughter, and the child they two had brought to light.

Eglantine had believed that at least she and her husband had shared an honest rapport, but clearly even that had been a lie.

The cur's letter was dated four months past.

My dearest Eglantine—

'Tis oft said that a man may not savor the view after a night of drinking and that is true enough of me on this morn. I have been foolish, not for the first time and probably not for the last, but I fear that this foolishness cannot be repaired.

Months past I took a wager, thinking it an easy one to win. 'Twas to ensure Esmeraude's future that I took this gamble, for I worry overmuch about our child's choices. I would have her wed a king, a prince, a lord of lords, and knew 'twas my responsibility to ensure she had the dowry to win the most deserving man to her side.

'Tis the irony of such matters that my deeds may well have precisely the opposite effect. 'Tis the way of the wine to make

me feel that Dame Fortune rides beside me, and more than once these past months, I have tried to set all to rights. Instead I have only made matters worse—last night, I lost the manor of Arnelaine itself.

I know 'tis not mine to lose, I know I had no right, but with the seal in my purse and the dice falling my way, I dared overmuch. 'Twas my intent to see this corrected, though I know now that 'tis a futile hope. After these past months of such efforts, there is naught left to my hand, naught with which I might wager, no honor left in my name which might compel others at least to courtesy.

This morn, I am faced with a dark realization. It is not unlikely that I shall fail in my quest to retrieve Arnelaine. This is no blight upon the man to whom I have lost your brother's holding, for this man of honor has granted me not only the opportunity to redress my error but the secrecy in which to do it. 'Tis by his generosity that we have been allowed to continue at Arnelaine as though naught was amiss, and to him I owe much.

Yet still, I write this confession to you, my own wife, the one soul destined to wring something from naught. If I succeed in correcting what I have done, then I shall burn this missive and you will never know the truth of my sorry secret. If you are reading these words, then 'tis because I have failed.

And you, you who loved me for what I pretended to be, will surely be dismayed. Though truly, Eglantine, if there is any who can make the most of little, 'tis you.

What I have to grant to you is little indeed. Here is my sole possession, the title to a distant holding, one which I have never seen. This Kinbeath was bestowed upon my father years ago. Truth be told, if any believed it had any value, I would have wagered it and likely you would not even hold it in your hand.

Kinbeath lies in distant Scotland, though its tale is perhaps worth the journey. 'Tis the way of the Celts to make a pagan wedding ceremony called a handfast. A couple pledge to live as one for a year and a day, and if all goes well, they swear at the end to keep all their days and nights together. 'Twas said by my father that this Kinbeath is believed a fortunate place to make such a vow, that locally all clamor to make their vows there.

Perhaps you and I should have made our pledges each to the other in Kinbeath. Perhaps then I would not be writing this missive, perhaps then I would not have failed so badly. Perhaps then you would regard me with other than disappointment in your eyes.

Perhaps then I might have been the man you once believed me to be.

But we did not and I am not. And instead of a fine fat dowry for Esmeraude, I leave you only the deed to a property held to be worthless, at least upon these shores.

Forgive me, Eglantine, if you can find it within your heart to do so. 'Twas not my intent to fail.

Eglantine ran her fingertip over Theobald's signature, the enclosed title falling to the floor unheeded. She traced the swirls of ink as tears obscured her vision, her heart aching with the memory of all the hopes she had once had.

She had been such a fool.

Unwitnessed, she buried her face in her hands and wept as never she permitted herself to do. Eglantine was alone but for her responsibilities and one worthless title, and felt more like a young girl than a woman widowed once again.

When thunder rumbled in the distance and the sky darkened, Eglantine straightened. She wiped her tears and found her composure once again.

She opened Reynaud's letter, every word feeding her dawning conviction to make a change in her circumstances.

My lady Eglantine—

Be advised that I shall arrive at Arnelaine in a fortnight's time. It is my understanding that your spouse has recently passed from this earth, and accordingly, arrangements have been made with the Abbess of Courbelle for your acceptance there as a novitiate. You are, however, welcome to linger at Arnelaine, as my guest, until the nuptials between Jacqueline and me are celebrated two months hence. I shall, with your certain agreement, be delighted to arrange for Esmeraude's marriage when she comes of age.

Please ensure that all is made ready for my arrival and that the keys to Arnelaine are entrusted to Jacqueline.

Reynaud had not signed his missive beyond a lazy R, but he had marked it heavily with red wax, imprinted so deeply with Arnelaine's seal that she could not have doubted the image. A second seal bore the arms of Charmonte, his home estate.

His letter motivated her as naught else might have done. Indeed, Eglantine's lips drew to a tight line at the sight of that seal.

So *this* was who had taken Theobald's wager! No wonder Theobald had been so evasive in naming the other man, for Eglantine had made no secret of her objections to Jacqueline's match.

Clearly, Reynaud de Charmonte paid no heed to Eglantine's objections to his marriage to her daughter and made to ensure that she had no right of protest.

And a *convent* for her! Eglantine would join no convent! How dare Reynaud make such an arrangement?

'Twas as if Eglantine were only so much baggage, and baggage that must be removed. Now the worst of her fears was confirmed. Although another lord might allow Guillaume to retain Arnelaine by the payment of Theobald's debts, Reynaud would not let the matter end so simply.

First he would ensure he had Jacqueline.

But a man who treated Eglantine in such manner would not make Jacqueline a fitting spouse. When he tired of his bride, would he dispose of her with such indifference as well? Eglantine guessed as much. As for Esmeraude, well, Eglantine heartily doubted that Reynaud's choice of spouse would suit her younger daughter any better than he himself suited Jacqueline!

She must ensure he did not win his way, for the sake of her daughters. Perhaps then Guillaume might regain his holding as well.

But what could she do?

Eglantine's first thought was to turn to her brother. But she had asked Guillaume repeatedly about Jacqueline's betrothal, and repeatedly he had quoted the law to her, albeit with apologies. 'Twas the way of a man of honor to uphold the law, and Eglantine knew that her brother would not be swayed to her side.

Men! Eglantine paced the chamber, hating the fact that her fate was yet again not her own.

There had been a time when she might have thought her friend Burke de Montvieux would champion her cause, but those days were gone. He was in love with his wife and enamored with his young son, and Eglantine knew she had no right to intrude on that happiness. Burke had persuaded her once of the merit of love; though that course had won her naught but trouble, Eglantine was tempted to find such love for her daughters.

What if even one of them might win the hand of a man like Burke?

'Twas a possibility that halted Eglantine's pacing. Aye, she

would not stand aside and let her daughters be compelled to repeat her own fate. They would not marry old men, they would
not be trapped in households hostile to them, they would not be
so much chattel in men's lives!

They would have the love of which Burke spoke so
eloquently.

Eglantine would ensure it. She crumpled Reynaud's missive
as though she could destroy his plans with that one gesture,
then flung the parchment across the room. She would not bow
to this man's will!

And she was not compelled to do so—because Theobald
had unwittingly granted her the means to make a difference.

'Twould not be an easy task, but the alternative was sufficiently unattractive to make her reckless. Eglantine picked
up the deed to faraway Kinbeath, a smile playing across
her lips.

She would take her daughters to Scotland, a place so distant that she could barely imagine it. Louis would go with
them, Eglantine was certain, for there was no future for him
beneath Reynaud's hand.

Aye, she would take any of the household willing to travel
with them, Reynaud's wishes be damned!

Once established at Kinbeath, Eglantine would launch her
own Bride Quest, not unlike that of the brothers Fitzgavin.
She straightened at the sheer good sense of the thought. Aye,
she would summon men to her court, she would persuade
them to undertake tests of valor, she would coax them to win
the hearts of their ladies fair!

Three particular ladies fair did come to mind. Eglantine
would ensure these men competed, the best of them winning the
hearts of her daughters three. 'Twould be just like an old *chanson*, just like the Bride Quest tale that already was recounted in
the halls hereabouts and in which Burke had participated.

Perhaps Theobald's legacy *would* bring more than he had

hoped. Eglantine lifted her chin and strode from the chamber, her footstep light with her brighter vision of the future. Perhaps she truly *could* wring something from naught.

For the sake of her daughters and their happiness, Eglantine certainly intended to try.

Chapter One

February 1177

EGLANTINE WAS GROWING TO LOATHE THEOBALD with a most uncharacteristic vigor.

Not only were they crossing a land of barbarians, but the weather was foul beyond expectation. They had traveled much longer and farther, under more primitive conditions, than Eglantine had ever expected.

And still they were not there. She had never imagined Christendom to be so very large. She was chilled to the bone, her wet wool traveling kirtle weighed more than could be imagined and, worst of all, her feet were nigh frozen. She cursed Theobald soundly beneath her breath as she rode, surprising herself with her creativity.

It could not be said that their passing went unnoticed. Eglantine traveled with a retinue of some fifty souls, including maids and squires, stablehands and scullery maids, cooks and a candle-maker, a seamstress and a saucemaker, a falconer and a stonecutter. She had borrowed a retinue of palfreys from Guillaume's stables, assuming that he would not want her to travel unprepared for every eventuality—along with, of course, the requisite trap and wagons, tents and pots, hunting dogs and tools.

The same rationale had prompted her to partake of her brother's treasury, though she had left him a note of apology for that. Her daughters' happiness, after all, rode in the balance, and Guillaume could well spare the coin.

But one eventuality for which Eglantine had not prepared was the cursed rain. 'Twas incessant, 'twas a burden
upon the soul. It turned the rough excuse for a road into
a river of mud, it frayed tempers thin, it prompted usually tranquil steeds to fight the bit and defy command.
'Twas no mystery why they found so few inhabitants in
these parts, nor indeed why Theobald's deed was held so
worthless.

Eglantine was more than prepared for a roof and a hearth
though none loomed ahead. "Surely, Louis, we draw near by
now?"

"I cannot say, my lady." The châtelain gestured to their local guide. "And he most certainly will not say."

The rough and rude individual hired to guide them was no
better than a crooked gnome from some child's tale, though
he kept a killing pace. He cackled incomprehensibly to himself and trotted ahead of the horses, his knobby knees moving in a blur, his pace one that the horses had trouble
matching in the mud.

Eglantine knew she had never seen a more ridiculous gar-
ment than his long yellow chemise. Leather sandals were
strapped to the guide's feet, but otherwise his legs were bare,
as crooked as the rest of him and decidedly hairy.

"In the manner of the Scots," Louis had supplied in response to Eglantine's incredulous stare upon introduction to
this creature. "The *leine chroich*, 'tis called, the saffron shirt,
though my pronunciation of the language of the Gaels may
be somewhat lacking. And I do question the availability of
saffron in such a cold clime. Perhaps they use other sources
for their dyes."

The man had been untroubled then by their obvious discussion of him and still did not appear to care that Eglantine conferred with Louis in familiar French. Louis had
taken it upon himself to develop a passing familiarity with

that language of the Gaels, a talent that had already served them well.

When they encountered other living souls, at least. Her palfrey's hooves made a sucking sound as the creature struggled to follow the guide. They passed yet another of the tall stones standing on end that seemed to fill this barren countryside, and Eglantine glared at it.

"One would think that even a land of barbarians could put this curious habit to better use," she commented to Louis. "Put a few of these stones together and one might have a wall, some thatching would make for a shelter far better than any we have enjoyed these few weeks."

"I believe I did warn you that 'twas not a land for tender sensibilities," Louis replied, and there was naught that might have been said to that.

Esmeraude began to wail, as she had done more or less constantly since leaving Arnelaine. Eglantine steeled herself against her own child's cry, her heart clenching in compassion. She knew all too well that her intervention would only make matters worse.

Eglantine cursed Theobald yet once again, this time for the child's dependence upon him alone. He had been so jealous of every moment Eglantine spent with the babe that it had seemed simpler to cede to his suggestion to use a wet nurse. But now Esmeraude was inconsolable without her papa or the wet nurse's teat. There was no prospect of either making an appearance soon in this sorry place.

Unless they had traveled all the way to hell. The faithless wet nurse earned a silent curse from Eglantine, too—they had not been long departed when it became clear the young girl lied about Esmeraude being weaned. Too late it was obvious that the wet nurse had not wanted to leave Crevy—and had been prepared to say whatever was necessary to so ensure it.

The toddler wailed, her cry echoing over the hills and setting the entire party's teeth on edge. Eglantine felt an ache begin to loom behind her temples. She hoped that Theobald *was* rotting in hell for his considerable list of sins.

Indeed, what else could go awry?

Their guide disappeared suddenly over a small rise ahead of them, his absence giving Eglantine a new fear. What if they did not draw near to Kinbeath at all? What if their guide led them astray? What if they had been led into a trap to be robbed?

Who would know?

Who would aid them? They were past the ends of the known world!

Eglantine and Louis exchanged a concerned look. Eglantine gave her steed her heels and crested the rise, with Louis fast behind.

But there was no one other than the guide lurking ahead. Eglantine was only briefly relieved, for her eye was drawn over the desolate landscape arrayed before her. The sea gleamed in the distance, the shadow of distant islands rising in the mist that shrouded the horizon. Birds wheeled overhead, their cries shrill.

They truly had come to the end of the world, for the sea continued to the very horizon.

The land stretched before her feet was rough and rugged, cut in sharp crags that fell into an angry sea. Another of those cursed stones stood on end just ahead, and at the edge of the point, a curious rounded tower stood, its roofline crumbling. The setting sun touched the stone with gold, as savage and forbidding a sight as she had ever seen.

"Ceinn-beithe," the guide croaked as he beamed at her, then gestured broadly to the land ahead.

Eglantine's heart sank to her chilled toes.

Despite his Gael pronunciation of the estate's name, she

immediately understood that they had arrived at their destination. Though the point itself was stony, a thick copse of trees grew a short distance away.

"But where is the manor?" she asked, fully expecting 'twas hidden by the trees.

The guide shrugged.

Eglantine frowned, in no mood for guessing games. "Where is the manor?" she demanded again, biting out each word even though she already guessed the truth. Her voice rose in frustration, though she knew that volume would not magically grant him understanding of her language. "The house? The dwelling? For the love of God, where is the stable? And the church? There must at least be a chapel!"

Louis translated but the guide shook his head slowly. He indicated the sky, then mimicked sleeping, his face on his folded hands, his smile beatific.

Eglantine understood him perfectly well. She swore with an eloquence that obviously startled her châtelain.

"It seems, my lady, that our guide heartily endorses slumber beneath the stars."

"This will not do! This cannot be so. We shall not sleep in the open air like barbarians." Eglantine reined in her temper with difficulty, heaved a deep breath, then continued with self-control more fitting of her position. "Louis, is our guide entirely certain that this is Kinbeath?"

The châtelain repeated the question in limping Gael and the guide nodded so emphatically that his meaning could not be missed. He launched into a monologue, complete with fulsome gesture, which obviously was an endorsement of the property and its charms, but Eglantine was not persuaded.

"What nonsense is this? *This* is Theobald's inheritance? It cannot be so!"

"If I may be so bold as to remind you, my lady, the title was held to be worthless."

Eglantine turned to her châtelain as a thought struck her. "Louis, can there be two holdings known as Kinbeath? Are we on the right estate?"

But the crooked little man shook his head and pointed, alien words falling quickly from his tongue.

Louis translated crisply. "Kinbeath, it seems, means the point of the birches, in the region's excuse for language. I am assured that not only were there once trees in abundance across the entire point, but that structure, known as a broch, is a fortification of considerable local renown." The older man cleared his throat. "Which perhaps is why those men have chosen to occupy it."

"Men?" Eglantine spun to look.

Only now she saw them, their garb blending in with the hues of the land, the shadows of the stones disguising their silhouettes and exact numbers. They watched her and her party, their stillness sending a chill down her spine.

There were quite a number of men. Large men. Dangerous-looking, unpredictable, barbarian men. Undoubtedly they were ruthless savages. Their uncompromising expressions did little to dissuade Eglantine of that conclusion. Indeed, she shivered.

Excitable chatter broke out in the ranks of her company, but Eglantine stared at the trespassers in silence and gritted her teeth. She had come all this way, faced every adversity, had her feet nigh frozen, only to be confronted with another challenge.

Would naught be simple in her life again?

But to turn back would be a surrender to Reynaud.

The price of comfort was still too high.

Indeed, Eglantine had faced worse foes than a ragtag company of illiterate men! No doubt they were lost, or vagrants who could be quickly encouraged to move elsewhere. If they wanted food or coin, she might share a small measure of bread. 'Twas better not to encourage beggars, after all, but she could afford to be somewhat charitable.

Indeed, they might be so awed by her manner that they would flee to whence they had come. One heard of such responses from barbarians faced with their betters. Louis cleared his throat pointedly, but Eglantine had no need for his advice in this moment.

She knew what she had to do.

She lifted her chin, giving her steed her heels. Lady of the manor, that was who she was, despite the state of her clothing and the absence of fine jewelry, despite the sorry condition of the manor she would claim. Her steed was not an old nag, and the creature seemed to sense her mood, for it stepped high with new vigor.

Eglantine felt every eye of her company follow her progress. The men before her folded their arms across their chests as they surveyed her approach. There were more of them than she had first realized.

Eglantine's heart began to hammer when one man stepped forward from the rest. He was tall and broad, wearing a saffron shirt of the same style as their crooked guide, though upon his broad shoulders, it had a certain élan. A length of wool was wound around his waist, the end cast over his shoulder. His bare legs were thickly muscled, his hair as black as midnight and all unruly waves. He was unshaven, unshod, and unamused.

The sight of him awakened a feminine awareness deep within Eglantine. Aye, she was not surprised that half the women she had seen in this land had been ripe with child, not if all the men were as ruggedly appealing as this one.

Fortunately, she was immune to the base allure of a barbarian. All the same, she noted that he was several hands taller than her and decided not to leave her saddle. That way she had the advantage of height.

And the ability to flee quickly, if necessary.

Aye, there was a glint of danger in this man's eyes, a determination in the line of his lips that did not bode well for her plan. He did not appear in the least bit intimidated—indeed, he seemed angered, as if *she* trespassed!

Though Eglantine knew that was not the case, there was a persuasiveness to the thought. The wind and the rain seemed to suit this man, seemed to make him look more aggressively male and more at home in this wild place, than she would ever be. Eglantine urged the steed forward at a quicker clip, as if to deny her uncertainties, and halted the beast with a flourish. She gripped the reins as the horse stamped.

The man propped his hands on his hips, tipping his head back to meet her gaze. His eyes were a stormy gray, not unlike the tempestuous sea behind him.

She had a sense that she faced a wild being, like the boars occasionally found in Crevy's woods, strong creatures that fought to their dying breath for their sole desire. The sole desire of the boars was to be free, to survive.

Eglantine wished that she knew what this man's sole desire might be.

His gaze swept over her assessingly, the appreciation in his eyes when his gaze met hers making Eglantine's flesh heat for the first time in days.

Aye, she knew what he desired.

A part of her shivered in response.

Two months amid barbarians and she became no better than they! Eglantine inhaled sharply and sat even taller, determined to maintain her noble bearing. She held his gaze with what she hoped was regal disdain, and braced herself for the inevitable vulgarity of his speech.

"Welcome to Ceinn-beithe, called Kinbeath by the Normans," he declared in smooth Norman French.

Eglantine barely kept her mouth from dropping open. Norman French was a vulgar approximation of true French, but she was temporarily silenced by this barbarian's fluency all the same.

"I am Duncan MacLaren, chieftain of Clan MacQuarrie, who holds sway over this land. I would suggest your party seek its amusement elsewhere, as you are trespassing."

Indignation quivered through Eglantine. "You may hold sway, but you do not hold title," she retorted with equal clarity, savoring the advantage of her educated speech. "Kinbeath is my holding by dint of law."

The hint of a smile touched his lips, though indeed no humor reached his eyes. The expression made Eglantine doubly wary of him.

This Duncan, she was forced to concede, looked like no man she had ever met before. Certainly none of her acquaintance had ever made her tingle with a mere glance!

Her uncharacteristic response obviously had more to do with her exhaustion than this man's presence. Indeed, in her experience, men were painfully predictable; surely he was no different.

"And how might you hold title to a land hereditary for eons?" Duncan's tone was mocking.

"Even hereditary land can be sold, as is more than clear, since this property was sold some ten summers past."

"Sold?" His brows drew together in a black furrow and he glared at her. "How can that be?"

Eglantine felt a quick stab of victory. She smiled coolly. "Surely even among barbarians, it is known that land can be traded for coin." A dangerous gleam claimed his eye, but Eglantine was not deterred. "This holding was sold to my family and passes now to me. By dint of law 'tis mine."

He took a hasty step toward her and it took all the fortitude within Eglantine not to retreat.

"Sold by whom?" His question was more of a growl, his eyes narrowed to dangerous slits.

"One Cormac MacQuarrie." Eglantine nodded as the name was clearly recognized by the man's companions. A whisper made its way through their ranks.

Her opponent, however, glowered at her. "This cannot be true!"

"Nonetheless 'tis." Eglantine shone her formal little smile over the company of men to no discernible effect. She would be gracious in victory, her fluttering pulse be damned. "I would suggest that you vacate my holding, as my party will require every last measure of it. We are quite numerous, as you may have noted."

She cast a deliberate eye over his party and nodded. "Much more numerous than your group of companions. Surely you can find another locale to better suit you?"

But this Duncan folded his arms across his chest. "I see no reason to move, purely on the assertion of a woman, a noble and a foreigner."

Eglantine's spine straightened at the list of her attributes, no less at how his tone cast them as liabilities. She glared at the man and was sorely tempted to embarrass him. "The king will endorse my claim."

Duncan arched a dark brow, unexpected mischief flashing in his eyes. "And we see so very much of good King William. Why, he could arrive at any moment." He repeated his assertion to his companions in their vulgar tongue and they laughed. That mocking smile claimed his lips as he met her gaze anew, a challenge lighting his eyes.

So, she was beyond the authority of the king. Eglantine should have expected no less.

But she was right and she knew it. And he expected her to simply back away, leaving him in control of her holding.

"Our lord king Dugall, King of the Isles, is rather unlikely to support your claim. He, in marked contrast, could be readily summoned." The cur smiled. "If the lady so desires."

Eglantine had not come so far as this to surrender to an arrogant pagan.

"There is no need for the king," she declared, "nor even his scribe, if you are lettered." Then she caught her breath and let her eyes widen in mock dismay. "But what is in my thoughts? How would a man learn to write in these remote lands?"

"Touché," he said wryly. There was no anger in his tone, and that smile played over his lips in a most disconcerting manner. "But of course I am lettered. A man's birthplace does not determine all he makes of himself."

Wretched creature! 'Twas twice he had surprised her, and Eglantine did not particularly care for the sensation.

And worse, she had a sense that she was amusing him, a most unwelcome situation. She was not in the habit of providing entertainment to rough men.

Eglantine unfurled the deed from her satchel. "Then, indeed, you may read the grant for yourself."

She expected the man to falter but he reached for it, and fearing suddenly that he would destroy it, she snatched it back.

His eyes flashed and she knew she had yet to truly see him angered. "How am I to read it unless you give it to me?"

"You will pledge to return it unscathed."

He smiled then. Eglantine's belly quivered, though she knew 'twas only because she faced a dangerous opponent. His gaze roamed over her once again, leaving her flesh oddly heated, and Eglantine acknowledged that the man posed an entirely different sort of threat than she had first imagined. He desired her—indeed, the most witless fool could not have misinterpreted the way he looked at her.

"And you would accept the pledge of a barbarian?" he asked, his tone almost teasing.

"Pledge on the hands of your father and your grandfather," Eglantine demanded, for she had learned from Louis that such a pledge was sacred to men in these parts.

Duncan arched a brow and she knew she had surprised him for a change. There was no chance to feel victorious, however, for he made the pledge and moved treacherously close to her. His gaze did not swerve from her own, and Eglantine was aware of naught but the simmering silver of his eyes.

Her breath caught as Duncan rested a hand upon her steed's bridle—as if he feared she would flee while he read—the evident strength of his tanned fingers snaring Eglantine's gaze. She cursed her feminine awareness of him.

Did she not know all she needed to know of men?

Aye, he was no different. With the deed in his hand, he forgot all else, his attention fixed on the document's contents. Eglantine breathed a sigh of relief that this at least conformed to expectation.

His thumb moved in a slow stroke across the front of her saddle, where he had gripped it, and Eglantine found herself transfixed by the motion of that tanned thumb. It moved slowly, as if memorizing the texture of the worn leather. An unwelcome part of her imagined that thumb sliding across flesh with the same deliberation, leaving a trail of heat in its wake.

Aye, there were some traits of men that were not without reward.

She flushed and straightened, forcing her thoughts back to more practical matters. Duncan frowned in concentration as he read the deed, his expression growing more ominous.

Until suddenly he smiled.

Eglantine blinked, but his delight was evident. There was a

sparkle in his eyes when he looked up at her, and Eglantine caught her breath at the change in his expression. On the verge of laughter, he looked young and playful.

'Twas not the response she had expected.

"'Tis signed by Cormac MacQuarrie," he said, as if this was of great import.

"Of course 'tis," Eglantine said crossly. "I already told you as much. Who is he?"

He looked away. "The former chieftain of the clan." His voice dropped low as he sobered. "He has been dead these two months."

He was so clearly grieved that Eglantine almost offered sympathy before she recalled that he wanted her land.

"If he were chieftain, that would indeed give him the right to sell the property, would it not?"

"It would." Duncan's gaze locked with Eglantine's once more and she was put in mind of the sea shimmering in the sunlight. "'Tis unfortunate that Cormac cannot provide an accounting of how this document came to be."

"No personal endorsement is necessary! His signature is *there*. I have the document and 'tis more than clear that he sold this land to another."

That roguish smile touched his lips fleetingly again. "Is it so clear as that, then?"

Eglantine's eyes narrowed. What did this vexing man know that she did not? 'Twas clear he knew *something*, and equally clear that he believed whatever 'twas to be to his advantage.

While Eglantine fought her urge to dispatch this Duncan to keep Theobald company in hell, the wind gusted suddenly. The skies launched an abrupt, cold, and intense volley of rain upon them.

And the ink ran down the parchment in Eglantine's hand.

"Nay!" Eglantine snatched up the deed in horror and shoved it beneath her cloak, hoping that the damage was not too extensive. She mopped at it beneath the shelter of her fur-lined cloak, relieved to see that only a measure of the text was now illegible.

Then she fired a lethal glance at her adversary. "I knew you would try to destroy it!"

Duncan shrugged amiably. "Perhaps 'tis the elements who would prefer not to endorse your claim."

"What madness is this?"

His eyes shone with unexpected devilry. "It has long been said that a ghost haunts this place—perhaps 'tis that phantom who challenges your suzerainty."

"A ghost!" Eglantine snorted. "Such tales are for children, and foolish ones at that." She tapped the document now safely out of the rain. "Any court would uphold my right, ghost or no ghost."

But Duncan eased closer, his voice dropping persuasively low. "Perhaps 'tis the souls of our forebears, whose blood stains the stones and whose tales are whispered by the wind, who would argue against your claim."

Eglantine shivered despite herself, then spared him a skeptical glance. "'Tis the law that is of import in this matter."

"Then seek yourself a court," Duncan suggested with a smug certainty she longed to defy. "I believe William's court is convened in Edinburgh, some weeks ride to the east."

"I know whence Edinburgh lies." Eglantine would never forget that town, for it had been the last place she had slept in warmth and dryness.

"Then I bid you a safe journey. Godspeed to you." Duncan bowed slightly, mockery in every line of his body, then turned to saunter back to his companions. Their confident grins exceeded Eglantine's tolerance.

"Nay Godspeed to you, Duncan MacLaren," she called after him, the determination in her voice obviously catching his ear. He glanced over his shoulder just in time to see her beckon regally to her company. Eglantine savored the sight of his surprise.

Then his gaze flew to her and Eglantine smiled. "We, of course, shall remain, precisely as planned. Kinbeath is mine by right of law, though you have every right to question that claim when next the king and his court pass this way." She widened her eyes deliberately. "Unless you choose to leave and seek that court immediately."

Duncan folded his arms across his chest anew, his humor dispelled. He looked as likely to move as the stones scattered across the point. "Is that a challenge that you would make?"

Eglantine lifted her chin. "Nay, 'tis a *guarantee* and one I shall keep."

His eyes shone, that smile tinging with what might have been admiration. Whatever 'twas, the sight made Eglantine's heart race anew. "And upon whose pledge do I have this challenge?" he demanded, his voice low once more.

"I am the countess Eglantine de Nemerres," Eglantine lied. Aye, though the title was hers no longer, she would take it as her own. And there was no estate that she knew of with such a name. This was her chance to foil any attempt Reynaud might make to follow Jacqueline here, by creating a new identity for herself. "I have come to establish my court upon the land to which I hold title."

Duncan's smile faded abruptly. "A court? Why found a court here?"

"Because 'tis my right. 'Tis here at Kinbeath that I shall found a holding to rival the finest in Christendom."

Duncan cast a dubious glance over the land, then looked back at her. Suddenly he threw back his head and laughed, the rich sound of his merriment echoing across the land.

Over *her* land. Eglantine fumed but her response made no impact on his laughter.

A madman, he could be naught else.

"I should like to witness that," he declared when he had exhausted his amusement, though his lips still twitched.

"Then leave Kinbeath to me and return in a year."

"Oh, nay. I should not wish to miss any of your triumph." Duncan's eyes gleamed in a most disconcerting manner and he strode closer, his hand landing upon her bridle.

He grinned up at her, at once the most engaging and unpredictable man Eglantine had ever encountered. "I shall indeed remain to watch, my lady Eglantine." Duncan tapped her knee boldly with a fingertip, his light touch sending sparks along her flesh. "Upon that you have *my* guarantee."

His hand rested boldly upon her knee. He stared up at her, his silver eyes dancing in challenge, as if he would dare her to move away. A glow spread from beneath the weight of his hand across Eglantine's flesh. It kindled a heat in her belly, a heat she could have comfortably been without. She stared into this man's eyes and remembered what 'twas like to claim pleasure herself.

"And, my lady," he murmured, his voice a low rumble of unwelcome intimacy, "the land is known as Ceinn-beithe."

"Kinbeath, I was told," she declared breathlessly.

"Then, Kin-beath, if you must," he insisted, those silvery eyes twinkling. He emphasized the soft "-th," the tip of his tongue pushing against his teeth, the sound slipping from his lips like a caress.

Eglantine felt her color rise, though 'twas not simply because she had mispronounced the name of her holding.

"Kinbeath," she echoed, suddenly aware of the harsh "-t" of the ending when the name fell from her lips. The sparkle in his eyes made her cheeks heat in mortification. Eglantine tried again, and again, despite a dawning awareness that she could not make that soft "-th" sound.

And Duncan, curse him, knew the truth all too well. He

grinned up at her, superior in his ability to properly say the name of a holding that Eglantine knew was her own.

"I could teach you to make the sound," he suggested, easing closer. His hand tightened on her knee, the knowing glint in those silvery eyes revealing his awareness of his effect upon her.

Aye, she knew what he wanted of her! Eglantine drew the reins up short and her horse stepped back abruptly.

Duncan smiled, folding his arms across his chest to watch her.

"It matters little what barbarians call my holding," she retorted. "Kinbeath is mine all the same." Then she smiled primly, granting him no opportunity to reply before she turned to issue orders to her company.

Eglantine could feel his gaze burning into her back, and her cursed knee was tingling from his touch. Aye, she could hear the way her name slipped across his tongue like a caress, his accent lingering exotically on the vowels.

Kinbea*th*. She played the sound in her thoughts and tried to move her tongue as he had done. Curse him! She could not make the sound—and 'twas vulgar of him to point out the truth!

Aye, Duncan was no more than a barbarian knave, enamored of his own charm. A coarse creature, common and base—indeed, he had no right to touch her! And he had no right upon her land. She would succeed in driving him from Kinbeath, she would secure her holding, if only to prove him utterly wrong.

'Twould be good for him.

And good for her to be rid of such trouble, she admitted silently, for she had no need of earthly temptations. 'Twas her daughters' futures that were her concern, her own liaisons with men a matter of the past.

Desire burned bright in her belly despite her resolve, as if 'twould remind Eglantine that Theobald was dead, not she. She sniffed as she approached her company, her chin held high. One touch of a barbarian and she forgot all she had ever known.

'Twould not happen again.

Chapter Two

EINN-BEITHE WAS A HEADLAND JUTTING INTO THE sea toward the isle of Mull. By legend, the point had once been thick with the birch trees for which it was named. There reputedly had once been a circle of stones here, and all had gathered to mark the rituals of passage.

But time had eroded both site and local memory. In these days, the point was devoid of trees and woad-painted priests, and but one of the great standing stones remained. 'Twas the largest, the eastern one, and it stood as a silent sentinel to the past of dimly recalled tales. Beyond, the trees still filled the space to the hills, a reminder that they had once grown thicker.

Duncan paced around the broch and considered his choices. The countess's arrival could have been his worst nightmare come true. A foreign noble not only held a title to Ceinn-beathe but had arrived to secure that claim and was intent on building a court.

He wished for the hundredth time that Cormac had not favored him with the responsibility of leading the clan. Cormac's choice made Duncan enemies among the very men he had to lead. More than one of them believed that Cormac's own blood son, Iain, should have been appointed chieftain, not the foster son who had come so late to the old chieftain's side.

And their support was critical if Duncan was to ensure the survival of Clan MacQuarrie. Dugall, King of the Isles, was a man disinclined to tolerate minor clans in his hegemony unless they could prove their military worth. Dugall wanted his perimeter secured and assigned the south to the men of Clan MacQuarrie—because Duncan alone had traveled south and knew much of the Anglo-Norman enemy.

Duncan had no choice but to succeed. He would not disservice Cormac's trust—but he had to make choices in his own way.

A bard, Duncan knew the value of tradition, language, rituals, and the tales a community of people tell of themselves. Ceinn-beithe was emblematic of their traditional way of life, a place valued for taking pledges. 'Twas a sacred spot, *their* sacred spot, and it could not be lost. So, Duncan had chosen Ceinn-beithe as his first objective and intended headquarters.

'Twas a happy coincidence that the site had strategic import as well, for it jutted into the sea, providing a view of incoming ships from west, north, and south. The broch was still defensible and of wide repute throughout the region.

The poet in Duncan understood what was at stake; the warrior within him knew what had to be done.

The Scottish king William, with his close ties to the Norman court, had a tendency to grant suzerainty of land to Norman lords, in marked defiance of the King of the Isles' claims to the same land. And once the Norman lords had built a fortification and armed it with knights, the land was difficult to reclaim.

Fortunately, the noble claiming this holding was neither Norman nor a knight. The countess was not only a woman, but undoubtedly one ill-prepared for the rigors of establishing a court here. The very fact that she traveled with such an enormous entourage did not hint at resilience.

And even more fortunately, the deed that she held was a forgery. Aye, Cormac MacQuarrie had taken pride in the fact that he was so illiterate that he could not even sign his name.

If the lady knew her deed was forged, Duncan doubted that she cared. Possession was the only law that troubled these arrogant nobles, and his challenge of her deed would not change that.

The better solution was simply to be rid of her.

"Well?" Gillemore demanded, matching his step to Duncan's own. "What does she desire?"

"She believes the land is hers to claim and means to build an abode here."

Gillemore spat in the grass. "Normans!"

"She is not Norman, Gillemore."

"Nay?"

"Nay, her French is too cleanly spoken and nigh difficult for me to comprehend. She is a foreigner, from farther abroad, perhaps a Frenchwoman."

"Bah! Nobles are all the same, seizing what they have no right to claim and forcing good people from their own land."

Though that might well be true in this instance, Duncan laid a hand on the older man's shoulder. "She will steal naught from us. If naught else, her foreign origins would leave her even less well prepared for the wildness of this place."

A hopeful light dawned in Gillemore's eyes, and Duncan realized that more of his men were following the conversation closely. "Aye?"

"Aye." Duncan's voice was firm. "Noblewomen loathe discomfort and travel only when necessary to secure their own selfish advantage. I have told her that we will not surrender Ceinn-beithe and she will not linger, particularly if the rain continues."

Gillemore, evidently encouraged, grinned and jabbed his

elbow into Duncan's ribs. "Aye, and what else did you learn of noblewomen, boy?"

Duncan smiled. "They have hearts wrought of stone, Gillemore, they are arrogant, they are selfish, and they spare no effort to turn others to their will. Though noblewomen may be beautiful, their beauty hides the darkness of their hearts."

Gillemore winked. "And we are led by the man who best understands these vipers." He clicked his tongue in satisfaction and walked away, hailing another to share the tale. Duncan was aware that more than one man's gaze rested assessingly upon him.

Norman or nay, this countess was precisely like the Norman noblewomen Duncan had met—haughty, cold, beautiful, manipulative. She had even shied from his touch, the condemnation in her eyes telling Duncan more than he needed to know of her opinion of him.

Not that he cared.

Nay, the issue of greater import was that she did not intend to leave immediately. Duncan recognized a formidable will when he met one, and if will alone could suffice, this countess would see the matter done.

But will alone could not establish a court. Duncan studied the lady for a long moment, as if he could unravel her motives as simply as that. The countess was slender, with a few tempting curves, her lips full and her manner crisp. To Duncan's dismay, she was possessed of startlingly green eyes, so clear that 'twas difficult to believe the woman had any capacity to lie. He would do well to recall that noblewomen were queens of deceit.

The Countess de Nemerres was tall for a woman, though still shorter than Duncan. She was probably fair of hair, though she kept her tresses demurely veiled, a habit that prompted unwelcome curiosity. Duncan told himself that the hue of her hair mattered naught, and could have believed it if he had not still been curious to know.

He deliberately wondered what had happened to the count, for there must have been such a man for her to hold her title of countess.

Had she expected to find her spouse established here already? Nay, no man would have surrendered the deed if he had planned to assert his claim first. And truly, the lady did not seem to expect a man to take her cause.

Duncan surmised that the count no longer strode this earth, though his widow seemed untroubled by her loss. The lady clearly had claimed the man's coin, for no expense had been spared in her retinue. What manner of widow would leave all she knew to make a new home abroad?

And then he guessed. What if this coolly composed countess had been the instrument of the count's demise?

Duncan's heart stilled. There was an intriguing possibility and one that certainly meshed with the selfish motivation of noblewomen. If she sought refuge from the law, that would explain her determination to stake a claim in this remote place. It would explain her determination to enforce even a deed that had no value.

He progressed no further in his thinking before a heavy hand landed on his shoulder.

"And so?" Iain demanded, scorn dripping from his words. "You do not appear to have dissuaded them from making camp."

"They will not persevere," Duncan replied with a shrug. "'Twill be but a day or two before they return to greater comfort."

"So we are to wait? Like women or dogs?" Iain made no effort to hide his disgust. "That is no way to secure a claim!"

Duncan granted his companion a disparaging glance, noting only then how his entire company watched this exchange as avidly as he watched the countess. "And what would you do?"

"Seize what is ours and make good our claim to the land!" A rumble of assent passed through the men. "We are men, not children, warriors who fight for what is rightly our own. We should slaughter them in their beds, we should seize the women for our pleasure, we should take their treasures for our own."

Duncan surveyed his opponent. "Aye? What manner of warrior slaughters women and children who cannot defend themselves?"

The men fell silent as color flooded Iain's face. "What manner of warrior stands aside while another seizes what should be his?" he retorted.

"Naught has been said of standing aside." Duncan's anger began to simmer. "There is naught to be lost in a measure of prudence. Should we move now, we might well find an army bent on revenge arriving with the sun."

Iain's lip curled. "Who would avenge this party?"

"Any noble might, for 'tis clear these are nobles of wealth, undoubtedly with many connections at court."

"One does not stir to war so readily as that."

"And what of the lady's spouse?" Duncan cast a hand toward the arrivals. "Does this not bear the look of half a household? Where are the knights and squires, the marshal, the ostler, the smith?"

Uncertainty dawned on the faces of his companions, and Duncan watched as Iain noted the change.

"No man would let his women travel unaccompanied," Iain snapped. "There will be no more."

Though Duncan suspected as much, he would be certain before he risked lives.

"No Gael would do as much, 'tis true, but 'tis too early to assume," he replied with authority. "The man might well have paused to raise a cup with his patron, with the king or another."

Iain remained visibly unconvinced.

Duncan continued with vigor. "He might have fallen ill, or lost a steed and thus be a day or two behind the lady's arrival. 'Twould not be the first time. He might well assume her safe enough with so much of his household in attendance. There could be a thousand reasons for his delay!"

Iain folded his arms across his chest. "Truly, Duncan, I always believed you made a better bard than a leader, and this day your tales prove me aright."

Duncan had had his fill of the insolence of Cormac's son.

"It matters not what you think of my leadership," he declared hotly. "I was chosen by Cormac and I am chieftain, regardless of your displeasure with the situation. 'Tis your duty to your father to support his choice. 'Tis your obligation to follow or leave, not to breed dissent among our numbers. We are weaker divided and you know it well."

"We are weaker poorly led."

"You would be weakest rashly led. For then you should all have to be buried and there would be none to do the labor."

"I say we attack by nightfall and make good our claim."

Duncan leaned closer, his words hot. "And what of the army who comes to enforce the lady's deed, which grants her the land?"

"What deed?" Iain was visibly shocked.

"She carries a deed, granting her title to Ceinn-beithe."

Glances of consternation were exchanged at this news and the men gathered closer. Iain frowned and stepped back.

Duncan continued, feeling the shift in Iain's support. "You would be murderers then and traitors under the king's own law, hunted men unwelcome at any court." He poked a finger into Iain's chest. "Even Dugall, King of the Isles, with his lack of affection for King William, would not rush to embrace a man upon whom he could not rely."

"We should seize the deed and shred it," Iain protested stridently. "That way there would be no tale of it forevermore."

"Destroying the deed will not remove the lady's claim, just as killing her party will not make their right in the law any less. There will be heirs, upon that you may rely, just as you may be sure that there was never a deed that existed without another to secure its claim." Duncan gave Iain a scathing glance. "Even *you* could not hope to kill them all and live to tell the tale."

The two men glared at each other.

Duncan took a step closer and lowered his voice. "Would you be mocked for all your days as a warrior who could not win his will from women without bloodshed?"

Iain's face darkened as the men began to chuckle.

"Cunning overcomes strength," Gillemore declared gleefully.

Though Gillemore's taste for proverbs could be annoying, Duncan welcomed this one.

"They will leave by the morn, by midday at the latest," Duncan informed his men. "No noblewoman will endure what she will undoubtedly see as harsh conditions. These are women raised in soft circumstances. We have but to wait to see Ceinn-beithe our own."

The men nodded and stepped back, appeased. Iain spat in the grass and strode away, his manner convincing Duncan that he had not heard the last of this trouble between them.

By dawn, Eglantine had persuaded herself that barbarian men possessed no allure whatsoever. That it had taken her the better part of the night to reach this conclusion was irrelevant, in her estimation; the important thing was that she had seen to the root of her own weakness and corrected the matter.

On their arrival, she had been troubled, tired, challenged, and facing only the first of the obstacles arrayed against her. And she was irked that their guide, having seen them to this wild place, had disappeared into the hills. It had not been easy to settle her company, given the inclement weather and the trials of both Alienor and Esmeraude. And there had been pledges to extricate from all involved that they not reveal her true name to anyone.

Siting a camp was not the easiest task, particularly in unfamiliar environs where one was uncertain of the pattern of rain and wind. Between herself and Louis, though, they had chosen a flat site a considerable distance from the broch that Duncan seemed unlikely to surrender. The pagan stone cast a shadow over the cluster of her company's tents, though Eglantine refused to see much import in that.

She had posted sentries for the night, distrusting Duncan and his men, whose numbers she could not accurately guess.

'Twas discomfort and anger that kept her awake that night. 'Twas guilt at involving her household in supporting her lie of being the Countess de Nemerres. 'Twas worry that she had not done enough to hide her destination, should Reynaud decide to pursue his betrothed.

'Twas not any tremble awakened by a heathen's rude touch that kept her from sleeping, nay, never that. Eglantine knew well enough that no rough man could be possessed of a whit of charm.

Even one who spoke some variant of French. She would spare no thought to the perfection of his pronounciation of Norman French, when she could not wring that cursed "-th" from her own lips.

She tried again in the privacy of her tent and muttered an

oath when the sound still would not fall from her lips. Eglantine swung from her pallet in frustration and paced.

How dare Duncan touch her knee! 'Twas only his appalling manners that caught her attention, that was the truth of it. Aye, he would be gone by this morn without doubt, bored and restless, seeking amusement elsewhere.

She most certainly would not provide the man's entertainment.

To be sure, she should be encouraged by the presence of Duncan and his men upon this land. If barbarians could survive in this barren place, then Eglantine, with her servants and supplies, most certainly could do so. That realization made her newly determined to see her will done. To be sure, she had had a shock the evening before, but she would still succeed.

A steady rain drummed on the roof of her tent as she dressed. She shivered at the chill in the air, then rubbed her feet, certain she would die a happy woman if they could be warm but once more.

Eglantine stepped out into a wet morning and compelled herself to find something about it that was not unpleasant. This was to be her home, after all, and she must make the best of matters. But for the life of her, she could find naught favorable in this gray, cold place that seemed to be wrought of rock and water and wind.

She stood and waited. Aye, there was something to be said for the tinge of salt in the wind. 'Twas invigorating, and she felt younger than her years.

'Twould have to do.

Given her thoughts, 'twas not surprising that Eglantine's gaze rose of its own accord to the broch, her heart hammering with hope that Duncan had chosen to leave.

But Dame Fortune had not smiled upon Eglantine this morn. Duncan was yet here. She could not pick him out from the ranks of his company, who already stirred. They were moving about, though she could not guess what they did at this hour.

Despite the rain. Eglantine stood and stared, her pulse skipping erratically. Disappointment, 'twas all. She had wished Duncan gone, yet he lingered. 'Twould be neither her first disappointment nor her last, she was certain.

She turned away and deliberately eyed her holding. She had hoped at least for a small manor, a shelter of some kind in this place, even a chapel, but other than that tumbling tower that Duncan occupied, there was not so much as a shed.

First, they had need of meat. She could not risk her vassals falling into ill health in this place, not before they had an herb garden flourishing, not before they had decent shelter. To hunt in the rain would be difficult, but that mattered naught. One did one's duties.

At that moment, Jacqueline stepped out of her tent, her smile bright. At fourteen summers of age, the girl was radiant in her innocence, and Eglantine watched her firstborn with pride. Jacqueline took a deep breath of the air, clearly unaware of her mother's presence so close by and oblivious to the poor weather. Jacqueline hugged herself and grinned, dancing in a little circle.

'Twas then she spied her mother.

She giggled and flushed as she had not done in a long time, flinging herself into Eglantine's embrace with childish abandon. "Oh, *Maman*, I love it here. Thank you so very much for bringing us away from Arnelaine."

Eglantine blinked even as her daughter kissed her warmly. "How can you love this wretched place?"

"How can you *not* love it?" Jacqueline crowed, lifting her hands to the sky. "'Tis wild and beautiful, 'tis peaceful and uncluttered."

"But the weather is most foul."

"Nay, *Maman*. 'Tis but a gentle rain." Jacqueline laughed and Eglantine supposed her skepticism was evident. "Look at the colors, feel the wind. There is no king, no court, no wicked obligations that must be kept." Jacqueline took a deep breath as if steeling herself for a foul deed. "I would aid you, *Maman,* however you might need my aid that we could stay."

"I go to hunt this morn," Eglantine admitted, knowing that would dispel her daughter's enthusiasm.

But the girl faltered for only a moment. "Let me come with you."

"But you hate the hunt!"

The girl lifted her chin, her lips set with resolve. "'Tis time I was of more assistance. You do too much for all of us, *Maman*."

Jacqueline smiled and 'twas as if the merry child she had been stood before Eglantine once more. Eglantine brushed the hair back from her daughter's temple with affection, pleased to see that the dread of Reynaud had already faded from her eyes.

'Twas worth any price, any hardship, to have her happy, carefree daughter back.

Eglantine slipped her arm around the girl's shoulders. "You shall have to feed Melusine the sweetmeats of the first kill," she teased, and Jacqueline grimaced comically.

"I shall do whatsoever is required," she said with a resolve Eglantine had not known she possessed.

Duncan had slept badly, with one ear cocked for the inevitable sounds of the countess's departure, sounds that never did carry to his ears. He was up well before the dawn, walking in the pearly mist as he pondered his choices. When the onslaught turned to a cold drizzle, his spirits lifted.

Aye, no countess would endure this! Duncan turned his

steps away from the wild coast and toward the lady's camp, intent on waving her farewell.

But few stirred in her camp. A trio of men simply armed stood around the smoldering fire, warming their hands and drinking some hot beverage. Duncan took the opportunity to slip closer unnoticed, as he could not have done while her vassals were awake.

The camp was considerable. In the midst of the haphazard settlement were three striped silk tents, their finery a notable contrast to their surroundings. He guessed one or all of these tents to be the abode of the lady herself.

No doubt the lady would slumber late in luxury. She would eventually rise and call for a bath, then order their departure after midday.

No sooner had the thought occurred to him than the lady proved him wrong. She emerged from her tent, stretched and arched her back, the move even observed at such distance making him keenly aware of her femininity. She was soon joined by a younger woman, perhaps one who had ridden behind her the day before, and they strode across the camp together.

Duncan was curious enough to trail behind, ensuring that he kept to the periphery of the camp and was not seen. His circuitous path meant that he fell a good bit behind the purposeful countess, and he rounded a corner in time to see her swing into her saddle.

But this was no departing party she led. Nay, only the other woman mounted a steed, the two women gathering their reins as the horses pranced impatiently. An older man clucked, then lifted something to the countess, who bent to receive it.

And Duncan understood as the countess gave her heels to her steed and rode toward him. She rode to the hunt!

The countess held her fist aloft, a hooded peregrine perched there with ribbons flying from its tethers. The bird was already wet, its feathers dark, though 'twas docile upon her hand. The lady was similarly dampened in the rain, her cloak hanging heavily over her shoulders.

Duncan moved into the shadows before she noted him, the image of her etched in his mind's eye. Her cloak had parted to reveal her kirtle wrought of a pale moss green, its hem and cuffs unadorned. A simple girdle emphasized the narrow span of her waist, the rough leather hunting glove making her appear particularly finely boned. As the horses cantered past his hiding spot, he felt a measure of admiration. She rode as if she were accustomed to the saddle, as if she were oblivious to the foul weather.

Duncan frowned. Surely she could not be so greedy for the thrill of the hunt that she would forget her own comfort? 'Twas hardly a morning when such activity could be enjoyed.

Although he had seen more than one noble unnaturally enamored of the hunt, so eager for entertainment that naught else could intervene.

'Twas precisely the sort of selfish indifference that Duncan loathed about the nobility. What irresponsibility to while away the morn with her falcon, as if she had no obligations to bear!

Duncan emerged from his spot to observe the departing countess. She rode with none but the other woman, a pair of boys running behind them.

If none would criticize the countess from her own household, he most certainly would do the honors. He strode after her, certain he would find an opportunity to have his say.

Here was Jacqueline's chance.

Her mother was not a woman of easy confidences and did not share anything of import where it might be overheard.

Ever since Eglantine had announced they would leave Arnelaine, Jacqueline had hoped this meant the breaking of her betrothal.

Eglantine had been evasive with details among the company, and truly, 'twas impossible to escape the listening ears of a company of such size while traveling. She had briskly changed the subject when asked once about Reynaud de Charmonte and been vague about her reasons for moving the household north.

Louis had been sour with disapproval, a fact that fed Jacqueline's hope that her mother had done something scandalous—such as destroy her daughter's betrothal agreement.

But there had been no chance to demand the fullness of the truth in privacy. Jacqueline had bitten her tongue all the way across France and the sea and most of Britain, awaiting her moment and itching with curiosity all the while. Every step persuaded her that she was right, but still she would hear the truth from her mother's lips.

And this was her chance. She rode to hunt in the silvery light just before the dawn, with her mother alone. Soon she would know for certain.

The raindrops hung on the deadened branches of the trees like crystals, then dropped on the thick bed of fallen leaves in a melody that no musician could repeat. Jacqueline had never guessed there could be so many hues of silver and gray, yet when she looked to the sea, she saw even more shades. The water was tinged with indigo and green and darkened to black, rife with shadows and secrets.

Even under other circumstances, Jacqueline would have done anything to remain in this wild yet oddly tranquil place. In her particular circumstances, she would do even more.

A pair of boys ran behind Eglantine's palfrey, laughing up at her, and that prized peregrine perched upon Eglantine's gloved fist. Her mother looked glorious and noble. She was gracious and lovely, composed and polite, and certain of what to say in every circumstance. Eglantine was perfect— and Jacqueline of late doubted that they shared any blood at all.

On this day, Jacqueline felt that she bumped along as elegantly as a lump of wet potter's clay. The contrast between her mother's smooth horsemanship and her own lack of grace was particularly strong.

Demons had claimed Jacqueline's body in the past year, for she accomplished naught with even her former measure of ease. At Arnelaine, she had fallen off steps that once she had leapt over, she had walked into doors, even now she burst into tears unexpectedly. She did not like the arrival of her courses, the eruption of her breasts, the changes in her body that made her look like a woman. She did not like the way men eyed her these days, as if she might make a fine meal.

Yet her mother had not only endured these changes but bore their mark elegantly. Where Jacqueline sprouted fulsome curves, her mother was lithe. While Jacqueline remained short, her mother was tall. While Jacqueline's hair was straight as sticks and the hue of straw, her mother's was wavy and honey-hued, like some gossamer confection of the angels.

To be sure, Jacqueline loved her mother—she merely wished that she was possessed so readily of such grace. Surely she might have inherited Eglantine's smooth assurance, instead of her father's shorter stature and awkward manner?

Jacqueline watched her mother talk to the peregrine, saw the hooded creature respond by bobbing its head. As long as she could recall, her mother had hunted with Melusine.

Jacqueline hated Melusine. More accurately, she hated what Melusine did—and she hated that her mother showed no fear of the terrifying creature. The bird was meant to kill, to tear and maim, and its cold eye instilled a healthy fear in Jacqueline.

Yet her mother cooed to it as if 'twere a harmless dove. Eglantine feared naught, while her daughter feared so very much.

The bird's festooned hood was removed and Melusine scanned the countryside with a steely purpose that made Jacqueline shiver. Her mother loosed the tethers and the hunting bird gave a cry. It took to the air, rising high to circle once over the women.

"She has been caged too long on this journey," her mother murmured. The raindrops briefly glinted off the bird, then its outspread wings were etched dark against the lightening sky. Jacqueline felt her usual measure of awe for its savage beauty.

"She is hungry." Eglantine tracked the bird's progress with her narrowed gaze. When the bird swooped and dove, talons extended, Jacqueline felt ill with the certainty of what was happening ahead.

Her mother, though, dug her heels into her steed with purpose, and she knew she had best do the same. By the time she caught up, her mother was dismounting with that enviable ease and striding toward the fresh kill.

Eglantine whistled, her peregrine so well trained that there was no need for the lure. With evident reluctance, the bird left the bloodied rabbit. It landed on Eglantine's upraised fist, the weight of impact making her hand momentarily dip to her waist.

Eglantine stroked the bird's throat, Melusine ruffling its feathers in what might have been pleasure. "Perhaps you might hood her, Jacqueline."

"Nay, not I!" Jacqueline eyed the dangerously sharp talons, the vicious beak, and backed away.

Her mother's level gaze seemed to see directly to her cowardice. "Then you would prefer to fetch the heart for her?"

Jacqueline's bile rose. She dreaded either option. She retrieved the hood with shaking fingers, but hesitated before the peregrine's cold gaze. "She will not let me do it."

"Of course she will. She is accustomed to it, after all." Eglantine's voice dropped and softened. "The secret is not to hesitate. She is a predator and alert to the scent of fear."

Still Jacqueline eyed the bird warily. It studied her coldly in return.

"You can do this if indeed you wish to aid me," her mother asserted softly, the confidence in her voice warming Jacqueline. "You have greater fortitude than you can begin to guess."

The warmth in her mother's eyes compelled Jacqueline to lift the hood. She moved quickly, surprised by her expertise, and hooded the bird without incident.

"Well done," Eglantine declared, the pair sharing a triumphant smile that buoyed the younger woman. "Now, don this extra glove and take Melusine."

Jacqueline's sense of victory was immediately dispelled. "Her talons will tear my flesh."

"Nay, the glove will protect you," Eglantine insisted. "Her grip will be tight, but you have only to move your fingers if 'tis too much to bear. Melusine knows her place."

Despite her doubts, Jacqueline believed the words. Her mother, after all, was always right.

A mere moment later, Jacqueline was holding the restless hunter on her own hand, her heart hammering in trepidation at the clench of those claws upon her fist. Eglantine moved quickly, taking her own dagger to gut the rabbit and remove the heart. She returned with the bloody souvenir in her gloved right hand and lifted her left fist for the bird.

"Ease her to my glove, just so," she urged in an undertone. "Exactly. Remove her hood slowly so as not to frighten her. See, she smells the meat!"

Jacqueline swallowed her gorge as the bird feasted greedily upon the treat, shaking it a little as if imagining a tussle. "You always feed Melusine from your hand."

"'Tis an old trick. It persuades her not to ignore the whistle because she could not survive without me."

"Surely that is a lie!"

"Surely 'tis. I cannot imagine that Melusine is so fool as to believe it, but she returns all the same. The falconer oft said she should be given cooked meat so as to deepen her dependence." Eglantine looked up quickly, a twinkle in her eye. "But I find it hard to believe that peregrines favor chicken stew with dumplings over their own fresh kill."

Jacqueline was startled that her mother did not abide by every rule she had been taught. "*You* broke the falconer's rule?"

"Oh, I have broken more than that!" Her mother's next comment was even more surprising. "I have broken the *law* in bringing us here, Jacqueline, and that is no small matter."

Jacqueline blinked, but 'twas yet her mother standing before her. "But why?"

"One must constantly steer a course, Jacqueline, between choices good and bad. 'Tis often difficult to decide what is the greater good, no less how to serve it." Her mother watched Jacqueline carefully over the peregrine as she considered that counsel. "You are sickened by this feeding."

'Twas not a question, but Jacqueline nodded. "I cannot bear to see innocent creatures die."

Her mother's gaze flicked to the bird then back to her daughter. "As such matters go, Melusine's killing is mercifully quick." She gave her daughter a stern look. "I am not fond of the hunt myself, but our company has traveled two months on slim rations. They have need of meat, of a hot stew in their bellies."

This Jacqueline understood better. "To ensure they do not fall ill?"

"Aye, and more than that. 'Twill prove to them that they have not traveled so far for naught. Meat is a symbol of home and hearth, of stability. 'Twill reassure more than their bellies."

Jacqueline almost smiled. "You sound as if they are your children."

Her mother's lips pursed. "'Tis the way of some to believe that noble birth confers only privilege. Your grandfather taught both me and your uncle that 'twas the mark of a true noble never to neglect his responsibilities. 'Tis our duty to ensure that our vassals are fed and clothed, have honest labor, and are defended against outside threat." She lifted one fair brow. "The greater good must be served, regardless of one's own preferences."

Jacqueline studied the bird, well aware of her mother's watchful gaze upon her, and decided to be bold. "How does calling yourself a countess serve the greater good? You have not been a countess since my father died—surely the title passes with the estate?"

Her mother laughed, much to Jacqueline's surprise. "Caught! You shall have to add 'liar' to my list of crimes."

Jacqueline stared at her mother. She took a deep breath then and asked, "What of Reynaud?"

Her mother eyed her for a long moment, then gestured to the boys to dress the first hare. She cried a command to the bird, which immediately took flight from her fist. She abruptly turned away, wiping her gloves on the grass, then shedding them as she straightened. Jacqueline feared that would be the end of their discussion, but her mother suddenly turned back to face her.

"Come. Melusine will not kill so soon after eating, and she will not flee after eating from my hand. Walk with me as I try to explain the inexplicable." Eglantine smiled wistfully at her daughter. "There was a time when I could simply tell you a thing was so because I said 'twas so, and you would have believed me. I see that those days are gone."

Chapter Three

JACQUELINE AND EGLANTINE WALKED IN SILENCE for a moment, the rain falling upon them like a soft mist. Its touch soothed Jacqueline's fears, though she watched her mother carefully, seeking some hint of her thoughts.

A rare frown pulled Eglantine's fair brows together. "I admit that matters might have been resolved differently had your father Robert lived to this day, or had Theobald not done as he did. But the truth in this is inescapable." Eglantine paused. "Do you know what happened fourteen summers past?"

"I was born?"

Her mother smiled in reminiscence. "That you were." She touched Jacqueline's cheek with a fingertip, marvel in her eyes. "My first child, and the light of all my days and nights thereafter. Never a greater gift could there have been. You have blossomed into beauty this past year, just as your grandfather predicted."

Her loving glance could not be interpreted as a lie, and Jacqueline felt herself blush. "But everything is so different . . ."

"You will become used to your beauty, Jacqueline."

"But I would rather look like you!"

"Me?" Her mother seemed surprised. "Just the sight of

you makes men's teeth ache with desire, child. You have curves and a lovely dimple and a sweetly generous nature." Eglantine kissed Jacqueline's temple. "This confusion will pass and you will see. Your grandfather, after all, was smitten at the sight of you, his first grandchild, and he fancied himself to have excellent regard for women. Do you remember him?"

"Nay."

"He had a stern eye and a robust laugh." Jacqueline thought she spied a tear in her mother's eye. "'Twas he who insisted I had named you wrongly and your name be changed."

This was news! "But what was my name?"

"I had called you Marie first and Jacqueline second. Jacqueline is your grandmother's given name, and seemed fitting as your grandfather said you were the image of her in youth." Eglantine paused to ponder. "How did he state it? Ah! That if you also possess his wife's disposition, 'twould be more fitting that you were named for her first and the Madonna second."

Jacqueline laughed along with her mother. "*Grandmère* does have a rare passion."

"Aye, that she does." Eglantine cast her daughter a side-long glance. "Do you know how old I was when you were born?"

Jacqueline shook her head.

"I was fourteen summers of age."

Jacqueline caught her breath, unable to imagine having a child at this moment of her own life. She half doubted her mother, but that woman smiled and nodded.

"Aye, 'tis true. 'Twas confusing to me, though perfectly predictable to all. I had been wed, after all, but ten months before."

Here was the tale of her parents' great love that Jacqueline had long desired to hear. "And you loved my father with all your heart and soul, just like a *chanson*!"

Her mother swallowed a laugh, her words wry. "I met him at the altar, Jacqueline, and 'twas not like a *chanson*. I was Robert's second wife. His first had died, though he had two children from that match."

"Alienor was one."

"Aye, as was Robert's son and heir. He was almost of an age with me, while Alienor was only four."

"Was she as spoiled and impossible then as she is now?" Jacqueline demanded, then caught her breath at her own lack of charity.

But Eglantine chuckled. "Aye, I believe she was."

Jacqueline looked at her mother with new eyes, struggling to think of Eglantine at her own age with a husband and a babe. And another woman's two children to raise, as well! A new wave of admiration swept through Jacqueline, buttressed by her own uncertainty that she could have managed as much.

They walked for a moment, then Jacqueline mustered her courage. "Why *did* you bring us here, *Maman*?"

Eglantine sighed. "Let me continue from the beginning. When my father commented on your beauty, your father saw fit to arrange your betrothal immediately."

"To Reynaud de Charmonte." Jacqueline could scarcely utter the man's name without bitterness falling from her tongue.

"Aye, he was Robert's friend."

Eglantine's mild manner, her apparent acceptance of this arrangement, was more than Jacqueline could bear. "But, *Maman,* how *could* you betroth me to such an old man? Even if you liked being wed to one, how could you do this to me?" Jacqueline clapped one hand over her mouth, certain she had said too much, but Eglantine eyed her steadily.

"Have I ever spoken poorly of your father to you?"

"Nay."

"Then I shall not begin to do so now." Eglantine walked away.

Jacqueline chased after her. "You let him do it!"

"I had no choice." Eglantine fairly marched through the grasses, and Jacqueline tripped more than once trying to match her pace. "At least, not then. My opinion was neither solicited nor welcomed in those days." She halted abruptly, scanning the sea as she took a deep breath.

Jacqueline stumbled to a halt, despairing that her body would ever follow her bidding again. Nay, she had been born to be short, buxom, and clumsy, of that there could be little doubt.

"What was my father like?"

"I barely recall," her mother admitted most unsatisfactorily. "Robert was thirty years my senior, a man active in protecting and expanding his estates." She smiled and shrugged. "Most of our encounters were abed and in the dark."

Jacqueline felt her cheeks heat, for she had never considered her parents' intimacy, and she could not hold her mother's gaze.

But Eglantine's words fell softly between them. "I could tell you that 'tis because of you that we journeyed here, that 'twas to save you from Reynaud that I launched this ordeal, but 'twould be a lie. 'Tis because of *me* that we are in this wretched place."

Jacqueline gaped at her mother, her heart stopping in dread. Surely she did not still have to wed that old toad?

"You know naught of what passed between your grandmother and me in those years of my first marriage for you were too young. 'Tis safe to say that I was deeply unhappy with her refusal to intervene in my own arranged betrothal, just as you are unhappy with me."

"Then how . . ."

Eglantine lifted a hand for silence, her voice flat, her eyes sad. "In hindsight, I see that she could not imagine that any ill would come of it, for her marriage had been arranged and she was deeply happy. All the same, I blush in recollection of the cruel things I said."

Her mother had been shrewish to her sweet grandmother? 'Twas impossible to believe, for they were so close.

"I could not condemn you to this match after my own experience." Eglantine turned to catch Jacqueline's gaze, the look in her eye as fierce as that of any peregrine. "But this choice was made for myself, for I would not have such bitterness, however briefly, between us. As a mother, I would not hear such accusations fall from the lips of my firstborn." She shook a finger at Jacqueline. "You will take no blame for my defiance, is that understood?

But Jacqueline understood only one part of what her mother implied. "I do not have to wed Reynaud?"

Her mother smiled. "We are here to ensure that you do not. None know our destination who were left behind—none but your grandmother whose lips are sealed forever. None whom we passed know our identity. I am a 'countess' to ensure that Reynaud never finds you. We do this, Jacqueline, so that you should not have to endure what I have already lived."

Eglantine lifted her chin and Jacqueline's mouth went dry. She saw her mother as a woman in her own right for the first time. She saw what Eglantine had known of marriage. She saw Eglantine's persistent hope, her conviction that better could be had and *must* be had, all for the elusive prize of Jacqueline's happiness.

They had left everything and everyone so that she would not have to wed Reynaud.

Jacqueline was humbled anew by her mother, though this

time by far more than grace and composure. 'Twas the self-lessness of her mother's character that shook her. The wind lifted the stray curls from Eglantine's braid, casting them against her cheeks, even as she held Jacqueline's gaze.

She suddenly wagged a finger at her astonished daughter. "But be aware of the truth in what I have always told you, Jacqueline. The first lie is easy—but it quickly requires another to support it. The web of deception I have begun will grow every day, though that will be my burden to bear." She touched Jacqueline's chin and kissed her cheeks, her voice turning husky. "But not yours, Jacqueline, not yours. This price is not yours to pay."

Jacqueline felt tears well in her eyes, though for once she was not ashamed of their appearance.

"I have learned but one thing in this life, Jacqueline," Eglantine said quietly, straightening like a queen. "One changes what one can, endures what one must, and prays for the best at every opportunity. I have made the change I can—now 'tis left to both of us to endure and pray for the best."

Jacqueline finally found her tongue. "Thank you, *Maman*!" she cried. Eglantine opened her arms and Jacqueline fell against her mother's chest. "I can never repay you for this, never never *never*!"

Eglantine kissed Jacqueline's brow gently. "Aye, you can, my child." She pulled back and surveyed Jacqueline. "You can find a true love, you can be happy, and you can prove my choice right." Her mother wrinkled her nose playfully. "You do know how I love to be proven right."

Jacqueline smiled through her tears. "I shall try my best, *Maman*."

Eglantine caught her close, her whisper hoarse. "A mother could ask for naught more."

Melusine screamed and Jacqueline pulled back to look

skyward. The bird circled above them and cried again, as if it would rebuke them. Eglantine laughed despite a suspicious shimmer in her eyes.

But her mother never wept, Jacqueline was certain of it.

"The greater good summons us to our labor anew, *Maman*," Jacqueline declared, and lifted her gloved fist for the bird. She would do whatever she could to ensure that they never returned to Crevy, or to Reynaud.

Even hunt.

As the predator landed heavily on her hand and her heart leapt in terror, Jacqueline knew even this was a small price to pay.

But they were not the only ones who hunted in that early morn. Eglantine straightened from the tenth rabbit that Melusine had killed, and a flicker of movement caught her eye. She spun quickly as the boy took the kill and saw a short shadow slip through the trees. It disappeared before she could discern precisely what 'twas. Four legs it had, though 'twas smaller of stature than the wolfhounds and moved with a stealth they did not possess.

The hunting dogs growled, the fur on the back of their necks bristling as they looked after the shadow. Eglantine exchanged a glance with Jacqueline, noting the girl's concern.

"What is it, *Maman*?"

Eglantine held up a hand for silence. The rain pattered on the ground and on the few deadened leaves still clinging to the trees. The branches of the trees rattled slightly in the wind, the sea sang in the distance as the surf broke against the shore. She heard naught else.

But there 'twas again.

'Twas no more than a dark fluttering between the tree trunks, at such a distance that it could not be readily observed. 'Twas smaller than either of the dogs accompanying them but fleet of foot. One of the dogs took a few steps forward and growled.

It could not be a fox, for such creatures avoided human contact. Her horse began to stamp, more troubled than the steed usually was. Its nostrils flared and its eyes widened, its fear telling Eglantine what she should have already guessed.

She eyed the blood of the butchered hares and knew 'twas a hungry predator that trailed them. Though she had only heard tales of wolves, she should have expected they would thrive in this remote place.

But because of her lack of foresight, Eglantine's small party was not equipped to face a wolf. They would cease the hunt and make do with the meat they had, and return to camp.

Melusine, though, cried from above before Eglantine could give an order. Eglantine turned and raised her fist with a whistle, but the bird had already spied her prey. Melusine dove, plummeting from the sky like a feathered spear, and the shadow moved like lightning in the same direction.

Three more shadows followed.

It seemed that hungry wolves were not fools.

"Nay!" Eglantine ran through the woods, hoping she would reach Melusine before the wolves did. They would kill the bird, of that she had no doubt, because Melusine would not allow her kill to be taken by any other than Eglantine. She gathered her skirts in two fistfuls and plunged through the forest, even as the boys shouted behind her. The dogs ran beside her, barking in anticipation of a fight.

Melusine gave a strangled cry. Eglantine burst into a small clearing to see the bird's talons buried deeply in an unfortunate hare. But the peregrine flapped awkwardly, her tether caught on a thorny shrub beneath her kill.

Four shadows separated themselves from the woods and

edged closer. Their eyes were cold, their gazes fixed upon Eglantine. She halted, uncertain what to do. The dogs snarled but she stayed them with a gesture, knowing that they would lose a battle with these wild creatures.

The largest wolf sidled closer to Melusine and the hare, one wary eye on Eglantine. The bird screamed outrage at the creature's boldness, the snagged tether impeding her ability to fight.

The wolf snarled at her and seemed to coil itself to spring. It was clearly not a stupid creature, for it had associated the bird's dive with freshly killed meat. Eglantine had heard many old tales of the cleverness of wolves, though she had never seen one. They had been driven from Crevy more than a century before.

Were they truly as fearsome as reputed? Did she have any options to save Melusine?

"It takes a particular kind of fool to step between a wolf and his meal."

Duncan MacLaren's words nigh made Eglantine jump from her skin. She spun to find him leaning against a tree, watchful and amused. Despite that, he looked no less wily, unpredictable, and dangerous than the wolf.

And no less inclined to pounce.

Jacqueline and the boys stood behind him, Jacqueline holding the reins of the steeds. Duncan evidently noted her glance for he shook his head. "I forbade them to come further. You are in peril here."

There was no heat in his words, and he seemed more interested in studying the wolf.

"Are they as vicious as they are reputed to be?"

His voice was deceptively soft. "Aye, when cornered, when hungered, when tempted."

"But I cannot leave Melusine to fend for herself. Her tether is caught, it inhibits her ability to defend herself, and that tether adorns her at my behest." Eglantine met Duncan's gaze, noting that he seemed surprised by her words. "How does one deceive a wolf?"

His smile was not without admiration. "Are you not afraid?"

"I am terrified. The beast seems wrought to fight, but that changes naught of my responsibility."

He pulled out his knife, cleaned its blade on his chemise. His eyes gleamed with intent, and he looked grimly purposeful. "'Tis not a task for a lady," he murmured, then moved with the same swift grace as the wolf. "Restrain your dogs."

The creature seemed to sense that it had met its match, for it crouched warily. The other three wolves backed away slightly, their poses cautious. Melusine flapped and struggled as Duncan eased toward her. He moved slowly but deliberately, with a grace and economy of movement Eglantine had not expected of him. His footsteps made no sound on the deadened grass.

When he stood half a dozen paces from the wolf, rabbit and peregrine midway between them, the wolf snarled a warning. It was claiming possession of the meat, of that Eglantine had no doubt.

Duncan stood still so long that Eglantine thought he had frozen in place. Just when she was convinced she could wait no longer, he lunged forward with the speed of lightning.

Duncan kicked the rabbit aside. The wolf leapt after the meat, its teeth flashing, not realizing that Duncan followed. He cut Melusine's tether without missing a step, then fell on the distracted wolf. The bird meanwhile flew high above. The wolf turned and snapped in surprise, but Duncan snatched at its snout and held it closed with one powerful hand. He drove his knife into its chest and jerked the blade hard.

The wolf sagged to the ground. Duncan wiped his blade

and sheathed it, meeting the gaze of each of the lingering trio of wolves as if challenging them.

They sniffed the air, then melted into the forest once more, becoming one with the shadows so quickly that they might not have been.

Duncan picked up the rabbit, examined it for damage, then offered it to Eglantine. "Your kill, my lady." He gave her a mocking bow.

And truly, the way he hunted made her activity look frivolrous and feminine. "I would have left them the rabbit."

He snorted. "And taught them that you are a source of food. 'Twould not be long before they entered your camp and feasted as they chose."

Eglantine had not thought of that. "I would never imagine that a wild creature would be so bold."

He smiled, then bent to gut the wolf with deft gestures. "They make much of opportunity."

She whistled and lifted her fist, relieved when Melusine immediately came to her. She hooded the bird and whispered to it, reassured to find it uninjured. She sensed that Duncan was watching her. "You have killed wolves before."

"Aye. Kill or be killed is often the choice of it." His eyes twinkled unexpectedly. "I have always preferred the former option."

"Will the others return?"

"Perhaps. Wolves are not unlike men, in that felling their leader leaves them uncertain how to proceed."

"I am surprised they do not linger to see what scraps you leave."

His features hardened. "They do not eat of their own."

'Twas as if he admired the savage creatures, and truly he seemed to have much in common with them. Perhaps they had an understanding of each other, all these wild creatures and men.

But a measure of civility was required. Eglantine took a deep breath. "I must thank you for your aid, no less for it being unexpected. I should think you would be relieved if I met with misfortune."

Duncan chuckled at that. "Ah, but, my lady, if you were to be killed here, there would be no one to lead your people away."

There was little she could say to that. She watched him work, curious at the difference in their ways. "Do you intend to eat its meat?"

"Nay. 'Tis strong and unfit for a meal." She saw that he trimmed the liver, dicing it in his hand before he tossed it toward her dogs. The hounds fell on the raw meat, consuming it with gusto. "There is little loss in giving your dogs a taste for wolf, if your cooks do not mind butchering it for them."

"Then there is no point in wasting it. I should be glad of the meat and 'twill be good for the dogs."

"Then 'tis yours." Leaving the offal on the ground, Duncan slung the wolf's carcass over his shoulder and strode back to her side, looking as if he did such deeds all the time.

The horses shied at the heavy scent of blood, but Jacqueline held their tethers fast. The boys regarded Duncan with undisguised admiration, and Eglantine could not completely hide how impressed she was by his courage and skill.

"I will keep only the pelt for myself." He held the tail toward her, daring her to touch it. "'Tis most soft."

She would not give him the satisfaction of balking at his challenge. Eglantine smiled coolly and touched the fur, its softness making her gasp. 'Twas a thousand shades of silver and gray, thick and luxuriant.

"More than one man has won a woman by offering her a bed heavy with such furs," Duncan murmured, a predatory gleam in his eyes. Eglantine felt that unwelcome heat of awareness once again, though she strove to hide her response.

She stepped back and eyed him. "Indeed? 'Twould be a simple woman who exchanged her future for no more than a few pelts." She marched away from him, mounting her steed and leading her party back to the camp. He strode along with them, silent and watchful, and she could not shake the sense that she had been rescued from one predator by another.

Duncan could not make sense of the fact that the countess would have sacrificed herself to save the bird. For a moment he had believed that her heart was not wrought of stone, that she had some compassion in her soul.

But then he realized the truth. A trained peregrine was an expensive frippery that none would be anxious to lose. Perhaps it had been a gift from a doting admirer, and she would have to answer for its loss.

Either way, she held the investment dear. And she was clearly one who loved the hunt at all costs, for this was not a morn that many would have ventured forth. 'Twas wet and damp, a morn that would have been better spent abed. Preferably abed with a dozen wolf pelts and a willing wench with soft thighs.

He wondered how soft Eglantine's thighs might be. Something heated in her gaze when he made suggestive commentary, the sight doing much to heat his own blood.

That she could bestow such a simmering glance, then put him out of her mind—as she clearly had—was sobering though. He had called her nature aright that first moment. She was manipulative, cold, and selfish.

He had best remember as much the next time she granted him such a look.

As they neared the awakening camp in silence, a child's cry rent the air. The countess turned her steed, seeking the child, her frustrated expression an ominous portent of that child's fate.

"Esmeraude!" she muttered.

The countess Eglantine dismounted with smooth economy, flung her reins to a servant, then strode toward the wailing child. She moved with lightning speed and was far closer to the child than he. Duncan cast aside the wolf carcass and darted after her, noting that even the maid bouncing the toddler looked alarmed by her lady's arrival.

If the countess struck that child, Duncan would see her pay!

"Give her to me," Eglantine commanded, much to the evident astonishment of the maid.

Closer proximity revealed that the child was richly garbed. She must be the unhappy toddler he had seen carried not far behind the countess upon her arrival.

Was this the lady's own child? If so, 'twas appalling—though not surprising—that her own babe was naught but an inconvenience to her.

"Enough is enough," declared the countess. The wide-eyed maid surrendered the child, who took one look at the noblewoman and screamed louder.

The child pounded her fists upon the countess and kicked savagely. Her face was red with fury. It sounded as if she wailed for "papa" though she was so distraught, 'twas hard to tell.

The child's blows made no apparent impact upon the countess, who stood as if wrought of stone. She must be very angry to so forget her own comfort.

Duncan pushed through the gathering throng even more quickly, fearing the worst.

"Esmeraude! Cease this nonsense," the countess said sternly. "I will no longer tolerate such behavior from my own blood."

'Twas her child!

But there was no triumph in calling matters aright, for the truth was too sad. Esmeraude clearly did not even recognize her own mother.

This countess must be one who thought others should raise her children. Duncan had never been able to believe that a woman with a shred of compassion could hand off her children after their birth and never trouble herself with them again—but he had seen it, time and again, in the south.

He did not like to see such behavior here. Why, this one could barely be weaned, yet the countess was slim and sleek. Clearly she was so vain that she refused to risk her figure in nursing her own child.

The countess gave the toddler a shake. "Esmeraude! We have had enough of these shows of temper."

Aye, the child could not be suffered to be inconvenient. 'Twas no wonder they all grew to be so cold when they were denied any love as children. Duncan's eyes narrowed, just as Esmeraude struck her mother's face so hard that she left a red handprint upon the countess's cheek.

The maid gasped and stepped away. The household froze, watching the countess for her inevitable retaliation.

But Duncan would not stand by. He stepped forward to intervene just as the lady put the child abruptly on the ground.

Duncan did not wait to see what she would do. Indeed, he did not so much as look at her. He crouched down beside the child, who was in such a frenzy that she did not even notice his presence. Esmeraude kicked and screamed, as if she would strike unseen adversaries, she bellowed loudly enough to wake the dead.

"Esmeraude," Duncan said firmly. "Now, there is a name befitting a princess."

Esmeraude, perhaps all of two summers old, stopped crying at the sound of his voice. She cast a wary glance about herself and immediately spied Duncan. She sat up, eyed him, sniffled, and hiccuped. The countess caught her breath, but Duncan would save his condemnation of her for later.

Aye, he looked forward to telling the lady his thoughts.

But for this moment, Duncan sat down on the grass, leaving a reasonable distance between himself and the child. He took a deep breath and spoke gently, for the child had undoubtedly seen enough abuse.

"Aye, I remember a song of a princess named Esmeraude." He glanced at the clearly curious child. "Would you like to hear it?"

Esmeraude nodded once, her expression turning coy. She granted him a half smile, obviously well aware of her own charm, and smoothed her kirtle over her dimpled knees.

Duncan fought to hide his surprise at her manner. "Well, you cannot cry or you will not hear the words." He spoke carefully, knowing she would find his French accented and difficult to comprehend. "You shall have to sit quietly or I shall halt the tale."

Esmeraude's lips pursed as she considered him. She was a pretty child and would undoubtedly become a lovely young woman. Her skin was fair, her face already heart-shaped. Her lips were so red 'twas as if they had been touched by carmine, their shape a perfect cupid's bow. Her eyes, a beguiling blue, were thickly lashed, her tousled curls the shade of flax.

"Tell! Sing now!" she insisted, raising her chin imperiously. This was one accustomed to having her way, of that there could be no doubt.

Duncan supposed he should have expected naught else.

At least, she had ceased to cry. And the countess had not struck the child. That was worth the telling of a tale. He turned to face the sea, rearranged the words to ensure that

'twas indeed about a princess named Esmeraude, then began
to sing.

> *There was a maiden Esmeraude,*
> *Her fairness paid sweet ode,*
> *In song from outside her abode,*
> *Beauteous charming Esmeraude.*

> *Esmeraude longed to know*
> *Who 'twas who sang so low.*
> *A kiss she vowed the man was owed,*
> *A kiss he'd have from Esmeraude.*

Esmeraude was clearly intrigued. She watched Duncan with
a hint of a smile touching her lips, her eyes shining, her
hands clasped.

> *None more surprised than Esmeraude—*
> *The minstrel proved to be a toad!*
> *He sang before her whole abode,*
> *Proving he crooned the sweet ode.*

> *The court whispered, but Esmeraude*
> *Her token did indeed bestow.*
> *All gasped when the small grey toad*
> *Became a prince, a fitting beau.*

> *The king, father of Esmeraude,*
> *Did upon the pair much wealth bestow.*
> *They wed and lived in a château,*
> *The toad prince and his Esmeraude.*

Esmeraude clapped her small hands with delight, easing
closer to Duncan. An appreciative ripple ran through the assembled company, though Duncan watched only the little girl.

"More!" she demanded, but he would not be another to satisfy this child's whim.

"Nay, that is enough for the moment."

"Again," Esmeraude insisted, offering him a pout that was probably supposed to be persuasive.

Duncan shook his head. He flicked a pointed glance at the countess and was surprised to find that her expression had softened. She looked for all the world like a relieved mother, one who adored her babe, though Duncan knew that could not be so.

She manipulated him apurpose and he had best remember as much. "Perhaps you should return to your mother."

Esmeraude looked crestfallen, but Duncan pushed to his feet, eager to put distance between himself and another noble-woman polishing her wares. The toddler looked from him to her mother, her attempts to summon tears so obvious that Duncan shook his head.

He hoped Esmeraude's thoughts would always remain so easily read, though he doubted that would be the case. Aye, she would learn from her mother, that much was certain, and would soon adopt the noblewoman's array of useful masks. Duncan felt his anger rise anew.

"I would speak with you," the countess said softly.

Her tone surprised Duncan. He reminded himself that the countess had wrought this situation herself, but still his anger wavered before her gentle manner. No doubt she knew 'twould be so, and he was annoyed with himself for being so readily manipulated.

Had he learned naught on his journey south?

Duncan's words were curt, his annoyance as much with himself as the countess. "What of the child?"

Eglantine smiled sadly, an expression that wrenched Duncan's poet's heart no less than her words. "I trust she would be happier without me."

"I shall take her, my lady," the maid offered, scooping up the child and cuddling her close. The countess nodded, then stepped toward Duncan. Her emerald eyes glowed with what might have been gratitude, had she been guileless. She led him away from her party, toward the coast.

"I must thank you for your kind intervention," she said, her gentle smile infuriating Duncan beyond anything else she might have done.

"'Twas naught." His tone was nigh insolent.

"Nay, 'twas most generous of you. You have a fine voice."

"Hardly that." Duncan snorted, then spoke his mind despite his reservations. "I feared you would strike the child in return for her boldness."

The lady seemed to stifle a laugh, though her gaze sobered. "Though I have been sorely tempted by Esmeraude to do so, and that more than once, abuse is not my way. 'Tis not her fault, after all, that she is so distressed."

"Nay, 'tis *yours*."

"Mine?" she said, new frost edging her tone.

"Aye, 'tis *you* who have failed in your duties. Clearly the child does not even recognize you, which speaks poorly of your role as mother."

She folded her arms across her chest, pushing her fine breasts to prominence beneath the wet cloak in a way that did naught to aid Duncan's thinking. "Indeed?"

"Indeed! I have seen much in my day, and little good of the nobility, but this is the first that I have witnessed a child unaware of her own parentage!" Duncan's voice grew louder. "'Tis no endorsement of your character, my lady, that much is certain!"

"Do tell," the countess invited coolly, her eyes narrowed to emerald slits.

Aye, she was insulted. A man less wise in the ways of noblewomen might conclude that he had wounded her, might beg forgiveness, might be fool enough to step anew into her trap.

But Duncan knew better.

"But then, what is one to expect from nobles? 'Tis clear enough that you, like all the others, think of naught beyond your own entertainment and comfort!"

"Which would explain my presence here?" Her words were crisply enunciated, as if she bit them off.

Duncan was not fooled. Nay, Ceinn-beithe was a prize of some kind for her, of that he was certain. He did not let himself be swayed from his argument, but propped his hands on his hips and scowled at her.

"Do not try to deny the truth of it to me! Were you not at the hunt so early on your first morn? How typical of a noblewoman to amuse herself while her villeins labor hard to ensure they have some food and shelter!"

He gestured to Esmeraude and her maid. "And how like a pampered noblewoman to leave the nursing and the raising of her children to those same villeins, lest she ruin her form or hamper her own pursuit of entertainment."

To Duncan's astonishment, the lady did not flee before his outburst. She did not cry, she did not flutter her lashes. She held her ground and glared back at him.

Duncan stepped forward in an attempt to intimidate her. "Aye, you mark my words, Countess, this land will not suit you well. There is no room here for noble and villein, for the land demands sacrifices from all."

"'Tis clear there are no nobles here, that much I will concede."

Duncan leaned closer. "Perhaps *you* should depart," he suggested in a low voice, "as you are the true foreigner, and leave your hardworking villeins behind. Why, I have half a mind to take that child from you, to ensure that she knows something of caring and trust before 'tis too late!"

Her eyes flashed. "I shall not argue your possession of half a mind."

A dull flush rose on Duncan's neck that her words could be so controlled. "Aye, is that not to be expected? I accuse you of casting aside your own children and you regard me with such composure—'tis as if I commented on the weather! Have you no passion in your soul? Is there no blood in your veins?"

She smiled a slow smile that infuriated Duncan. "I assure you that there is blood in my veins. I was, however, raised to show impeccable manners—clearly not your own good fortune." One fair brow lifted. "Therefore, given your eloquent clarification of your sentiments, it would be inappropriate to invite you and your men to share our repast, as was my intent just moments past."

"A repast your villeins will labor to provide for your pleasure!"

She nodded. "Aye, Gerhard and Gunther will labor hard to skin the rabbits and ensure they are stewed; however, they assured me that they were most grateful for the meat."

Duncan's eyes narrowed. "How could they not be grateful when to hunt fulfills their lady's pleasure? 'Twould be less than prudent to respond in any other way."

"You are mistaken again," she snapped, her voice rising for the first time, "for the hunt is a responsibility, not a pleasure for me. Had I the choice, I would never hunt, but 'tis my obligation to provide for those beneath my hand. My household had need of a hot stew after our journey. And it is, after all, my *right* to hunt upon my holding."

Duncan blinked. She hunted purely to ensure her company had a hot meal? That could hardly be called selfishness. Indeed, 'twas almost . . . maternal. And she had not fled from his accusations, nor even his fury, she had not wept.

She had faced him proudly and defended herself.

Duncan was startled to realize that she was the first woman he had encountered of any class to do as much.

He had always longed to meet a woman who could argue like a man, who would not tremble when he shouted, who knew that he would never strike her, notwithstanding his bellows.

'Twas disconcerting to have met such a woman in this countess.

His anger drained out of him, as quickly as always it did, the lady's manner leaving him with too many unanswered questions, the most pressing of which was why she had come here.

'Twas suddenly imperative that he know. Duncan noted now that she wore plain leather boots, heavy boots, wrought like those of a man and unadorned with frippery. Her kirtle was simply cut, of good-quality wool, its embroidery far from lavish. She wore no jewels. He noted now aspects of her appearance he had not seen immediately.

The countess's features were unadorned by kohl or carmine, her fingers devoid of rings. She was garbed simply, as if she had risen quickly and hastened to fulfill her obligations to her household.

Had he misjudged Eglantine, Countess de Nemerres?

The lady, however, did not look inclined to confess her secrets to him. She inclined her head slightly, her tone formal. "I wish you good day, Duncan MacLaren, and Godspeed in your departure." She pivoted and walked away, her back perfectly straight.

"One last question, my lady countess," Duncan cried after her.

She cast a glance over her shoulder. "I owe you naught."

"Why does Esmeraude fear her own mother's touch?"

Eglantine turned then to survey him, the flame burning in her eyes enough to steal Duncan's breath away. "That is not your concern."

Duncan smiled, liking how her eyes snapped. "You are

afraid to tell me the truth," he charged, his manner deliberately provocative.

He provoked far more than anticipated.

Eglantine's eyes flashed like fiery emeralds, the fury in her expression making his pulse thunder. Far from retreating demurely, the lady stormed back toward him, a vengeful goddess taken flesh.

Duncan was entranced.

Chapter Four

HE LADY DID NOT SHARE HIS MOOD. SHE HALTED BE-
fore him, tipped up her chin—clearly undaunted
by the difference in their height—and jabbed her
finger into his chest to make her point.

"I am afraid of *naught*!" she spat. "And I am certainly not
afraid of an uncivilized, troublemaking, unpredictable, vulgar . . ." She sputtered, momentarily at a loss, and Duncan
grinned.

Ye gods, but he could well sympathize with the sense of
being so angry that words did not fall readily from the lips.

"Barbarian," he supplied helpfully, feeling a startling affin-
ity for this woman. Indeed, an admiring grin curved his lips,
clearly doing naught to improve the lady's temper.

"Aye!" Her eyes flashed dangerously. "A *barbarian* like
you!" She caught her breath, her breasts rising as she gritted
her teeth and glared.

She was magnificent. Duncan touched the curve of her
cheek with one calloused finger, though he half expected
she would smote him for such boldness. Eglantine inhaled
sharply. Her skin was softer than soft, but her eyes hardened.

"How *dare* you?" she demanded breathlessly, and swatted
at his hand. She was trembling with anger, but she did not
step away. Indeed, she leaned closer. "You shall not touch me
again, are we understood?"

Nay, she would surrender naught without a fight, this one. The prospect emboldened him as naught else could have done.

Could he drive her from Ceinn-beithe with his touch?

'Twas worth a try. There were none from her camp within range to intervene—indeed, her vassals seemed intent on pursuing their own labor and ignoring the lady.

Perfect.

"Oh, I would dare more, far more than that," Duncan vowed in a low voice. He moved quickly, capturing her chin with one hand and bending close. "Does my pledge strike fear into your heart, my lady Eglantine?"

Her eyes narrowed, but not quickly enough to hide the heat of her response. "Nay!"

"Good." He whispered against her lips, deliberately trying to infuriate her. "For 'tis the way of barbarians to take what they desire." Duncan brushed his lips quickly across hers, knowing 'twould take her precious little time to recover.

"And you know what I desire," he murmured, before claiming her with a thorough kiss, the exquisite taste of her nigh making his head spin.

Duncan's head did spin when Eglantine slapped him, hard.

"Shameless rogue!" Her eyes snapped as he fingered his jaw. 'Twas he who inadvertently took a step back, though the lady immediately took a step to follow. "Have you no manners at all in this no-man's land? Do you not know your place, or respect the rights of a woman to say aye or nay?"

"And what would you say to my invitation, Countess Eglantine?" Duncan demanded with a grin. "Aye or nay?"

"Nay! Of course!"

He gently tapped the tip of her nose with his fingertip. "But your eyes say aye." He noted how she caught her breath, his gaze drawn to the ripe curve of her breasts. He boldly let his hand fall to cup one breast, knowing she would not tolerate such familiarity.

He was startled that the curve of her fit his hand so perfectly that they might have been each wrought for the other.

"You!" Eglantine exhaled in a low hiss, grasped his wrist, and flung his hand away. Duncan had the wits to take a step back before she could slap him again.

"Tell me of the child," he coaxed, telling himself that he fared well in provoking her. "Tell me why she fears you. Is it because you are a stranger to her?"

Eglantine's hands clenched into fists as she stared at him, her gaze hot, her cheeks red. How could he have imagined her to be wrought of frost? The lady's passion raged like an inferno, and Duncan wanted to touch her again—though not to drive her away.

"I owe you no answers," she spat. "I owe you *naught*, Duncan MacLaren—I owe you *no* explanation and no kisses and no 'aye or nay,' and I would suggest you not forget the truth of that."

With that, Eglantine spun and stalked away, leaving one captivated man in her wake.

She pivoted when she was a dozen paces away to jab her finger through the air at him. "And leave my land," she demanded. "You are not welcome at Kinbeath now, if indeed you ever were."

The countess left Duncan no opportunity to reply before she marched back to her camp.

Duncan most certainly would not leave Ceinn-beithe so readily as that. Aye, he had named Eglantine's temperament wrong. 'Twas blood, hot blood, that coursed through her veins, that much was more than certain.

What had driven her here? Duncan wanted to know. And why did her own child fear her? What had happened to the count? And who, of course, had forged that deed? Within the tangle of mysteries lay the key to driving her away, to securing this holding for his own.

Duncan was honest enough to admit to himself that he was somewhat less interested in seeing this lady depart yet. 'Twas just her mysteries that intrigued him, and once he understood her better, his fascination would fade.

But his gaze clung to her figure overlong all the same.

"If that be a woman you believe wrought of stone, lad," Gillemore commented, startling Duncan, "then I should be wary of meeting one you call fiery."

Duncan chuckled, then clapped one hand on the older man's shoulder. "I shall drive her away yet, Gillemore. She is not one who takes kindly to being denied her will."

Gillemore harumphed. "Aye, mind she takes naught of you with her when she leaves, lad."

"There is no fear of that," Duncan declared with confidence, though he ran his tongue across his lip as he walked, tasting Eglantine again.

He wanted more. One sample of her sweetness would not suffice. Would Eglantine writhe beneath a man, would she demand as much as she gave—or would she lie back like a corpse once she chose to surrender? Was her show of passion a ploy or a glimpse of her true character?

Duncan did not know and was sorely tempted to find out—if only to ensure that he chose the best strategy to drive the lady away. That was it. Aye, he would attend that meal—the one to which Eglantine had pointedly *not* invited him. With any luck, his presence alone would infuriate the lady yet further.

Duncan could hardly wait.

Eglantine hated losing her temper.

Nay, she *never* lost her temper. 'Twas out of the question. She was not Esmeraude, blessed with Theobald's charm and his stormy temperament. Nay, not she.

Eglantine was tranquil. Eglantine was collected. Eglantine

never so much as raised her voice; she turned chaos to order everywhere she went.

Her blood most certainly did not boil.

Although on this day, it gave a fair impression of doing so. Aye, she seethed, as never she had seethed before. She had been stern with Esmeraude when softness would have won greater results—a mistake for which she would certainly pay, even though it could readily be blamed upon her exhaustion. Worse, she had shouted at and struck another.

One who deserved no less, but still.

Her loss of composure was all because of that same irksome ruffian, a man who had no right remaining on her land, a man whose moods shifted like the shades of the sea, a man who tested her mettle then *laughed* when she responded.

A rogue who kissed her, when he had no right even to address her. She never felt lust either, not Eglantine; she never burned with desire. A man's touch was pleasant, no more than that, and occasionally gratifying. Men did not make sensible Eglantine simmer.

Though on this day, she nigh expected to see steam rise from her flesh.

Had it not been for the obvious annoyance of dealing with Duncan MacLaren, she might have assumed she had fallen ill with some foul disease. Indeed, 'twas amazing to Eglantine that in the course of one short day, her murderous intent should have shifted almost entirely from Theobald to a man she had only just met.

And trebled in intensity.

No less, she could not ignore the burn upon her lips, a brand left by Duncan's provocative kiss. A stolen kiss. Such audacity was beyond belief.

And she, shameless wanton that she had evidently become, had wanted more. She was no trembling virgin in these days, and though her marriages had been dutiful arrangements, there had been nights of passion and pleasure. Eglantine admitted to herself that she missed the weight of a man's hand upon her flesh.

Not often. But once in a while.

But she was beyond marriageable years, and certainly not one for casual liaisons. 'Twould be a poor example for her daughters, and truly, she had not been raised herself with low moral standards.

Nay, her daughters' matches were her sole goal, their satisfaction would be her own. She told herself that twice, to no effect. Eglantine took a deep, shuddering breath and willed the tingle deep in her belly to silence.

It ignored her, and heated like a coal on the smith's forge.

She could not be caught in the allure of a barbarian, not she. She could and would steel herself against the man's rough appeal. She only had need of one night's good sleep to shore up her defenses, and she would have it this night.

The problem of Duncan MacLaren settled, she set herself to organizing with terrifying efficiency.

Esmeraude was Eglantine's primary concern. The child had had her chance to mourn her papa but now must come to terms with the way matters would remain. Eglantine knew that she had erred in her approach this morning. She would have to begin again, begin more gently. Yet as Eglantine watched her daughter play with Célie, she knew she was not yet prepared for another battle of wills.

Eglantine rubbed her brow, cursed the rain, and wished with all her heart that something would turn in her favor.

First, she would discuss the construction plans with Xavier, then she would oversee the meal. Once all were sated and calm, Esmeraude would be moved into Eglantine's own tent. Célie, of course, would join them as well, though likely none of them would sleep this night.

Perhaps on the morrow, or on the night after that.

But 'twould be the beginning of the establishment of trust between mother and child. Sooner or later Esmeraude would accept her circumstances and her mother. Eglantine knew she could outwait the child.

She was the patient one, after all.

'Twas no coincidence that 'twas Theobald who recognized her own ability to make the most of little. Eglantine sighed, wishing he had not left her quite so complete a challenge, then summoned a smile as she sought Xavier.

Patience and perseverance would bring their own rewards.

Xavier was prepared to undertake his own feat of patience and perseverance in the building of their manor. He was excited about the site he had chosen and spoke with enthusiasm of the shelter from the wind to be had here, as well as the large stones already scattered around the site. He intended to add to their number with smaller rocks from the vicinity.

Indeed, the boys aiding him had already assembled an impressive pile, and even as the stocky man spoke to Eglantine, he fitted one or two smaller ones into place. 'Twas as if he could not bear to be parted from his project.

His scheme was to make a floor of the stones, then a low wall that would rise to Eglantine's hip or so. That stone wall would hold large logs upright every three strides. At the roofline, Xavier intended to build a frame with timber, then complete the walls with more stripped trees set vertically.

Louis listened carefully, hands folded behind his back, his periodic questions incisive. Eglantine tried to envision the structure, so different from the stone or wattle-and-daub that she had known.

Anything would be better than a tent. And a stone floor strewn with herbs had a strong appeal. 'Twould be a marvel to rise without dirt or mud underfoot.

She spared a glance at the tower Duncan and his men

had claimed, and Xavier expressed his opinion that 'twould indeed make a defensible retreat. Louis contributed his knowledge that such structures were evidently built with storerooms beneath, that the occupants might better withstand a seige. None mentioned that they would only be able to investigate it fully and use it once 'twas reclaimed from Duncan's band.

Xavier and Louis agreed that the walls of the manor should be of double thickness to halt the wind, which even now had a bite as it swept in from the sea. Xavier etched the site of the fireplace with his toe, more or less in the middle of this hall, and described a roof of the stripped boughs overlaid and lashed with straw. Louis suggested an enlargement of the fireplace, to better allow for cooking, and the two men discussed the possibilities.

Xavier intended to build one hall of moderate size—again, he etched the dimensions in the ground with his toe—then add to the manor, room by room. In this way, he explained proudly, they would all have some measure of shelter soon, yet by the autumn the structure would boast four or perhaps five chambers. This would better shelter their ranks for the winter and allow for some division of tasks and accommodation among the rooms.

Eglantine was impressed by Xavier's plan and said as much, her praise making the older man's ears redden as he grinned. She suggested that this first hall be the largest of the chambers and serve as the central hall of the finished structure to ensure the heat of the fire was used to best advantage. Both Louis and Xavier had agreed that this was sound.

All in all, their planning took a considerable measure of the day. The glow behind the clouds that marked the position of the sun had sunk toward the horizon by the time they were in agreement. They had only just fallen silent when Gunther began to hammer upon an empty pot.

"Come for your vittles!" he roared. "Our ladyship has hunted this day and there is hot rabbit stew for all."

"And fresh bread," Xavier amended with a satisfied sniff of the air. "'Twill be welcome indeed on a day such as this." He bowed to Eglantine, then summoned his boys and made his way to the fire.

"A most prudent choice, my lady," Louis declared with rare warmth. "The meat will do much to lift our household's spirits."

Eglantine cast him a smile. "Despite their being in this wretched place?"

Louis did not smile. "'Tis even more remote than I anticipated."

Eglantine sighed. "Aye, 'tis that. And truly, there will be more potatoes than meat in that stew." She eyed her châtelain, knowing he had the experience to best answer her fear. "Do you think we can make a home in this place, Louis?"

Louis pursed his lips and looked away, his gaze moving over the mist shrouding the hills and coast. "'Tis nearly spring and we might fare well enough, but my concern is for next winter. Xavier makes a fine plan for our shelter, and there is wood aplenty for the fire . . ."

"But?"

"But what shall we eat, my lady? Can one fish the sea in the winter? I know naught of such matters." Frustration creased the older man's brow. "Can one hunt here in the winter, or will the creatures move elsewhere? 'Tis beyond my experience to summon a guess. And we have no crops, nor do we know if any of the seed we brought can grow in this wretched place."

Eglantine halted, her heart chilling. "You think we cannot prosper here."

Louis arched a brow. "If I may be so bold, my lady, you risk the lives of many dependent upon you in this venture and that with no good chance of success. I should suggest that we make plans to return home to Arnelaine, or at least to Crevy . . ."

The very suggestion angered Eglantine. "Return? 'Twould be impossible!"

"No less impossible than traveling to this land of heathens in the first place."

Eglantine folded her arms across her chest and considered the man she trusted to run her household. "Louis, I thought your approval was implied by your accompaniment."

"You thought wrongly, my lady."

"Then why *did* you accompany me?"

He scowled with a characteristic ferocity that had frightened her when she was but a child. Not so now—Eglantine held both her ground and his gaze. "'Twas my pledge," he muttered.

"I would have absolved you of your duties, Louis, had I guessed the fullness of your objections."

Louis glared at her, the suggestion obviously so offensive that he could not hide his response. "Some duties are not so readily shed as that, my lady. Not only was I born to serve your family, but I swore an oath to serve you to the full extent of my capabilities. My pledge is not a worthless one and I shall uphold it to my dying breath." His eyes flashed. "With or without your absolution."

'Twas the closest they had ever come to an argument, and Eglantine struggled to keep her tone level. 'Twas that cursed Duncan who had unsettled her, and she knew it well. "Your loyalty is not in question, Louis."

"Nor is your intellect, my lady." The châtelain took a steadying breath and continued in a more even tone. "I would respectfully suggest you abandon this folly and return to France."

"And surrender Jacqueline to Reynaud?" Eglantine watched

Louis's determination falter, for he too was fond of Jacqueline. She touched his arm and leaned closer. "She deserves better, Louis, and you know the truth of it as well as I."

"She is too young to die in the wilderness," he argued grimly.

"As am I." Eglantine smiled but again Louis did not.

"I fear that you indulge her overmuch, my lady." Louis heaved a sigh. "She would become accustomed to Reynaud in time."

Eglantine's smile faded. "I do not believe so."

"'Tis the way of things, my lady, and you, of all women, should know the truth of it."

"'Tis because I know the truth of it that we are here, Louis."

The older man hid his surprise quickly, though his gaze lingered upon his mistress.

"I survived my marriage to Robert, Louis, and I shall survive what little Theobald has left me." Eglantine pointed to Duncan's group of ruffians in the distance. "*They* manage to live here—surely we can do as much."

"They have been bred to hardship, not to the leisure of plying a spindle and choosing jewelry," the châtelain retorted crisply, clearly unpersuaded. "They are *men*, my lady."

Eglantine shook her head. "Surely you recall my father's insistence that I could succeed at any task as well as a man."

"Aye, I remember." Louis coughed delicately into his hand. "But I would wager that he did not expect you to believe it." His gaze met hers, sudden humor gleaming there.

Eglantine laughed. "We shall manage, Louis, I shall ensure it."

"With respect, my lady, it may not be your choice."

Eglantine squared her shoulders, knowing she would prove all these men wrong. "You are right about our need for suitable seed, of course, and similarly about our ignorance of this place. But that does not mean that there is naught to be done about it."

"God in heaven, my lady, what do you mean to do now?" Exasperation tinged the châtelain's tone, but Eglantine was undeterred.

"We shall use the resources at hand, of course." Eglantine pursed her lips, disliking that she should require any favor from the likes of Duncan but knowing there was no choice. She cast a bright smile at Louis. "I shall seek advice from those who do survive in these parts."

"It appears that you shall shortly have your opportunity," he muttered darkly.

Eglantine turned, only to find Duncan and his party of men converging upon her household's line for stew. Carrying their own bowls and spoons, they looked unlikely to be swayed from their course. Gunther and Gerhard glared at the men disapprovingly, to no discernible effect.

Indeed, Duncan stared outright at Eglantine, as if he would dare her to deny his men the meal. They were not the most reputable-looking troupe, and indeed, Eglantine already knew their leader to be both bold and troublesome.

Alienor, already near the stewpot, giggled as a fair-haired man behind Duncan eyed her appraisingly. The girl flushed and sidled closer to him, as if she would tempt Eglantine to throttle her.

Indeed, Alienor had competition for that honor at this moment, for Duncan halted a few paces away to address Eglantine.

"My lady countess," he declared, executing a flawless bow. "We gladly accept your invitation to join your meal."

"Invitation?" Louis echoed from slightly behind her, but Eglantine had no time to explain.

She picked up her skirts and marched toward the infuriating rogue. Before the meal was consumed, she would have answers to Louis's questions and a guarantee of Duncan's immediate departure.

Eglantine would gladly pay for both with a measure of rabbit stew.

The countess was magnificent.

Aye, Eglantine's eyes flashed as she strode toward Duncan, all fire and steely purpose. She appeared not to have noticed that her hood had fallen back.

But her hair, 'twas her hair that stole Duncan's breath away. She had abandoned her veil over the course of this day, and her hair hung behind her, ostensibly braided but already escaping its bounds. 'Twas indeed blond, of the same hue as honey.

A thousand small curls surrounded the countess's flushed cheeks, the wavy nature of her tresses was untamed. The misty rain seemed only to heighten her femininity, to make her skin glow as if 'twere kissed by dew, to coax the loose tendrils of her hair to curl. Her beauty touched Duncan deep inside, even as he recounted all the reasons he should be indifferent to her allure.

But Duncan stared, unwelcome desire heating his blood. His mouth went dry. He found his heart pounding, but told himself 'twas only because he expected a merry battle. He folded his arms across his chest and held his ground.

She halted before him, flinging her skirts to the ground with impatience even as she granted him a look that would kill a lesser man. "You, sir, are insolent beyond belief."

Duncan stifled a chuckle. "Me?" he asked, all wide-eyed innocence.

"Aye, you!" The lady lifted a brow regally. "You know full well that I did not invite you to join our meal, just as you know that 'twould be beyond rude for me to deny you hospitality now that you have joined us."

"But fortunately for me and my men, you were raised a noblewoman and your manners are far finer than mine. I know this, for you have explained it to me just this very morn."

Eglantine regarded him warily, clearly uncertain whether he mocked her. "And as you are hungered, you would take advantage of my courtesy."

"You came close to inviting us."

Anger tinged her words. "But I did *not* do so."

Their gazes locked for a long hot moment. Again, Duncan was assailed with curiosity, the desire to know what she would grant abed—and what she would demand in return.

"I should let you starve," she said with low heat. "I should make you watch us lick the pot clean, like dogs forbidden to beg from the board." Her eyes had darkened to a deep emerald hue.

"Even a barbarian can imagine a finer use for a lady's tongue," he murmured suggestively.

The countess pinkened slightly but did not demurely drop her gaze as he might have expected. Nay, she was wrought of sterner stuff than the others he had met. Despite himself, Duncan admired her.

"You will not shock me with lewd commentary," she muttered.

A raven-haired demoiselle giggled before Duncan could reply, and Eglantine pivoted to cast a quelling look toward the girl. She ignored the countess, and Duncan watched Eglantine's lips thin with disapproval.

He might as well have disappeared from her side, but Duncan would not be dismissed so readily as that. He snared a loose tendril of Eglantine's hair before she could pursue the girl and wound it proprietarily around his finger. Duncan heard the lady's breath catch at his boldness, but he had pledged to drive her away with his touch, after all.

"'Twas not my intent to shock you," he murmured, letting his finger slide along the curve of her cheek.

Her eyes widened, but she did not move away. He watched the light play in the gold of her hair, then eased that curl behind her ear, letting his fingertips trail over her flesh. She trembled slightly, the crimson hue of her cheeks revealing her awareness of him even as she stared after the demoiselle.

Duncan bent to whisper against her cheek. "I sought only to learn whether we were of like mind in this. What would you give, Eglantine, to be rid of me? What might I give you, to persuade you to be gone? Or truly, could we create an alliance that would serve us both well?"

His words seemed to prompt her to action. "Rogue!" she cried, and stepped back, that alluring fire burning anew in her gaze. "I will not cede to your base desires—" Her gaze flicked back over the assembly before she could continue, then she shook a finger in the air. *"Alienor!"*

Duncan spun to find the demoiselle standing very close to Iain. That man looked far from innocent, though this Alienor's expression was defiant when she turned.

"You will stay away from these men, as I have repeatedly bidden you," Eglantine insisted, and marched in pursuit of her errant charge. Duncan wondered what relation was between the women, for 'twas clear Eglantine felt responsible for the girl's behavior. She caught the girl's arm and urged her away from Duncan's men, her head bent toward the girl as she chided her.

When the girl was safely surrounded by a cluster of maids, that group given emphatic instruction from the countess, the countess returned to Duncan's side with purpose in her stride.

Her exasperation was more than clear.

"They must all leave, this very day." She fixed a determined glance upon Duncan. "Departure of your party is the price of the stew."

Duncan did not care for the countess's offer. "Nay!"

"Then you shall not partake of the meal." The lady lifted her hand and gave rapid instructions to her cook. Iain offered his bowl, but the cook put the lid firmly on the pot. As Iain swore and reached for the lid, the man beside the cook hastily drew a blade.

Duncan watched his men being denied a hot meal that was directly before them. A quick survey revealed that their allegiance to him wavered anew. Iain made a sour comment, the content of which Duncan could not hear, though he watched the ranks of his men part once more. They all looked to him expectantly.

Curse the lady for this trick!

Duncan scowled at Eglantine. "Do not refuse them a meal at this moment, whether they be barbarians to you or nay. 'Twould be uncharitable."

She sniffed. "I have surrendered enough alms on this journey and now must protect my own."

"'Twould be cruel not to share."

"'Tis foolish to feed beggars and dogs, lest they linger."

Duncan felt his lips tighten. "They are men and you know it well."

Her eyes narrowed. "If I share, you and your men shall depart immediately after the meal."

Duncan scoffed. "Ceinn-beithe for a meal? You place a high value upon this stew."

Eglantine's eyes twinkled unexpectedly and Duncan was intrigued that her temper fled as swiftly as his own was wont to do. "I have great faith in the capabilities of my cook and baker. I grant you my assurance that the bread is most fine."

"Well, Duncan?" Iain cried in Gael. "Are we merely to salivate while you ogle the woman?"

Duncan spared his foster brother a dark glance, then met Eglantine's gaze. "Let the men eat while we wager."

"Nay." She folded her arms across her chest, as resolute as any man could be. "Your departure is the only term to which you must agree. No negotiation is necessary."

Stubborn creature! Duncan took a step closer, but she was not visibly intimidated. "You are about to deny twenty hungry men a hot meal, twenty men you call barbarians, twenty men who were prepared to shed blood to win this land, twenty men who were prepared to seize what they believed to be theirs last evening. 'Twould seem to me to be more clever to cultivate their goodwill before retiring to your bed on this night." He arched a brow. "But do not let me influence your decision."

Eglantine considered him for only a moment, then she swore with surprising vigor.

"You will not make a habit of this," she charged. "And be warned that I shall demand fair compensation for this concession." She then waved the cooks onward.

At least the woman possessed a measure of sense. The men grunted approval as meat was ladled into their bowls, but Duncan captured the lady's elbow before she could return to the group.

He had only just begun to vex her, after all.

He led her toward the broch, dropping his voice. "And I return the generosity of your gesture by showing you the marvel of this broch."

"I should like to see it." In a move he was beginning to see as typical of her, the countess pulled her arm from his grip and marched determinedly ahead of him. 'Twas as if she had been merely waiting for an opportunity to study the structure, for she scanned it purposefully as she walked. "'Tis for defense, is it not?"

"Aye."

"And how old is it?"

"A thousand years old, maybe two."

Her eyes widened.

"Aye, originally it would have been taller . . ."

"With a roof?"

"Aye, and galleries. You will see." Duncan smiled, offering her his hand as they reached the rubble at the foot of the tower. She ignored him—though he did not doubt she saw his gesture—hefting her skirts and striding onward untroubled by the rough terrain.

The wall of the crumbling broch still stood the height of four men. Duncan gestured into the shadows but the lady regarded him warily.

"You will not touch me again, not when I am at a disadvantage in unfamiliar circumstances."

Duncan grinned down at her. "Perhaps I should ask for a similar pledge, as you are so impassioned in my presence." He leaned closer, liking how she caught her breath. "But then, all I have is yours to sample, my lady countess. Will you take your compense for the meal in pleasure?"

Her eyes flashed. "Insufferable creature!" Then she ducked through the doorway. Duncan chuckled and followed, nearly running into her where she stood just inside the shelter of the shadows. He caught her shoulders in his hands and knew 'twas a mark of her awe that she didn't pull away.

"How ingenious," she murmured.

'Twas just so. The walls of this broch, like so many others, had been built of double thickness. Between the inner and outer walls of fitted stone, slabs of stone had been laid horizontally. The ends of these stones had been built right into the walls as the tower was constructed. As a result, there was a permanent floor that wound around the tower in an ascending spiral.

The inner wall was punctured by the occasional doorway, providing access from that sloping ramp to the central courtyard. Spaces for the timbers that would have supported the floor could be seen in the stonework at two levels, though now they were only empty holes. The central chamber stood open to the elements, a yawning cavity filled with stones and the occasional stubborn tuft of greenery.

There was a single point of entry at the ground level, the door in which they stood, and a small chamber for a guard built into the wall directly to their right.

The countess turned to face him, her features alight. He felt a momentary surge of pride, both that she appreciated this treasure and that he had shown it to her.

Her words, though, destroyed any sense of triumph. "You should surrender this immediately to me."

Duncan laughed, though in truth her presumption annoyed him. "Why? To satisfy your whim alone?"

"Because the land is mine and you know it well." She spoke crisply. "And this would clearly make a fine fortress. You owe me no less."

"I owe you naught on the basis of a forged deed." He had not intended to say as much, but once the words left his lips, he watched her carefully.

The lady was clearly shocked, though she recovered well. Had she not been noble, Duncan would have been certain that she had not known.

Then she quickly shook her head. "'Twould clearly be to your advantage to convince me to leave, and 'tis only your word I have upon this forgery."

"The others could testify to the fact that Cormac never could sign his name."

"They have the same motivation as you." The lady shrugged in turn. "Nay, I shall believe in the deed until you prove beyond a shred of doubt any lack of validity to me."

She leaned closer, eyes shining. "Why do you not seek a court, Duncan MacLaren? I understand William's court is convened in Edinburgh, some week's ride east of here."

Duncan felt his own reluctant smile. 'Twas strange to have them both think the other guilty of similar schemes. He felt new respect for the lady's quick wits. "I would guess your doubt will not be readily dispelled."

The lady laughed, a sight so fetching that Duncan's heart skipped a beat. "'Twould be sorely inconvenient to me to be cast from this holding. And indeed, there are few in my household who would welcome a repetition of our journey here."

"Then why did you come?" She paused to study him. Duncan found himself eager to know the truth. "I cannot fathom why you would trouble yourself, let alone uproot all who depend upon you."

"Why should I confide in you, when you are the one who can cost me my heart's desire?" Her voice was low, her choice of words feeding Duncan's curiosity.

"Ceinn-beithe is your heart's desire?"

The lady's smile flashed. "Aye. The key to it." Then she fell silent. 'Twas clear she thought her confession sufficient, though Duncan did not share her view.

And he was not sufficiently well mannered to let the lady be.

"How so?" he prompted.

Eglantine straightened. "I owe you no explanation, Duncan MacLaren."

Duncan folded his arms across his chest and regarded her indulgently. She was so evasive that he guessed the matter was of import. Or 'twould tell much of her nature.

Which made him only more determined to know. She might have stepped past him to return to the camp, but he moved squarely into her path. He folded his arms across his chest, blocking the opening more effectively than any wooden portal.

He smiled as she assessed the situation, then took a step back. Her expression conceded naught. "Perhaps your reasons will be so compelling that I will readily cede the land to you."

Eglantine choked back her surprised laughter. "You would not!"

Duncan grinned, liking that she did not fear him. "Perhaps not. But surely, 'tis worth the effort. 'Tis no life of ease you have here, and the journey must have been arduous. Why not remain in safety and comfort at your home?"

Eglantine assessed him for a long moment, then sighed. "Because I had no other choice." Her gaze slid away and her lips tightened. "I had naught but this title and three unwed daughters."

Duncan frowned in shock, then called himself a fool for so readily feeling sympathy for the lady. No doubt her definition of "naught" was vastly different from his own. And Alienor could not be her daughter—the two could not be five years apart in age!

Nay, she tried to manipulate him with a lie.

"Is that why you would cease Alienor's flirting? Because her value will be reduced to any suitor without her maidenhead?"

Eglantine's eyes flashed. "How like a man to state the truth so coarsely! For what 'tis worth, Alienor has been cheated of her dowry. She is left with only her beauty and her virginity with which to make a match fitting of her birthright."

Duncan could not help but shake his head, the scheming ways of these nobles not readily forgotten. "A fitting match would be one with a wealthy lord, some decades her senior, some old knight finally come into his inheritance and desiring an heir?"

"A fitting match would be a man who makes her heart sing," Eglantine retorted unexpectedly and with heat. "A man who cares for her happiness, for her comfort, for her safety. A man who loves her with all his heart and soul. A man with whom she will be happy for all her days and nights."

'Twas such a poetic whim that Duncan knew not what to say.

Chapter Five

UNCAN STARED AT THE LADY, WATCHING FRUSTRA-
tion flicker across her features. He was certain he
had heard her wrongly and wished heartily that she
would elaborate.

But Eglantine was clearly not prepared to confide more of
her secret desire.

"Do you pledge to me that this comrade of yours"—she
waved her hand in Iain's general direction as she held Duncan's gaze—"is a man who will honor Alienor, pledge marriage to her, and ensure her happiness for all his days and
nights?"

Duncan could not find it within him to so guarantee his
foster brother's intent. The man was a virtual stranger to him
these days. He shook his head. "Nay, I cannot."

"Then for the sake of Alienor, for the sake of a woman
who knows not what she does nor even what price she will
pay for any dalliance with him, ensure his departure from
this place. Do this, Duncan MacLaren, do this noble deed before damage is done that cannot be repaired."

It had been a long time since anyone had appealed to Duncan's honor, and he found himself instinctively wanting to
fulfill Eglantine's appeal. 'Twould be the right deed to do, of
that he had no doubt.

But did she toy with him apurpose?

He granted her his best grin, intent on provoking her once more, for 'twas when provoked that she revealed her character most clearly. "And if I ensure Iain's departure, what will you grant to me?"

"The meal is ample exchange for your departure as well."

"Not to me."

Eglantine's expression turned wary. "What is this?"

"I will not leave Ceinn-beithe." Duncan spoke firmly. "I will not surrender a hereditary holding to a foreigner, especially on the basis of a deed supposedly signed by a man who never could sign his name."

"Have you heard naught I said?" She flung out her hands in frustration. "Have you no honor in your soul? Your men cannot stay!"

"You will not be rid of us so readily as that, my lady, even though you tell a fine tale." He caught her shoulders in his hands, but she folded her arms across her chest and leaned away from him. A spark lit in her eyes, though, and Duncan stifled a smile.

He was not the only one who enjoyed their matching of wits. "Do not tell me that you will be disappointed that I will remain."

Eglantine swore under her breath with a fluency that no longer surprised him, then eyed him accusingly. Duncan could not help but grin, for he both admired her fire and looked forward to whatever she might say.

An unexpected thread of humor ran beneath her words when she did speak. "I should have guessed that you would not make matters easy."

Duncan chuckled. "'Tis not my way." His thumbs moved of their own volition in slow circles against her shoulders, and the heat of her flesh rose through the wet wool of her kirtle.

They stared at each other, Eglantine's smile fading to naught. Duncan forgot the source of their disagreement.

Though the rain had slowed to a light drizzle, she was nigh as wet from the rain as he. The scent of her skin mingled with the odor of the damp wool, the combination warm and intoxicating. Duncan spied the pert peaks of her nipples and wondered whether 'twas the chill or his presence that prompted their state.

The very thought made his blood simmer anew. He met Eglantine's gaze and found an answering heat in those emerald depths. Aye, on this one matter they two were in perfect consensus. He could well imagine taking the lady to her tent, peeling the wet clothes from her flesh, and kissing her until she was rosy from head to toe. She would not be shy, not this Eglantine, she would not hesitate to demand her due; she would both please and be pleased.

He knew it, and he wanted to do that pleasing.

Duncan tried to pull her closer, but Eglantine resisted. "What is *your* heart's desire?" she asked, her voice catching on the words. "Surely you owe me the fair trade of your tale?"

Duncan sobered. Her gaze searched his, as if his answer would tell her much of him. He half smiled, knowing with complete certainty the only thing he sought and suspecting it would tell her much indeed.

"Truth," he declared. "The truth is all that I have ever desired." Aye, truth from this lady would be a fine beginning. He could not dismiss his sense that she misled him, leaving matters half unsaid that he wrought the wrong conclusion.

"Truth." Eglantine stared at him but did not step away, and 'twas clear he had not responded as she expected. Her lips parted, as if in invitation, their softness drawing his gaze.

Duncan caught his breath, and their gazes locked anew. The assembly was naught but a distant murmur, the mist crept from the sea to cloak their ankles, the rain had gentled though it yet fell.

The truth was that he wanted her, and given his own declaration, Duncan found that urge impossible to deny.

"'Tis not the truth you desire from me," she declared suddenly, color tinging her cheeks. She straightened imperiously. "Let me pass." She lifted a hand to urge him aside when he did not move, but Duncan caught her fingers in his.

"And what is it that you truly desire from me?" he demanded, letting his voice drop low with provocation. She hesitated and he deliberately ran his thumb across her palm. He kept his gaze fixed on hers as he bent and kissed her palm.

The lady shivered and hastily pulled her hand away. "Your immediate departure. 'Tis *all* I desire." Even the words sounded breathless.

"Liar," he murmured. He could not resist the urge to touch her. He cupped her shoulder in his hand and, when she did not recoil, slid that hand up her throat to cup her jaw. The lady did not retreat. Indeed, she swallowed when he stared at her rosy mouth, then her tongue slipped across the fullness of her lips. He felt her tremble.

Perhaps this at least was honest between them.

Eglantine was so very soft, softer than he had ever imagined flesh could be. But beneath the softness of her jaw was the uncompromising bone. He felt that her teeth were clenched, her breath held, and he slid his thumb along her jaw in a coaxing caress. She exhaled shakily and closed her eyes, but Duncan did not miss how she trembled, nor how reluctantly her face turned to his palm.

If she had told him the truth, then she was the woman he had always dreamed of finding. A woman unafraid of his temper, a woman who knew he would hurt none, a woman with a poet's heart as whimsical as his own, a woman for whom no half measure would do.

If she lied, he was a fool to be seduced by her beauty and her deceit.

He had always been a man cursed with too much hope.

Duncan felt Eglantine's pulse beneath his thumb, saw the thousand questions light her fine eyes. He was aware that she was far smaller than he, so delicately wrought that he could have snapped her neck in his hands if he had so desired.

But he did not so desire, and she knew it well.

"Let me pass," she demanded tightly, her eyes demanding something entirely different.

Duncan smiled. "There is a toll of a kiss to pass through this portal."

"Liar."

He grinned. "Nay, 'tis an old tale, one entwined with the history of this place."

"I have no time for whimsical tales."

"Indeed? I had thought you would want to know the history of Ceinn-beithe, particularly how 'tis prized for mating. Is that not of import to your daughters?"

"I know already that Ceinn-beithe is a fortunate place for a handfast."

"Do you know why?"

Eglantine shook her head, her wariness making him smile.

"But one kiss and the tale is yours."

She assessed him, her gaze slipping to his lips then back to meet his gaze. Then she shrugged, apparently insouciant, but he was not fooled. "I suppose I have naught to lose, as I am given to understand that a barbarian will take what he is not willingly accorded."

Duncan laughed. His heart swelled that Eglantine trusted him to take no more than she desired to grant. Even in their brief acquaintance, she had seen that his temper was naught but harmless noise. No other had been so perceptive, no other had accepted him as he was.

Not even Mhairi.

Perhaps Eglantine truly was afraid of naught. Perhaps this was a lie. Either way, she stood fearlessly, waiting and watching, soft and strong at the same time. Daring him to take that kiss.

And he would dare.

The lady was irresistible. Duncan had no choice but to surrender to temptation. He drew her against him, his chest tightening with desire as her curves pressed against his chest.

"One kiss, and thence your tale," she reiterated firmly.

"Unless, of course, you beg for more." Her eyes flashed at his audacity and her lips parted, no doubt to loose a recrimination, but Duncan did not grant her the chance.

Eglantine had been a fool to confide even a measure of her reasons for coming to Kinbeath, yet she was more a fool to let Duncan touch her.

Still she could not step away. How could she resist a man whose aim was so noble as the truth? A nigh-impossible objective, a goal for a dreamer, yet he had uttered it with a conviction that tempted her to believe.

And his touch tempted her to do far more than that. He was not what she expected, that much was certain. The skin of the wolf she had seen stretched within the broch to dry, a reminder both of his ability to conquer such a beast and his suggestions as to how the fur might best be enjoyed. She had never seen a man hunt like an animal—certainly not a man who also sang to pacify a child.

She wanted to know how he kissed, though she told herself that curiosity about one's opponent was healthy. The more she knew of him, the more effectively she could drive him from her estate.

She forgot that part when his lips closed over hers. She

knew she should fight him, she had every intention of giving him less than the willing kiss he wanted.

But his chest was muscled and broad, his hands strong. He was rough and the most aggressively masculine man she had ever encountered—but he touched her as if she were wrought of glass. He caught her close, cradling her against his chest as if to protect her from all the ills of the world.

For Eglantine, who had waged her own battles, his protectiveness was irresistible.

If he had assaulted her, if he had forced his will, if he had tried to seduce her with his touch, Eglantine would have fought him tooth and nail for the right to choose.

But his lips met hers gently, reverently, coaxing her to join him in this embrace. 'Twas a concession on his part, and Eglantine knew it well.

He knew intuitively how best to disarm her. Aye, in her days and nights, she had been forced, she had been claimed, she had been savored—but Eglantine had rarely been seduced.

And never by a man who looked like a barbarian, sang like an angel, and dreamed like a poet.

She could smell Duncan's skin, feel the rasp of his whiskers upon her skin. Duncan's warm hands cupped her face, as if she were a fragile prize, not a competitor for the land he would have for his own. His hands slid down her back, as if he would memorize every curve of her and savor it, then he cupped her buttocks in his hands and drew her against his strength. The hardness of him, the sheer size of him, made Eglantine's breath catch in her throat.

And 'twas then she recalled that competitors were what they were. The conquest of her was but a game to him, and her own body traitorously played on his side.

Eglantine pulled away abruptly. Duncan let her go and she was shocked to realize that she had expected naught else. His stormy gray gaze trailed from her lips, which burned with new vigor, to her eyes, which undoubtedly revealed too much.

His expression was so intense that Eglantine nigh could feel his gaze slip over her. She certainly could still feel the imprint of his erection against her belly, and she yearned, as she had seldom yearned in her life, to feel his heat inside her.

How would Duncan love a woman? Thoroughly, Eglantine would wager. Slowly, ensuring that she remembered not only with whom she coupled but the splendor of the mating for all the rest of her life.

She was a fool to be so tempted by something so fleeting as lust. Duncan rubbed finger and thumb together absently, as if reliving the touch of her flesh beneath his hand, and Eglantine had difficulties catching her breath. The languorous movement of his strong fingers captured both her gaze and her imagination.

Aye, this man knew how to coax the embers to flames. This man would sacrifice all to pleasure. Eglantine's mouth went dry with her certainty of his passion, her conviction that he would suffer no half measures.

But he told her a tale. Truth was not his heart's desire, it could not be. 'Twas not honesty of any kind he desired—'twas her holding and naught else.

She had best recall *that* truth.

"Why do you want Kinbeath?" she demanded.

Duncan folded his arms across his chest, his gaze meeting hers once again. "I told you already."

"Nay, you did not. I would have recalled."

One brow rose and his lips tugged in a crooked smile. "'Tis clear you would not have done so, Eglantine, for I *did* tell you."

When he looked at her like that, as if he would prefer to have her to rabbit stew, Eglantine could barely recall her own name. When he uttered her name like an invocation to pleasure, she could barely string two thoughts in a row, much less recall some passing comment he had made.

She felt her cheeks heat and took refuge in sharpness. "Then tell me again."

"Ceinn-beithe is haunted by the souls of our forebears, whose blood stains the stones and whose tales are whispered by the wind." Duncan watched her closely as he spoke, his lips quirking when she started in recognition of the words.

"You said 'twas a hereditary holding."

Duncan nodded. "A legacy for our children, a cornerstone for our clan, a place of such import that it cannot be readily surrendered, a place I cannot suffer to see lost."

His words evoked images from a *chanson* or heroic saga. Eglantine refused to be readily swayed, particularly at the reality she had found.

"And the tale of handfasting?"

His eyes narrowed as he looked into the distance, at the sea.

"Once there was a man and a woman, son of one chieftain and daughter of another. Their families were engaged in a fearsome battle of vengeance that continued for generations and had no prospect of resolution. 'Tis said that the gods tired of this incessant bickering, that they believed they were poorly served by men so occupied in war. So, 'twas by their intervention that this man and woman met, no less that they fell in love.

"The happy couple met secretly as often as they could, and finally they could bear the subterfuge no longer. They met here, at the broch of Kinbeath, and exchanged a pledge of eternal love. They kissed beneath this very portal, sealing their troth each to the other, and then they loved all the night through.

"'Tis the way of young lovers to believe that all solutions lie within their power and that all ills can be set to rights.

These two believed that their fathers could be swayed to peace, purely to ensure their own happy match."

"They were wrong," Eglantine guessed.

Duncan shrugged. "There are those who say 'twas no less than the divine plan of the gods. The woman returned home and confessed to the loss of her maidenhead. Her father demanded retribution and refused to hear her entreaties that she might wed. He assembled a party for war, a greater and more fearsome party than ever his people had seen. He told his daughter that her deed would see the end of this feud, but not in the way she imagined. He would see her beloved and his family slaughtered for the insult.

"The man, meanwhile, returned to his father's hall and asked permission to wed the woman he desired. This was accepted, until he confessed her name. His father claimed that his son had been bewitched and assembled his own party for war, an equally fearsome and numerous party. 'Tis said that when both fathers offered sacrifices in preparation for war, the gods shunned their offerings.

"But they were not deterred. The ground trembled as the two parties marched closer. The sea churned and the wind raged, a storm gathered as if all the elements of the earth would protest this fight. The fathers did not care. They personally led their men to the field and, on recognizing each other, charged into battle.

"They shouted at each other as they met, hurling insults and threats, ignoring the entreaties of their children and the inclement weather. They raised their swords as one, and suddenly the sky parted with a roar. A bolt of lightning was flung down from the displeased gods and struck their crossed blades.

"The fathers fell back, stunned, their weapons were destroyed. Indeed, their sword arms were never fit to raise a blade again. And thus, said the tellers of tales, were the gods avenged for the refusal of men to cede to their greater plans."

"And the couple?"

"Pledged their handfast here at Kinbeath, where they had met and exchanged that first kiss of peace. They lived long, they ruled their fathers' unified peoples in peace and prosperity, they had many children of beauty and skill. And so, 'tis said, that to make a pledge of handfast here at Kinbeath is to claim a measure of that couple's good fortune." He smiled mischievously. "And to exchange a kiss beneath the arch of this portal is a portent of a good match indeed."

He had tricked her, but Eglantine would not let some pagan tale dictate her future. "Nonsense!"

"Not to my people." Duncan looked grim. "This holding is greatly prized and will not be willingly surrendered to any foreigner."

"Greatly prized?" Eglantine knew he but made a tale to suit his own ends. "A legacy sold for hard coin by your former chieftain, a cornerstone so critical that there is not so much as a shed erected upon it." She made a sound of exasperation. "There is no manor, no chapel, there are no crops or any sign there have ever been any. There is no hint that any have resided here in centuries!"

Duncan's features set. "Not all places of import are residences."

"But 'tis clear it has been neglected in the past. Why should I believe that Kinbeath is of such import to you now?"

"Because everything changes." Duncan's eyes narrowed and he folded his arms across his chest. He looked most unlikely to change his thinking. "Because everything of import could be lost."

Eglantine heaved a sigh. "We are not going to agree upon this, certainly not as long as you talk like a troubador instead of negotiate like the chieftain we both know you to be."

Duncan smiled suddenly. "But I am a bard first, Eglantine, and a chieftain against my own desire."

She gaped at him, astonished by this confession, but he headed back toward the group they had left. She had a fleeting sense that he sought to distract her from any queries about himself.

Then he chose the perfect words to make her forget their conversation. "It seems Alienor does not share your desire to preserve her chastity."

Eglantine hastened after him, dreading what she would see. Alienor, not surprisingly, had freed herself from the circle of maids and flirted anew with Duncan's men.

"I shall kill her with my bare hands," she muttered without intending to do so. Duncan chuckled behind her, but Eglantine pivoted to warn him. "And should so much as a hair upon her head be tainted by you or your men, I shall take a penance from your hide for the transgression."

Duncan winked at her, then made a mocking bow. "I shall look forward to it."

Eglantine felt her color rise. "Barbarian!" she managed, then whirled to retrieve her stepdaughter, Duncan's laughter echoing in her ears.

"Eglantine!" He called after her, and she glanced back to find him looking unpredictable and dangerous. He spoke so low that she had to take a step back to hear his murmured words. "You should understand, my lady, that we call this season *faoilleach gavri.*" His eyes glinted with unwelcome mischief that Eglantine knew better than to trust.

"And what is that to mean?"

"The *winter deadmonth* would be a literal translation." Duncan grinned rakishly. "But 'tis known as the *loving month* among many here." He took a step closer, his eyes gleaming with new challenge. "But perhaps you already guessed as much, for you seem to be seeking a lover to keep you warm. Are you cold, alone in your fine bed each night, my Eglantine?"

"How dare you!" How could he know? Eglantine hated that she was losing her temper again, yet was powerless to keep her voice from rising. "You presume overmuch."

Duncan folded his arms across his chest, his expression hardening. "While you promise much with your kiss yet deliver naught. 'Tis typical, is it naught, for women of your ilk?"

"You know naught of me!"

"Aye, but I know this. Should Alienor similarly seek comfort among my men, she will find it." Duncan leaned closer, his eyes dark. "And I will not chastise any who fulfill her demand."

Eglantine swore, much to his evident amusement, then stalked back to her camp. She had to be rid of Duncan MacLaren, that much was clear.

But, God in heaven, could she drive such an impossible creature away?

Duncan lingered on the spot, still hot from Eglantine's kiss. She had shaken him, in more ways than one, and he was in no hurry to rejoin his men. 'Twas a kiss he intended to remember, regardless of what happened between them after this point.

He watched as she strode directly toward Alienor, the pretty pouting demoiselle with hair of raven hue. Eglantine was a woman who did not hesitate to resolve matters herself, and he liked that. He smiled, noting how the countess said little to Alienor but won quick results. The maiden was returned to the care of her maids and effectively separated from Duncan's men.

A second maiden, somewhat smaller than the other and with flaxen hair, was dressed with equal expense and lingered nearby. This was the one who had hunted with Eglantine this morning, so must be another of her daughters. Even from this distance, the two demoiselles appeared as different as chalk and cheese, as much a question of their coloring as their manner.

And they both looked too old to be Eglantine's own children.

Another lie. Duncan let his lips settle into a grim line.

Alienor made a retort, whatever she said uttered with obvious challenge, her arms folded across her chest as she waited for her mother to reply. Eglantine flung a hand toward Duncan's men as she explained something— undoubtedly the threat they posed to tender sensibilities— but Alienor stared at Duncan's men long after the countess had bustled away.

This one was trouble, Duncan wagered, and he did not envy Eglantine such a charge. 'Twould be no small battle to ensure that such a willful one kept her virginity.

If Alienor truly had no dowry and no betrothed, then Duncan had to admit that Eglantine showed good sense in protecting the girl's assets. Duncan had seen more than one penniless woman with neither spouse nor maidenhead be scorned in Norman society, despite her noble birth. Alienor would do well to wed soon, for she was not so young as nobles oft preferred their brides.

But Eglantine's tale could not be the truth; she would find no willing suitors in this place for her daughters, particularly ones who met her standards.

'Twas a lie, and a lie concocted purely to twist Duncan to her will.

He did not appreciate how close she had come to success.

All the same, the crimes of the mother were not those of the children. Duncan might not be inclined to leave, he might enjoy striking fear into Eglantine's breast when he was angered, but in truth, he would attempt to keep his men from ruining those daughters. For the futures of those maidens, if naught else.

Eglantine clearly was taking no chances. Duncan watched her discuss the arrangements of the camp with several of the men, who nodded. The tents of the household were already set up encircling three tents wrought of striped silk, evidently those of Eglantine and her daughters, undoubtedly settled thus by her specific direction. On this evening, she had other more humble tents moved, so that more surrounded the silk ones and added another sentry.

Duncan half smiled to himself at the troublesome one's obvious displeasure with her circumstances. Alienor stamped her foot and raised her voice in demand, but the countess ignored her.

When Duncan's men left the group and began to saunter back toward him, Alienor cried out. Several of the men turned. She opened her arms in a beckoning gesture and called something that was snatched away by the wind.

"Oh, I will have me a bit of that," Reinald muttered under his breath. Reinald fancied himself a man of charm and good looks, and truly, there were women from here to Inverness ready to support that claim. He might have stepped closer, but Duncan laid a hand on his shoulder.

"Do not be making more trouble than we have," he counseled.

Iain, ever close and watchful, snorted beneath his breath. "Aye, Duncan is afraid of what the countess might say to him."

The men chuckled, but Duncan granted his opponent a cool glance. "Nay, this is one of the lady's daughters and naught good will come if she is seduced."

"Naught good to who?" Reinald muttered with a wicked grin. He lifted a hand to wave to Alienor, who smiled radiantly in return. Eglantine noted the exchange and glared at Duncan before forcibly escorting Alienor from view.

"We still know little of the countess's alliances. Dugall

will have little good to say to us if your lust provokes a confrontation with the king of Scotland himself."

"Over a girl?" Reinald scoffed.

"Over an asset," Duncan corrected. "The girl's value is at stake, and the countess will not suffer any compromise lightly. Indeed, she has just told me as much."

"What value?" Reinald demanded. "A woman's worth is in the sons she bears."

"Nay, this demoiselle will be worth less as a bride were she sampled first, for noblemen value the maidenhead."

Reinald snorted and spat on the grass. "Aye? Well, I would not give an old pebble for a woman on her first time. Give me a whore or a widow who knows what she is about, and I shall sleep the sleep of a sated man!"

The men laughed in agreement, the talk shifting to the willing whores of Dugall's household before Iain stepped forward, challenge bright in his eyes.

"Would that have been before or after the lady shared her charms with you?" he demanded, and the men fell silent. "Aye, a blind man could not have missed the liaison betwixt the two of you. 'Tis a curious course you make in securing Ceinn-beithe, Duncan, in seducing the woman who should be our opponent. Is that why you do not let her be driven from the land? Because you would sample her assets first?"

Duncan felt his color rise as the men watched. Some looked surprised, some displeased, though it seemed that Iain had been the most observant of them all.

Gillemore cackled to himself, shaking a finger at Duncan. "Aye, there is more than one way to see a rabbit skinned, that much is certain. Our Duncan will *charm* the deed and the land from the lady, of that there can be no doubt!"

Reinald laughed and clapped Duncan on the back. "'Tis clever, that is. Why bloodshed when there can be pleasure?"

"And indeed, once Duncan holds the deed, then the law too

will be upon our side. Surely there can be naught better than that?"

"Surely Dugall will be pleased!"

"Surely then, the lady's party will quickly leave!"

"And we have not to lift a blade." The men laughed, and Duncan was content to let them believe what they would while he sought the elusive truth.

Iain, though, spat in the grass. "If this is your plan," he said coldly, "I think it folly indeed." The men might have argued with him, but Iain held up a hand. "You must all recall that we have but half the tale and rely solely upon Duncan for even that much. Indeed, he could have said anything to the woman in that foreign tongue, and we would not know the truth of it."

"He has no reason to lie to us," Gillemore protested.

"Nay?" Iain asked.

"Nay!" Duncan retorted.

"And Duncan has been honest since first he joined us," Gillemore continued. He grimaced. "'Tis perhaps the boy's greatest flaw."

"I thank you for that," Duncan said, prompting another chuckle from his companions.

But Iain would not leave the matter be. "Perhaps Duncan means to ally with this woman and see his own bed made in the bargain." He folded his arms across his chest. " 'Twould not be the first time he saw to his own advantage, devil take the rest."

Silence fell among the men. Duncan fixed Iain with a cold glance. "On the contrary, I have always put the needs of others ahead of my own."

"Liar!" Iain charged.

"'Tis no lie!" Duncan roared.

"I shall not stand aside and let you claim a fortune, after you have won your advantage with lies." Iain bellowed. "I shall not watch you see to your pleasure while we beg for vittles!" He shook a finger at Duncan. "I grant three days, Duncan MacLaren, to you and your reputed charm. Three days, no more, to win the deed from this foreigner, destroy it, and see her party gone from Ceinn-beithe."

Duncan put his hands on his hips and stepped closer. "And then?" His words were low and heated, a dangerous tone that a wiser man might have heeded.

Iain did not. "And then I shall lead the clan and I shall take that leadership by force."

Iain cast a glance over the company, some of whom nodded approvingly. "I shall take it with the assent of the clan, for they will know that they have no leader in you. I shall reclaim Ceinn-beithe and I shall pledge my service to Dugall, King of the Isles, as the chieftain of the Clan MacQuarrie." He poked his finger toward the sea. "Then I shall honor the rest of your pledge to Dugall and see the south secured, no matter the cost!"

The lady's kiss had indeed cost Duncan dearly and he was angered that he could have been so foolish. She might well win her desire, if dissent separated his men.

"You will do no such thing!" he retorted. "You have no right!"

"I have every right!" Iain replied, his face reddening. "I am the chieftain of Clan MacQuarrie!"

"And I should have been! I am the son of Cormac MacQuarrie, the rightful heir to the role of chieftain. 'Tis you who had no right to steal what should have been mine!"

"'Twas granted to me, and that willingly!"

"You already stole once from my family!" Iain was livid. "I shall not stand aside and watch you steal again."

'Twas but half the tale. Duncan could not say a word against Cormac, not after the friendship that had bound them together, not after all the good that man had done him. He took a deep breath.

"You know that is not the truth," he allowed himself to say.

"Aye, 'tis the coward's way to dodge a fight." Iain sneered. "You twisted my father to your will rather than labor for the prizes you would have for your own. I will not watch you turn the entire clan against me."

Duncan folded his arms across his chest. "'Tis you who damage your position, with lies and by fomenting dissent."

Iain held up his fingers. "Three days."

"Be warned—I will not let you do this, Iain MacCormac."

Iain smiled coldly. "Then I shall delight in killing you first, Duncan MacLaren." His smile broadened but was no more friendly for all of that. "Unless, of course, you manage to succeed."

Chapter Six

GILLEMORE MIGHT HAVE SAID SOMETHING, BUT DUN-can stalked in the opposite direction.

Oh, he could wrap his hands around Iain's neck with pleasure, for what that man wrought these days—at least he might have, had they not been so close once long ago.

But that had been before . . . before Cormac found fault with Iain, before the boy went away, before Iain was shocked by the evidence that his father favored Duncan over him. Before Duncan had been made chieftain at Cormac's request.

Fostership to a hundred and blood to twenty, that was what Gillemore oft said of the considerable affection that oft grew between a man and his foster son, even at the expense of his own blood son. Indeed, there had been a rare bond between Duncan and Cormac, one that transcended any lack of blood between them. Duncan knew the old man loved his son, knew he wanted naught but the best for him, knew that he had finally accepted that Iain was not the warrior he had hoped he might be.

But none could tell Iain that now. He was too embittered by his losses.

Perhaps Duncan should have seen the strains in the family who adopted him as their own. But he had been too glad to find a home to question the conditions. Duncan shoved a hand through his hair and stared out to sea, haunted by memories and tormented by his choices. Aye, he had made more than one error in his days.

Did he make another in being tempted to trust the countess Eglantine?

He sorely regretted that kiss, that much could not be changed. But he would win compensation from the countess, he would drive her from this place with haste, regardless of what he had to do to succeed.

He had little choice.

The moon rose in the clearing sky, even as Duncan doubted anew the old man's choice. How could he win Iain's wager? How could he ensure there was no bloodshed? How could he seduce the deed from Eglantine?

Yet how could he fail the task assigned by the King of the Isles, when failure would mean the elimination or the subjugation of Cormac's heritage? How could Duncan not try to unite the clan beneath his hand, as Cormac desired?

It seemed he was doomed to fail the old man yet again.

He would not think of Mhairi. Duncan rubbed his face in frustration and stared into the mist shrouding the isles, knowing he would not sleep this night.

"She is a rare one, that much is certain," Gillemore declared, setting himself beside Duncan.

"Who?" Duncan asked, though he knew full well who the older man meant. In truth, he welcomed the distraction from his thoughts.

"That countess." Gillemore rubbed his hands together, then blew upon them. "As vexing as a new filly but strong enough to run all the way to Edinburgh, aye?"

Duncan smiled. "I expect as much."

Gillemore wrinkled his nose. "But burdened with such an ugly name for such a bonny face. Eglantine." He grimaced. "It sounds like a foul brew."

Duncan found himself grinning. "'Tis apt enough for her."

"Aye?"

"Aye. In her own tongue, it means a wild rose." He nudged the other man. "The kind with thorns as doughty as a briar."

Gillemore chuckled. "Then it does fit well enough, for the lady's beauty is as rare as a rose's bloom." He watched the younger man knowingly. "She is stronger than you guess, Duncan, like those stubborn flowers. Be careful, lad, or she will claim more than Ceinn-beithe from you."

Gillemore gave Duncan's shoulder a hearty squeeze. "An early match is oft a poor one and a late match a blind one."

"I make no match, Gillemore."

"Do you not, lad?" The older man shook his head. "Love and a cough are not well hid, Duncan MacLaren, but a man is never well served by a love blind to consequences. Take your desire of this one but do not compromise your own goals."

'Twas good counsel as so oft this man's was. Duncan smiled and grasped Gillemore's hand. "Aye, I will."

Then the older man was gone, whistling through his teeth as he went.

And Duncan was left, recalling a poor match and wondering about a blind one. He was certain 'twould be Mhairi's ghost who tormented him this night, but 'twas the vision of another woman who stood resolute in his mind's eye.

A noblewoman with hair like spun honey, with silken skin and a warrior's resolve. 'Twas because he desired her that Eglantine so interfered in his thoughts, Duncan knew it well.

And there was but one way to be cured of that affliction, for mystery alone fed desire. No woman held sway over a man once he had tasted her charms fully, 'twas well known.

He would have to seduce Eglantine.

For the good of his clear thinking of course.

Eglantine suspected that Duncan lied about the forgery of the deed.

'Twas the simplest way to be rid of her, to seize Kinbeath,

and he was not a man to trouble himself with finesse when a blunt solution would serve his ends. Clearly there was no way to prove his falsehood for what 'twas without leaving the holding to seek the confirmation of a king—and once he seized possession of the land, 'twould be nigh impossible to reclaim it.

Eglantine would not fall for his ruse.

Even if her heart wondered whether Theobald could have disappointed her again. 'Twould not have been out of character, that much she had to admit. Oh, she could see him, delighted with himself as he concocted a false deed, certain that 'twould appease her.

But Duncan lied. Duncan! He wanted Ceinn-beithe. Eglantine already knew that he wore the cloak of civilization lightly, if at all.

And she had learned precious little from him on this night, naught of crops and survival despite her determination to do so. The man took pleasure in provoking her, and showed remarkable skill in distracting her from matters at hand.

The "loving month" indeed. Eglantine clicked her tongue in disgust, hating how her flesh heated directly to her toes, hating even more how appealing the thought of a lover was in this chill clime. Nay, not a lover, but Duncan.

But she would not consider the merits of welcoming Duncan to her bed to ensure her warmth, though he did volunteer as much.

The man had a rare insolence about him, that much was clear.

Eglantine deliberately forced Duncan MacLaren from her mind, ignored the cluster of Duncan's men silhouetted by the fading sun, and set to work. Her daughters had to move, and she had best ensure 'twas done aright.

At least the rain was halting. Perhaps her luck changed after running awry for so long. Eglantine shook her head and smiled at the unlikely prospect of that.

Célie had already moved Esmeraude's belongings into Eglantine's tent, and she could hear the two of them playing as the maid prepared the child for bed. Previously Jacqueline and Alienor had shared the third tent with their maids, but Jacqueline was more than happy to move into the newly empty tent.

There was Jacqueline to move and Alienor to pacify, the next day's menu to review with Louis, and sentries to be posted. Eglantine worked through her evening tasks diligently, dreading the inevitable confrontation with Esmeraude.

But her fortunes had indeed changed, if only slightly. She finally entered her tent to find not only a brazier glowing with welcome heat, but her daughter already sound asleep in Célie's arms. The women shared a smile and Eglantine brushed a curl back from her little cherub's brow before climbing into the welcome luxury of her own bed. The tent nigh glowed golden within; 'twas a dry and peaceful sanctuary.

And warm enough, she told herself, even without a lover in her bed.

Though still Eglantine was not to have that single night of sound sleep. Just as her eyes drifted closed, a man sang in the distance and the sound made her sit bolt upright. His deep voice sent chills down her spine, though maid and babe slumbered on untroubled. She gripped the linens, knowing full well who 'twas.

Curse him! The man would even deny her sleep!

Eglantine thumped the pillows and dropped back onto the mattress, drawing the linens high over her ears. She squeezed her eyes shut, determined not to listen to him, but the song wound its way not only to her ears. Its mournful tune made her heart ache, though Eglantine could not understand the words. She found herself wondering what Duncan had lost, for his song sounded as if 'twas wrung from the depths of his soul.

Then she realized how readily he had distracted her. A pox upon Duncan MacLaren! She would forget him and his lies if 'twas the last thing she did. No doubt he wanted only to ensure she did not sleep well—so that she would be a less worthy opponent on the morrow.

Eglantine would give him no such satisfaction. Nay, she would arise early and hunt once more, fulfilling her responsibilities to her vassals.

Though this time she would not venture so far afield.

Duncan returned from his walk along the shore while the sky was yet dark. He had not slept the night, he was rumpled and damp and in a foul temper. But 'twas not the sleeplessness that soured his mood—and 'twas not because he had been haunted by Mhairi and his errors in the past.

Nay, 'twas Eglantine who had kept him from sleep, and that rankled. 'Twas Eglantine with her hot kisses and her flashing eyes, with her slender curves, her mysteries, and her steely determination who invaded his thoughts and awakened his desire.

Even when he sang of Mhairi.

Duncan flicked a glance at Eglantine's already spreading settlement. The woman won her way in this, and he was fool enough to be her pawn. She had not left; she showed no signs of departing. The weather had turned to her favor, while Duncan's men grew increasingly impatient with his decisions.

But 'twas not within Duncan to attack women, much less to countenance bloodshed in the first place. He was not a warrior, he was not an intuitive leader of men, and he wondered anew at Cormac's choice.

But while he took the noble course, the walls rose slowly but steadily on the hall that would be her court. 'Twould not be long before Eglantine was settled permanently here, her claim fortified and defensible.

'Twould not be long before 'twas too late.

Duncan had to do something and he had to do it now.

And then it came to him, as clearly as if Cormac himself had whispered in his ear. If you have but one eye, look with the eye you have got.

Duncan smiled. Aye, he was a bard and a fine one at that. He would win this battle with a tale. And he had already planted the seed of it, as if it had been his plan all along.

He pulled the knife from his belt and crept closer to the sleeping settlement. He steered a wide berth around the cooks who were arguing good-naturedly, picking out the places where he could make the most damage with the least work. One sentry dozed, a second hovered near the cooks. The third and fourth were easily avoided.

Duncan would make trouble as only a Gael storyteller could—by feigning the presence of an offended ghost. Should the household's superstitions be stirred, even the pragmatic countess would not be able to keep her vassals here.

And Eglantine could not survive in this place alone.

Duncan bent and quickly pulled a strategic trio of tent pegs from the ground. He cut guy lines so that a mere thread remained, and pulled more pegs while keeping out of sight. The wind rose as he worked, as if 'twould aid him in this, and he knew that he had made the right decision.

By the time he had swept silently through the camp and a fitful gust of wind finished his labor, Duncan was sitting amid his men as if he had been there all the night long. He stood up, apparently startled by the sounds of tents collapsing and chaos being wrought.

But his smile at the cries of dismay revealed his hand to more than one of his companions.

Alienor screamed when her tent fell upon her. She won a mouthful of silk for her efforts and struggled, furious at the ineptitude of Eglantine's vassals. She abandoned her maid and finally crawled into the sunlight.

The laughter of the local men halted her while she was yet on all fours. The camp was in confusion, tents falling, women crying out, and men running, but Duncan and his men stood and laughed at their antics.

They had left their camp to watch what they undoubtedly deemed entertainment, and stood not far outside the perimeter of Eglantine's camp. The sentries seemed to have forgotten their duties in the urge to help, and Duncan's rough group of men pointed and howled. 'Twas true that no one was hurt, but Alienor's face burned with embarrassment.

She looked far from her best. She stood, though, and spared the men a haughty glance before casting her disheveled braid over her shoulder. A tall fair man ceased his laughter and she could nigh feel his gaze upon her.

'Twas then that Alienor realized she wore only her sheer chemise. Instead of modestly hiding her charms, she turned and glared at the man for his boldness.

And he smiled, appreciation tinging his expression.

Alienor had an idea. Aye, she knew what she wanted, and she knew she would not find it here. She was fast under the thumb of Eglantine and did not care for that in the least. Alienor wanted a spouse, and though a barbarian was not her first choice, there were few other options hereabouts.

She eyed Duncan MacLaren with new appreciation. He was not hard upon the eyes. And Alienor had seen Eglantine eyeing him with interest the day before. There was infinite appeal in claiming something—or someone—that Eglantine desired.

'Twould be fitting recompense, to Alienor's thinking.

She had no doubt of the power of her own considerable charms. Eglantine was ancient, after all, widowed and prim and scarred by childbirth. Alienor was young, unsullied and willing.

Alienor did not intend to let subtlety lose the battle. She cast back her hair and boldly walked across the camp, loosening her braid as she picked her way through the disorder. She was well aware of how those black tresses accentuated the fairness of her skin, how the pallor of just awakening would make her eyes look more vividly blue. She ignored her maid's cry of protest and kept her gaze fixed upon Duncan as she walked.

He folded his arms across his chest, his fair companion making a comment to which he did not reply. Indeed, Duncan's eyes narrowed in a most unwelcoming manner. But Alienor did not care. She granted him her finest smile.

"Good morn to you," she said, breathless to be directly before the object of her desire.

Duncan was even taller and more mysterious at close proximity, his eyes filled with a hundred tales. Alienor could well imagine that he kissed like a god, and she shivered as she imagined his hands upon her flesh.

And he was a chieftain, the most important man hereabouts, which was of equal significance to Alienor. 'Twas high time she had another man in her life like her father, a man who understood that women needed luxuries, a man who would pamper her as she deserved, a man who would steal her from beneath Eglantine's strict demands. She was due to be lavished with gifts and masculine attention.

Aye, Alienor was certain that Duncan knew much of stealing and spoiling women.

"I am Alienor," she declared.

"So I understand." Duncan regarded her with amusement, some shadow in his eyes not entirely welcoming. Indeed, he reminded her of her stepmother, always prepared to be disapproving.

Alienor put one hand on his arm, intent on capturing his attention in a less parental way. "Are you wed?"

"Nay." Duncan lifted her hand, none too gently, and removed it.

"Betrothed?"

He cast her a quelling glance. "Nay."

"Nor am I." When he frowned instead of returning her brilliant smile, Alienor tossed her hair. Duncan spoke tersely to his men, his gaze lazily roving over the settlement.

And avoiding her. He was only *feigning* indifference, Alienor knew it well. She had only to prompt his jealousy to change his tune. She spared the man on Duncan's left—the fair one, the appreciative one—that same smile. He smiled eagerly down at her, his gaze trailing over her sheer chemise.

Duncan said something fast and foreign, and the other man's smile faded. Alienor did not need to understand the words to feel triumphant, though; her ploy had worked! Duncan was defending her as his woman.

She leaned toward him and batted her eyelashes provocatively. "I do hope our meager meal yesterday was sufficient," she murmured. "A man of this wild land like you must be accustomed to more hearty fare."

"'Twas a fine stew," Duncan said, his tone noncommittal. "And a finer meal than we might have had otherwise. The countess was most gracious to share."

"The countess," she scoffed, then rolled her eyes at the absurdity of the title. "If anyone should be called countess, it should be me. My father would have wished it to be so."

'Twas not entirely true, for the title passed to her elder brother and hence to his wife, but Alienor noted with pleasure that she had snared Duncan's attention.

"Indeed?" he asked.

"Indeed."

"And what happened to your father?"

Alienor shrugged. "He died, as old men are wont to do. I must say 'twas most troubling for me and the beginning of all my woes . . ." She tried to force a tear to win his sympathy, but Duncan frowned in a most unsympathetic way.

"Your father died of old age?"

"Nay, not precisely. He choked on a chicken bone at the board." Alienor winced at the banality of the truth. "Eglantine tried to aid him—doubtless she was in no hurry to be widowed—but he cast her off, insisting that only his châtelain might aid him. That man came to his side too late. He was ancient and could scarcely walk, much less run." Alienor did manage to find a tear and let her lip tremble as that tear spilled to her cheek. "'Twas horrible for me, for I was a mere child . . ."

"Did you witness this?" Duncan interrupted sharply.

"Aye, I was there."

"And your mother tried to aid him, in truth?"

"Aye, Eglantine did," Alienor allowed, her tone turning cross for she did not wish to speak of Eglantine. "But she is not my mother."

"She said she was." Duncan studied Alienor as if he thought she might be lying. 'Twas not the most flattering response he might have shown, and Alienor lifted her chin.

"She is my *step*mother. My father wed her when I was four summers of age." The old jealousy that had raged through Alienor in those early years of her father's second marriage claimed her again, and she hoped Duncan did not glimpse it before she managed to conceal it once more. He watched her steadily, though, his gaze assessing. "Eglantine left the household when my father died."

Duncan frowned, puzzling this through. "But Esmeraude is her own daughter?"

"As is Jacqueline." Alienor tried to keep the resentment from her voice and failed. "Jacqueline was born to Eglantine and my father a year or so after they were wed. Esmeraude is the child of Eglantine and Theobald."

Duncan's eyes narrowed and Alienor feared he saw too much.

"'Twas no concern to me when Jacqueline was born, you understand," she insisted, "for my father always loved me more than any other."

But Duncan did indeed seem to read more into Alienor's words than she intended. "Because 'twas Eglantine you resented," he suggested softly.

And the words fell from her lips before Alienor could stop them. "She stole my father's eye away!"

"Yet you make your home with her."

Alienor glared at him. "I had no choice."

"How so?"

She folded her arms across her chest and tapped her toe, desperately trying to calculate how she might chart the conversation's course back to herself and her desires and their entangled future.

"In my darkest moment of despair, when I most had need of a chivalrous man, my elder brother showed that he was not that man. So, too, did my betrothed, who showed the lack of foresight to die before our nuptials. His family kept my dowry, and I was left with naught but the garb upon my back. This was contrary to my father's will for my future, but none saw beyond their own greed."

Alienor let her breath catch, knowing a show of vulnerability might win her much. "They *cheated* me, and none came to my aid!"

Her companion seemed unstirred by this confession—which only meant she had not put sufficient emotion into her words.

Alienor boldly placed her hand upon his chest. She could feel his heartbeat beneath her fingertips and was pleased that she conjured a maidenly flush.

She tipped up her face, opening her eyes wide to hold his

skeptical gaze. "I knew that somewhere in Christendom there would be a man for me, a bold man who would care naught for my lack of dowry, a man who would but gaze into my eyes and know that we were destined to be together for all time . . ."

Duncan eyed her warily. "But in the interim, you asked Eglantine to provide for you?"

The man had no romance in his soul, 'twas clear. Alienor's lips tightened as she eyed him. "She owed me no less."

"Indeed?" Duncan laughed beneath his breath. He eyed Alienor, his expression knowing. "Because you so sweetly welcomed her to your father's home?"

Alienor flushed scarlet. 'Twas as if the man peered into her memories and saw the toads that had found their way to Eglantine's bed, the fine bridal chemises that had been shredded, the gold chain of the lady's heirloom amulet that had been willfully broken and left scattered across the floor.

"She deserved no less than what she won," Alienor muttered.

Duncan's gaze did not waver. "Because your father loved her?"

"He never loved her!" Alienor cried. "He but lusted for her, and she tricked him into marriage. She *tempted* him and made him forget my mother's precious memory!"

"She cannot have been old enough to have been a temptress."

"Fourteen is old enough when sin is in the blood," Alienor said darkly. "Everything changed when she came! My father nigh forgot about me—'twas unfair! 'Twas justice served that she was never happy in our home, justice that my father was furious at the arrival of another daughter and spurned Eglantine, justice that my brother cast Eglantine from the gates before my father was even laid to rest."

Duncan arched a brow in surprise. "It would seem a small comfort to let a widow witness her spouse's funeral."

"'Twas a family event and she was not family."

"What a fine brood you are. 'Tis no credit that your brother treated his father's widow even more shamefully than he treated you."

"Nay, I bore the brunt of his malice!"

"And what of Jacqueline? Had she no right to attend her father's funeral?"

Alienor could not hold Duncan's gaze. Indeed, this conversation did not proceed as she had hoped. She tapped her toe impatiently, wondering why Duncan persisted in talking about old and withered Eglantine when she, ripe and lovely Alienor, was directly before him.

Perhaps the man was blind as well as unromantic.

"It seems the lady bore much in your household," he commented quietly.

Alienor exhaled noisily, annoyed with his insistence upon this mistaken conclusion. "I bore the brunt of it." She pointed emphatically to herself. "*I* did. *I* was the one cheated of a dowry, of a father's love, of a spouse and a life of ease. *I* was the one poorly served." Her tears came in earnest this time, a testament to the ordeal she had suffered, at least from her own perspective.

"The lady Eglantine," Duncan said, "has shown you more charity than your behavior toward her deserves. If you wish to find that man of whom you dream, you might take a lesson from the countess."

He snapped his fingers at his companion, spoke rapidly, then strode away. He gathered the other men with a word here and another word there, clearly oblivious to Alienor's dismay.

Oh, he was insufferable! How could he not be touched by her tears? How could he not take her side? How could he champion wretched Eglantine at Alienor's expense?

But the fair man was not so unappreciative. Though he took a step away at Duncan's command, he lingered.

Alienor spared him a cutting glance. "And what do you stare at?" she snapped, wiping her tears with her fingertips, then covering the shadows of her breasts with her hands. "Go away!"

He smiled at her, then touched his heart. "Iain MacCormac," he said, his accent so thick that it took Alienor a moment to comprehend that he confided his name.

"I do not care who you are," she retorted. "Duncan is the man for me. I will have a rich man, a man of influence and power, a man who will treat me as I deserve." She cast a scathing glance over this man, to make her point clear.

"Nay Duncan," he growled, his low words making her shiver. He jabbed himself in the chest with his thumb. "Iain MacQuarrie."

No man would tell Alienor what she wanted. Even if this man's fair good looks and his intense manner made her pulse skip, he was of no repute.

"Nay Iain MacQuarrie," she corrected sharply, but he laughed again, as if he knew better than she. He stepped closer and caught her shoulders in a sudden move that Alienor had not anticipated.

Then he kissed her, his mouth warm and firm upon her own. She trembled, though whether from indignation or pleasure even she could not say. Iain slanted his mouth across hers and tasted her more fully, pulling her closer so that her breasts bumped against his chest.

Duncan cried a warning and Iain reluctantly ended his kiss.

But his blue gaze bored into Alienor's own. He murmured something low and hot in the language of the Gaels, then rubbed the rough edge of his thumb across her cheek in a blatantly possessive gesture. He whispered his own name again as if he would bid her to recall it.

Alienor glared at him. Who did he think he was? She made to kick him for his audacity, but he danced out of range.

That he laughed at her was no balm to her pride.

"Cursed creature!" she cried. Iain winked as if he guessed her thoughts and did not care. Then he was gone, striding after Duncan and leaving Alienor standing alone.

But she could not catch her breath and she could not slow the hammering of her heart. Her fists were clenched and her breasts ached for something she could not name. Alienor took an impatient breath, not pleased to be so readily forgotten when she was all atingle. She glared at Iain's back, then returned to her dismayed maid in a huff.

She knew 'twas Iain who called her name, but Alienor ignored his cry. She had no interest in a man who thought he could tell her what to do. She would have Duncan and no other.

Even if he did not possess eyes of startling blue.

Chapter Seven

EGLANTINE RETURNED TO CHAOS THAT EVEN SHE doubted could be made aright.

She could not believe that her camp could be cast in such disarray, but her eyes did not deceive. The entire household scurried like frenzied ants, tents lay collapsed and wagons were spilled. Palfreys and goats wandered untethered through the melee, even the hens had been loosed from their temporary pen. She strode through the disorder, quickly determined that none was injured, and noted the tent pegs pulled from the ground.

Then she was shown not one, not two, but a dozen guy lines cleanly cut almost through. The last cord in each had snapped, no doubt by the weight of the tents in question shifting, but would never have broken without the initial cut.

And Eglantine knew instinctively who was responsible. Her gaze rose to one Duncan MacLaren, who loitered with his men and grinned.

Shameless rogue! If he thought she would demurely let this insult pass, he was mistaken indeed. Eglantine stalked out to meet him, knowing her anger showed.

"I would have thought that such petty vandalism would be beneath you," she said by way of greeting.

"Me?" Duncan's eyes widened in mock alarm. "You think me responsible for this?"

"Who else might it be?"

"No doubt, my lady, you are unaware of the caprice of the winds in these places. They gust most unpredictably. But then, you would not be accustomed to such vigorous winds in France." His eyes narrowed, his gaze flicking over her as if he would wring secrets from her very soul. "You are on foreign shores, after all, and much must be unfathomable."

"And most unwelcome upon them, clearly." Eglantine arched a brow. "Do the winds in this land come equipped with knives, as well? There are guy lines cut almost through and though I have no doubt that the wind finished the task, it most certainly did not begin it."

She thought the corner of his mouth quirked mischievously before Duncan whistled through his teeth. "Oh, my lady, I fear this could be dire indeed." He frowned with evident concern and laid claim to her elbow. "You must let me see one."

He had that unpredictable look again, and Eglantine feared she stepped directly into the trap he had set for her. But surely there could be no harm in this?

She wished she knew for certain. But she did not, and his thumb moved across the inside of her elbow with such persuasive ease that she could not think as clearly as she would have liked. She found herself accompanying him back to the site of the damage, realizing his intent only when her entire household gathered around.

"Oh, this is most serious," Duncan proclaimed, his tone prompting Eglantine's vassals to eye each other in consternation.

"Aye, 'tis willful destruction."

"Nay, worse." Duncan frowned and shook his head. "I warned you well, my lady, that this was a sacred place to our forebears. I warned you that there might be ancient souls displeased with your presence here. But you did not heed my counsel and now a toll must be paid."

Eglantine felt the shiver run through her company. She pulled her arm from his gentle grip, not wanting them to look as if they stood together, and glared at him.

"Ridiculous," she said crisply. "All souls go to heaven, hell, or purgatory, as their circumstance dictates. There are no souls lingering hereabout, ancient or otherwise." Her priest nodded agreement with this recounting of doctrine, but Duncan shook his head.

"Perhaps not in France, my lady, but we have older traditions here." Duncan raised his gaze to scan the horizon, his eyes narrowing as if he saw the shadows of events long past. "Perhaps 'tis because of our heathen roots, the history of our faith in these parts, the bloody course of our past."

The assembly leaned closer, eyes rounded, and Duncan warmed to his theme. Oh, he told a fine tale, she would give him that!

His voice dropped low and he looked the villeins in the eye, each in succession, as if he would persuade them of the truth of this claim. Eglantine tapped her toe, impatient with his nonsense, but the assembly was rapt.

"Once there stood an entire circle of stones upon this land where you now build your abode. That one remaining was but the largest, the one on the eastern side of the circle. 'Tis said that there was the altar, that there was where the pagan priests made their blood sacrifices to their hungered gods."

The company shivered, though Eglantine rolled her eyes. "Foolery to frighten children to their beds, 'tis no more than that."

"Oh, my lady, you are brave indeed to so challenge what all know to be true." Duncan nodded grimly and Eglantine was disgusted at the way her vassals hung on his every word, greedy for gruesome detail. "'Tis said among us that those souls who leave matters unfinished in their lives do not pass to the beyond. They linger, hovering, influencing the circumstances of the living, insisting that those incomplete matters be resolved before they can rest in peace."

He fingered his chin as he looked toward the great stone, the company following his glance. "What secrets does this stone recall?" he mused, though none noted how Eglantine rolled her eyes. "What tragedies and marvels has it witnessed? I cannot help but imagine that those unfortunates who were sacrificed upon these stones had need of such resolution. Surely they would linger near the place of their demise, insistent upon seeing justice done."

He had every one of them snared beneath his spell. Her vassals edged closer to each other, as if the sun was not enough to warm them in this place. Eglantine made to interrupt, but Duncan touched his fingers to her lips with such familiarity that she was momentarily startled.

'Twas long enough to suit him. He fingered the broken rope and let it fall from his fingers, his expression grim. "So many centuries they have waited in solitude, so many centuries they have longed for revenge. Can one blame them for seizing upon the first so bold as to build a keep upon the site of their misfortune?" He shuddered and stood. "Who knows what toll they ultimately will demand? In truth, I fear for you all—though you have acted in ignorance, you may well be forced to pay some gruesome price."

A chattering broke out in the ranks of Eglantine's vassals, and she wished she could consign Duncan to that same state of lingering between this world and the next.

It took but a trio of heartbeats before the appeals began.

"My lady, we must abandon the construction."

"My lady, we must move camp."

"My lady, we beg of you, do not trouble these souls any longer."

"Perhaps," Louis interjected crisply, "'twould behoove us to return to Crevy."

Eglantine spun in horror to eye her châtelain, never having expected him to correct her before the company. There was a glint of determination in Louis's eye, though, and she knew he did not believe Duncan's tale.

But he seized the opportunity to express his opinion of what should be done. Eglantine gritted her teeth, fully intending to have words with the older man over his so-called loyalty to her family.

The company rallied behind the châtelain, their gazes fixed expectantly upon Eglantine. She had but a glimpse of the wicked twinkle in Duncan's eye, but 'twas enough to spark her temper.

He enjoyed the havoc he wreaked on her!

"This man lies to us all," Eglantine declared with such fervor that her company was visibly startled. "Are you so witless that you do not see his hand in this? 'Twas a mortal hand that cut these ropes and pulled these pegs, 'tis a mortal man who wishes us to leave that he might make his claim to this land. He contests ownership of this holding, after all, and 'tis in his interests to see us gone." Eglantine lifted her chin and glared at Duncan. "I will not be such a coward as to cede to his game."

The company rallied slightly at her words, but the seeds of doubt were sown. The damage was done. Eglantine knew that reason would sink with the sun this night and that her vassals would lie awake whispering in fear. She knew that Duncan would not cease his manipulation of events, and she knew that if he were not halted, her support among her own superstitious vassals would erode.

And he would claim Kinbeath in the end. Eglantine was not prepared to let him win so readily as that.

She would fight fire with fire. She hailed the priest and beckoned to him. "Father, we have need of a mass."

"Aye, my lady." The priest of Arnelaine bowed deeply.

"'Twas the edict of none less than Pope Gregory to consecrate the heathen shrines of Britannia to the service of Our Lord. With your permission, we shall celebrate the mass at noon at the great stone."

An apprehensive shiver rolled over the company, but Eglantine smiled with confidence and spoke before Duncan could interject a word. "I have always admired the clear thinking of Pope Gregory. Make it so, if you please."

The assembly dispersed, chattering avidly as they returned to their duties. The priest chose a few to aid him and strode toward the stone, his crucifix held before him and his black robes blowing in the wind.

Eglantine left Duncan without another word, so irked with his game that she had no interest in whatever he was clearly schooling himself to say. She spoke with Louis, though to no avail—he believed he served the ultimate welfare of the family by expressing his doubts.

His tone made it clear that he thought Eglantine risked all for no good reason. 'Twas not an argument she could win. She saw Esmeraude playing with Célie, a reminder of another battle in which Eglantine took the losing side. Alienor swept past Eglantine and headed directly for the camp of Duncan's men, prompting her stepmother to sigh with exasperation.

Could anything else go awry?

First matters first. Eglantine's gaze was drawn unwillingly to Duncan, joking with his men. He stood with his muscled legs braced against the rock, as much a part of this place as she was not. Her heart skipped when he lifted a hand to her in silent salute.

As if she would welcome his company after what he had done! Eglantine stalked in the opposite direction. She had to find an alternative, a more enduring solution to the problem and the presence of Duncan MacLaren. She glanced back in time to see Alienor preen before Duncan as he watched, a small smile playing over her lips.

And with sudden certainty, she *knew*.

Eglantine had hoped French knights would compete for her daughters' hands. But then, there was a paucity of knights in this region, and Kinbeath was considerably farther from civilization than Eglantine had expected. 'Twould take years to build the manor, perhaps even longer to build a reputation that would coax men to Eglantine's court.

And Alienor grew no younger. Indeed, she should have been wed years past, but the death of her betrothed and the loss of her dowry had destroyed her father's plan.

Duncan *was* the chieftain of the Clan MacQuarrie, so evidently a man of some affluence and influence in these lands. He spoke Norman French and thus could converse with Alienor, an apparently distinguishing characteristic in these parts. He was far from foul to look upon, Eglantine conceded, ignoring the unruly skip of her heart. He was not without charms—he could sing, he had shown compassion with Esmeraude.

Alienor clearly found him appealing. Perhaps they two would suit each other—her demanding nature might pass for honesty in his estimation. Aye, and Alienor could certainly benefit from a match with a man nigh as stubborn as herself.

Certainly such a course would resolve the issue of their respective claims, for a marriage between Eglantine's family and Duncan's clan would merge the ambitions of both groups. 'Twould halt this nonsensical competition between them and ensure all could labor together for the benefit of all.

'Twas perfect. Something needled Eglantine about the solution, but she deliberately ignored her doubts. No doubt Duncan would agree with such a sensible proposition. Aye, once he had a woman in his bed, he would cease his attempts to seduce her, as well.

For some reason which did not bear exploration, Eglantine did not want to think overmuch of that.

Aye, as soon as she set the camp to rights again, she would propose the arrangement. The matter must be presented delicately. Duncan would surely be delighted that she thought so highly of him as to surrender her daughter to his hand.

■

Contrary to Eglantine's expectations, Duncan was infuriated.

She sent for him shortly after midday, and Duncan expected naught good. Indeed, 'twas unlike her to send another to retrieve him, instead of simply hunting him down herself, and he assumed 'twas no good portent. He came to her tent, as bidden, braced for her fury and a lecture on the inappropriateness of fostering superstition, no less meddling with the beliefs of her vassals.

But the lady surprised him yet again.

She received him with a gracious smile, like a queen at her court. She wore a kirtle he had not seen before, its rich green hue making her eyes yet more like emeralds. Her hair was secured behind a sheer pale veil, making her look disconcertingly unfamiliar and remote by dint of her formal attire. She appeared slender and regal and unapproachable in such garb, even more foreign than she had thus far.

In contrast, he felt somewhat less than presentable. Aye, Duncan was well aware that his shirt had need of a scrub—as did all the rest of him—and his whiskers had need of a scrape. The tower his men occupied offered somewhat primitive accommodations, and they had not intended to linger here, after all.

Coals glowed upon an ornate brazier near the lady's feet, rugs were thick beneath his feet. The silken walls of the tent shimmered as they moved slightly in the wind, the filtered sunlight painted the rugs in striped patterns. A thick mattress piled high with pillows lurked behind the lady, the fine texture and varied colors of the cloth beyond what was seen locally.

Duncan was awed. Eglantine had wrought a court out of naught. She proved her ascendancy and her birthright in the same moment she made Duncan painfully aware of his lack of one.

'Twas a game of power and one artfully played.

While he hovered on the threshold, feeling large, male, and unkempt, Eglantine donned a fur-lined cloak and a pair of gloves wrought of finest leather. "I would have you show me all of Ceinn-beithe," she said with a sweetness he knew better than to trust.

This composed creature might have been a stranger. Even her features seemed unfamiliar, her expression so demure that she might have been the twin of his countess.

Duncan raised a brow. "I beg your pardon."

The lady gave undue attention to her gloves. "I assume you can ride? I have ordered a steed saddled for you, as well as my own palfrey." She met his gaze, her own sharp with challenge. "I would hope you have no issues with this."

She had a scheme, of that Duncan was certain. Though he was curious, he was more interested in how her plan meshed with his own. He had pledged to seduce the lady, and truly, there were better places to do so than within her camp.

He smiled, knowing his expression was predatory. "I should be delighted to show you *my* Ceinn-beithe."

And then she surprised him again. "Your specific claim to Ceinn-beithe will be moot when you wed Alienor."

She brushed past him, leaving him standing with his mouth open in shock. She had the manner of a woman who has resolved everything to her own satisfaction.

Duncan charged after her. "What nonsense is this?"

"You need not look so astonished, 'tis perfectly good

sense." Eglantine smiled at him as sweetly as a madonna and continued to argue her case. "Now bite your tongue. I shall not discuss the matter before my vassals."

The woman was naught if not determined.

Duncan was so angered by Eglantine's presumption that he needed time to find words for his outrage. They mounted the horses held ready and rode from the camp in strained silence. Their steeds climbed the low roll of hills that buttressed the land to the east.

Then Duncan knew precisely where he would take her. He seized the reins of her palfrey and touched his heels to the flanks of the steed she had supplied for him.

"What are you doing?"

Duncan said naught but rode.

"As you can undoubtedly appreciate, this course makes perfect sense," Eglantine declared with crisp efficiency, obviously taking his silence for some measure of agreement. "If our families are united, then this tedious competition . . ."

"It makes *no* sense," Duncan interrupted, speaking somewhat more loudly than necessary.

Eglantine blinked but was typically untroubled by his volume. "Of course, 'tis somewhat of a surprise to you, but should you pause to consider the advantages . . ."

Duncan glared at her. "There are no advantages to be had in wedding a child!"

Eglantine cleared her throat gently. "Alienor is eight and ten years of age. She is a woman fully."

Duncan snorted. "She is an ungrateful wretch of a child with naught good to recommend her character."

Eglantine's eyes widened at his blunt assessment. Then she smiled, the way she leaned forward to pat his forearm in such a maternal fashion doing naught to aid matters. "I think perhaps that in your surprise at my generous offer, you underestimate Alienor's assets. She can be somewhat temperamental, but I would think that a man of your nature would appreciate her honesty."

"A barbarian is what you mean," Duncan corrected, his anger rising with every word she uttered.

Eglantine laughed beneath her breath, a winsome twinkle appearing in those green depths. Desire joined Duncan's simmering anger and coaxed it to boil.

How could she conclude that she could chart the course of his life, that she could conveniently be rid of him by saddling him with Alienor?

Duncan gritted his teeth, inclined to be anything but convenient.

"One never doubts Alienor's desire certainly, but she is young and beautiful and not too old to bear a son for a man of such a position as yourself."

"She is but a child!" Duncan roared. He coaxed his horse to a gallop, and hers was compelled to match his pace since he yet held her reins.

"There is no need to shout and alarm the horses."

"There is every need to shout!" Duncan halted the horse in a small clearing, then bounded from his saddle. Eglantine regarded him from her saddle like a queen who was shocked at the outspoken manner of one of her minions. "How dare you imagine that you could rid yourself of that selfish creature by foisting her upon me!"

"I had thought you might be of like mind."

"You thought wrongly! I have no lust for children, no desire for women who think only of themselves, and no interest in blushing virgins who come unwillingly to bed!"

Eglantine rolled her eyes. "I hardly think that Alienor could be considered reluctant to rid herself of her virginity," she said with a touch of the incisiveness he had come to expect from her.

The very glimpse of the Eglantine he knew vastly encouraged Duncan. "But I shall not do the deed!" he cried. "You may find another hapless fool to do your bidding in this!"

Eglantine's eyes flashed and she too dismounted, her own words rising in volume. "'Tis not a case of doing my bidding, but of finding a suitable solution for all."

"This solution does not suit me!"

"Well, perhaps it should!" Eglantine shouted back. "Perhaps you are a witless fool, after all! What manner of man would refuse a noble bride, a young beauty like Alienor? What manner of fool would choose dissent over peace?"

Duncan was sorely tempted to give her a shake. "A man who knows what he wants, no more than that."

"Aye?" Eglantine, unafraid, tilted her chin in challenge. "And what is it that you want, Duncan MacLaren? What lofty ambition have you that Alienor is not good enough to fulfill?" She flung out her hand. "Tell me what good reason you might have to spurn this fine offer."

Though he appreciated that he could shout without Eglantine fleeing like a startled hare, in this moment Duncan was irritated that she paid so little attention to his anger. He let his voice drop low and noted the answering flicker in her eyes with satisfaction.

And something else. She caught her breath but did not step away from him.

"Let me make myself understood, my lady Eglantine." He growled. "I have seen one commanded to wed to suit another's convenience once already in this life, and I will not be part of such a plan again."

She was blessedly silent, her gaze fixed upon him. Aye, he had her full attention. Duncan liked that Eglantine did not flinch. He liked her trust and he liked her bravery. He caught her elbows in his hands, lifted her to her toes, and drew her closer, liking the heat that dawned in her eyes.

"A wise man learns from error, Eglantine," Duncan said

softly. "If ever I wed, 'twill be solely for my desire and convenience."

"How like a man," she whispered, "to wed solely to sate his lust."

"How like you to twist all I say into what 'tis not."

Eglantine arched a brow, inviting him to explain, the wary light in her eyes telling him she expected little persuasive.

Duncan smiled despite himself, her response dismissing his temper. He let his thumbs move across the smooth wool of her kirtle, let his palms slide up her arms to cup her shoulders, and leaned close enough that he could hear her catch her breath.

"If ever I wed, my lady Eglantine, 'twill be to a woman without whom I cannot draw a breath, a woman who has laid claim to my heart, a woman from whom I cannot bear to be parted."

Her lips quirked. "And you shall cast her over your shoulder in good barbarian fashion."

"I shall woo her until there is naught in her heart but me."

Eglantine swallowed visibly as she stared up at him. "Then woo Alienor," she suggested, her voice catching on the words.

Duncan let his gaze drift to her lips and he flexed his fingers as he drew her closer. She caught her breath, her lips parting, and he knew with sudden clarity what he did want. "Nay, Eglantine," he whispered, his lips a finger's breadth from her own. "I cannot woo Alienor. 'Twould be far too simple to live without her presence."

Eglantine almost laughed. "You and your whimsy. Tell me where you will find a bride of finer birthright, of more noble lineage, of more beauty than Alienor?"

Duncan smiled, the word rising to his lips with such ease that he knew 'twas the truth. "Here."

Duncan felt Eglantine shiver when he claimed her lips

with his. He pulled her against his chest. 'Twas no gentle salute he offered this time, but a kiss demanding her surrender, a kiss demanding that she loose the passion he knew slumbered within her.

And 'twas but a moment before the lady leaned against him. She opened her mouth to him and Duncan did not need to be invited twice. Duncan's heart pounded in triumph and he tasted her fully, loving how she met him touch for touch. He discarded her veil impatiently, marveling at how finely she was wrought even as he pushed one hand through the thick silk of her hair.

She was magnificent.

He claimed her lips hungrily again. Duncan did not know whether he had provoked her into showing her true desire, or whether she twisted him to her own purposes. He was provoked enough himself that he did not care.

And neither, it seemed, did Eglantine. Her slender hands were in his own hair, her fingertips running over his face, her tongue between his teeth. 'Twas as if a storm had been unleashed, the passion he had glimpsed afore compelling her to seize her share of pleasure.

Duncan was only too happy to aid in that pursuit. His blood was thundering, his body was hard. And 'twas no lie that he desired this woman. He kissed Eglantine's cheek, her eyelids, her temple, her ear, eager to sample her everywhere. He nuzzled her throat, kissing her in that achingly soft place beneath her ear, and the lady moaned. Eglantine twisted her tongue in Duncan's ear, her breathless gasp of his name enough to drive him wild.

With only one thought, he swept her into his arms and made for the crumbling structure that had been his destination. "The horses," she whispered, but he shook his head.

"They are not stupid enough to flee." He smiled crookedly for her. "And if they are, you are better without them."

"What is this place?"

"A chapel built by a hermit monk some five centuries ago." He ducked beneath the low sill of the stone doorway, blinking at the darkness within. "'Tis dry here and sheltered from the wind." The ceiling was low, compelling him to crouch as he balanced Eglantine on his knees. 'Twas no bigger than a noble's bed within, but 'twould more than do.

He smiled. "'Tis unfortunate the pelt of the wolf is not yet cured."

"'Tis but squirrel," she said huskily, loosening her cloak and revealing the fur lining. "But perhaps 'twill do."

The confirmation of her willingness was more than he expected. Duncan caught Eglantine's nape in one hand, holding her close, his fingers buried in the soft shimmer of her hair. His other hand caressed the length of her, her curves pressed against him from shoulder to toe. She made a cry in her throat when he found her nipple and arched when he rolled that peak between his finger and thumb.

Her lips parted and her lashes fluttered against her cheek as he cupped her breast in his hand. He bent and grazed his teeth across the peak, and she shivered, his touch clearly penetrating the wool of her kirtle.

'Twas not enough.

He broke his kiss to study Eglantine, noting her shining eyes, reddened lips, and flushed cheeks. He caught his breath that her gaze was fixed wonderingly upon him, and, indeed, he wondered what she saw that filled her eyes with marvel. Her breath came quickly and she held his gaze as he coaxed that nipple to a tighter peak with finger and thumb.

He drew back to watch her and was astounded only now that she had permitted him such familiarity. Desire coursed thick and hot through Duncan's veins. He would be the next between her thighs, of that he was certain.

Though the lady would agree to it first.

"You lied to me, Eglantine," he murmured.

"Nay," she insisted, her gaze unswerving.

"Aye." Duncan whispered. "In this moment, you do indeed owe me aye or nay."

It nigh killed him to wait, to feel her softness beneath him, to know that he could coax her with his touch to submit, to be convinced that without consent, she was not his to take.

But wait Duncan did.

The lady had already labeled him a savage, and he would not prove her aright. He would not take more than she offered. His thumb moved persuasively across her taut nipple, 'twas true, as if his touch alone would coax her to cede all. Her breath caught and Duncan was not above using any advantage to win her to his side.

Eglantine studied him for a moment that seemed to stretch through eternity, her pulse pounding beneath his hand.

Then she abruptly gripped his neck and pulled him closer, offering her lips and the sweet curve of her throat. Characteristically, the lady made her choice and did not linger over the decision.

"Aye," she whispered hoarsely against his flesh. "God help me for my weakness, but I can say naught else."

Duncan claimed her lips, even as awe flooded through him. He had asked her for honesty but never expected this much.

He had no intent of giving Eglantine the opportunity to reconsider.

Eglantine told herself that ceding to Duncan was the only way to ensure his surrender of Kinbeath. Aye, he had but one interest, the interest of a man seeking conquest, and once he had sated his desire, he would be gone.

She did not truly believe it. She did not want to consider her own weakness, her own burden of desire, certainly not her growing sense that her life was wrought of responsibility alone.

Nay, she wanted to *feel*. Duncan seemed intent on ensuring she did precisely that. The lace at the neck of her kirtle was already loosed, the tie of her chemise similarly undone. Eglantine shivered as Duncan pushed the unwelcome cloth aside, exposing her breasts to the cool air. She saw heat flicker in his eyes and felt a surge of nigh-forgotten feminine pride.

Then his lips closed over her nipple and she forgot all but sensation. His tongue flicked over the peak, urging it to tighten further, his touch sending a surge of heat straight to her toes. The warmth of his hand closed over her knee and eased over her garter, the touch of his palm upon her bare thigh more delicious than she could have believed.

Eglantine's heart was thundering, her mouth was dry. She wanted as she had never wanted before. She pushed her hands into the thickness of Duncan's unruly hair, letting the waves wind around her fingers. She gripped the back of his neck as his teeth grazed her nipple and arched against his strength, wanting only more.

His questing hand slipped through the hair at the top of her thighs as he lifted his head and met her gaze. His fingers parted her, his hand landing with a surety that made her jump. And he smiled at the wetness he found.

"Tell me what you desire, Eglantine," he whispered, his eyes gleaming as his fingers worked. Eglantine writhed, certain she had never burned with a lust of such vigor before. She gripped his shoulders, her nails digging deep, her nipples taut. His hand closed around her waist possessively, his lips grazed her chin, her earlobe. "Tell me," he urged.

"You know the truth of it."

She felt his smile against her flesh and nigh swooned when he licked her earlobe. "Aye, I could guess, but I would have the tale from your lips." His tongue teased her ear, his persuasive fingers making her moan. "Tell me, Eglantine."

"I want pleasure."

Duncan chuckled, his breath warm against her neck. "No more than that?" He rolled his hips against her, letting her feel the fullness of his erection. "How would you be pleasured, Eglantine?"

"'Tis vulgar to converse in this moment," she charged, breathlessness stealing any indignation from her tone.

Duncan laughed and drew back to watch her. "But I am a barbarian, am I not?" He had that unpredictable look about him, but Eglantine had only a moment to recognize the fact of it before his heat was suddenly gone.

He slid beneath her skirts, cupped her buttocks in his hands, and closed his mouth over her.

Eglantine moaned, powerless to keep silent, and lifted herself against him like a wanton. She had never felt such an intimate kiss—and she did not want it to cease anytime soon.

Duncan's tongue rolled against her, exploring, teasing, coaxing her ardor to a crescendo. He held her fast in those great strong hands, though Eglantine writhed and twisted. She felt the brush of his teeth, his nose, the roughness of the whiskers on his chin, but all served only to further enflame her.

And his tongue, oh, his tongue had a wicked skill.

Her desire rose to heights previously unscaled, there was an inferno blazing unchecked beneath her flesh, and her hips began to buck of their own accord. She gripped the breadth of Duncan's shoulders and heard herself cry out as pleasure washed over her in a sudden wave.

Before she could catch her breath, he was crawling over her, his eyes burning with his own desire. He laced his fingers through hers and stretched her arms over her head, bending to suckle her breast anew. Eglantine found herself moaning, her fingers gripping his tightly as her desire roared once more. He sampled one breast then the other, gazing upon her with satisfaction when the nipples were drawn to peaks.

Then his gaze locked with hers and his weight settled between her thighs. She caught her breath at the size of him, the hardness of him, pressed against her, and she *wanted*.

"Your eyes are telling tales again, Eglantine," he murmured, with no small measure of pride. He smiled and rolled his hips against her. "But tell me what you desire."

"You," she whispered before she could stop herself.

Duncan arched his dark brow, tempting her to surprise him in turn.

"You, your heat inside me, filling me as none other has ever done," she declared, her pulse racing at her own boldness. "Take me, Duncan, and please me again while I am wrapped around you."

His eyes flashed as he bent to kiss her and nigh devoured her in his urgency. He caught her hands in one of his now, his other hand fairly tearing cloth in his haste to have it out of the way. Eglantine returned his kiss hungrily, greedily, hardly aware of the bareness of her thighs before he was atop her again. She felt the rough tickle of the hair upon his legs, then parted her own, arching against him as she offered what they both desired.

He eased within her, filling her completely. He gave a ragged sigh, his gaze dark as it locked with her own. "Eglantine," he whispered, the single word filled with wonder. His fingertips eased the hair from her brow, his erection swelled within her.

And Eglantine felt more powerful than she had in all her days and nights. This man who had granted her pleasure fit to melt her bones, this rough man who could seize any trinket he desired, wanted a gift of pleasure that only she could give. She smiled and lifted her hips against him in silent demand.

He grinned, his teeth flashing suddenly. "Do you not ask what I want?"

Eglantine chuckled despite herself. "I know what you want."

But Duncan's eyes filled with mischief. "Do you?"

Eglantine considered him for a moment, then decided to indulge him. She gripped the back of his neck and drew him closer, deliberately echoing his pose and question. "Tell me what you desire, Duncan," she whispered, then flicked her tongue across his ear.

He shivered in a most satisfactory fashion and eased deeper within her. "Pleasure," he acknowledged, his voice strained.

Eglantine slipped her hands beneath his chemise, liking the smooth heat of his flesh beneath her hands. "What else?" she demanded, nipping the corded strength of his neck with her teeth. "Tell me."

Duncan began to move, his rhythm coaxing the embers of Eglantine's own desire to burn anew. When he looked at her, his eyes had darkened to the hue of slate.

"Your eyes tell tales," she teased, then ran a possessive hand through his hair. "Tell me what you desire, Duncan."

His eyes flashed and he gripped her buttocks tightly once more. "You," he declared. "And you know it well, my lady Eglantine. I want you wrapped around me, I want you to scream with your release. I would have you claw my back and fair devour me. I would have you sated in my embrace."

He eased within her to the hilt, his shoulders trembling with the force of his control. He watched her closely, as if he feared he had moved too deep too fast—though Eglantine gasped at the size of him, his heat was welcome indeed. "And I would have you sate me, in turn."

Eglantine smiled up at him and watched relief filter into his expression. She reached up, pushed an errant curl from

his brow, and framed his face in her hands. "I want all you
have to give," she whispered, liking the flame that lit in his
eyes. "And, Duncan, I want it now."

He laughed suddenly, as if she had surprised him, then
braced himself over her on his elbows. He cupped her face in
his hands and kissed her with new intensity even as he
moved within her. And Eglantine writhed anew, loving the
heat of him within her, the weight of his hand upon her
breast, the fervor of his kisses.

"I want you and me to find pleasure together," Duncan
whispered against her temple. His hand slipped between
them, his thumb seeking the bead of her desire, and soon
Eglantine arched against him once more. She could feel him
shaking with the effort of pacing himself and was touched
beyond all else at his concern.

Then again, his touch obliterated all thought. Eglantine
rose against him, she gripped his shoulders, she writhed and
moaned and wanted more. She nipped at his neck with her
teeth and twined her legs around his waist, bucking against
him in silent demand.

Duncan moaned, he moved with increasing speed, he held
her fast. 'Twas a ride unlike any other Eglantine had shared,
and truly, she did not recognize her own unrestrained response. But it felt absolutely right. They moved together as if
they had loved a thousand nights before. Their gazes locked
and Eglantine watched the storm gather in Duncan's eyes. She
saw the heat rise in him and felt an answering heat within herself. He drove deeper and moved faster, she twisted against
him and moaned aloud.

And a heartbeat later, they crested the peak as one. Her
breath caught as her name slipped over Duncan's lips.

"Mine," he whispered against her throat. He rained kisses
along her throat. "Eglantine is all mine."

Far from arguing with the possessive claim, Eglantine

found curious pleasure in it. She closed her eyes and fell back, holding Duncan fast against her chest, the thunder of his pulse indistinguishable from her own. She smiled at the realization that she was warm to her toes for the first time in months.

Then she found the wits to wonder what she had done. Eglantine stared at his dark hair curled between her fingers, felt his breath upon her throat, and saw the marks of her teeth upon his flesh. Horror coiled cold in her belly.

What manner of savage had she become?

Chapter Eight

UNCAN HAD TASTED PARADISE AND WAS LOATH TO move. Indeed, he could have fallen asleep readily here, cosseted in Eglantine's soft fur-lined cloak and her even softer embrace. His eyes drifted closed, he breathed deeply of the perfume of her flesh, and he let himself ease toward slumber.

Eglantine, however, had markedly different ideas.

"Get up," she said abruptly, her words crisper than Duncan might have thought appropriate. He frowned and snuggled deeper.

Aye, the woman was softer than silk and her hair smelled like flowers in summer sunlight. He smiled against her flesh, his lips finding the ripe curve of her breast. He kissed her, cupping her fullness in his hand, then licked the tightening nipple.

Another mating of the ilk of that first one would not be all bad, to Duncan's thinking.

But Eglantine shoved his shoulder and made a growl of frustration. "Get up and get off of me."

This was the woman with whom he had just shared such pleasure? Duncan could not believe his ears. He pushed his weight to his elbows and regarded her warily.

She looked like the woman who had pulled him closer. Her hair was a tousle the hue of wild honey, her cheeks were flushed, and her lips were ruddy.

Her words, though, were harsh.

"Off!" she insisted, squirming in a way that did naught to encourage him to leave. She glared at him, those green eyes snapping with something other than passion. "'Tis time enough you departed—and make no mistake, you will not be welcomed within my camp again."

Duncan felt his eyes narrow, and he did not move. "Forgive me, but did you see another woman in this chapel? I could have sworn the woman in my embrace found sufficient pleasure that she would not be in any haste to see me gone."

If Eglantine's cheeks had been flushed before, now they burned scarlet. "The *wanton* in your embrace is what you mean. The woman so lacking in moral fiber that she could not turn you aside. She turns you aside now!" She moved her knee in a very definite and unwelcome fashion.

For the sake of personal protection, Duncan rolled away, then stood. He was not, however, prepared to leave.

Not without an explanation.

Eglantine hauled down her skirts and laced her bodice with shaking fingers, hastening to stand, as well. She granted him a wide berth and marched out into the thin sunlight, leaving him glowering behind her.

"What nonsense is this?" he demanded impatiently. "You were pleased, I ensured as much."

"Aye, and so were you!" She turned to face him, her gaze flicking over his disheveled garb before she averted her face. Duncan realized his chest was nigh bare and his tartan less than well wrapped, but did not care.

There were more important issues to be resolved.

"I did not argue the truth of it. We both were pleased, or so I believed." He stepped after her, intending to cajole her with his touch.

But Eglantine danced away. Her gaze met his in challenge.

"What game is this?" he asked with a frown. "'Twas you who said you desired me within you, was it not? 'Twas you who wished to be filled with my heat."

Though he might not have believed it possible, her cheeks turned yet a deeper red. "But a month among barbarians and I become one, as well! What does this place do to civilized souls?"

She was embarrassed at her own passion, no more than that. Duncan heaved a sigh of relief. Fortunately, he shared no similar qualms. He had heard tales of women regretting their passion, though he would never have expected Eglantine to be so shy.

Duncan smiled and took a step closer, disliking how the lady still shrank from his touch. "This place awakens our true nature," he suggested, then ran one finger down her arm. "It grants all souls the chance to display their true nature, to wear their passion, to be honest with one another."

Eglantine shivered so elaborately that he suspected her show of distaste was feigned. "It makes barbarians of us all. You have wrought a barbarian of me." She grimaced, her gaze flicking to the chapel, then away. "Truly, dogs show more restraint in satisfying their desires."

"And of what value is restraint?" Duncan demanded. He caught her shoulders in his hands before she could step away. She trembled in his grip but did not flinch. "What possible evil is there in what we just shared, Eglantine? We desired each other, we confessed as much, and we chose to indulge that desire. 'Tis healthy."

Now her eyes flashed in truth. "Healthy? 'Tis *savage*! 'Tis undisciplined and unrestrained and—"

"And satisfying beyond all else." Duncan bent and kissed her quickly, but she put her hands on his chest and pushed him away.

"And now you would make yourself a place in my bed.

Once granted, you assume my favors are yours to sample whensoever you desire. You are wrong, Duncan MacLaren, you are wrong in this." She shook her head angrily. "I may have faltered once, but I shall not do so again. I swear it upon the grave of my father and his father before him. I am not wrought of weak fiber, and I will not become a woman prey to every desire, like a straw cast into the wind. I will not become a savage, a . . ."

"A barbarian," he supplied, much less amused than he had been before.

The lady lifted her chin. "'Tis you who name it aright. Now leave me be." She folded her arms across her chest and glared at him. "For good."

But Duncan caught the lady's chin and cupped its softness in his hand. He could feel her trembling, though whether 'twas with anger or fear, he could not say.

And he would not guess, lest he guess wrongly. Nay, Duncan had no taste for a woman's fear. "I will leave you on this day, Eglantine. Your arguments have a rare gift for irking me—if I lingered, I would shout and no doubt matters would be twisted yet worse than they are now."

Her lips tightened as she stared at him, and Duncan felt that ire rise. "But I will not leave you be for good, for what we shared was finer than fine and I know that I will not be alone in yearning for another taste of such sweetness."

"'Twill not happen again."

"'Twill happen again," Duncan corrected. "On that you may rely." He hauled her close, wrapped his arms around her. "Mark my words, Eglantine, 'twill be you who invites me to your bed again," he whispered, then kissed her thoroughly, regretting with all his heart that this sweet encounter had ended so poorly. Aye, he was shaken to his toes and ill prepared to match wits with this beguiling woman.

He was stunned when he lifted his head to find her wondrous eyes filled with tears.

"Truly it could be said that I have naught to lose, for I am a shy virgin no longer." Her voice was low and hot, her gaze burning. "I have been loved and I have been claimed and I have even come to love in return."

Eglantine's eyes glittered with those unshed tears that Duncan knew she would never let fall. "You could take what you desired of me, and 'tis clear enough that mine own weakness would betray me. But I will not willingly cede the only thing that is truly mine." She raised a fist to her heart. "Aye or nay remains with me alone."

Duncan stared down at her, astonished by her confession and understanding her response a bit better. He recalled now those two men in her life and wondered which of them had forced her, which had stolen her right to decline his attentions. "You have never been wooed," he suggested quietly.

Eglantine laughed without humor, her gaze suddenly hard. "Men do not woo what is theirs to take."

Anger shot through Duncan that she would consider all men to be of the same ilk as the one rogue who had served her poorly. "Perhaps some men do not, but a man of merit does woo the woman he intends to keep," he declared hotly. "When I see fit to woo a woman, 'twill be the one who so captures my heart that I would keep her by my side for all my days and nights."

He glared at a delightfully disheveled Eglantine. "And that partnership will be wrought of mutual consent and naught more than that. You may call a show of passion savage, but I call it honest, and, in truth, I will be happy with naught less."

And without waiting for her reply, he strode out of the chapel, and marched back toward his steed. He waited for

Eglantine to mount and returned to the camp with her though he kept his distance and left her in silence once there.

Indeed, he did not trust himself to speak with any measure of temperance.

Eglantine was worried.

The camp had quieted to the muted sounds of the final labor of the day, the villeins' voices had fallen to whispers, the sea lapped rhythmically against the shore. Half a dozen villeins huddled around the glowing embers of the fire, laughing and sharing gossip. The sky was awash in a thousand rich hues, the sun having indiscriminately smeared every hue in the rainbow across it before dipping beyond the blackness of the sea.

But Eglantine hesitated outside the silk shimmer of her tent, deaf to all but the chortle and splash of Esmeraude inside as Célie bathed her before bed. There would be no respite from her duty this night.

Yet she was poorly prepared to face Esmeraude's iron will. She had spent the better part of the day cloistered in her tent, haranguing herself for her own weakness and wishing she could undo what she had done. She felt jangled as she never was, unsettled and on edge, and she knew 'twas because of Duncan.

Beneath his touch, she became another woman, a woman who surrendered to desire and passion, a woman unlike the woman she knew herself to be. Was she not widely reputed to be a woman of rare composure? Dispassionate? Aye, she had heard the tales that Theobald had thawed the ice maiden of Crevy. Though once she had thought she loved that man, Eglantine had never begged Theobald to fill her with his heat.

His touch had been less loathsome than that of Robert, but mating was hardly an event she eagerly sought. It could have its pleasures, though they were not consistently won.

And they had never been so shattering as the pleasure she had found this day with Duncan.

As if that were not disconcerting enough, Eglantine yearned for more. She wanted to loose that passionate side of herself again, to touch Duncan again, to surrender to sensation again.

And now she faced another challenge that could be avoided no longer.

Esmeraude.

The child's goodwill would not be readily won. Nay, Esmeraude had always known her own mind and had no qualms expressing her opinions from the first morn she saw daylight. Esmeraude was a child of extremes, wrought of sunlight and storm; she was alternately so charming as to be angelic and so temperamental that she might have been the spawn of demons. Worse, she had been so very close to Theobald.

Like to like, Eglantine supposed. The startling thing about Esmeraude was that her smile tempted even the most beleaguered soul to forgive all her transgressions.

Her father's child indeed. Eglantine knew she would never understand the forces that flowed through her youngest, just as she had never fully understood Theobald. But he had called Eglantine his rock in a turbulent sea—perhaps she could be the same to Esmeraude.

And truly, she had more understanding of passion since coming to this place than ever in her days.

Eglantine thanked the scullery maid who brought her the cup of warmed goat milk and heaved a sigh, knowing the moment could be delayed no longer.

"She shall adore you upon sight, my lady," the girl said offering her an encouraging smile.

Eglantine smiled at this endorsement, though she did not share the girl's optimism. "I thank you again." The girl bowed and ducked into the shadows of the night.

Eglantine fingered her chemise, wondering in hindsight whether it made sense to approach Esmeraude in simpler garb. She had thought she might seem less imposing in her chemise, with her hair unbound, though in this moment she doubted all her choices.

But delay would win her naught.

Eglantine lifted her chin, cast one glance over her shoulder, and froze. A man stood not twenty paces from her, beyond the circle of the tents yet silhouetted by the sunset, his arms folded across his chest. Her heart pounded in recognition. Though he was wreathed in shadows, Eglantine had no doubt that he watched her.

She similarly had no doubt that 'twas Duncan. The sentry hovered nearby, disapproving, but Duncan came no closer.

He neither moved nor spoke, simply watched. 'Twas as if he could not stay away from her, though she knew that was whimsy.

He but wanted more, as all men wanted more.

As she wanted more. Eglantine's mouth went dry. Duncan seemed intent on reminding her of his presence, as if he did not guess how large he loomed in her thoughts. Perhaps he hoped to compel her to abandon the sanctuary of the camp and speak to him again.

But even now Duncan looked resolute, dangerous, and unpredictable. The way his features were wreathed in shadow did naught to dispel that impression that he too was beyond comprehension—as Theobald had been. Eglantine knew the risk of approaching him, knew her own response was but tentatively contained.

Yet an errant part of her yearned to join him, to repeat their deed of earlier this day, to confirm his touch was like that of no other. She shook her head. No doubt that was what he wanted of her. Just as she told her daughters, a man come without a ring desired but one thing.

Eglantine had never imagined that she would be one to surrender it, much less that she would do so with such abandon.

When Eglantine might have turned her back upon him, Duncan lifted a hand in silent salute. She had a sudden sense that he would merely hearten her for the task ahead. Eglantine caught her breath. How could he know how uncertain she was?

Eglantine was oddly convinced that he did know. Her breath caught in her throat and she wished she could see his eyes. But then she remembered the truth of it and turned away.

She was alone, as she was always alone, and her responsibilities were hers to resolve.

Alone.

Eglantine lifted the flap of the striped tent, one of a trio of silk tents her father had had made for her and her girls. A lump rose in her throat as she missed her father with sudden intensity. He had been so good with the girls, so instinctive in guessing the right course. He had been a better father than either of her spouses. She realized now that her father would have had no tolerance for Theobald or that man's suggestions for Esmeraude.

Her father would have seen through Theobald's thin charm as she had not. Her father would not have made this mistake and, further, his counsel would have saved Eglantine from making it and several more. 'Twas true that he had arranged her match with Robert but he had believed his decision best; especially given his happiness with her mother.

But he was gone, along with his uncompromising love, his protectiveness, his essential goodness. Eglantine reminded herself that she had been fortunate indeed to have such a man as her father. She smiled to herself, recalling how she had once foolishly believed that all men were like her father.

She could not have been more mistaken.

But thinking upon it would not change the past.

Eglantine took a deep breath and crossed the threshold. The pair within the tent had just finished the toddler's bath, and Esmeraude looked like a mischievous imp in the warm light. Her damp curls were stuck to her brow and she was playing with Célie. In other circumstances, Eglantine might have smiled at her babe's antics.

But not this night.

"Esmeraude," she said quietly, and stepped into the golden circle cast by the single oil lantern in the tent. Both maid and child looked up, Esmeraude's giggles fading abruptly. The toddler stared at her with obvious trepidation.

Eglantine's heart contracted that her own child should fear her. Only now she appreciated how simple matters had been with Jacqueline, how readily the bond between they two had been established. She had never had to fight for her child's affection before.

She only hoped she would proceed aright. All her conviction that she could be Esmeraude's rock ebbed away before the toddler's suspicious expression, and a lump rose in her throat.

Eglantine lifted the cup she carried before the child could cry. "I have brought your milk, Esmeraude, and 'tis warm."

Esmeraude reached for the cup with chubby fingers. Though the goat milk did not offer the comfort of her nurse-maid's breast, she was coming to see it as the closest substitute. Indeed, she had had little choice.

"Give it now."

At least she wanted the milk. "Nay, Esmeraude." Eglantine deliberately kept her voice low and even. "I shall hold the cup for you. Come sit upon my knee."

Esmeraude's face crumpled and Eglantine's heart hammered as she hastened on, hating how her words became tinged with urgency. She sounded desperate to her own ears. "I know you miss your papa, Esmeraude, but he will not return. 'Tis not an easy fact, but 'tis the truth." Eglantine stepped closer, her knuckles white where she gripped the cup. "'Twill not change with your tears, Esmeraude."

The way the child shrank away from Eglantine offered no encouragement, but she could not lose this encounter.

"I understand, Esmeraude, that you are frightened, but I will not hurt you. I swear it to you." Eglantine smiled, though it nigh killed her to appear so tranquil when so much was at stake. "'Tis your choice alone."

Esmeraude eyed her for a long moment, her grip fast upon the maid. "Célie bring milk," she tried once more, though her voice held less conviction.

"Nay," Eglantine argued gently. "*Maman* brings milk from this night forth." She curved her hand around the cup and arched a brow. "And indeed, it grows cold."

Esmeraude huffed. Her mouth worked silently as she watched Eglantine. Clearly she gauged the potential value of crying. Something in Eglantine's regard must have dissuaded her, for she reached again with that hand.

"Milk now!"

Eglantine shook her head. She seated herself upon her own bed and patted her lap. "Of course you can have the milk now. You have but to come here."

Esmeraude's brows knotted and she clung to the maid's hand. "Célie," she insisted. Aye, the maid had become the one issue of certainty in her life, but 'twas not a role that should be filled by a maid. Though Eglantine appreciated all the girl had done, she could stand aside no longer.

She was Esmeraude's mother. Though Theobald had done his best to undermine that fact, he was dead and she would do what she knew was right.

"Of course Célie will remain," Eglantine promised softly. She smiled for the child. "Come for your milk. There is no reason why you cannot hold Célie's hand while you drink it."

She held Esmeraude's gaze for an endless moment, certain she would burst if she did not take a breath, but terrified to move and frighten the toddler.

Abruptly Esmeraude chose to cross the floor. How like her to suddenly make up her mind, then plunge ahead with no regrets or second thoughts! She paused before Eglantine and eyed her anew, too serious for a child.

"Up," Esmeraude commanded imperiously, certain that all the world existed to do her bidding. She lifted her arms to the hovering maid.

Eglantine drew a shaking breath of relief and the women exchanged a glance. Eglantine indicated the full cup of milk. "Célie, if you would lift Esmeraude I should appreciate it."

The maid smiled and hefted Esmeraude in her arms. She kissed the toddler on the tip of her nose, making Esmeraude giggle and wipe at the embrace. Then she placed the child in Eglantine's lap, the affection between them making Eglantine all the more aware of what she had sacrificed.

Then the weight of Esmeraude was upon her thighs and the sweet smell of a clean little one made Eglantine smile. It had been so long since she had cradled Jacqueline thus! She longed to cuddle Esmeraude close but knew that right would have to be earned.

Indeed, Esmeraude was reluctant, her posture stiff and her expression wary. She sat away from Eglantine, minimizing the contact between them. The milk proved to be a far more powerful lure than Eglantine had realized. The toddler reached for the cup, locked her hands around it, and promptly bumped her upper lip against the rim.

Her tears welled and she began to cry, though she would not suffer the cup to be taken away. She fussed, her face reddening as the tears flowed.

Eglantine soothed her with wordless cooing, the sound coming to her lips of old habit. She rocked the toddler and shared another glance with Célie. "Esmeraude is tired this night."

"She wants the milk but cannot manage the cup well as yet," Célie confided. "This one loved the breast too well."

"Ah, so did her sister Jacqueline," Eglantine said.

Esmeraude let herself be soothed, clearly too upset to realize who 'twas who cradled her close. When she did, her eyes widened in dismay.

"Did I not promise not to hurt you?" Eglantine asked, winning a cautious nod from her daughter. "Then let me aid you, Esmeraude. Let me show you a trick that Jacqueline used when she first took the cup."

Esmeraude snuffled. "Jacqueline is big."

"Aye, now she is a young woman, but once she was a little girl, just like you." Eglantine smiled. "And she loved both milk and breast as much as you do. Each night I held the cup for her, too." She patted her upper arm. "If you lean back here, I will aid you. 'Twill work, you will see, just as it worked for Jacqueline."

Esmeraude looked to Célie, who nodded. "Your *maman* knows."

The toddler wriggled backward, settling herself uncertainly against Eglantine's arm. Eglantine pretended she did not note her daughter's wariness, and curled her arm around Esmeraude.

Eglantine smiled at her. "Ease back just thus, aye, there 'tis. Now, you hold the cup and I shall steady it. 'Tis still warm." She ensured there was no bump against the lip this time and felt Esmeraude sag in relief as the warm milk crossed her lips. Eglantine forced her own posture to be at ease, knowing that the child would sense her tension.

Esmeraude sipped, her blue eyes bright as she studied her mother. After a long draw of milk, she pulled slightly back from the cup. "Tell a Papa story," she demanded.

Eglantine looked to the maid in confusion.

"My lord Theobald used to tell her tales while she nursed."

Eglantine blinked. A tale? She was no storyteller, that much was certain. Indeed, she seldom remembered fanciful tales, though she enjoyed listening to them. She knew but one, the one she was living.

'Twould have to do.

Eglantine settled back on her pallet. "Once upon a time, there was a very pretty demoiselle, who had two older sisters."

"Esmeraude," the toddler insisted, nestling closer. She sipped the milk diligently, her gaze fixed intently on her mother.

Eglantine smiled. "Aye, her name was Esmeraude. How did you guess as much?"

Esmeraude chortled, blowing a few bubbles in her milk. "Tell it!" Her fingers caught Eglantine's hair and she stared at the lock of blond hair for a long moment before resolutely closing her fist around it.

'Twas a start. "Well, this Esmeraude also had a *maman* and a papa . . ."

"And they lived in a castle."

"Who tells this tale?" Eglantine asked with mock indignation, as Theobald might have done at his most charming. Esmeraude giggled again, looking unrepentant. "Indeed, you seem to know all of the tale already."

When Eglantine related a tale about the pretty demoiselle Esmeraude who lost her beloved father at a young age but went on to find happiness in life and win the heart of a valiant knight, she felt her daughter snuggle more closely in her arms.

As Eglantine concluded her tale she tickled her daughter's chin and asked, "Do you know the ending?"

Esmeraude smiled proudly. "They lived happily ever after."

"Aye, they did." Eglantine bent and kissed her daughter's brow, using the ending her mother had always given to a tale. "And if I am not mistaken, they are happy together still."

"And he was never a toad," Esmeraude added as her own embellishment, the reminder of Duncan's tale making Célie laugh aloud.

"Would you not wed a toad?"

"Nay, not me!"

"Or kiss him?"

Esmeraude made a face, then dimpled as they laughed together. Oh, this was a rare gift! Eglantine eyed her happy daughter and could not believe she had made such progress already.

But victory was to be short-lived. The toddler poked Eglantine, her expression a quelling one.

"Another story," she insisted, and Eglantine's worries returned.

"But I do not know another story." Fear clutched her heart. Would she lose what progress had been made?

"A song." Esmeraude nodded at her own suggestion.

Eglantine grimaced, her gaze flying to Célie. "I cannot believe, Esmeraude, that any song that might pass my lips would please you." She met her daughter's gaze steadily. "I cannot sing, child, and if I tried, 'twould pain us all."

Esmeraude sucked her thumb as she regarded her mother. She patted Eglantine's breast, evidently just discovering it, and her eyes widened hopefully. "Milk?" she asked around her thumb, and Eglantine hated that she could not offer that, either.

Just when matters had been proceeding so well. There was no chance of milk filling her breast, nor of another tale appearing in her practical thoughts. If only she had the gift of song!

But before Eglantine could reply, a familiar male voice began to hum. 'Twas Duncan, she knew it well, and he was not far away. Eglantine frowned, for he must have entered the camp to have come so very close.

The cheek of him! His very proximity made her tingle in a most unwelcome way.

Then he began to sing softly, the words obviously Gael as they were incomprehensible to Eglantine. But the tune was familiar. 'Twas the ballad he had sung before and 'twas clear he meant to sing it again.

For her child. Eglantine sagged in relief. She could not imagine what Duncan's motivation might be, but as much as she would prefer to avoid him, she would have to see him thanked.

Her cheeks heated with a sudden certainty of what a man like Duncan would demand in trade.

His voice grew louder, the melody filling their ears, the words wrapping around their hearts. 'Twas an achingly beautiful tune, sung by a man with an achingly beautiful voice.

Eglantine wondered what 'twas about. Again she noted the yearning in Duncan's voice that could not be ignored. Did he sing for a child? A lost child? A lost love?

Did he yearn for a woman compelled to wed another?

The very idea made a lump rise in Eglantine's throat. Had Duncan found and lost a great love? He was not a man who would take such a loss in stride, she would guess, and she wondered if that lay at the root of his determination to woo the woman of his choice.

She would not speculate on how well Duncan might woo a woman.

But she would savor this gift. Eglantine and Célie rearranged the pillows on Eglantine's pallet. She leaned back, Esmeraude cradled against her chest, the toddler sucking less diligently on that thumb as her eyelids drooped. The maid snuffed the lantern and curled up on her own pallet as Esmeraude's eyes closed.

Eglantine's heart skipped as Duncan's voice rose and fell,

like the rhythm of the sea, his song spinning a colorful tapestry that enfolded Eglantine and her child.

Her child, who feared her no longer, at least on this night. Eglantine held Esmeraude close, treasuring the child's warmth.

Finally, something went aright.

Perhaps this place was not so dreadful, after all. Eglantine noted how the last colors of the sunset tinged the sheer silk over her head, and watched the silk billow in the wind from the sea. Aye, when the weather was fair, Kinbeath was pretty enough. 'Twas wild, to be sure, but splendid in a way that neatly cultivated fields could never be.

Much as an unpredictable man with eyes as changeable as the sea could be splendid in a way that a nobleman could not be. Eglantine closed her eyes and found the image of Duncan, eyes ablaze, as he demanded her aye or nay.

Neither Robert nor Theobald had ever asked her permission to take what was their marital due. Was it merely the lack of vows between them that prompted Duncan's courtesy?

Eglantine could not imagine so. Perhaps he was a barbarian in some ways—but in others, he had a rare grace. Had she ever been pleasured so thoroughly? In his absence, Eglantine could admit the truth. And she knew she had never seen such reverence in a man's expression when he touched her flesh.

'Twas only human to yearn for more. Eglantine heaved a sigh and let the sound of the waves mingle with Duncan's voice to ease the last of the tension from her shoulders.

God in heaven, but the man could sing.

Eglantine smiled as her feet began to warm. 'Twas almost civilized here, in this moment, though no doubt it would soon rain in chilly torrents again. Her thumb stroked Esmeraude's soft curls and she thought of angels, strong angels with stormy eyes, deep voices, and broad shoulders.

Angels singing sad ballads.

When Duncan's song faded, along with the last glimmer of the sunset, 'twas not only Esmeraude who had fallen asleep.

And 'twas not only the toddler who smiled at her dreams.

In the dark of the night, Eglantine had a reminder of the lesser joys of sleeping with a small child. Her eyes flew open as she felt the bed become wet, and not with water. Her cherub had turned back into an earthly being after all.

Chapter Nine

DUNCAN SAT ON THE ROCKS LONG AFTER EGLANtine's tale ended and watched the moon rise high. Far behind him, her camp slumbered. Far ahead of him, the broch was a shadow against the blackness of the night, his own company slumbering there.

A thousand stars were scattered across the sky, looking close enough to be plucked. The dark waves lapped at his feet, lulling him with their rhythm.

'Twas a night made for magic, a night upon which any dream might come true. He watched a star shoot across the heavens, wondering what wish he should make, and knew it involved Eglantine and her fur-lined cloak.

And her teeth against his flesh.

Duncan had long believed that Mhairi haunted him, but Cormac's lost daughter could not come close to Eglantine's power to torment. He had never met a woman who blazed like Eglantine, never met a woman who could sear his soul with her touch.

But Eglantine had avoided him the rest of this day. He had caught but one glimpse of her, earlier this evening, with her hair unbound and her expression oddly vulnerable. He had been nigh felled by a desire to hold her close, to fight her dragons, to assail whatever stood in her path.

He did not want her to shun him. He wanted to touch her

again. He wanted to talk to her. He wanted to finish that argument, if need be, then reconcile abed.

Eglantine, however, insisted upon slaying her dragons alone. Still her tale echoed through his thoughts, explaining so much, while the words she did not utter explained so much more.

He wanted to injure the man who had sired Esmeraude and found himself disappointed that the man was already dead.

'Twas then he heard a faint splash.

He turned, expecting to see naught, and froze. A vision wrought of moonlight and unaware of his presence, Eglantine eased to the edge of the sea. Her hair was unfurled around her shoulders and shimmered silver beneath the moon's caressing light. A heavy cloak was wrapped around her, the collar high against the chill. She bent hesitantly, clearly not trusting the sea, and Duncan smiled at the caution of Eglantine.

She dipped something into the inky waves. Duncan dared to turn fully, moving silently, half afraid she would flee, half afraid she was naught but a vision wrought by his restless thoughts.

But 'twas Eglantine, not surprisingly immune to his fanciful mood. Aye, she scrubbed a length of pale cloth with purpose, then bent to rinse it again.

Ever pragmatic, that was his countess.

Duncan smiled.

"If 'tis a stain left by the fey, 'twill not come out so readily as that," he called softly. The lady started despite his low tone, spun, then caught her breath when she spied him.

Their gazes held for a long moment, though her features were half shadowed. She held the dripping cloth protectively before herself, and spoke formally.

"I would thank you for the ballad this night, for 'twas most fortuitously timed."

Duncan inclined his head in acknowledgment. "I would speak with you, after this day."

Eglantine ignored his entreaty and did not move. "Is it the same song you sang last eve?"

"Aye." Duncan noted that she did not draw near to him. "Were you injured this day? 'Twas not my intent, Eglantine . . ."

"I was not hurt," she retorted, then lifted her chin as she changed the topic. "What is the song about? I did not understand the words."

Duncan shrugged dismissively. "'Tis naught but an old tale." He stood, relieved when she lingered. "Eglantine, I would speak with you this night . . ."

Eglantine shook her head. "I doubt 'tis merely an old song. 'Tis sad, I would wager a tale of love and loss. 'Tis a tale that lies too close to your heart to be merely some old tale, Duncan. You do not fool me."

Duncan looked away, wanting her to stay but not wanting to share the truth of this. "'Tis naught. I but prefer old tales."

"Liar," she charged softly.

Duncan scowled, disliking the charge no less than the fact that in this case, 'twas true. "What of the tale you told this night? Was it a lie, or a fiction concocted to ease a child?"

Eglantine's defiance crumbled, vulnerability making a fleeting appearance. "You heard?"

"Aye."

She caught her breath and tried to hide her dismay. "'Twas not your right."

"Nay, 'twas not," he acknowledged, then took a step closer. "Is it true?"

Eglantine heaved a sigh and looked across the water in turn. Her admission was so low that 'twould have been lost in the lap of the sea if Duncan had not been listening so closely.

"Aye. More or less." She rubbed her brow and might have turned away, but Duncan lunged forward and caught at her elbow.

"How did he ensure the babe loved him best?" He was surprised to hear the thrum of anger in his words. "'Twas what you said in your tale and I heard the ache in your words. How dare he treat you with such disregard, after you had borne him a child?"

Eglantine also appeared surprised by his response. She met his gaze questioningly.

"Theobald indulged Esmeraude overmuch, 'tis all." She sighed. "And like all children, she preferred the sweet to the stern."

"Tell me more of it."

"I am tired," she insisted, then frowned and would have abandoned him there.

The offer came so impulsively to Duncan's lips that 'twas uttered before he considered it. "I will translate the song for you first."

"Why should I indulge you again?"

Duncan spared her his most winning smile. "Because I truly want to know. I confessed to you already, Eglantine, that I have a rare passion for the truth."

He tingled at the heat that lit her gaze. Then she shook her head and glanced back toward her tent. "You are a man of rare persistence, Duncan MacLaren," she charged, though there was no recrimination in her tone.

He grinned. "Stubborn, Cormac called it, but then he was not a man to gild either rose or thorn." A wistful smile touched Eglantine's lips and Duncan was encouraged that she did not hasten away.

"You were fond of this Cormac."

Duncan nodded, unashamed of this. "Aye. He was uncommonly good to me."

"You heard how the child fought me," she said softly. "I suppose I owe you some due for your aid."

Unspeakably relieved, Duncan gestured to his smooth seating as though 'twas a fine throne. Eglantine hovered as she considered the spot, poised like a doe prepared to flee.

"'Tis cold. Perhaps the morrow would be better for such tales."

"Now or not at all." Duncan held her gaze steadily, wishing he knew how to reassure her. "My tale is long. You had best be seated."

She sat abruptly as if 'twas a trial to be endured. She averted her features from Duncan and folded her hands tightly together.

"You must not think poorly of Theobald," she said, the words falling in a breathless rush, and he was astounded that she would defend the man.

Was this her guilt speaking? Duncan could not guess.

"Theobald had long wanted a child of his own blood. Esmeraude was his first and his only. He saw the closeness I had with Jacqueline and wanted a measure of that himself."

"But surely she had to be nursed?"

Eglantine's words were flat. "He preferred that she should have nursemaids, as they could be changed at frequent intervals." She pleated her cloak hastily, frowning down at her busy fingers seemingly unaware of what they did. "He insisted that she be granted every frippery, but 'tis not good for a child to be undisciplined, to be so spoiled."

Duncan's anger gained new vigor at more signs of the man's selfishness. "And so 'twas left to you to decline the child."

Eglantine nodded, her head bowed. "Someone had to say nay. 'Tis only human nature that Esmeraude preferred her papa, he who granted her all. And he, he wished only to be loved best."

"And so Esmeraude was devastated when he died."

Eglantine smiled softly. "Who could hold a candle to such an indulgent parent?"

Duncan's heart clenched. He placed one hand on Eglantine's shoulder, unable to stop himself from offering sympathy where 'twas clearly due. Eglantine had felt as much pain from this as Esmeraude, of that Duncan had no doubt. "You take the blame for another's crime, Eglantine."

"Nay. I should have known better."

"'Twas *his* fault," he argued heatedly. "No father should have asked as much. 'Twas wrong of him, and the wrong of you blaming yourself does not make it right."

She looked up, clearly surprised by his defense of her.

"Love is not a commodity to be hoarded, Eglantine, though I suspect you know as much." Duncan smiled for her, shaken by the uncertainty lingering in her eyes. "You took great strides this night in making your repair."

Eglantine's smile did not light her eyes. "'Twould have all been lost without your song. I thank you again for your aid."

He studied her, watching the moonlight play over her features. "Why did you come to Ceinn-beithe?" he asked quietly, sensing that she would not deny him the truth on this night. The moonlight seemed to have softened her formidable defenses, or perhaps it had been Esmeraude's acceptance that had done as much.

Eglantine sighed. "For my daughters. I came to grant Alienor, Jacqueline, and Esmeraude the chance to each find a man who loved her with all his heart and soul. I would have them wed for love, not obligation. I would have them find happiness in marriage, even as I did not."

Duncan blinked. 'Twas a noble quest fitting of an old tale, an objective so selfless that it snared Duncan's heart as surely as the lady's clear green gaze.

'Twas a goal that appealed so deeply to him that he could

not summon an agreement to his lips, so surprised
was he to hear such frivolity fall from the lips of practical
Eglantine.

"I know 'tis madness," she said forcefully, obviously mis-
interpreting his silence as censure. "I know it defies convention, but surely there is naught amiss in a mother wanting to
ensure her children's happiness?" Eglantine took a deep
breath and folded her arms across her chest.

"And 'tis not so foolish as that," she insisted, clearly expecting him to argue with her. "Some people are so fortunate
as to wed for love. My own brother is smitten with his bride.
And his friend pursued his love to the ends of the earth, for
the image of that lady was burned so deeply upon his heart
that he could not be happy with another."

"This sounds like an old tale," Duncan ventured.

"Aye." A smile touched Eglantine's lips, then was gone.
"'Tis a stirring tale and mine own inspiration." To Duncan's
surprise, the lady's eyes clouded with tears. She raised a
clenched fist to her heart. "My daughters deserve that manner of love, that manner of marriage. I have brought them to
the ends of Christendom to grant them that opportunity.

"You may mock my intent to launch a bride quest from
Kinbeath." She struggled to pronounce the "-th," the effort
clearly vexing her, and Duncan cursed himself for his earlier
teasing. "You may even mock my foolishness in having such
a dream for my daughters. But I have lived the alternative,
and I shall see them happily wed to deserving men, if 'tis the
last deed I achieve in this life."

Duncan surveyed her in silence, humbled by her selflessness. There was no doubt in his mind that she shared the
truth with him, no doubt that this was her real objective.

"You ask naught for yourself."

Eglantine stared at him steadily. "I have no dreams for myself any longer."

'Twas the saddest claim that Duncan had ever heard.

"Whyever not?"

"I am too aged for dreams." Eglantine blinked quickly as if clearing her eyes of tears and continued hastily. "I have said too much this night, and 'tis clear I have need of sleep. If you do not mean to share your song with me, then I shall retire." She made to rise, but Duncan halted her with a touch.

He knew he had no right to do as much, not after eavesdropping on her own story and winning this further confession from her. And he did not want to. Nay, Eglantine's choice was fitting of a bard's tale—and 'twas a choice that could only snare the heart of the bard Duncan was.

His intuition told him what he must do, though the boldness of the idea made his heart pound.

'Twas just like an old fable—once what is sought is forgotten, 'tis always found. Duncan had long ago ceased to search for a bride and partner—and he had found the woman of his heart in the most unlikely of places.

He did not intend to let her go. Her heart was wounded, but Duncan knew that he held the perfect balm.

'Twas time he began to woo Eglantine.

Eglantine thought Duncan would share his song with her, but instead he laid claim to her hand. He held it gently within his own, and she could not help but note the contrast between his broad roughened palm and the smallness of her own hand.

'Twas better than thinking of the shiver his touch launched over her flesh.

He stroked her hand with his thumb, frowning as he sought the words, looking so concerned that she did not have it within her to draw away. Then Duncan looked up suddenly. "My lady Eglantine, I would ask that you consider me to be the first suitor to call at your court."

Whatever Eglantine had expected him to say, 'twas not that. She stared at him but Duncan appeared to be as earnest as she had ever seen him. "You?"

He scowled and she knew she had insulted him. "Aye, *me*. I am the chieftain of Clan MacQuarrie, the closest equivalent to a lord of the manor in these parts." His grip tightened ever so slightly upon her hand, emphasizing his words with his touch. "I am eligible, I am of an age to wed, and I seek a bride."

"You." Still it made no sense. "But you declined Alienor this very day. Indeed, you were most insulted . . ." Eglantine's words faded, but Duncan lifted her hand to his lips. She shivered as he pressed a kiss to her palm, his gaze fixed upon her.

"I would not court Alienor." His expression was determined, his gaze intense, as he closed her fingers deliberately over the heat of his kiss.

Eglantine had some difficulty marshaling her thoughts. "You protested Alienor because of her age," she managed to say.

Duncan smiled and folded her hand between his two larger ones, his touch warming her to her toes. "Among other attributes." One brow rose roguishly. "Or lack of them."

Eglantine shook her head, not seeing the humor. "But Jacqueline is yet younger."

"I do not court Jacqueline either," he said silkily.

Eglantine could not draw a full breath into her chest and marveled at this man's ability to addle her thoughts. Suddenly she was all too aware that she had donned naught but her cloak this night, that the fur lining brushed directly against her skin.

And Duncan held her hand as if he would never let it go. Eglantine was sorely tempted to lean on him, to confide in him, to indulge her instinct that this man was most like her father of all the men she had known. The moonlight wrought illusions, persuading her that he would ensure his woman's safety, her health, her happiness.

But that was madness.

Was it not?

"Fret not, my lady." Duncan smiled slowly, his voice low and reassuring. "I shall prove to you that I am the ilk of man you seek. I shall prove to you that I am a man who understands the fragile treasure of dreams."

Aye, she more than half believed it, in this moment at least. Eglantine stared into the stormy gray of his eyes and feared she would lose what was left of her resistance.

"The song," she whispered unevenly.

Duncan studied her before he turned away. He braced his elbows upon his knees and stared over the shimmer of the sea. Though he looked to have slipped away to another place and time, Eglantine was very aware of his heat beside her own.

Then he began to sing and Eglantine closed her eyes, deliberately pushing all from her awareness but the rich splendor of his voice.

> *Ceinn-beithe is old and its stones remember all*
> *Its circle in old days every handfast did call*
> *But one mating these stones ne'er did see*
> *And that was the pledge of the maiden Mhairi.*
>
> *Mhairi was stubborn, stubborn and proud*
> *And she refused to wed the man her father had chose*
> *Instead she would decide whose bride she would be*
> *She vowed to have only her love Ruaraidh.*
>
> *Down came her father and he stood at the door*
> *Saying "Mhairi, you are trying the tricks of a whore,*

You care nothing for a man who cares so much for thee
You must marry my choice and leave Ruaraidh.

"For your Ruaraidh is barely but a man
Although he may be pretty but where are his lands?
Your betrothed's lands are broad and
his towers they run high
You must marry my choice and leave Ruaraidh."

Eglantine was glad her eyes were closed for she felt a measure
of privacy from Duncan's perceptiveness. She folded her hands
together, her fingers knotting tightly. Aye, she could sympathize
with Mhairi well enough, though she had not been so fortunate
as to have a true love when her own nuptials were called.

Mhairi would not cede to her father's bidding
To Ceinn-beithe no man on the isle could her bring
The blessing of that place her own match denied
She swore 'twould show she was no willing bride.

"You who are my father may compel me to marry
But this betrothed I will ne'er bear his seed
To a son or a daughter I will ne'er bow my knee
For I will die if denied my love Ruaraidh."

The sentiment made Eglantine's heart pound. This was what
she desired for her daughters, after all. Perhaps she had mis-
understood his intent, though she could not imagine how.
She slanted a glance toward Duncan, noting the absorption
revealed in his expression. Was that why he had chosen this
song? Was it truly the same song he had sung before, or had
he changed it once he had heard her tale?

How far could she trust him?

Indeed, could she trust him at all?

"Come to me, my Mhairi, my honey and my sweet
To stile you, my mistress, it would be so sweet"

So cried her husband when Mhairi missed their feast
But Mhairi had naught good in reply to his pleas.

"Be it mistress or Mhairi, 'tis all the same to me
But in your bed, my husband, I never will be."
And down came her father and he spoke with a frown
Saying "You who are her maidens—
go loosen up her gown."

But Mhairi fell down to the floor
And lay pale before his knee
Saying "Father, look, I'm dying
For my love Ruaraidh."

Eglantine raised one hand to her lips in horror, but Duncan did not so much as glance her way. His voice dropped lower, the words making her eyes prick with tears.

The day that Mhairi married
was the day that Mhairi died
And the day that young Ruaraidh came home on the tide
And down came her maidens all wringing their hands
Saying "Oh you were so long, so long upon the sands

"They have married your Mhairi and now she lies dead."
His heart struck cold, Ruaraidh bowed his head.
He kissed Mhairi's cold lips while he wept
And soon 'twas more than Mhairi who there lay dead.

Ceinn-beithe is old and its stones remember all
Its circle in old days every handfast did call
But one marriage these stones ne'er did see
And ill-fated was the match of maid Mhairi.

Duncan held the last note, then slowly turned to face Eglantine beside him.

"That is beautiful," she whispered in wonder.

He shrugged, dull red creeping up his neck. "'Tis more lovely in the original Gael."

"Then it must be a marvel indeed."

His gaze brightened so that Eglantine could not hold it, not without knowing his thoughts. She turned and stared over the water, hugging her knees, haunted by the tune and her sense that 'twas more than a mere story to him. But where was the key to understanding Duncan in this recounting? In the choice of tale itself?

Or had he known the star-crossed lovers?

Or was he but a bard, as he claimed, who dug into his trove of songs and presented the first one that came to hand? Eglantine did not know, and worse, she did not know how to find out.

"But a poor fellow can do no more than his best," Duncan muttered. He smiled thinly when Eglantine glanced his way. "'Tis an old saying oft recounted by one of my men."

"The song does sound better in your tongue, less dire and more melodic." Eglantine nodded. "More passionate."

"Aye. Each tongue has its own music, its own range." Duncan frowned, as if he might say more, then slanted her an unexpected grin. Eglantine sensed that he deliberately changed the subject, but her heart lurched painfully all the same.

That dark hair hung unruly over his brow, the glint of mischief in his eyes hinting that he knew the turmoil of her thoughts, no less that he was responsible for their muddled state. He eased closer, his shoulder bumping hers companionably, and Eglantine's mouth went dry.

"'Tis the way of the Gael to linger upon the price of love gone awry." He surveyed her, that perceptiveness in his gaze. "And you seem to know much of that subject yourself. Why did you cede to this Theobald?"

"He was my husband and thus owed my dutiful agreement."

Duncan laughed aloud, the merry sound making her own lips twitch. "That, I wager, would not have stopped your heated disagreement."

Their gazes locked for a telling moment, then Eglantine shook her head and looked away. "I loved him. Have you never granted a loved one their desire, simply because 'twas within your power to do so?"

'Twas Duncan's turn to avert his gaze and frown. "Aye." He slanted a quick glance her way. "But it seems that I am not the only one to have regretted such a course."

Eglantine could not catch her breath, nor could she look away from his darkened gaze. Eglantine saw his hand rise and knew he meant to touch her, knew she would melt against him if he did so.

But the reminder of Theobald was too close. Surely she had enough evidence of her poor fortune with men?

She inched away quickly, not trusting herself to resist him if his hand landed upon her, and asked the first question that fell from her lips. "Why do you alone speak French of your men?"

Duncan's hand fell. The change in his expression revealed all too well that Eglantine had touched upon a subject he would prefer to avoid.

To her surprise, he answered. "Because I alone traveled south."

"Where did you go?"

"South." His lips flattened to a grim line.

"Where in the south?" He did not reply, so Eglantine suggested possibilities, intending only to prompt him. "Norman England? France? Spain?"

"South." He gave her a look that was undoubtedly supposed to be a deterrent to further questioning.

Eglantine was not deterred. Here was something of import to him, and she meant to know the truth. "Why did you go?"

"'Twas time."

"There must have been a specific reason . . ."

She got no further before Duncan pushed to his feet, effectively ending their conversation. "If you will excuse me, 'tis late." He turned and left, his footsteps so fleet that Eglantine wondered whether he feared she would pursue him.

Or demand his honesty.

But that was madness. Duncan was afraid of naught, and he certainly was not afraid of her. Eglantine reluctantly wrung out her chemise one last time and looked after Duncan.

But he was gone. For the first time in recent encounters, he had not kissed her. Eglantine was honest enough with herself to admit she was disappointed.

The wolves howled in the distance, as foreign and unpredictable as the man who had just left her side. Eglantine shivered, then hastened back to her bed. Truly, she had to ensure she had more sleep. The deprivation was beginning to affect her good temper.

Not to mention her judgment.

The lady's timing had not been the best.

No sooner had Duncan realized that she was the one he sought than Eglantine managed to awaken his unwelcome memories of Mhairi. Aye, there was a tale that would tempt a man to avoid nuptials for all his days and nights, a poor augury for marital bliss indeed.

He walked along the shore as had become his wont, savoring the sounds of wind and wave, the muted music of night, the distant warbling of the wolves. 'Twas a long time before he freed himself of the grip of guilt, so long that new clouds had obscured the moon and rain was promised by the wind.

But Eglantine was not like Mhairi. She was not an innocent maiden, she was not fragile of spirit and delicate of build, she was certainly not besotted with him without cause.

She certainly would never make the foolish choice Mhairi had made. Nay, not Eglantine. Duncan smiled to himself. The lady was wrought of sterner stuff than Mhairi had been.

Duncan heaved a sigh and returned to the broch, ducking into the passageway just as the rain began to patter on the stones overhead. Gillemore grunted and kicked the small fire back to life, the embers belching smoke into the small space before they began to flicker.

And 'twas only then, as the flames vied with the first fingers of dawn to cast light around the broch, that Duncan realized something was amiss.

Aye, Iain was gone.

Eglantine awakened when Célie shook her shoulder. She had lain awake half the night, then slept badly, falling into a deep slumber only when the rain began to fall on the roof of the tent. 'Twas chill and damp again, and Eglantine was certain morning had come too soon.

Indeed, 'twas barely light.

"My lady, you must come." Célie's voice was low and urgent. "Gunter and Gerhard are upset beyond all else."

Eglantine pushed the weight of her hair from her face and sat up in confusion. "Gunter and Gerhard are the most tranquil souls in all the household. Are you certain of this?"

"Aye, my lady." Célie nodded hastily. "Their stores have been plundered, and all are certain 'tis the labor of the restless souls who desire us gone from this place."

Eglantine swung her legs from the bed, wincing at the cold of the air for a moment before she hauled on her kirtle. She laced the sides with impatient fingers, her anger beginning to hum.

What nonsense did the moonlight make! Had Duncan deliberately distracted her while his men wreaked havoc? Or had he fled her side after enchanting her with his tale only to put her entire company's survival at risk?

Oh, she had been a fool to trust him, however briefly!

"There is but one soul who desires us gone from this place, Célie," she said sharply. "And he is not dead." She spared the startled girl an ominous glance. "But then, I have not finished with him as yet."

Leaving the maid behind, Eglantine strode from the tent.

'Twas far worse than she had imagined.

The sacks of flour had been cut open, their contents scattered across the ground and already joined to the mud underfoot. Grain had been spilled similarly, a remaining trail indicating that much had been dumped into the sea. Pots and pans had been scattered in the woods; the tinder and firewood so painstakingly gathered had been cast into the rain and rendered useless.

The fowl had been released, only their cries discernible in the woods. Most undoubtedly had fallen prey to the wildlife resident here. God alone knew what had happened to the goats, and Esmeraude was already crying for milk. Even the rabbits left to hang had been cut down and left for the ravens, which made a hearty feast of it even as Eglantine watched. Most of the villeins did not know where to begin to set matters to rights and merely wandered through the mess, shaking their heads.

Gunter and Gerhard were particularly disheartened. They sat side by side, their gazes glazed, their expressions shocked. There was not so much as a fire kindled or a pot of water put on to boil.

And speculation ran rampant through the ranks of the

household. The maids huddled together, cackling like troubled hens. Everywhere she turned, Eglantine heard whispers, whispers that halted when her presence was noted.

The trio of sentries bowed low before her, their apologies hasty and incoherent. "My lady, we slept, I cannot imagine why."

Eglantine touched their brows, frowning at the sluggishness of their speech. "You drank something before the night?"

"Aye, a cup of grog to keep us warm. Gunther made the brew."

Eglantine demanded an ingredient list from the cook, surprised to find no sedatives among the herbs he listed. "Did you serve it immediately?"

"Nay, my lady, 'twas too hot. I left it there." And he pointed to the makeshift table at the edge of his kitchen space.

"And whence were you?"

He pointed to the opposing table. "We began the bread last eve, as always."

Aye, Eglantine could see how someone could have sidled up to the table with the grog, someone who had crept stealthily through the evening shadows. Someone intent on sprinkling an herb or two into the mix that their deeds might not be interrupted.

Someone, indeed.

The priest murmured his rosary over and over again, more folk than usual joining him in his morning prayers. The men nodded sagely and scanned the horizon, as if expecting spectres to appear at any moment. All watched their lady arrive and waited expectantly.

Save Louis, who stood with his lips pursed and his eyes downcast, his shredded ledger in his hands. The treasury trunk had had its lock shattered, apparently before it disappeared into the night.

Its contents were gone with it, all save the ledger, as was the deed to Ceinn-beithe.

"Did you not have the trunk with you, Louis?"

"Aye, my lady, as is my wont and my responsibility. Sadly, I made the miscalculation of sharing in the grog last evening, for I was chilled to the bone."

The châtelain fairly exuded disapproval of this circumstance, and Eglantine knew he was nigh bursting to observe that had they left sooner, this would not have befallen them. She would not ask for his opinion—and, she hoped his manners would compel him to keep it to himself.

For her own part, Eglantine was so angry that her hands shook. Duncan toyed with her apurpose.

And worse, she had been fool enough to forget their competing desires, and that because of his charm. Aye, the man knew his touch troubled her, he knew his kisses unsettled her, he knew this and he persisted.

Because he wanted her to surrender Kinbeath to him. 'Twas so blessedly simple. She had already surrendered more than had been her intent, that much was certain.

She knew that Duncan would stop at naught to see his goal achieved. Clearly he had lied to her the night before. This man wanted no bride and no quest. He wanted Kinbeath alone.

"We have had another visit from the restless souls, my lady," murmured Gerhard. He shook his head. "And I know not how we shall recover from this."

"We shall recover from this travesty by pursuing justice," Eglantine said crisply.

"From the dead?"

"'Twas no restless soul who wrought such destruction but a party of men who are very much alive." Her company stirred and eased closer. "Though I do not underestimate the power of souls, mine own father taught me to look first in the realm of men for the source of trouble." Several chuckled at this and a few comments were exchanged about the good character of the late Lord of Crevy-sur-Seine.

Eglantine warmed to her theme. "Who indeed wants us gone from this place? Who indeed understands what stores we need most and how best to destroy them? 'Tis no specter who wreaks such damage but a troop of barbarians." Eglantine turned and pointed a finger that quivered with anger at Duncan's party, who only now stirred sleepily. "Look how late they slumber—no doubt this labor left them overtired!"

Her vassals muttered impatiently, throwing more than one ugly glance toward the broch. "And who are they to oust us from land that is rightfully deeded to my hand? 'Tis they who are in breach of the law, 'tis they who shall pay a reckoning!"

"Aye, my lady!" A cheer rose from the assembly, though Louis shook his head.

"With what shall they pay it, my lady?" he asked quietly.

"Firstly with the return of the coin they have stolen from us." Eglantine gritted her teeth and glared first at her châtelain, then at Duncan's camp. "Then with the labor of their own hands, if need be. I shall have a penance from them, that much is certain, or there shall be more blood shed on Kinbeath, whether 'tis on that cursed stone or not."

The company cheered.

Enough was enough. She would demand an audience with whichever king held suzerainty over this land, both if necessary! 'Twas time the law was summoned to resolve this issue.

'Twas somewhat galling that she had need of directions to one king from Duncan, but she was angry enough to not care. Eglantine lifted her hand. "Let us demand compensation! Let us demand justice! Let us demand the king's own ear and the assertion of the king's law. We are the rightful tenants of Kinbeath. Let us demand acknowledgment of our legal right!"

Her household roared approval. Eglantine turned and strode toward the intruders' camp, determined to declare her intent.

Aye, with the involvement of a king, any king, this contest would be resolved once and for all.

Chapter Ten

UNCAN WAS HAVING A MARVELOUS DREAM.

It could have been naught else. Even in sleep he knew 'twas improbable that Eglantine should try to seduce him, but still he was loath to awaken.

Duncan sighed with satisfaction as Eglantine leaned over him, the softness of her breast against his arm. Her breath upon his ear made him shiver, her hair trailed against his face and he reveled in its silken touch. The countess kissed his cheek gently, granting further confirmation that 'twas a dream.

For the real countess was not so timid as this. The incongruity of that caught Duncan's attention, for 'twas unlike a dream to be less passionate than what a man might find awake.

What if he did not dream?

Duncan opened one eye warily, noted the chill in the air and the sound of rain. Then he saw that the curl trailing across his face was ebony of hue.

'Twas not Eglantine!

Duncan sat up with a jolt, the sight before him making his eyes widen in dismay even as he eased backward.

"I do not kiss so badly as that," Alienor said with a pout. She sat back on her heels, looking disheveled. She had unfurled her hair from her braid, the dark tresses hanging loose over her shoulders and falling to her waist. She evidently wore naught but a chemise beneath her cloak. Her feet were bare, her expression tempting, the shadows visible through the opening of her cloak promising many pleasures. Many a man might have seized what she offered.

But Duncan stared at his visitor in horror. "Ye gods, what is this you do?" he muttered.

Alienor smiled coyly and crept closer.

Duncan looked wildly around the broch, but his men slept soundly. He would wager his last coin that Eglantine did not know her stepdaughter was here.

And that she would not be pleased to learn the truth.

"You must return to your tent," he advised in a low whisper. The determination in the girl's eyes told Duncan that she had no more intent of heeding him than she did Eglantine. "Truly, 'tis imperative—"

"I shall have a kiss first," she whispered, smiling as she unclasped her cloak and let it fall behind her. Truly, the chemise was so fine that it hid naught. She crawled toward him, her eyes glowing and her breasts fairly spilling from her chemise. "Do you not desire me, Duncan? Do you not wish to claim me as your own?"

'Twould be rude to make his feelings clear, and worse, Duncan sensed this woman-child would not take the truth well. "'Tis inappropriate for you to be here," he advised sternly, keeping his gaze resolutely above her amply displayed bosom. "Have you no care for your reputation, or even your chastity?"

Alienor rolled her eyes. "I would be rid of chastity and glad of it, if such sacrifice won me a true man." Duncan's back encountered the wall and Alienor knelt directly before him. She shook out her hair, her fingers falling to the ties of her chemise even as she smiled.

"My men will see you," Duncan muttered.

Her smile broadened. "Then you had best ensure they know I am yours."

Duncan seized her hand before she could display her breasts, then knotted the tie with a vengeance. He did a poor job of it, not accustomed to such finery, and the chemise still gaped open when he was done. He brushed past her, picked up her cloak, and flung it at her.

"You must return to your mother's camp," he declared, fighting to keep his voice low enough that his men did not awaken. "You have no place here, and I seek no woman to make my own."

Alienor's eyes flashed. "Whyever not?" Her expression turned coy, her hand landed on his shoulder. "I could change your thinking in this . . ."

Duncan stood and pulled the girl to her feet. "You will change naught with your childish games."

"I am no child! I am a woman fully grown. What man would decline what I offer?" Alienor demanded, then she exhaled in a low hiss. "Are you the manner of man who prefers boys?" Her voice rose waspishly, proving his earlier conclusion aright. "Aye, there are plenty of such men at a king's court, but I had expected to find true men here, men who know of pleasing women and fighting for all they desire." She lifted her chin in challenge. "What manner of man are you, Duncan MacLaren?"

"A man with no desire to take a child as a bride." He gripped her elbow, snatched up her cloak, and marched her out of the broch.

"Oh, you sound like Eglantine. Always right, always thinking of duty and obligation, never sparing a moment for innocent revelry . . ."

"The revelry you propose is far from innocent."

Alienor tossed her hair. "I offered naught but a kiss."

"In such circumstances, only a fool would imagine that a kiss would be all she would pay." Duncan glared at the defiant girl. "You are fortunate indeed, Alienor, for a less noble man would have taken what you offered and more, leaving you with naught but blood on your thighs." Her eyes widened only briefly before her lips set mutinously. "What then of the marriage you would make? What then should Eglantine say?"

Alienor glanced over Duncan's shoulder toward her mother's camp. A disconcertingly smug smile curved her lips. "Why do you not ask her?"

Duncan pivoted to find Eglantine closing upon them, most of her household on her heels. It seemed that news had traveled fast, for the lady's expression was dark and she strode toward him with determination.

She looked furious enough to flay him with her bare hands. Duncan hoped that he would have the opportunity to explain the truth of it, but did not doubt the lady would have her say.

He stepped deliberately in front of Alienor, for he would hide her state from the entire household. But the girl did not share his concerns for her modesty. She stepped around him, then pressed against his side.

"Fool! Do you want all the assembly to see your nudity?" Duncan demanded, glancing down in time to see Alienor pull her chemise so the front gaped. The rain had already soaked the thin fabric, rendering it so sheer that the girl's charms were visible to all.

Indeed her eyes lit with devilry. "What shall you tell Eglantine?" she whispered. "And what will she believe?" She wriggled closer then turned to face her stepmother with a triumphant smile. "I am not a woman to go lacking in what I desire, Duncan, and you had best know the truth of it before we are wed."

Duncan swore under his breath. He had to admit that his suit for Eglantine's hand seemed unlikely to be won.

If Eglantine had thought she was as angry as ever she could be, she quickly learned differently. Aye, for Alienor appeared at Duncan's side and granted her stepmother another unwelcome revelation. There was no disputing the girl's dress or its import—Duncan held her gaze unrepentantly and Eglantine had not a doubt what he had done.

The shameless cur! This was sordid beyond belief! What manner of man went from mother to daughter, and with such haste? 'Twas good that Eglantine was so furious, for otherwise she might have been ill.

"This is unforgivable," she declared. Alienor huddled closer to her lover, but Eglantine saved her fury for the one who should have known better. "You will depart this very morning, you will not return, and you will not sully Kinbeath with your presence any longer."

Duncan folded his arms across his chest. "Again you are quick to leap to conclusions, my Eglantine . . ."

"I am not *your* Eglantine!"

"I would argue the point."

"I would argue naught with you. Get yourself gone!"

But Duncan's eyes narrowed. "You have tried to dispatch me afore—what do you believe has changed this day?"

"*All* has changed. You have despoiled my daughter and claimed what was not yours to claim." Eglantine took a deep breath. "Unless you two were wed last eve without my awareness?"

"We could be wed now, Eglantine, if it pleased you," Alienor offered.

"It does not please *me*," Duncan snapped, sparing an exasperated glance for the girl. "We will not be wed on this day or any other."

Eglantine was indignant. "You would not make right what you have done? You take her maidenhead, even knowing she seeks a spouse, and then would leave her to pay the price? Even I did not imagine that you could be so base!"

Duncan's eyes flashed. "I took naught!"

"That was not freely offered," Alienor amended with a coy smile.

Duncan turned a look of such fury upon her that the girl took a step back. "Fetch your cloak," he ordered. "And leave us be. You aid naught in this discussion."

"Alienor," Eglantine interjected, troubled by the intensity of Duncan's tone. The girl met her gaze defiantly. "Tell me true—did Duncan take your maidenhead or nay?"

Alienor tossed her hair back over her shoulder, ensuring that all could see her pert young breasts through her sodden chemise. "He took my maidenhead," she declared with a bravado that oft meant she lied. "He sampled all I had to offer."

Eglantine frowned, uncertain of the reason for her doubts. Did she read Alienor aright in guessing that the girl lied? Or did she merely *wish* that the girl lied? She looked to Duncan, to find his expression newly grim.

"Eglantine, I took naught," he insisted. "She accosted me in my bed, but I put her aside. Alienor is as virginal as she was on your arrival, or if she is not, 'twas not I who did the deed." His silver gaze bore into her own, compelling her to believe him. "I swear it to you."

Eglantine hesitated, but Alienor did not. She smiled, her expression arch, and trailed her fingertips down Duncan's arm. He did not so much as glance her way. "There is naught to fear, my love. My stepmother is not so witless that she will stand in the way of lovers true. Indeed, we have only to set the date for our nuptials to see this resolved."

"There will be no nuptials!" Duncan roared.

"Aye, there will not," Eglantine agreed. The two halted to stare at her, Alienor with loathing and Duncan with surprise. "True lovers or nay, I would not permit any of my daughters to wed a thief, no less a man who would willfully force a company to starve. Such cruelty is no good portent of a husband's character."

"What nonsense is this?" Duncan demanded, taking a step toward her.

But Eglantine was not fooled by his apparent confusion.

"Do not play the innocent with me," she retorted. "Our stores have been plundered this past night, purportedly by restless spirits anxious to have us gone. There is naught to eat and naught to sow, yet we both know that no spirits were responsible for this willful destruction. The deed to Kinbeath has been stolen and the treasury raided bare." She took a step closer. "There is but one who wants us gone at all costs, and he stands before me."

"You are wrong, Eglantine."

"I have had sufficient of your tales to satisfy," she interrupted, sparing no chance that he might charm her anew. "'Tis time this matter be taken to a court and be resolved fully. Kinbeath is mine, I had the deed to prove it while you have naught but tales. You have not only obstructed my settlement here but in damaging the stores have put my company's health and survival at risk. I shall have reparation from your king."

Duncan shook his head. "'Tis clear that you are ill-disposed to listening to reason this morn."

"'Tis clear that I finally understand the character of my opponent."

He studied her for a long moment, his eyes alight with that unruly fire that she knew better than to trust. When he spoke, his words flowed low. "A king cannot hear a case without claimants." He offered her his hand, the broad palm looking warm and inviting despite all she knew. "As 'tis your command, you and I shall depart this very morn to the court of Dugall, King of the Isles."

Eglantine laughed under her breath and stepped back. "I should think not!"

"There is no other way to resolve this."

Eglantine forced herself to be cynical, for she dared not

soften her stance in the least. "Aye, I know your resolution—
I should depart in your company and not return. I can well
imagine the tale." She affected the pose of a conqueror returning, shrugging with chagrin. "How unfortunate that the
countess Eglantine met with an accident en route."

"I should never permit you to be harmed!" Duncan
protested hotly.

"Indeed." Eglantine silenced him with a look that could
cut stone. "And what have you achieved this morn?"

Duncan opened his mouth and closed it again, his lips
tightening to a thin line. "I told you I am innocent of both
charges."

"And I say you lie."

"Nay, Eglantine, you know better than that." He reached
for her shoulders, but Eglantine evaded his touch. "Eglantine, you draw incorrect conclusions. I did not plunder your
stores. I did not despoil your daughter. I did not empty your
treasury. What desire have I for a deed of no value? Would
you not grant me so much as a hearing, after all that has
passed between us?"

"After all that has passed between us, I expected no
shadow of doubt to fall upon your intent. 'Twas clear I was
wrong in that." With that, she spun to return to her company,
surprised to find that she was shaking.

Aye, 'twas unlike her to become so angry. The man summoned the worst of her to the surface.

"Eglantine!" Duncan bellowed. "You will grant me a
hearing!"

She paused and schooled her expression, hoping she could
ensure that her disappointment did not show. She had been a
fool to give even a meager measure of trust to a man again.
"The king shall grant you a hearing. I must ensure that we
survive until you return."

"Aye? And who will argue your case?" Eglantine glanced

back to find Duncan looking disgruntled and formidable. His legs were braced against the rock, his arms crossed, his dark brows drawn together in a scowl. He arched one brow suddenly, his expression changing briefly to mischief. "Since you do not deign to accompany me to the king's court?"

Eglantine held his gaze, well aware that he felt he had been unfairly judged. "Louis shall accompany you, of course. As my châtelain, he is fully vested with the power of the house to negotiate." She turned away then before she could be swayed further, and led Alienor back toward their own camp.

"Eglantine!" Duncan roared. "You will discuss this with *me*!"

But she would not. She dared not do so. Her household surrounded her, as if they would protect her from Duncan and his men, though Eglantine knew that he could force his way to her side.

But he did not lend chase. She looked back, once, and noted that he argued heatedly with Louis, who looked as pinch-lipped as that man could be.

Aye, she was of no further interest to Duncan now that she refused to do his bidding.

Célie met her, bouncing a teary Esmeraude upon her hip.

"Milk!" The hungry toddler reached for Eglantine, who caught her close and held her tight, rocking on her feet as she tried to soothe her.

"My lady, what shall we do without the goats?" Célie asked. "They are not to be found and Esmeraude is hungered."

"Let us go to Gunther and Gerhard," she suggested, knowing full well that the toddler was listening. "Esmeraude grows so big these days, perhaps 'tis time she had the same porridge in the morn as all of us."

Esmeraude sniffled once more, then locked her hands around Eglantine's neck, evidently reassured that she was becoming a big girl. Eglantine kissed her daughter's brow and smoothed back her hair, unable to deny the unwelcome fact that Duncan had aided her in reestablishing this fragile bond.

Aye, she owed him thanks for that and naught more—and truly, he had had thanks enough from her already.

The woman was vexing, Duncan would grant her that.

But in her place, he would have wrought the same conclusions, and truly Alienor had done naught to aid matters. He did not know who had destroyed the stores or plundered her treasury, but it had not been him, nor had it been done at his dictate.

And the timing of Iain's absence was notable.

Duncan knew Eglantine well enough to know that words would not suffice in this—'twould be his deeds that spoke the truth. He needed to provide her compensation for her loss, a reasonable request given the circumstances, and that could be won only at Dugall's court.

He needed to prove that his pledges were not empty ones, as those of that rogue Theobald had clearly been.

Which meant that Duncan had to find the real culprit—he guessed that Iain could be found worming his way into Dugall's favor. Aye, 'twould be there and only there that Iain might win a redress of what he considered to be the injustice of Cormac appointing Duncan his heir.

Duncan did not truly care whether he was chieftain of Clan MacQuarrie, though he doubted he would win his true desire without that title. Aye, he would still woo his countess Eglantine, but it seemed that events would follow a different order than he might have preferred.

Truly, Eglantine had already derived the best solution to their competing claims, that of merging the claims through marriage. But Duncan would wed Eglantine, not one of her daughters, to forge that bond. He knew he could persuade Dugall to approve the match, for that man had a king's fondness for wealthy foreign blood. He and Eglantine would make a traditional handfast, here at Ceinn-beithe, where 'twould be well favored by the Fates. Then he would have a year and a day to woo her and win her, a year and a day of certainty that she would be by his side.

Duncan did not doubt it could be done. The true challenge would lie in convincing Eglantine even to make the handfast in the first place. Duncan knew better than to expect anything to be simple with this woman.

Indeed, 'twas a fair measure of what he liked about her.

He decided to leave a small group behind at Ceinn-beithe and take the rest of his party along to Dugall's court.

Gillemore offered to remain, much to Duncan's surprise.

"Do you not wish to be out of the rain? It cannot be good for your knees."

"Ah, my knees are as hale as any man's." The older man grinned. "Where there is a cow, there will be a woman; and where there is a woman, there will be temptation. I will stay to ensure that naught happens that could make matters worse." Gillemore spared Reinald a dark glance. "For I am better fit for such a labor than some of us."

All the men laughed aloud at that.

"Oh I should give them trouble such as they have never had before," Reinald jested, to much laughter.

"But there is no cow, Gillemore," another observed. "Does that mean they are not women?" The chatter broke out in earnest, insults and jests flying fast. The men were doubtless glad to be traveling again.

Duncan shook his head with relief as he checked the small boats they had stowed among the rocks. Aye, 'twould be good to have Reinald under his own eye. The last thing he needed was another issue between himself and Eglantine.

He glanced up from the hull of the first boat to find her châtelain hovering on the perimeter of his party. 'Twas clear the older man knew his role, and equally clear that he did not understand what the men said to each other in Gael.

'Twould be a long trip for Louis, Duncan imagined, but the choice had not been his to make.

'Twas the older man left by Duncan who found the goats, and that before Duncan's party had even departed.

He was a gruff and rough individual, his hands calloused and his features burnished by the wind. He fair glowered at Eglantine as he drove the goats toward her, and so fierce was his expression that she did not immediately guess his intent. He gestured to the creatures and loosed a spate of Gael that made all draw back and regard him warily. Esmeraude hovered behind Eglantine, too curious to hide herself away but clutching her mother's skirts for protection.

The man uttered something that could only have been a curse, seized a pail, and set to milking the first of the goats. The beast chewed complacently while he worked, his touch evidently experienced and more gentle than his manner.

When done with the first, his scowl deepened as he surveyed the household still watching him in silence. Indeed, he filled the silence and then some, his hands flying as he commented thoroughly on the situation. He pointed emphatically to the goats' teats hanging so low.

And Eglantine understood that he was irked that the creatures had missed their milking. 'Twas true enough that the creatures would be uncomfortable, and one bleated plaintively in complaint.

"Didier, aid the man. He speaks aright, for the goats have need of milking." Eglantine addressed one of the boys who aided Gunther and Gerhard; he immediately hunkered down to milk the third goat.

Duncan's man had already begun to milk the second, but he did not miss her deed. Eglantine won a grunt for her efforts and a litany of Gael. It seemed to rhyme, like a saying of some kind. Though she could not fathom what he had said, there was an echo of approval in his words that needed no translation.

He stood finally, his task completed, and brushed his hands upon the length of wool wrapped about his hips. His feet were bare, his legs more hairy than she might have imagined possible. His stature was surprisingly small, though Eglantine realized as much only when he paused directly before her.

"Gillemore," he said, tapping one fist upon his heart and repeating what was clearly his name. His bushy brows were shot with silver and seemed thick enough to have a life of their own. He regarded her warily from beneath them, and Eglantine knew she was being assessed. Then he offered the pail of milk to her and inclined his head slightly. He spoke again, the words incomprehensible as his intent was not.

Eglantine inclined her head as she accepted the heavy pail. "I thank you for your aid in this, Gillemore," she said warmly. "I feared the goats lost for good and heartily appreciate your assistance. 'Tis most unexpected."

He nodded, his expression somber, and she wondered how much he had understood of her words. How did she proceed from here? She set the bucket by her feet, a tug on her skirts revealing Esmeraude's curiosity.

"Milk!" the toddler exclaimed with undisguised delight. She cupped her hand and dipped into the pail before she could be stopped, then attempted to drink from her fingers before the milk ran through them. More milk spread on her face and down the front of her kirtle than made it into her mouth, but she looked so pleased that 'twould have been impossible to chide her.

Esmeraude turned a glorious smile on Gillemore, even as the milk dripped from her chin. She abruptly dipped both hands into the bucket, cupped them together, and offered a taste of the milk to him. "Milk is good," she informed him solemnly.

The older man was clearly charmed. He fought a smile and lost, then dropped to one knee. He cupped his own hands together and Esmeraude poured the milk into them. Gillemore drank the milk, making a great show of sighing with satisfaction and wiping his mouth with the back of his hand. He murmured contentment, as if he had sampled the finest fare in Christendom. His eyes twinkled and he smiled at the child, his approval clear in his thanks to her.

Esmeraude was suitably proud of herself for making another conquest. She hugged Eglantine's knee and bit her lip as she eyed Gillemore coyly. "You tell a story?" she asked, then stretched out her hand in appeal. "A story for me?"

Eglantine bent and scooped up the toddler. "Do not trouble Gillemore for a tale," she said softly. "He has found the goats and brought you milk, which is a fine labor indeed."

The toddler frowned, not pleased with this news. "A story! A song!"

"Hush, I shall tell you a story," Eglantine offered, searching her memory even now for some tale she could tell. Indeed, she had best become used to amusing Esmeraude herself, for there would be no timely songs from Duncan now.

Or perhaps ever again. As much as she wanted a resolution to their stalemate, Eglantine could not say she would be glad never to see the rogue again. He was not without his own charms—but 'twas good that she knew those charms were not for her. She hefted Esmeraude—who was getting heavy for such deeds—and made for her tent, well aware that the toddler waved at Gillemore over her shoulder and that Duncan's man watched her go.

Adversity showed the true nature of Eglantine's daughters, if naught else. Alienor pouted, insisting that she had been despoiled and, further, that her *true* mother and father would have ensured that Duncan paid the price for his deed, instead of letting him sail away never to return. Eglantine abandoned the girl to her sulking, having no patience for such recriminations when there was so much else to be resolved.

Jacqueline rose admirably to the occasion. Eglantine found her daughter using veils pilfered from her own collection, patiently sifting the dirt from the flour. Gunther and Gerhard had sufficiently recovered their spirit to aid her appreciatively. Jacqueline flushed when Eglantine arrived.

"I know 'twas your favored one, *Maman,* but 'twas the veil of finest weave and the greater good would be served."

"You show splendid good sense as always, Jacqueline, in putting it to good use." Eglantine smiled. "Indeed, 'tis foolery to try to wear a veil in this land of unruly winds. I am glad to be rid of it."

The two shared a smile, then Gunther brought a small bowl of porridge sweetened with the last of the honey for Esmeraude. That child showed every measure of her charm, undoubtedly determined to prove herself as "big" a girl as her mother had suggested. She rocked amiably between Eglantine's knees as Eglantine held the bowl, humming cheerfully and tapping her spoon in the bowl as she ate.

All smiled at her as they passed. Truly, Esmeraude could charm the sun from the sky, when she desired to do so.

'Twas not long before Eglantine heard Duncan's men calling to each other, and she could not help but watch. The waves splashed as they urged the small boats into the sea and their laughter was hearty and deep. She did not mean to pick out Duncan's silhouette, yet 'twas precisely what she did.

From the angle of the sunlight, 'twas impossible to tell whether he looked back. Though Eglantine told herself 'twas a good thing, her heart still felt leaden. She knew that she had cursedly poor luck with men—had this interval with Duncan not proven the truth of it?

But what if Duncan did not lie to her?

What if he never returned?

Who knew whether she would ever have the opportunity to grant Duncan the hearing he had requested? Eglantine had the urge to run after him, to cry for him to halt, to have that honesty between them that he so coveted, but she did not do so. If he lied, as all men had lied to her, then such a deed would only show her to be a fool.

So she held her ground, but watched him sail away because she was too weak to deny herself one last sight of Duncan MacLaren.

'Twas only when the small boats disappeared in the haze hugging the horizon that Eglantine permitted her shoulders to sag. She rubbed her brow and could not imagine how she might have wrought a situation any worse from what Theobald had granted to her. Her eyes filled with tears as surveyed her humble surroundings and thought longingly of home.

Home. It seemed so distant from this wild place. She recalled Arnelaine's fields, Crevy's towers, the meadow beyond the woods, and the sparkle of the millstream. She smiled in recollection of her mother's smile, her brother's gruff protectiveness of his sweet bride.

Brigid should have had her child by now—the realization made Eglantine feel the tug of home more ardently. She wished that she had not missed that arrival, then wondered whether the babe was a boy or a girl. Guillaume would not care, and that certainty made her smile broaden.

As long as Brigid was fine. Oh, he probably paced a trench in Crevy's stone floors while she labored to bring the babe to light; that would be Guillaume. Eglantine's smile faded to naught. She hoped with sudden fervor that all *had* gone well.

New doubts needled her. Perhaps she should have lingered,

been there for Brigid's delivery. Indeed, the shock of her departure would have troubled sensitive Brigid. And who else could have come?

What if Eglantine's mother had been ill, as was so often the case in the winters of late—or worse, if her mother chose to meddle rather than to aid, as was often her wont? Brigid had no other family nearby, save Burke's Alys.

What if the babe came early and Guillaume was yet at court?

Eglantine fretted, seeing another duty she had failed to fulfill when 'twas too late to make amends. How could she have stayed, though, and left Jacqueline prey to Reynaud? 'Twas a muddle of poor choices she had been granted and that was the truth of it. Indeed, it seemed that no matter what choice she made, there was a disappointment to be borne.

But there was no point in dwelling upon what could not be fixed. Eglantine pressed a kiss to Esmeraude's brow and was grateful for one victory in her life. She prayed for not only the best, not only that both Brigid and babe were hale, but that her brother would forgive her all.

Indeed, there was little else she could do from here.

Chapter Eleven

GUILLAUME, FOR HIS PART, WAS NOT IN A FORGIV-
ing mood.

Indeed, he ranted in Crevy's hall as never he had
ranted before. He paced and he shouted and his staff eased
back against the walls, putting as much distance between
themselves and their raging lord as possible. Even his mother
had the good sense to hold her tongue, which was something
indeed.

Guillaume raved because the babe was late. Not only was
it late commencing the labor, but it lingered over the task. He
began to suspect that the babe had no inclination of coming
forth into the world at all. Aye, this babe was taking longer
than all the babes in Christendom had taken in sum!

And worst of all, there was naught Guillaume could do
about it.

His wife screamed far above him, she raged in pain at a
volume quite unlike her docile self, and he could do naught
to make this easier.

Much less faster.

So, he paced and he growled and he snapped at anyone
fool enough to venture close to his side. He had been home
a fortnight, having feared the babe would have arrived
sooner but powerless to free himself from the king's grip.
He had galloped through the gates, relieved to find Brigid

nigh bursting at the seams. She had burst into tears at the sight of him, and it had seemed the child awaited its father's return.

But each subsequent day had made Guillaume fear that something was sorely amiss. His mother insisted that first children were apt to be tardy, but he fretted all the same.

Such was the state of his thoughts that Guillaume had barely noted how Eglantine had plundered his treasury and his stables. He had avoided his mother's worries about his errant sister, no less her insistence that someone should ensure Eglantine was well. That last comment was made repeatedly, with hard glances at Guillaume each time, but he was preoccupied with his own concerns. He knew well enough that Eglantine was strong, Eglantine was determined, Eglantine could fend for herself.

Brigid, however, was soft and vulnerable. Brigid needed him.

And now she cried out in pain, striving to deliver the babe that he had planted in her belly. Guillaume tugged at his hair and paced the hall again. He had done all he could, he had sent for Alys and Burke, he had summoned a midwife, and now he could only wait.

'Twas not a role he relished.

"Where is Burke?" he demanded in frustration. "And why does he not hasten? Surely every steed in his stable cannot have been struck lame at this time! Indeed, a man could walk from Montvieux, or even from Villonne, in the time he has taken!"

His mother cleared her throat. "It has been but a day since you sent word—"

Guillaume flung out his hands and spun to face her. "It has been an eternity!"

She lifted one brow, as much censure as she ever granted, and pushed to her feet. "I have told you well that the first will take its own time."

"But someone must do something! I can bear it no longer!"

"*Alors,* I shall take a honeycomb to Brigid. 'Tis a treat she favors well enough, and perhaps 'twill take her thoughts from the pain, *non*?"

"A honeycomb will do naught to ease her labors!" Guillaume roared, realizing only when his mother's eyes widened that 'twas the first time he had ever shouted at her.

Her mouth opened and closed again, before she turned away. Her skirts flared behind her as she snapped her fingers at her staff and climbed the stairs, her silence as cutting as anything she might have said.

Before Guillaume could follow and apologize, his châtelain stepped into the hall. "Chevalier Burke de Montvieux, Lord de Villonne, and his lady wife, Alys, to see you, my lord."

"Burke!" Guillaume approached his friend with open arms. "What took you so very long?"

The knight rolled his eyes and grinned. "Has she labored for more than an hour?" he jested as he clasped Guillaume's hand.

Brigid screamed, a most effective interruption and one that had all in the hall wincing. Alys, her fair hair bound back and her belly only slightly rounded, appeared somewhat alarmed.

'Twas only then that Guillaume realized his insensitivity in summoning her of all people to a birthing. But naught would go awry here, would it? He bowed low, all the same, for it had not been his intent to recall hurtful memories to these good friends. "Alys, I do apologize . . ."

She forced a smile and squeezed Burke's hand. "Perhaps the formalities are best left for later," she suggested, visibly squaring her shoulders. "I would hasten to Brigid."

Burke's eyes lit with concern. "I will go with you," he suggested, obviously following Guillaume's thoughts.

But Alys shook her head. "Brigid would be mortified by your presence. I shall attend her myself and all will be fine."

"You will be far from alone in that chamber." Guillaume tried to jest. "There must be a fair crowd there by now. Indeed, my mother intended to feed Brigid honeycomb."

"In this moment?" Alys's eyes widened in surprise, then she shook her head. "Only the Lady of Crevy would do as much," she murmured with affection, then bustled to the solar. Burke's gaze followed his wife's progress and his eyes narrowed.

"Burke, in my haste, I forgot . . ."

But Burke held up a hand. "Alys would not have missed this." A smile touched his lips. "She has a fondness for Brigid that no sorry event can undermine."

The small boy beside Burke, no more than three summers of age, watched Guillaume solemnly. He was a handsome boy and shared his father's coloring, though his eyes were the clear green of his mother's. "Why does the lady scream, Papa?"

Burke ruffled his son's hair. "Ah, because she labors mightily. 'Tis not for you to concern yourself, Bayard. You remember Guillaume, do you not?" Guillaume appreciated that his old friend tried to distract both the child and himself from the proceedings above. "You may not recall this, Bayard, but Guillaume is your godfather."

The boy bowed low, his father beaming at his fine manners. "'Tis an honor to make your acquaintance once more, my Lord de Crevy-sur-Seine."

Guillaume smiled. It seemed but yesterday that he and Brigid had pledged to raise this boy as their own should the need arise, that Guillaume had pledged to ensure the true faith burned bright in this small soul. How the years had flown!

"I believe you might call me your Uncle Guillaume," he suggested, hunkering down before the boy. "Has your father taught you to play draughts?"

An impish grin lit Bayard's features and he leaned closer to whisper. "Aye, and I best him most every time!"

"Ah, well, your father was always a poor player," Guillaume declared even as Burke choked at this undeserved assault on his skills. Guillaume winked. "For I used to best him most every time as well."

"You cannot best me, sir," the boy claimed with confidence.

Guillaume grinned, guessing this would pass the time admirably. "Aye? It shall not be for lack of trying!"

Alys paused on the threshold of the solar and took a deep breath. She would not remember, she would not think of her own ordeal with her first.

She would not think of that tiny little girl, that impossibly small babe, drawing her last breath in her own arms. Brigid would bear a healthy child, she knew it well, and naught would go awry.

But Alys's palms were damp as she stepped into the chamber. She was not unfamiliar with birthing and its ordeal, but she was shocked by what she found in the solar all the same. Her cousin was as pale as a winter moon, and there was an astonishing amount of blood upon the linens. The portly midwife sat back, her expression grim, and wiped her brow with the back of one hand.

"'Twill be one or the other of them," she informed Alys tartly. "Or perhaps neither at all." She pushed to her feet and wiped her bloody hands upon her apron. "'Tis in God's hands now."

'Twas clear the woman meant to leave. "What nonsense is this?" Alys demanded, seizing the woman's elbow. "She has not labored long, has she?"

"One night and one day," Lady Crevy supplied. That lady sat on the windowsill, nibbling worriedly on a honeycomb. Her eyes were wide, her expression uncommonly sober.

Alys gave the midwife's arm a shake. "You cannot leave her!"

"There is little point in my lingering."

"But what is amiss?"

The woman shrugged. "I do not know. I am only recently come to this task. 'Twas Berthe of the village who deigned to teach me, but she has gone and died afore my apprenticeship was done." She shrugged again. "The easy ones, they are no trouble to me. Out they come and a body has but to catch them and cut the cord." She looked to Brigid and shook her head. "This one does not come out."

Alys muttered a curse and bent to touch Brigid's cheek. Her cousin was pale, too pale, and her breathing was shallow. Brigid's pulse was strong at her throat, though, and her lashes fluttered for only a moment before she opened her eyes.

"Alys." The name left her lips like a sigh. "I am so glad you are here." She licked her lips and her voice was uncommonly soft. The stutter that had once plagued her speech had faded to naught beneath Guillaume's affection. "You have traveled far—did Guillaume grant you a cup of wine to parch your thirst?"

"Brigid, I have come to aid you, not to drink your wine." Alys leaned closer. "How do you feel?"

"Oh, it hurts." Brigid gripped Alys's hand, a flicker of fear in the depths of her eyes. "Something is amiss, Alys." She whispered, as if she feared to frighten the others in the solar. "It hurts overmuch and naught is changing. Should the babe not come forth? I am so very tired."

Alys's heart clenched, but she forced herself to smile cheerfully. "It always hurts, Brigid. And it always takes longer than can be believed."

"Alys." Brigid's eyes flew open and tears shone within them. "Alys, aid me. Do not let my babe die. Guillaume is so anxious for a son."

Alys blinked back tears of her own, and she squeezed her cousin's hand tightly. "Let me see what can be done."

Brigid's features contorted as another contraction seized her. Her hand clenched around Alys's fingers and her scream nigh rent the walls.

But even as she moved to look, Alys knew it had been too long since the last contraction. By now, with this much blood, the contractions should be close together, one fast after the other, and the babe should be showing its crown.

"I cannot bear the sound," the midwife muttered as she covered her ears.

"Do not let her leave!" the Lady Crevy cried, but Alys cared naught for that one's aid.

"It matters not," she said crisply, and reached beneath the blood-soaked linens. She would have much to say to Guillaume later over the fitness of that midwife—indeed, she would not allow the woman into Villonne's stables.

Something *was* amiss—and Brigid grew too tired to aid herself. 'Twas clear her womb despaired of bringing the child forth. But why?

And if the choice truly must be made between mother and babe, which would Guillaume have her choose? Brigid, Alys decided, Brigid without a doubt. But she eyed her cousin's pallor and feared they might not have even that choice. Alys looked, but there was indeed no sign of the babe.

'Twas no time to be squeamish, if she meant to ensure that this babe survived as her own first had not. Alys gritted her teeth and reached into her cousin's warmth. She cooed to Brigid, making reassuring noises, though she was unaware whether it made any difference. The sound of Brigid's heavy breathing filled the solar.

Alys closed her eyes, feeling her way, her heart skipping as she felt the curve of the babe's head. 'Twas so still, she feared 'twas too late for the child.

But Brigid's belly rippled, another contraction gathering, and the child squirmed against Alys's hand.

Her own heart leapt with hope and she patted her cousin's belly. "Do not push, Brigid—scream, scream down the walls, but hold the babe tight within you for a moment."

"Aye, Alys," Brigid huffed, then another cry of pain was torn from within her. The midwife cursed and fled at the sound, and Guillaume was probably green about the gills. Lady Crevy came anxiously to Alys's side. Alys felt their movements, she sensed the maids drawing closer in dismay, but her attention was fixed on the child.

And then she felt the cord.

'Twas wrapped around the babe's shoulder, as it should not be, keeping the child from leaving the womb. Alys felt a surge of relief that matters were so simple.

"Brigid, the cord is around the babe's shoulder. I shall ease it aside, but you must aid me. Do not push until 'tis done."

"Aye, Alys, aye, Alys." Brigid puffed, her fingers clawing at the linens as another contraction gathered.

"Lady Crevy, you might hold her hand. And someone bathe her brow, for 'twill aid naught if she grows too hot." All leapt to do Alys's bidding, no doubt grateful for any task to occupy their hands.

But the cord was not so readily moved as that. Alys eased its thickness over a slick shoulder, amazed at the size of the child. There was little room to work, to be sure, and the cord seemed to fight her efforts. The babe, though, struggled beneath her hands, as if it too would choose to survive. 'Twas stronger than she had hoped, even after all of this, and Alys's hope flared.

It took her two contractions to work the babe's shoulder free, and she was trembling when the next contraction gathered. "Now you must push, Brigid, push with all your strength. Spare naught to scream."

Lady Crevy kissed Brigid's hand, then held it to her heart. "I give you my strength, *ma petite,*" she murmured. "We push together, you and I, *non*? The first, it always is reluctant to see the light."

Brigid's body rippled with the force of the contraction before she could do more than nod agreement. She gritted her teeth and arched off the pallet, her grip so tight that Lady Crevy's fingers turned white.

Alys pulled on the slippery child, coaxing it farther than it might have come on its own. She was relieved that the cord did not seem to impede its progress any further, but the contraction ended all too soon.

"My lady, I see the head!" one maid cried, and the others gathered closer. Their enthusiasm helped Brigid to rally, though her gaze fixed on Alys.

"Again, as the last," Alys counseled. "'Tis almost done, Brigid."

"The babe is fine?"

Alys smiled. "It fights to see the light."

"A fighter, *non*?" Lady Crevy kissed Brigid's brow. "'Tis a fine knight and heir to Crevy you carry, *ma petite. Encore,* we push."

Brigid nodded, took a deep breath, and bared her teeth as a contraction rolled through her once more.

And the child fairly leapt into Alys's arms, its expression tormented. "'Tis a boy," she cried, and cleared its face with haste.

The maids hovered breathlessly. The babe's eyes were squeezed tightly shut, his tiny fists clenched. He arched back against Alys's hand and let loose a cry so hale that Alys fairly wept in her relief.

"'Tis a boy, Brigid," she said past the lump in her throat. "A fine healthy boy, just as Lady Crevy predicted."

The maids cheered. Brigid collapsed with a sigh, her skin

nigh as white as the linens even as the tears streamed over her cheeks. "Quinn," she whispered weakly. "I told Guillaume we should name a boy Quinn."

"'Tis a fine name, *ma petite*." Lady Crevy wiped the tears from her own eyes, then kissed her daughter-in-law's brow. "You have done most well," she whispered, then barked orders for cleaning the bed, the babe, and Brigid.

"*Ma petite* must have a hearty beef broth—she has lost too much strength." She clucked, snapping her fingers impatiently all the while. "Bring her eggs. And veal! 'Tis good for the blood, *non*? Tell Beauregard that his chick has need of especial care."

'Twas well known at Crevy that the large gruff chef Beauregard had a soft spot for Brigid, and the comment prompted more than one welcome smile. Alys had no doubt that the finest calf in the meadow would be slaughtered this very day for that veal.

Lady Crevy kissed Brigid's brow. "We shall see you hale in no time at all, *ma petite*." She straightened and flicked her hands at the maids. "Hasten yourselves! Clean this chamber. The babe must be washed, the mother cleaned. My son will arrive shortly to visit his son, of that you may have no doubt, and all must be made ready!"

But Guillaume was already there. He hovered in the doorway, his features haggard, his eyes filled with concern. Alys felt her tears rise as Brigid's face lit at the sight of him.

Brigid offered her hand to her spouse, though it hung limply in her exhaustion. "Come see your son, Guillaume," she said softly.

"I came to see my wife." 'Twas clear that Guillaume too noted the toll the birth had taken on his wife. "I feared to lose you," he whispered hoarsely, his gaze flicking to Alys. "She is fine? She will be fine?"

The cousins shared a warm glance, tinged with considerable

relief. "Brigid is tired but fine. She will need to lie abed for some days, for she has lost much blood. And she has need of sleep after such a task."

"But I will be fine, because Alys came." The cleaned infant was laid on Brigid's breast, and she cuddled him close as yet another tear leaked from beneath her lashes. "He is big, Alys, is he not?"

"Aye, a very healthy boy."

Guillaume sat tentatively on the side of the mattress, his eyes filled with the wonder of both wife and son, and Alys knew 'twas time she left. She spied Burke in the shadows of the corridor outside the solar and excused herself. But one glance and she knew they both recalled the arrival of their first.

At moments like this, the loss hung on Alys's heart like a leaden weight. She would never forget that tiny girl, never so long as she drew breath.

She took shelter in Burke's embrace, trembling only once his arms had closed tightly around her. "Oh, Burke, I feared to lose them both."

"'Twas close?" he murmured into her hair.

"Too close. The cord was tangled around the babe. If we had not come, Burke . . ."

"But we did come." He tipped her chin with one finger. His lips quirked, coaxing her to smile. "We came, and you aided Brigid, and all has come aright."

Alys shuddered. "But I could not help thinking of our first . . ."

"You know that my mother has said that the first often is lost. She was a fine girl, but too small, Alys." His arms were tight around her, as they had been in that trying moment. "'Twas neither your fault nor mine that she came too soon. And now we have Bayard, as healthy and hale a child as ever there could be."

"Aye." Alys breathed deeply of his scent, taking reassurance as always from his strength. "And another coming."

"Perhaps another girl." Burke kissed her brow.

"Do you desire a daughter?"

"I desire my wife hale, first and foremost. If the babe is healthy, too, then that would be also welcome. I care no more for its gender than the hue of its eyes."

Alys leaned against his chest, savoring the thrum of his heartbeat, then realized what she did. She pulled away and surveyed herself ruefully. "I am a wretched mess."

Burke's eyes glowed. "Because you had heart enough to give aid."

Alys felt her color rise beneath her spouse's warm regard and knew he would always have this power to dispel the shadows for her. "Where is Bayard? I would hug him tightly in this moment."

"He plays a game with the châtelain." Burke sobered. "I was not certain what he would see here, so left him behind." He smiled. "Though 'tis good to have one's fears prove unfounded."

Alys's hand curved over her own belly, her thoughts turning in an obvious direction, and the warmth of Burke's hand immediately closed over her own.

"'Twill not happen to you, Alys," he said as if he alone could will it to be so. "Bayard's birth was without incident. Such troubles are behind us."

"It could happen to anyone, Burke, and we both know it well." She interlaced her fingers with his own. "Thanks be to God that your service upon the king is completed and that you will be home when this one arrives."

His lips tightened and she knew he would tell her something that she did not want to hear.

"There is something I must confess, Alys," he said heavily.

"Burke? You *will* be home?"

He folded her hands into his and met her gaze steadily. "Aye, I will be home, Alys, but I must leave in the interim."

"Burke!"

"I only just pledged as much to Guillaume. His sister Eglantine has fled Arnelaine with her daughters while he was at court. She has taken much from Guillaume's household, as if she would make a home elsewhere. He cannot understand that she would make such a choice, not unless something were terribly amiss. 'Tis not like Eglantine to be frivolous."

"Why would she leave Arnelaine?"

Burke shrugged. "Her spouse Theobald did die last fall, and Guillaume confirmed that he gambled overmuch. Perhaps her debts were too large, but I cannot fathom why she did not turn to her family. And there is an issue before the king's own court to be resolved. One of Eglantine's daughters was pledged to Reynaud de Charmonte, and that man demands either his bride or paid restitution for the insult. Guillaume would know the truth of Eglantine's intent before he pays the fee."

"What manner of man is this Reynaud?"

"I know him not, though your father might be acquainted with him."

Alys wrinkled her nose in disgust. "They are of an age?"

"I gather as much."

"But Eglantine's daughters are so young!"

"You know how such things are arranged in some families."

Aye, Alys did. "But where could she have gone? One cannot simply claim land without a deed or travel incessantly. Who would shelter her? Is there more family?"

Burke shook his head. "Nay. But Lady Crevy has admitted that Theobald left Eglantine a title for lands in Scotland. She knows naught but the name of the holding and has as much as confessed that Eglantine has fled there. She did, by the way, swear Guillaume to secrecy, for she is betraying Eglantine's trust in admitting as much."

"'Tis her worry that broke her silence."

"Aye and rightly so."

Alys guessed the direction of this conversation and cared naught for it. "But Eglantine has made her choice, Burke. 'Tis none of your concern."

"Alys, 'tis not that simple. The family fears for her survival. Guillaume would pursue her, merely to ensure that all is indeed well, but he feared even moments past to leave Brigid. Brigid's recovery will be a long one, we both see the truth of it, Alys. And we both have witnessed the impact of Guillaume's absences upon Brigid's health."

Alys felt her own tears rise. She knew Burke would do the gallant deed, she knew he would do this favor for his friend, and truly she could not slight the generosity of his nature.

But still she wished he would not go. "Oh, Burke."

"And Lady Crevy is most distressed. Alys, I would remain home by my own choice, but these are good friends, friends of a lifetime. Eglantine I have known since we were children. I, too, worry for her safety."

"She is the one who took that wager to seduce you, is she not?"

Burke grinned and kissed her hand. "She had not a chance of success, since you already held my heart in thrall."

Alys heaved a sigh as she recalled more of Eglantine. "She was the one who came to the funeral for our daughter," she said heavily, her gaze misting with tears. "She was the one who was round with her own child and spoke so compassionately to me of the risks we all face."

"Aye, that was she."

There was little Alys remembered of the day they laid their first child to rest in Villonne's cemetery, but Eglantine had touched her heart with her expression of sympathy.

'Twould not be right to reward such kindness with selfishness.

"Alys, you are stronger than Brigid," Burke argued softly,

unaware that Alys already shared his view. "You have your father at Villonne to aid you and my mother at Montvieux."

Alys rolled her eyes, then smiled. "Do not wish Margaux upon me in this moment, I beg of you."

Burke grinned in turn, for his mother's sharp tongue was of wide renown. Then he sobered as he gave her fingers a squeeze. "You are but five months along, Alys. I pledge to you that I shall return before your time."

"You shall have to ride like the wind."

He smiled that slow smile that always warmed her to her toes. "For my lady's favor, I could do naught less." He caught her close, his lips against her ear. "I swear it to you, Alys, by all we both hold holy. I shall return, I shall hold your hand, I shall never let you face this labor alone. 'Tis wrought of the deed we shared, and I will share this with you as well."

Alys clung to him. She knew Burke would keep his word—'twas much of what she loved about him. 'Twas not within him, though, to retreat on a promise made to a friend, to leave Guillaume fretting of his sister's fate, to not make all right that he could.

'Twas another trait Alys loved about him.

"I shall miss you sorely," she whispered, hating the unevenness of her words. She pulled back to look into his eyes, her hands rising to frame the handsome visage she knew so well. "I love you, Burke. Though your chivalrous tendencies can be vexing indeed, I would have you be no other way."

He kissed her deeply in his relief, only the sound of a man clearing his throat drawing them apart.

"They always do as much," Bayard told Guillaume's châtelain.

The older man fought a smile even as he bowed. "Do you believe, my lady Alys, that my presence would be unwelcome in the solar at this time?"

She smiled. "'Tis a boy. Are you curious to see him, as well?"

"Aye, that I am, but a more pressing matter calls." The châtelain sobered. "My lord Guillaume has a guest."

"Surely this guest could be waylaid for the moment?" Burke asked quietly.

The châtelain shook his head. "Reynaud de Charmonte is not so readily dissuaded as that. He claims he is come for his payment for Arnelaine's seal."

Burke and Alys exchanged a glance. Alys guessed that this Reynaud had come for more than that, and she had no desire to meet him. She excused herself on the basis of her dirtied kirtle. Then she caught her son in her arms and lifted him high, while Burke waylaid his curiosity about doings in the solar with a challenge for draughts.

They adjourned to the kitchens to play a rousing game, one that Burke soundly lost by his own design. Beauregard treated them all to fresh dumplings and a new keg of ale, the cook in an expansive mood now that his mistress was well.

But there was a shadow on Crevy despite the arrival of an heir. There were men in the kitchens, strangers employed by Reynaud, men who said little but drank a great deal of that ale. Guillaume was cloistered long with the visiting lord, his expression strained when they met at the board that evening.

And when Alys waved farewell to Burke three days later, Reynaud was yet at Crevy, demanding better terms for Arnelaine's seal.

Chapter Twelve

TO DUNCAN'S DISMAY, HE WAS EXPECTED AT Dugall's court.

And not to be honored. Indeed, a pair of burly guards met his coracle and seized his elbows the moment he set foot upon Mull's shore. Duncan felt the châtelain Louis's surprise, but he had greater troubles than interpreting events for Eglantine's servant. It was only a day and a half since they had left Ceinn-beithe, Dugall's high court on the isle of Mull being a short journey away by boat.

Dugall, King of the Isles, was the eldest son of Somerled, the lord of Argyll and the Western Isles. Somerled had conquered the Hebridean islands from the Norwegian kings, married the daughter of Olaf the Red, and prompted the memory of many old tales by uniting the ancient kingdom of Dalriada under his hand once more.

The Scottish king David had coexisted with Somerled, with few altercations. However, the ascent of David's son, Malcolm IV, to the Scottish throne as a boy of twelve had prompted ambitious souls to challenge the succession. 'Twas no small thing that Somerled's sister was wed to Malcolm MacHeth, a man of Moray who became the earl of Ross.

By 1160 the Scottish king Malcolm and Somerled had been sufficiently reconciled for Somerled to spend Christmas at the king's court in Perth. But then Malcolm had attempted to divest Somerled's brother-in-law of the earldom of Ross in favor of his own brother-in-law and the peace had ended. Somerled had attacked the mainland of Scotland, sailing up the Clyde River and landing at Renfrew in 1164, in an attempt to stem the westward advance of the Anglo-Norman nobility. He died in that battle, along with one of his sons.

Somerled's son, Dugall, however, had been crowned King of the Isles as a boy. After the loss at Renfrew, Somerled's territories were divided among his three surviving sons: Dugall, Reginald, and Angus.

Meanwhile, Malcolm IV had died in 1165, and the Scottish crown had passed to his brother William, known as the Lion. Bred of a Norman mother and a father of the line of Malcolm Canmore, much of his expectations of the world were shaped by the French and thus the Norman court. His most notable accomplishment thus far had been to challenge the suzerainty of the English king Henry II over Northumberland. The border lands had been contested again in 1174, and William had been defeated and captured at Alnwick.

The humiliating result of this was the Treaty of Falaise, which made the Scottish king a vassal of the English king and dictated the surrender of four major castles, if temporarily, to the English king.

'Twas not a loss that fostered the support of those already dubious of the Scottish king's suzerainty. However, William, his ambitions of southern expansion effectively curtailed, had cast his eye over the western territories. 'Twas not anticipated that he would be so bold again to attack openly, but the Norman tradition of granting deeds to knights and lords, who then built fortified castles upon those lands, was not unknown even here.

And 'twas certainly known to William, who had virtually grown up in the Anglo-Norman courts.

Judging by his reception, Duncan saw that Dugall was
evidently displeased with him, which neatly revealed where
Iain had fled. Duncan did not protest as he was marched in
the direction of Dugall's hall without a word of explanation.
He could well imagine what tales had been told in his absence and at his expense.

His own explanation would be saved for the ears of the
King of the Isles. He would need all his skills for telling tales
in order to see his hide whole by the end of this interview.

All fell silent in the smoky hall as Duncan was thrust into
its shadows. He could hear the dozens who normally attended the king breathing in the darkness and felt the weight
of their gazes. Dugall surveyed him coldly.

The king sat in his high seat on the far side of the hall, a
mug of ale cupped in his hands, a woman and a hunting dog
curled at his feet. The firelight flickered over the harsh lines
of the king's visage, for this was not a ruler content to remain
in the comfort of his court. Dugall fought himself and fought
often, having no compunction to kill when it served his
needs.

And in this moment, Dugall regarded Duncan with something akin to loathing.

Iain's golden hair caught the light as he stepped forward
from the shadows behind Dugall's chair. He murmured
something to the king, his expression exultant as he met
Duncan's gaze. Dugall almost smiled, his gaze unswerving
from Duncan.

"I hear tell that you have failed me," the king said by way
of introduction. The sentries shoved Duncan forward, releas-
ing his elbows so abruptly that he fairly stumbled into the
center of the hall. All assembled there watched with bright
eyes, no doubt expecting a cruel judgment from the king for
such a failure.

Duncan again felt the weight of Cormac's unorthodox

choice in naming him as chieftain. He was not a man of war like Dugall, nor even a bloodthirsty fool like Iain. He glanced around the hall, noting now the familiar faces of other battle-hungry chieftains.

With sudden clarity, he understood why Cormac had chosen him as his successor. With so many men of war gathered, bloodshed could be the only result.

But 'twas not always the better result.

And here was Duncan's chance to prove it.

Dugall scowled. "Unless you have secured Ceinn-beithe since the departure of Cormac's own son?"

Duncan lifted his chin and smiled with a confidence he was far from feeling. "Nay, as yet I have not."

Iain spread his hands, as if this were confession enough, but Duncan cleared his throat. "But that does not mean that the battle is over."

"There has been no battle!" Iain cried. "He is too much a coward to unsheath his blade and do what must be done!"

"Aye, I refuse to slaughter women in their beds, like a common vagabond," Duncan retorted. "There are other ways to see a victory assured."

"Then tell me of them," the king invited silkily. There was no mistaking the import of the hard light in his gaze, and Duncan understood that his liege lord would not be readily persuaded to abandon a course of warfare.

Duncan knew that Dugall was interested only in the tactical import of Ceinn-beithe. There was no doubt in his heart that Dugall could muster an army this very day, that this king would strike the telling blow himself if need be to see his hegemony secured. He had one chance to persuade the king to stay his hand, one chance to ensure that Eglantine and her household were not slaughtered to see the land regained.

'Twas more than enough incentive to argue his best.

Duncan bowed low, striving to appear at ease. "My lord king, I would review what has transpired for your benefit alone. Shortly after our arrival at Ceinn-beithe, a party arrived to stake a claim upon it. 'Twas a noblewoman who came to secure a holding, a countess from France and in possession of a legal title."

"A title? I granted no such title!"

"Aye, but another king did, and did so with the certitude that his will would be served." Duncan paused for a moment to let Dugall consider who that king must be. "And this 'twas that made me pause. In addition, the lady arrived with all the accoutrements of a household but with no knights. I suspected that her spouse and militia would follow behind. Had we moved hastily, as Cormac's son advised, that man undoubtedly would have retaliated."

Dugall pursed his lips in consideration.

"But no men came!" Iain interjected. "There were no knights and no militia. This household and their riches are ours for the taking." He sneered. "Should we have had a leader who was man enough to order an attack."

Duncan shook his head, avoiding the obvious retort. "Nay, one must consider all the possibilities, and with a household so numerous as this lady's and a party so small as our own, 'twould have been impossible to ensure that none fled to give word of any attack. She had already visited the court of William of Scotland, so her vassals would know the way. No doubt that man had granted his approval to her enterprise— and if word came that she had been slaughtered in your name, a great war could have erupted between yourself and William of Scotland."

"He has no authority here," Dugall declared, but consideration had dawned in his eyes.

"Nay, but without your counsel, my lord king, I was reluctant to begin a war."

"You should have sent for approval immediately," Iain advised. "I would have come to your court, my lord king!"

Duncan arched a brow as he held Iain's hot gaze. "But I have always found it prudent to know the strengths and weaknesses of one's opponent, rather than acting in haste. How would your decision have been served, my lord king, by half of the tale?"

Iain spat into the rushes. "A company of women has but one asset to share, and you would not even permit us that."

A chuckle rolled through the company, a chuckle not shared by Duncan, the king, or the woman sitting at the king's feet.

Duncan waited for silence to return before he spoke. "There once was a time you spoke highly of women, Iain, and honored their beauty with treasures wrought by your own hand." Iain flushed at this charge, and Duncan continued gently. "And your father, I know well, was proud of what you wrought. Would he be proud of what you have wrought in these days?"

"You have no right to speak of my father!"

"As his chosen successor, I have every right to speak of him, and as your foster brother, I have every concern for your choices and your fortune."

"My father had no pride in me, 'tis clear, for he appointed you his successor." Iain turned away and folded his arms stubbornly across his chest.

Duncan returned his address to the king, knowing the issues between himself and Iain would not be readily resolved. "Someone has seen fit to destroy much of the foodstuff brought by this party. Their treasury also has been robbed. The countess demands compensation for her loss—she sends her man to our lord king Dugall to make her claim."

Duncan gestured to Louis, who had also been brought to the hall. That man bowed, evidently guessing why he was being indicated.

"I have no doubt she has similarly sent word to William, and his envoys will be fast across the mountains."

Dugall growled and tapped his cup upon the arm of his chair. "You should know that rash choices are seldom good ones," he said to Iain, then frowned at Duncan. "But your leisure no better. We shall have to act quickly to ensure all is settled before William sends reinforcements for this wrongful claim."

"Aye? But what point is there in warfare here?" Duncan demanded. "Surely there is more to be lost than gained?"

The king's eyes narrowed, but he did not interrupt.

"These new arrivals have talents," he continued. "Could we not use the skills of stonemasons, of cooks and bakers, of weavers and spinners, of herdsmen and hunters? They are people unafraid to labor and determined to build a settlement upon that land, regardless of the cost. Would it not increase the glory of our king to have a village there? Would it not increase the glory of our lord king to have a settlement of Norman sophistication beneath his hand?"

A murmur of consideration rolled through the company. Dugall rubbed his chin.

"What of the opportunity for trade?" Duncan asked. "Ceinnbeithe could be a fine port. 'Twould be defensible, situated as 'tis within the embrace of the islands, yet the waters of its bay run deep enough for the great ships of the continent. What prosperity could be found in trade for all of our lord king's people?"

"We have naught to trade," snapped an old chieftain.

"Have we not? What of the work of our jewelers?" Iain stiffened, but Duncan did not acknowledge his obvious interest. "I tell you that I have seen little of such splendor in my own travels, and indeed, I sold my one brooch too early on my own venture. I could have sold it a hundred times and for far greater coin. What of the wool of the sheep that thrive here? Everywhere I traveled, the women complained of the cost of English wool and Flemish weaving."

Whispers broke out in the company, the ayes and nays evenly mixed.

Duncan turned and spread his hands, appealing to the company. "What better way to prove that we are more than a tribe of barbarians lost on the edge of Christendom than to create a thriving port, a colony of artisans, a source of revenue for our lord king's coffers?"

"'Twill be of merit only if that holding is loyal to our king," Iain argued, stepping neatly into the trap Duncan had set for him. "A fortified opponent so close at hand would be poor asset indeed."

Duncan smiled, folding his arms across his chest. Indeed, the tide turned in his favor. "Iain speaks the truth in this. And what is the finest way to secure an alliance?"

"Marriage," the king declared, though the shrewd light in his eyes did not diminish.

"Aye, marriage." Duncan nodded and voiced his plan with a confidence he was far from feeling. "And what better man to ensure this alliance than a man known beyond doubt to be committed not only to the goodwill of our lord king but to the increase of his wealth and glory?"

He jabbed a finger at his own chest and took a step closer to the king. "I would surrender myself to this task. I would make a handfast with this countess. I would pledge Ceinn-beithe to the service of the King of the Isles, and I would make it into the settlement described. In this way, its assets would be the king's own."

The assembly whispered to each other, Dugall stroked his chin and studied Duncan. "Cormac did indeed make a most uncommon choice," he murmured, then sipped of his ale.

'Twas Iain who snorted and voiced Duncan's greatest fears. "With respect, this is no plan, my lord, but a ploy to stall for time. With each passing moment, this countess settles more on Ceinn-beithe. She builds a fortress, she would plant crops, she will soon be impossible to dislodge. What reason has she to take Duncan as her spouse? Indeed, she will not have him! Her sponsor, King William, would hardly endorse such a choice! And a handfast endures for but a year and a day."

"But Ceinn-beithe is known for granting uncommon fortune and longevity upon the matches pledged there," Duncan argued. "Who can say what a year and a day might bring?"

"Nonsense!" Iain drove his fist into his palm, his voice rising as he stepped farther into the light. "We must move immediately to secure our right to this ancestral land! We must make amends for Duncan's errors, we must make war as the men we are. If she has lost her treasury and stores, good! Let us complete what has begun! William plots shrewdly in sending a woman to do a man's task, but he plots to steal our land all the same. We must eliminate her party before 'tis too late."

"'Twas Cormac MacQuarrie who signed the deed she holds," Duncan declared, and the company gasped as one.

"What?" Iain cried. "Why? You lie, for he would not do such a thing!"

Duncan shrugged, choosing to hold his own counsel on that document's authenticity. "I saw the deed and I saw his name upon it." He looked to the king. "Is it so unlikely that Cormac had a similar vision for Ceinn-beithe?"

"He was clearly one filled with surprises." The king's words were wryly spoken, and Duncan guessed he referred to more than the deed itself. A whisper of new endorsement made its way around the room, for Cormac had been respected by his fellows.

The king frowned and drank deeply of his ale. The woman

hastened to fill his cup as he drummed his fingers upon the arm of his chair and watched Duncan. The assembly held their collective breath as the king set his cup aside and pushed to his feet. He surveyed his company sternly before he spoke.

"I am not persuaded of the wisdom of this course," he declared, and Duncan's heart sank to his toes. What of Eglantine?

"But, my lord king . . ."

The king held up one hand. "You have said more than your share, Duncan MacLaren, though the truth of it is that I cannot surmise the truth without the evidence of my own eyes. We depart with the dawn five days hence for Ceinn-beithe. Prepare for battle."

He granted Duncan a sharp look. "You will have one chance and one chance only to see your way in this. Should the woman refuse your suit or refuse to pledge all she has to me, then we shall take Ceinn-beithe by force. She can remain only if she willingly cedes all to you."

He placed one hand on Iain's shoulder. "And with your failure, Duncan, now or a year hence, the chieftainship of Clan MacQuarrie shall pass to Cormac's blood son." The king lifted his hands to the company. "This is my decision, before the witness of all of you. Let it be so."

Duncan bowed his head, his thoughts flying like quicksilver. There was not a doubt within him that Eglantine would never surrender all she held to him, particularly now when she blamed him—however wrongly—for so much. Yet he knew he would have no chance to make a case, much less to persuade her of how much was at stake.

He would have to deceive her, for her own survival. 'Twould not be readily done and 'twas a poor way to begin a marriage, but Duncan had no choice. He could not let the people beneath her hand be wounded, he could not see her

lose all she had struggled to build. He could not let his lady
be killed, whatever the price.

She was the one who heralded the honor of serving the
greater good.

Duncan had been gone a fortnight, but much to Eglantine's
dismay, the passing of time did not diminish how large he
loomed in her thoughts. He might as well have remained, for
she felt his presence so often and thought of him so much—
and looked for his return more frequently than she should.

The weather had improved, the sun showing its face for
more of the days and longer each day, the air warmed and the
wind lost some of its bite. The first part of the manor had
been completed the previous day, and though 'twas somewhat crooked and the thatch more uneven where they had begun than where they finished, all had given a hearty cheer.

They had celebrated heartily the night before, all sharing
in the last cask of wine and gathering around the manor's first
fire. It had begun to rain, and the water had leaked through the
thatch in more than one place, but naught so small as that
could diminish their merriment.

They made a home here and all knew it well. Eglantine
was fiercely proud of her vassals and their accomplishments.

Her daughters fared equally well. Jacqueline positively
bloomed in this new place; she was more cheerful and outgoing
with every passing day. Esmeraude toddled here and there,
winding her way through knees as if 'twas all a game of hide
and seek. She slept with Eglantine more nights than not, the
two sharing a quiet time together each night while Esmeraude
drank her milk. Eglantine looked forward to those moments,
and found she knew more tales than she had believed. Or else
Esmeraude was less harsh a critic than she had expected. Both
girls had color in their cheeks and stars in their eyes as they
never had before.

It seemed that Kinbeath suited them.

And though she might never have expected as much, it suited Eglantine. She had abandoned her veils completely, fastening her hair in a sturdy braid each morn. She had simplified her garb, choosing plain kirtles over those with any embroidery, and wore her heavy boots all the time.

She found herself laboring beside her villeins, for 'twas foolery to not lend a hand when there was so much to be done. And, indeed, Eglantine learned more of the people beneath her hand than ever she had before. To be sure, they still regarded her as their lady, but she and her daughters mingled more readily with the company and the line betwixt noble and vassal was oft blurred.

Eglantine found that she preferred the affection and camaraderie to the stiffness of ceremony that had once characterized their relations. She would never have known this sense of community had she remained in Arnelaine, and, indeed, the awareness that all were reliant upon each other lessened her own burden of responsibility.

For the first time in all her days, the backs of her hands turned a pale golden hue, and Eglantine, contrary to all she had been taught, was not ashamed. Indeed, the tan had a look of vitality to it that she welcomed. She felt more vigorous than she had ever before, and Jacqueline's was not the only laughter that rang out more frequently than previously. They all labored hard, they ate heartily, and they slept well, each day showing more progress in wringing a home from this corner of wilderness.

And each day Duncan's words echoed in Eglantine's thoughts. He had been right to claim that there was no place for nobles here, that all must labor together to survive. A part of Eglantine wanted him to witness that she was not the frivolous noblewoman he had first thought her to be—though she told herself that 'twas only to show him wrong in that.

Her heart called her a liar. There was more reason than that to desire to see Duncan again. Aye, she would see him to prove to her errant heart that he had no hold over her, that any affection she felt for any man was doomed to fade like a flower plucked and left to wilt. That was the truth of it.

That sunny morn after their celebration, when Eglantine was rethatching the weaknesses of the roof, someone cried of ships. Her cursed heart leapt to her throat at the sight of small boats bobbing across the silver sheen of the sea. She shaded her eyes, the men no more than silhouettes against the brightness of the water, and tried to discern Duncan's broad shoulders before she could halt herself.

There were so many men, so many boats, so many glints of metal in the sunlight that for a moment she feared another party came, and one with warlike intent.

But then a man who could only be Duncan charged into the sea, the sunlight lighting his ebony hair with blue, his manner characteristically impatient to be at his destination. He hauled the boat to the shore, Louis's prim posture in that vessel clearly recognizable. Duncan strode over the rocks as if they were no obstacle at all and headed directly for her. He grinned, fully aware that she watched him, and quickened his pace.

God in heaven, but absence had only increased his allure. Eglantine's heart hammered and it seemed she could not move. Her gaze slipped over him, greedily devouring details she had not forgotten. His shoulders were as broad, his legs as muscled, there was more of a tan upon his flesh.

His dark hair lifted in the wind and he halted below her, propping his hands upon his hips. He grinned up at her, as cocky and irresistible as only Duncan could be, his eyes glinting with that wild light of unpredictability.

Her mouth went dry. There was not a word upon her tongue, and she stared at him like some witless child.

'Twas only because she had been proven wrong, of course.

"I never thought I should see the day that my countess Eglantine was struck speechless," he teased. "She must indeed have missed me."

"I thought you would not return," she said, hating how the words tumbled together. "You were so loath to do the honorable deed of wedding Alienor."

"Alienor lies and you know it well," he said so firmly that she could not doubt him. He reached for her, his smile warming her to her toes. "Come down from the roof, my Eglantine, come and give me a welcome." His voice fell so low that she knew 'twas no salutary handshake he would offer in greeting.

"I will not!"

"Eglantine, this is no jest." He growled, his warning most unexpected.

Eglantine's gaze flicked over the men who trailed behind him, and she noted that they were indeed fiercely attired. "Where is Louis?"

"He follows anon. He caught a chill, and that was the reason for our delay—the healer at Dugall's court would not suffer him to leave until the phlegm had cleared." Duncan braced a hand against the low edge of the roof, those fingers close to Eglantine's ankle. His eyes gleamed. "Did you miss me, Eglantine?"

She caught her breath and moved her foot farther away. "What news of the king?"

Duncan moved his hand quickly and caught her ankle in his gentle grip. He grinned up at her as he tugged, evidently well aware of the thunder of her pulse. "The king arrives with us, for he would ensure his will is done."

She slipped farther down the sloped roof, closer to his embrace, her skirts catching on the thatch. Duncan, to her amazement, did not savor the view, but pulled the cloth hastily over her legs. "What will?"

"He would have you and I make an agreement." Eglantine's skepticism must have shown, for Duncan chuckled before she could protest. "A treaty of a year and a day, Eglantine, no more than that, and a pledge of goodwill to see our differences of opinion resolved."

'Twas an odd period of time, and Eglantine knew she had heard it mentioned once before in the recent past. Was it that these Gaels had a preference for it, over a year? She could not recall, not with Duncan gazing at her as if she were the most marvelous creature in all of Christendom. She suspected 'twas unimportant, but her failure to remember niggled at her.

How odd that a king would not merely grant the holding to Duncan and banish her.

"Aye?" she asked. "And what happens at the end of that time? I have little expectation that we shall agree on anything, be it today, tomorrow, or in a year and a day."

"I would argue that view." Duncan's grin widened with confidence that made her own certainty waver. Aye, the man could charm the moon from the heavens, that much was certain. "But the pledge must be made without delay."

"What if we do not agree?" Eglantine demanded, sensing that he was avoiding something of import.

Duncan glared at her, his eyes suddenly bright. "We *will* agree, upon that you have my pledge." His thumb moved leisurely across the tender flesh inside her ankle, and Eglantine nigh forgot the course of her own thoughts.

The unpredictable light appeared once more in his eyes and her heart skipped a beat. "I would have my kiss now, Eglantine," he suggested softly, even as a company of men drew close.

Curse the man! He knew his effect upon her all too well. Eglantine folded her arms across her chest and strove to look indifferent. Her gaze flicked between Duncan and those men arriving. One man stood taller than the others, the gestures of the others revealing his status as his garb did not.

"Why on earth would we make such a treaty?" she asked, suspicion in her tone. "And why would you believe that we might ever agree upon anything of import? You will not even admit to what you took from Alienor."

Duncan swore. He caught at her ankles and fairly hauled her from the roof despite her squeal of protest, setting her down before himself before he glowered down at her. "I did not touch Alienor, though indeed she touched me. I have pledged this to you, Eglantine, and 'tis irksome indeed that you continue to question my word." His gaze bored into hers. "'Tis not the time for such matters."

Eglantine lifted her chin. "I say 'tis. And still Alienor insists of your deed."

"Alienor lies, and I shall prove the truth of it to you." His brow darkened ominously. "*After* we make this pledge of treaty. Eglantine, it must be done, and it must be done now."

She folded her arms across her chest. "I fail to see the reason for such haste. What decision was made regarding compensation for the destroyed stores?"

Duncan's lips quirked. "I think you will have few complaints of the gifts brought from the King of the Isles in recompense. Eglantine, for the love of God, trust me in this and make this pledge now."

He was so determined that Eglantine wondered what was at stake. She might have asked, but the tall man of regal bearing halted at Duncan's side. His hair was a ruddy gold, his features lined, his flesh tanned. He looked to be forty summers of age, and his cold gaze flicked assessingly over Eglantine.

Duncan gave her a sharp look, then took her hand, as if she were garbed in her finest. Gael rolled from his tongue, her own name and the appellation "countess" clear enough to Eglantine's ears.

The king took Eglantine's hand and kissed its back with so cursory a gesture that she shivered. His gaze roved over their manor and his lips thinned.

What was amiss?

"My lady," Louis croaked, his voice nigh indistinguishable. He hastened toward her, his progress impeded by a large matronly woman who seemed determined to enforce him to move slowly. Louis shook her off with an effort and waved to Eglantine. "My lady, I must have a word with you."

The king made another comment to Duncan, then snapped his fingers imperiously.

"My lord king would have us make the pledge now," Duncan informed her.

"But I would speak with Louis . . ."

"*After,* Eglantine. 'Twill take but a moment." That light was in Duncan's eyes again, and Eglantine had a sense that she should not be so biddable in this.

She looked to Louis, who made great haste toward her. "You have but to agree, my lady!" he called hoarsely, and the king's head turned sharply.

A crisp command fell from his lips and Louis's progress was restrained. "Duncan, what is awry? What is the import of this?"

Duncan glared at her anew and gave her fingers a squeeze as he spoke through his teeth. "Eglantine, for the love of God, simply do this thing."

Something was sorely wrong. Duncan folded her hand within his and matched his step to the long strides of the king. Eglantine tried to extricate her hand from Duncan's grip. His fingers would not be moved, though his grip was deceptively gentle.

She watched as that matron pounced upon Louis, then held a wineskin to his lips. The two argued heatedly, then Louis rolled his eyes and took a swig of her offering clearly to be rid of her. He grimaced and coughed, doubling over with his efforts.

Then Duncan tugged her around and Eglantine realized she stood with him before that great sentinel stone. Duncan took her right hand in his right hand, his left enfolding her left. The warmth of his touch coursed through her and she found herself staring into his eyes. His expression was resolute and so somber that she wondered anew at the import of this pledge. They faced each other, the king beside them, the household and king's party gathered around.

'Twas a most odd pose for agreeing to a treaty.

Eglantine opened her mouth to protest, but the king began to speak and even though his was another tongue, she had been too well bred to interrupt a monarch. He intoned a short pledge in Gael, which Duncan repeated, his intense gaze burning into her own. Duncan squeezed her hands when 'twas her turn as if he would compel the words to fall from her lips.

Eglantine hesitated.

"Trust me," Duncan mouthed silently.

Eglantine might have chosen not to do so, but a trio of the king's men took obvious note of her hesitation. They elbowed each other, one drawing his blade from its scabbard with undisguised delight. Eglantine looked to Duncan in horror and noted anew the grim set of his lips. His grip was so tight that her fingers turned numb, the force of his will undeniable.

The king repeated the words, impatience tinging his tone, and Eglantine made her choice. What power indeed could these few words hold? She swallowed, then repeated the pledge more haltingly.

'Twas only when the last word crossed her lips that the tension left Duncan's features. He smiled down at her, evidently happy with whatever they had wrought, then to her astonishment bent and kissed her soundly.

The king hooted loud, as did all of the recently arrived company, the fervor of Duncan's embrace driving all else from Eglantine's thoughts. This was no chaste touch to seal an agreement, this was a kiss more fitting of nuptials.

Nuptials!

'Twas then that Eglantine remembered where she had heard that length of time dictated afore. Theobald's letter spoke of Kinbeath being perceived as lucky for handfastings, a kind of heathen marital pledge lasting for a year and a day. God in heaven, it could be no coincidence.

She pulled herself from Duncan's embrace and glared at him. "Tell me that was not a handfasting pledge," she demanded.

"I cannot do so," he admitted, his eyes narrowing. "For that is what 'twas, but, Eglantine—"

"You wretched cur!" she cried, and pushed Duncan so suddenly that he was not prepared for her assault. The company laughed, though whether 'twas at her or Duncan, she did not care. Eglantine pushed him again, knowing full well she could not hurt him, but frustrated beyond compare.

It helped naught that Duncan chuckled for the king. "A feisty bride, my lord king. She is naught but spirited." He repeated the claim in Gael.

The king replied coldly.

Duncan roared too genially for the circumstances. He caught Eglantine against him and kissed her hard, lifting his head only for a moment. "Trust me, Eglantine, and cease your fighting for the sake of the greater good," he muttered through gritted teeth.

He would have kissed her again, no doubt to silence her, but Eglantine was infuriated by his audacity. She swung at him and again, forcing him to back away from her, his hands raised before himself.

Still he tried to make light of her anger, jesting with the king, a response that did naught to win Eglantine's cooperation.

"Eglantine, perhaps you recall that 'twas your own idea to see our competing claims for Kinbeath settled with marriage."

"Oh! 'Twas my idea that you would wed *Alienor*, you vexing creature!" she cried, and gave him a hearty shove. Duncan's smile faded as he lost his footing. He teetered for a moment on the lip of the cliff though Eglantine knew she had not pushed him so hard as that.

He began to fall and she snatched for him instinctively. His grin flashed briefly, telling her she had done precisely what he expected, then he caught her around the waist. She had the definite sense that he jumped from the cliff. Though 'twas not far to the water, Eglantine was no swimmer and would have screamed, but Duncan kissed her soundly as they fell.

The water was cursed cold, the pool beside the point remarkably still. Eglantine came up sputtering. 'Twas shallow enough that she could stand and not so far a fall that either of them was hurt. Duncan surfaced not far from her, cast a glance over her, and grinned wickedly.

"There is naught to heat a man's blood like a woman of spirit," he cried, his cheerful words infuriating Eglantine. His yellow linen shirt clung to his flesh so lovingly that naught was left to her imagination, his muscles rippled as he closed the distance between them once more.

"You wretched creature!" She grabbed a fistful of his hair and shoved his head under the surface so quickly that he sputtered in turn. "I cannot believe you would so deceive me as this!" The company laughed, but Duncan broke the surface with a dangerous gleam in his eyes.

Eglantine's breath caught at the purpose in his eyes and she took a wary step back.

Duncan shook the water from his hair, then appraised her slowly. "Are you cold, my Eglantine, or is your passion borne of something other than anger?" He reached and flicked a fingertip across her tightened nipple, his bold move before the entire company shocking her no less than his words. "Aye, she is willing enough!" he roared.

Eglantine might have shoved him anew, but he caught her in his arms, the warm strength of him pressing against her from head to toe. Eglantine cursed her own traitorous pulse for leaping at his touch.

"I bade you trust me," he growled for her ears alone.

"Aye, and where has it gotten me? In the midst of a pagan marriage, which mercifully is of no import in the eyes of God or the law." She wriggled against him, which did naught but make her more aware of his lean strength. "I decry this match before 'tis begun . . ."

His eyes flashed. The company roared as Duncan swung one leg behind her knees. Eglantine fell with a whoop and a splash, taking a mouthful of seawater even as Duncan tumbled with her.

"How dare you?" she cried when she could.

"How else am I to silence you?" he growled, and wrestled when she might have fled. They both tumbled into the water once more.

And when they came to the surface again, Eglantine found Duncan's hand warm over her mouth. He sheltered her from the view of the company above, his eyes bright.

"Now, listen, Eglantine, and listen well. Dugall desires Ceinn-beithe secured as his own and meant to seize it with bloodshed. He has nigh a hundred men with him to make good his claim, and he will kill all to see the matter done."

Eglantine's eyes widened in horror, though Duncan continued to speak with low heat.

"But I insisted there was another way, that I would hand-fast to you and we would both pledge all of Ceinn-beithe to him to secure his hegemony thus."

"You deceived me," she charged through his fingers. Her words were muddled, but he evidently guessed what she said.

"Aye, for the greater good. I but thought to save the hides of you, your daughters, and your vassals. All has nearly come untangled thanks to your quick tongue." He shook his head, sorely burdened with the trial of her. "I knew you would decline but also knew there would be no chance to discuss the matter." His eyes flashed. "I should have guessed you would not merely put your trust in me."

"There is no reason for me to trust in you." She pulled his hand away yet kept her own voice low.

"Would you see your vassals slaughtered this very day?"

"You know I would not." She was in a corner and Eglantine knew it well. She did not have to like it, nor did she have to readily agree with the man who had squarely placed her there. If only his touch did not addle her thoughts so!

If only she knew for certain whether he was guilty of destroying the stores and taking Alienor's maidenhead.

"Then do this thing. And feign some delight in the deed."

"'Tis but a temporary solution," she complained. "In a year and a day we shall be in the same predicament. What difference if your king takes his toll now or then?"

"There is enormous difference and you know it well," Duncan snapped. "All could change in a year—this king could be overthrown, you could decide against occupying Kinbeath, William could come to your aid."

He paused significantly and Eglantine's gaze raised to meet his. His eyes had darkened to a stormy hue and his voice dropped low. "Or you and I might truly make a match of this."

A gull cried as she stared up at him, and Eglantine nigh forgot all on the cliff above who watched them avidly. There was naught but Duncan, his conviction, his darkened gaze. Her heart began to thrum and she desperately wanted to believe in him.

Even though Eglantine knew that she was not destined for

the kind of loving marriage she desired for her daughters, Duncan had the power to tempt her faith.

Duncan smiled crookedly and heaved a sigh. "Now, use the wits with which you have been blessed, Eglantine, and make your choice before 'tis too late."

Aye, she would use her wits and remember her doubts. She would save her vassals but cede no more than the pledge she had already made. Indeed, she had little choice but to agree with him.

But she would never be fool enough to love Duncan MacLaren.

Eglantine smiled slowly and twined her arms around Duncan's neck. His eyes narrowed, as if he knew not what to expect from her, and Eglantine laughed in complete understanding of that sense. She pitched her voice so that it would carry to those above, yet low enough to sound intimate.

"Ah, Duncan, forgive my anger," she declared. "But what woman would not be vexed to have to wait all these days and nights for you?" She heard Duncan catch his breath before she arched against him and kissed him boldly.

He hesitated but a moment before he caught her close, and Eglantine sighed with satisfaction, her fingers tangling in his hair as he returned her embrace.

God in heaven, but she had missed his kiss.

Chapter Thirteen

UNCAN DID NOT KNOW PRECISELY WHAT HE HAD said to persuade Eglantine and he did not care. He was too startled that she had agreed—'twas unlike the lady to readily reconcile herself to his will.

It could only be a good portent. Eglantine was his woman— at least for a year and a day. And in that year and a day, he would woo her and win her, Duncan knew it to be so.

A fortnight from her side had done naught to diminish Eglantine's appeal. Duncan had known the truth of it the first moment he spied her on that roof, and his heart pounded fit to burst.

He had seen naught but Eglantine, slender, strong, and struck by sunlight, her lips parted in surprise. She was tanned and glowing, more hale and more beautiful than he had recalled. There had been something in the depths of her emerald eyes when he halted below her, some measure of delight that persuaded Duncan that he did not love alone.

Aye, Duncan was smitten for the first time in all his days and could have imagined naught better. Eglantine had agreed, and now she kissed him as if she would suck the very marrow from his bones.

Duncan caught Eglantine around the waist and held her close, loving how her tongue tangled with his and her heart pounded against his own. If not for the catcalls from the men above, he might have forgotten their audience and sampled the lady's charms without delay.

Instead he reluctantly lifted his head, smiling at the flush in her cheeks and the sparkle in her eyes. She smiled back at him, and his pulse leapt.

"Did I feign interest well enough?" she whispered. Her eyes sparkled with a rare mischief that tempted Duncan to cast her over his shoulder and make for privacy.

Instead, he cupped her chin in his hand and let his thumb slide over the fullness of her bottom lip. "Surely 'tis not completely feigned?" he murmured. He brushed his lips across hers and she shivered in a most satisfactory way, then pushed away from him and averted her face, no doubt deliberately veiling her response.

"'Tis cold," she said, replacing playfulness with her usual reserve. "We should seek warmer garb before we fall ill."

Duncan caught at her hand and pulled her back against him, not liking her retreat. "Do not flee from me, Eglantine. I would have honesty between us, if naught else."

"And what is honest in the beginning of this?" she charged.

"What is here." Duncan tapped his heart. "'Twas you who said that one only finds treasures when they are sought no longer. Grant me the year and a day in honesty, Eglantine, this is all I ask of you."

She hesitated and his hopes plummeted, but still he argued his own case. "A man's worth is in his deeds, and I will prove my worth to you. Already I vowed to woo you and would take this handfast to do as much. I will find men for your daughters, Eglantine, men befitting your standards."

Duncan swallowed, his gaze locking with hers. "And the choice of aye or nay, my Eglantine, will always remain with you. I will take naught that you do not willingly offer, upon that you already have my solemn oath."

She studied him in silence, then averted her face. "Truly, Duncan, I would expect naught less." She turned to make for the shore, her sodden kirtle hampering her progress so that Duncan easily caught up with her. He scooped her into his arms, to hearty approval from Dugall's men, and strode for the shore.

"You should not do this," she protested, but Duncan cast her a confident grin.

"I but feign interest as you do," he teased, intrigued when a blush stained her cheeks.

"I do this for my vassals and their survival," she said crisply, though she draped an arm around his neck, no doubt for the benefit of those who watched. She smiled up at him, though her tone was chilly. "You had best recall the truth of it."

"You protest overmuch, my Eglantine. This course is not without advantage to you and me."

She flushed scarlet and seemed again at a loss for words.

"Honesty, Eglantine," he murmured. "'Tis the least that should be between us for this time."

She heaved a sigh, finding her footing as he set her down, though he stubbornly kept his arm around her waist. They climbed the last of the rocks together, her hand clasped in his, and Duncan saw the assembly surging forward to congratulate them.

In the last moment they might not be overheard, the lady slanted him an intent glance, then nodded once. "You speak aright in this, Duncan. And in truth, I do not feign pleasure beneath your touch." She held his gaze steadily as Duncan's heart nigh stopped. "I desire you, as you desire me, though there is naught but lust at root of it."

Eglantine desired him!

"But desire is not enough. I will not couple with you, regardless of whether your king expects it, regardless of whether your own desire demands it. I choose nay, Duncan, for the sake of the issues between us. You had best reconcile yourself to that." She watched him absorb this news, then turned to greet the company.

Issues. Duncan blinked as he named them all. He would see Iain admit his crime and apologize, though he could not imagine how 'twould be done. And Alienor, the gods only knew how the truth could be had from that creature. He wished he might guess what had happened to that forged deed.

For somehow, Duncan had to persuade Eglantine of his innocence. She required proof and he would find it for her.

Her daughter Jacqueline fell upon her then, her eyes sparkling and her cheeks pinkening as she glanced from her mother to Duncan. "Oh, congratulations, *Maman*!"

The girl, whom Duncan had not yet met, hugged Eglantine with enthusiasm and evident delight. She curtsied deeply when introduced to Duncan and blushed furiously when he kissed the back of her hand.

She shared her mother's coloring, and Duncan suspected Eglantine's beauty had been much the same at this age. But where Eglantine was tall and slender, Jacqueline was all lush curves and stood only as high as her mother's shoulder.

"She is lovely," he murmured, his hand falling to the back of Eglantine's waist. "As beautiful and gracious as her mother."

But Eglantine's maternal smile faded, her gaze flicking over the company of men. "I hope 'twill not bring her more trouble," she murmured enigmatically. Before Duncan could ask, her gaze rose and she frowned.

Duncan followed her glance to Alienor, who hung back, her expression sullen. How Duncan wished he could unmake the nuisance this one had contrived! She and Eglantine shared a glance, until Alienor tossed her hair and stomped away.

"I did not touch her, Eglantine," Duncan muttered, his annoyance at the fore once more.

"So you have pledged," the lady ceded, her tone neutral.

"Aye, but do you believe that vow?" he demanded impatiently.

Eglantine pursed her lips. "Her manner is not inconsistent with that of a liar." 'Twas a small concession, but more than Duncan had expected.

"My lady, I would speak with you," Louis declared, coughing soundly after his words. Indeed, the man did not sound hale as yet, and Duncan regretted that he had fallen ill.

Would Eglantine hold him accountable for this, as well?

But the lady evidently did not. She smiled for the older man. "Your counsel was good, Louis, and I heartily appreciate it." Eglantine seized the châtelain's elbow and led him toward the camp. "And though I am certain that you have accomplished much in your journey to the king's court and have much news to share, 'twill keep. On this day you must ensure your own health, which I understand has suffered greatly in your loyal service."

Eglantine had a company escorting the châtelain toward the fire before he knew what he was about, his croaking protests no match for her efficiency. Duncan grinned, enjoying the sight of that man being briskly dispatched at his lady's bidding.

"A hot broth is what he needs and soundly to bed." Eglantine pivoted and lifted a hand. "Gunther, is there a drop of *eau-de-vie* left? I imagine Louis has need of its heat and perhaps a warm stone wrapped in his bed."

Little Esmeraude, to Duncan's delight, came directly to him and took his hand. "Do you have a song?" she asked hopefully. "No one sings for me anymore."

Duncan smiled down at the child, pleased to find favor somewhere in this company. "Aye, I have a song for you, Esmeraude. This night will be filled with tales and songs, unless I miss my guess, perhaps even enough to grant your fill."

She grinned and gripped his hand expectantly, her trust and acceptance touching him. "Now?"

But Duncan was to taste his lady's efficiency, as well. "Not now, Esmeraude. First, Duncan must change his garb," Eglantine said crisply.

"I will dry," Duncan protested, guessing he would lose this battle.

He earned a sharp look for his trouble. "There is bite in the wind and 'twould not do for any to fall ill this day."

"I have naught else to wear."

"Then something suitable will be found." Eglantine paused to take a breath and survey the company, and a heartbeat later, she had dispatched vassals to arrange appropriate seating and refreshment for the visiting king.

Gerhard had scampered away to arrange the finest meal of which he and Gunther were capable on such short notice, maids were moving the belongings of Alienor back into the tent with Jacqueline so that silk tent could be pitched at a suitable distance to house the visiting king. Eglantine had moved her vassals into the recently completed hall, ensuring their comfort before her own, as Duncan knew was typical of the lady. At her bidding, fires were stoked and hot brews were poured, the visitors were made welcome, and dry clothing was brought for Duncan.

The company, in the twinkling of an eye, was a blur of activity, all under the direction of Eglantine. The lady showed no signs of changing her own garb, and Duncan waited, intent on ensuring her good health as vigorously as she ensured his.

Indeed, it had been a long time since any had cared whether

he fell ill. Even her brisk concern cast a warm glow around Duncan's heart—'twas not all bad being one of Eglantine's responsibilities. 'Twas progress, and he would savor it as such.

"I should keep a tight hold upon this one," Gillemore muttered once he and Duncan had greeted each other again.

Duncan smiled and tightened his fingers around Esmeraude's as his conviction strengthened a hundred times. "Aye, Gillemore, I intend to do so."

A wedding feast! Alienor could have spit in frustration even as the festivities unfolded around her. How like Eglantine to ruin everything. She stamped her feet as she strode through the company, making disruptions wherever she could.

She kicked a vessel of new ale on her way past and ignored the cries of dismay behind her as it spilled. She bumped her hip against a table of fresh bread, more than satisfied when two dark loaves fell to the ground. She surreptitiously tripped a servant, who hastened with such a burden of mugs that he could not see his feet.

These deeds did naught to assuage her temper. Eglantine had always hated Alienor, the girl knew it well, and truly who would not be jealous of Alienor's beauty and charm?

'Twas loathsome how her aged crone of a stepmother snatched the only man of merit in these parts, even after all her claims that she would ensure her daughters wed great men. Ha! Typically, Eglantine was selfish in ensuring her own bed was warm first.

Alienor huffed. Eglantine might have stolen Duncan away, but Alienor would see that match did not endure. She was not entirely certain what she might do, not with Duncan's gaze fixed upon Eglantine with such enthusiasm, but she would do *something*.

There had to be some way to see her ends achieved. She

watched the new arrivals with a scowl, earning an answering glare from one of them. He was tall and not too hard upon the eyes, though he was even more ancient than Eglantine and far too ancient to be granting her such a look. Alienor lifted her chin and glared back at him for his cheek.

"Alienor!" Jacqueline chided, so close beside her that Alienor jumped. "'Tis vulgar of you to stare so boldly at the king."

"King? What king?"

Jacqueline rolled her eyes. "Do you listen to naught around you? That is Dugall, lord King of the Isles, come to witness the handfast of *Maman* and Duncan. Is it not wondrously romantic?" Jacqueline asked, her expression dreamy. "I knew *Maman* had a fancy for someone, for there have been stars in her eyes from our first arrival. Now we know not only that 'tis Duncan, but that he loves her, as well. And Theobald's letter did declare that Kinbeath granted good fortune to those handfasts pledged upon its site. Would it not be wondrous if 'twere so?"

A *king*? That word alone snared Alienor's attention.

A king was far better than a mere chieftain, even a king of whom no one had ever heard. To be sure, he was not the king of France, or even of Sicily, but he must be a prince among men. And she was not likely to have many kings from whom to choose in this wretched place.

The first inkling of a plan came to Alienor and she held the king's interested gaze, letting a coy smile slip over her lips. For an aged king, he was not so bad in appearance—indeed, he might be infirm and never demand more than her hand upon his knee.

Surely a king would shower his bride with riches and jewels? Such finery would be worth even his gnarled hands upon her! He murmured something to one of his men, then smiled at Alienor, lifting his chalice in silent salute.

Typically oblivious of such adult subtleties, Jacqueline sighed contentment. "Perhaps he will make her happy."

"Who?" Alienor eyed Jacqueline without comprehension. "Who will make who happy?"

Jacqueline rolled her eyes. "Perhaps Duncan will make *Maman* happy. In all honesty, Alienor, there are times when you might be as deaf as a stone. Now, hasten yourself. Your belongings are to be moved, that your tent might be granted for the pleasure of the king."

Alienor laughed lightly, knowing that 'twould be more than her tent granted to that man's pleasure. Aye, she had erred in not seeing the matter completed afore with Duncan.

She would not make the same mistake again. She waved to the king when Jacqueline turned away, knowing full well that his gaze followed her departure. There was a bounce in her step as she dreamed of her pending life as Queen of the Isles.

There was a title with a fitting resonance for her.

Eglantine could not have imagined that a man clad in Gunther's best—though still well-worn—boots, an old tabard of Louis's that was too narrow through the shoulders for him, and a pair of chausses cut for a man much greater in breadth could have made her heart pound.

But Duncan did. He looked as ruggedly masculine as ever, his borrowed garb doing naught to diminish his appeal. His belt and scabbard still hung around his hips, his hair was still wild. And his smile made Eglantine catch her breath. He would never be a courtier, even in the finest garb to be had, for there was an air of a renegade about him that could not be disguised.

She would be wise to be wary of his charms.

But Eglantine was surprised to realize that she preferred Duncan in his usual garments, however unfamiliar and barbaric she had once thought them to be. They suited him better.

She missed the sight of his strong bare legs, and that thought made her smile.

They would make an odd pair, she realized too late to make a difference, for she had donned her finest for this feast. 'Twas worth the effort to see the flame light in Duncan's eyes. He stood tall and straight as he waited for her, indifferent to the change of his garb, only a glimmer of doubt in his eyes when Eglantine took his hand.

"Do not tell me I have dressed in the wrong order," he teased, his eyes twinkling. "I must look more a beggar than a bridegroom. Or a bard paying favor to the bride."

"Nay, not so bad as that."

"Not even beside such finery as this?" He bent and kissed her fingertips with a flair that few noblemen could match. His gaze was warm. "You look most elegant, Eglantine."

Her intent to steel herself against him was failing miserably, though Eglantine fought to hide her response. She guessed that Duncan noted the flutter of her pulse at her throat and had no doubt he discerned that she had taken care with her appearance. He most assuredly concluded 'twas for his benefit.

He would not be far wrong if he did. Certainly he was responsible for the flush in her cheeks. "It seemed fitting for the company of a king."

"Indeed." He smiled. "Then I shall make my gratitude to the king known, for his presence has supplied me with a most winsome lady by my side."

Eglantine pulled her hand from his. "I said nay, Duncan."

His lips thinned, his gaze hardening. "And you have my pledge that I shall take naught which is not freely offered. I am a man of my word, Eglantine, whatever you might choose to believe to the contrary." With that, he placed her hand upon his elbow with undue ceremony and led her to the board.

Eglantine could not help but feel she had been unfair.

'Twas not the finest wedding feast ever seen. Their meal was simple, and they had only thin ale with which to celebrate. This King Dugall looked skeptical of the proceedings, but Eglantine did her best to act the besotted bride. Duncan ate stoically beside her, making no attempt to coax her smile. 'Twas unlike him to be surly and she knew she had pushed him too far. Indeed, she could fairly feel him simmering.

And what was she to believe? Was she to bed him simply for the pleasure of it, all other issues forgotten?

The idea had an alarming appeal. Eglantine's mouth went dry as she considered her circumstances. To be sure, she would never love a man again, for love brought only weakness and vulnerability to a woman. Look how she had erred by loving Theobald! And look how that love had faded, leaving her in a tepid marriage to an untrustworthy rogue.

'Twas clear that her desire for Duncan was lust alone and that 'twould not endure. But she was no virgin and she owed her chastity to no man—and she had just pledged to share her household with Duncan for a year and a day.

Eglantine risked a glance his way to find his features set. She recalled how his eyes had lit when he suggested they might make a true match of this handfast, and her pulse quickened. But nay, 'twould never happen; she knew love did not linger so long as that.

But what harm was there truly in letting Duncan share her bed? She was sorely tempted to feel him atop her once more, to indulge her desire to its fullest. Surely then 'twould fade more quickly and this irksome ability of Duncan to muddle her thoughts would disappear.

Or was she merely trying to justify her weakness? Eglantine did not know, and the truth of it was annoying. The skies darkened over the sea and isles, the fire leapt high and painted their faces with flickering shadows, the silence stretching long between the supposedly happy couple as all celebrated around them.

It seemed they did a poor job of persuading Dugall of the sincerity of this. Eglantine laid her hand on Duncan's knee and murmured as much, winning a dark glance for her words.

"A cheud sgeul air, fear an taighe," Gillemore cried before Duncan could reply, lifting his mug high. *"Is sgeul gu lath' air an aoidh!"*

"What does that mean?" she whispered to Duncan, taking the moment to lean her breast against his arm.

He caught his breath and slanted a simmering glance her way. "The first story from the host, and tales from the guest 'til morning." Duncan shook a finger at Esmeraude, who nestled against Eglantine. "'Tis here you will have your fill of tales, Esmeraude."

The child bounced with delight and Eglantine slipped an arm around her shoulders, feeling denied when Duncan said naught further to her. Duncan got to his feet, folded his hands behind his back, and sang.

'Twas a moment before she realized he sang in French, but a heartbeat later before she wondered why.

Immediately she knew—'twas for Esmeraude. He was singing a lovely ballad about a woman who lived in the sea to delight her youngest daughter.

Esmeraude was not the only one enthralled by Duncan's song. Aye, Eglantine could have listened to his singing for an eternity. As Duncan held the last note, Eglantine imagined that it echoed long over the sea. He finished to resounding silence, then took his seat, his gaze fixed on the board before him. Applause broke suddenly and swelled beyond expectation, all beginning to chatter at once. Esmeraude sighed with satisfaction, then yawned sleepily, Célie quickly appearing to lift the child high.

Eglantine laid her hand upon Duncan's and he glanced up, no doubt noting the tears gathered in her gaze. "Your gift is rare, Duncan," she admitted. "For your tales have a power to touch the heart."

He studied her in silence, his expression unfathomable.

"Do you always sing of love?"

"Aye," he admitted gruffly, and took a deep draft of the ale.

"Why?"

"Because 'tis love that matters beyond all else."

She recalled the other song he had sung for her and the poignancy of his singing. This time she did not have the same sense that he sang a tale he had lived. "Who was Mhairi?" she asked before she could think better of asking.

The question clearly startled Duncan for he failed to hide his response. "It matters not," he said, and frowned.

Eglantine laid a hand on his thigh and felt his muscles clench. "How can it not matter if 'tis the only subject you will not discuss?" she chided quietly. He flicked her a glance of such dismay that she might have laughed under other circumstances. Truly this man had no ability to lie. "Did you love her?"

Duncan heaved a sigh. "Nay, I never loved Mhairi, though there was a time when I heartily wished I did."

Eglantine guessed. "She loved you."

His lips tightened. "Aye, beyond belief and without encouragement." He placed his hand over hers, his heat lingering there only a moment before he moved her hand back to her own lap. "Does that sate your curiosity?"

"Nay."

He almost smiled, then shook his head. "I should have guessed 'twould not be so simple as that." He slanted a silvery glance her way. "Matters seldom are, with you."

"Nor with you." Eglantine smiled, a sense of intimacy

enfolding her despite the presence of the company. "Tell me of Mhairi, Duncan. Please. I should like to know."

He held her gaze for so long that she grew certain he would refuse. Then he frowned, letting his voice drop as the celebration continued around them. "Mhairi was Cormac's daughter, though she was no more than a child when I came to this place. Cormac took me in as his foster son, though he had no obligation to do so, and in gratitude, I served him as well as I was able."

"But what of your family?"

"I know not who they were." He shrugged as if it did not matter, but Eglantine was not fooled. "I took the name MacLaren rather than be without a name at all. The Mac-Larens have no blood hereabouts, and who would know the truth of it? And I was always alone, traveling, learning songs, listening to tales. When Cormac claimed me as his foster son, I suddenly had a family, and I was proud to have both brother and sister."

"Brother?"

"Ah, you may have noted Iain in my party, the tall fair man. He is Cormac's son, and for a time we were insepara-ble. See, there he is beside the king, complaining of all my failures and weaknesses."

Eglantine frowned in confusion even as her gaze slipped over the man in question, but Duncan continued. "At any rate, it came time for Mhairi to wed. Cormac made the arrangements with another chieftain who desired both her and an alliance. Mhairi, however, refused to wed him."

"Because she wanted you."

"Aye, but I had naught to offer her—I did not even love her!—and Cormac insisted upon this alliance. Mhairi was the light of his days, he loved her as few men love their daughters, and he wanted every luxury for her. And I be-lieved he was right in this, that this chieftain's affection and wealth would serve Mhairi well. But Mhairi would hear naught of it—she even tried to persuade me to her cause. So I left, for I thought to make matters more easy for all involved. I, like Cormac, thought she was but being willful."

His expression was grim and Eglantine found herself recalling the tale he had recounted in song. "She refused him," she guessed.

Duncan shook his head, then shoved one hand through his hair. "Worse. She refused, she and Cormac argued, and Cormac carried her bodily to priest and betrothed. She fought him every step of the way and 'twas said to have been quite a scene. But after the ceremony Mhairi seemed to have calmed. All thought she had accepted her fate, now that 'twas done. She was sent to her chambers to prepare for her spouse, while the men drank his health."

He swallowed. "She killed herself there, with the dagger her father had once given to her as a gift, rather than let the match be consummated."

Eglantine felt her lips part in surprise. Duncan frowned and looked away, his distress at this recollection so evident that Eglantine's heart ached for him. "I returned but two days later, expecting all to be well and finding the opposite."

"And Cormac?"

Duncan heaved a sigh. "Was never again the same. He faded and grew small. There are those who say he died of a heart broken in two." He frowned and pushed to his feet, his tone brusque. "There, you have your tale, Eglantine, and I have need of more ale."

Eglantine laid a hand upon his arm, her own heart stirring with compassion. "I see that you blame yourself for this, though the fault is not yours to bear."

"How could I not blame myself!" Duncan snapped, his eyes flashing. "The man who sheltered me lost his sole daughter because of me! I should have spoken to her, I

should have persuaded her." Duncan sat down heavily and
drained his cup though 'twas already empty. He cast it onto
the board. "I should have loved her. 'Twould have been the
least I could do for the man to whom I owed so much!"

Oh, Eglantine knew what 'twas to blame oneself overmuch
for what had happened in the past. But Duncan had done
naught wrong—he had been true to his heart. 'Twas Mhairi
who had acted impulsively and Cormac who had seen naught
but his own desire.

"You are no more to blame for Mhairi's foolish choices
than I am for the course of Alienor."

Duncan grimaced. "Let us not discuss Alienor again."

Compassion flowed through Eglantine, his pain at his
role in this tragedy showing her that she had judged him
as harshly as he had judged himself. But Duncan had
pledged himself to her and her goals, he had aided her with
Esmeraude.

The least she could offer him was solace.

Eglantine cupped Duncan's face in her hand, then kissed
his cheek, smiling at his astonishment. "Come to my bed,
husband," she said, her voice loud enough that all might hear.
"I grow impatient for your heat."

She made to tug him to his feet, but Duncan resisted, his
scowl filled with uncertainty. "Eglantine, what is this that
you do? I am in no mood to suffer games."

She smiled for him alone, hoping he could see that she
had no intent to cheat him. 'Twas not like Eglantine
to make an impulsive choice, but she knew that this
was the right one, just as fleeing Arnelaine had been the
right choice despite her haste in choosing it. "I say *aye*,
Duncan, though I never imagined I should have to say it
twice."

His eyes flashed and he was on his feet in a heartbeat, his
haste making Eglantine laugh beneath her breath. The com-

pany hooted in approval, taking up some lewd drinking song in Gael with vigor. Eglantine did not care.

"I know not why you have changed your thinking." Duncan then scooped her into his arms. "But I shall not grant you the chance to change it again."

Indeed, 'twas a fair enough exchange.

Chapter Fourteen

GLANTINE'S TENT HAD BEEN PREPARED FOR THEM, the snowy linens turned down and the coals in the brazier lit. 'Twas quieter here, the raucous sounds of the celebrating company fainter with distance.

Duncan eased Eglantine to her feet, letting her slide down the length of him. He let the lady see his admiration for her, then bent to capture her lips with his.

Gently. He tasted her surprise then smiled at her own surge of ardor. Eglantine's lips parted, her hands framed his own face. She arched against him in silent demand and the heat rose between them, but Duncan touched no more than her face.

He kissed her lingeringly all the same, his fingertips sliding beneath her chin where her pulse thundered in perfect echo of his own. When Duncan lifted his head, her mouth clung to his and his name slipped from her lips like a sigh. She stretched to her toes, to kiss him again, but Duncan smiled.

"There is no need to hasten, my Eglantine," he murmured. "'Twill only be the first night of our handfasting this once, and I would savor every moment of it." He loved how her eyes widened in surprise at that, loved how she shivered as his fingertips eased down the length of her throat.

Duncan swallowed as his gaze drifted over her. She was

more finely wrought than he could believe, her skin so soft, its golden hue making her look even more like a goddess who deigned to let her toes touch the earth. On a night such as this, when so many marvels had already occurred, a goddess might even grant the most heartfelt wish of a mere mortal.

Duncan touched her temple and dared to ask. "May I see your hair unbound?"

"Of course." Eglantine nodded and smiled in turn, her hands rising to make quick work of the tie.

"Nay, grant me the honor of unfurling it." Duncan caught her hands in his, kissed her palms. Eglantine shrugged and he took the end of her braid in his own fingers. He untied the tether slowly then let his fingers slide into the thick silk of her hair.

The golden tresses curled around his fingers as he worked the braid loose, increment by increment. Her hair spilled over his hands, his wrists, his arms in a golden waterfall that shimmered in the light of the braziers. It smelled of sunshine and flowers, of Eglantine's own scent mingled with the wind.

Duncan caught his breath. "'Tis a treasure fitting of a king's horde," he whispered, lifting a handful of her hair to his lips.

Their gazes met, the shimmer of desire in Eglantine's green gaze making Duncan's pulse quicken. His body urged haste but he forced himself to move with leisure.

"I would see you garbed in naught but your hair's splendor," he breathed.

Eglantine not only seemed inclined to indulge him, but, again, she would have seen the matter done in short order.

Once more Duncan halted her busy fingers, then stood but a handspan from her as he loosed the knot in her girdle. "Let me," he urged. "I would see all of you, explore all of you, taste all of you, my Eglantine."

Eglantine's breasts rose and fell, revealing her awareness of him, and her eyes widened. But she did not move away. She stood as Duncan set to unfastening the neck and sides of her kirtle.

He folded his hands around her shoulders, savoring their strong curve. "I like that you are not wrought small," he confessed. "I like your strength, Eglantine, your vigor and your passion." He kissed her again and she rose against him, meeting him touch for touch and fueling his desire.

When he lifted his head, they both were breathing heavily. Duncan swallowed and smiled for her, then eased the weight of the wool from her shoulders, bending to kiss each increment of flesh as 'twas revealed. The whisper of his breath made her shiver and she arched her neck back, offering herself to him.

Duncan accepted. He kissed her ear, her throat, the smooth curve at the crest of her shoulder. He tasted the hollows around her collarbone and ran his tongue across her sweetly scented skin. He let his lips linger on the flutter of her pulse, reassured that she responded thus to him.

Eglantine clutched his nape and murmured his name. Knowing he could not continue with such restraint, Duncan left her chemise, easing the kirtle away with a thoroughness the task did not demand, running his hands over her as if he would memorize her curves with his touch. Her nipples beaded and her fists clenched, but Eglantine granted him his will. Their gazes locked as he traced the curve of her buttocks, before his hands ran over the length of her thighs. The heat in the tent rose by the time he knelt before her, and he could smell the scent of her desire.

Eglantine gripped his shoulders as she swayed slightly on her feet. "Duncan, I would have you hasten."

But he shook his head. "Not this time."

When the wool pooled around her ankles, he stood once

more, cupped her buttocks, and lifted her against himself. He kissed her soundly, then swung her in his arms and lay her upon the bed. She reached for him but Duncan evaded her touch with a smile.

"Patience," he chided, shaking a finger at her. Eglantine laughed lightly and lay back. He removed her boots and cast them aside, intrigued by the finery of her stockings. He ran his fingers up the slender strength of her legs, past her knees, and watched as her cheeks pinkened as his fingers brushed her thighs. Duncan could smell her, he knew the import of the glitter in her eyes, but he forced himself to take this slowly.

'Twas more difficult than he had expected.

He untied her garters with deliberation, then bent to kiss the inside of her thigh. Eglantine shuddered. She was impossibly soft and sweet and Duncan lingered there, running his tongue beneath the edge of the garter, raining kisses upon the dimple in her knee.

Eglantine moaned. Duncan slipped his fingers beneath one stocking, easing it lower with excruciating slowness. He kissed each measure of her bared to his gaze, nipping and laving each curve with his tongue.

He repeated his attentions upon her other leg, noting how Eglantine rubbed her hips against the mattress when he paid particular heed to her feet. He was harder than ever he had been, everything within him urging him to hasten when he slid beneath her sheer chemise. She parted her thighs, tempting him with the sight of her, but Duncan gritted his teeth and held his course.

He eased up the length of her, rolled his tongue within her navel as his hands folded around her waist. He eased the linen higher as he progressed, baring her to the golden light and his gaze.

She was perfection. His kisses fell on the tiny lines on her belly that evidenced the children she had borne, a mark of her selflessness. The similar lines upon her breasts, wrought of giving Jacqueline her breast, won the caress of a fingertip. Her nipples were ruddy and taut, their peaks the shape of a child's mouth. Duncan closed his mouth over her and Eglantine arched against him with a cry. Her hand locked in his hair, her breast filled his hand, her hip bumped against his erection.

Duncan pulled away, his own fist clenched in the linens. He heaved a ragged sigh and looked upon his flushed and willing partner, his golden goddess made flesh, and shook with desire.

Eglantine smiled and pushed him to his back. "My turn," she whispered, and set to unclothing him with the same leisurely thoroughness. He watched her as she moved, intrigued by her grace, amused by her wonder. Her kisses set him on fire, the caress of her fingertips drove him mad, the sight of her was more than he could endure.

He caught his breath when she closed her hand around him. Duncan thought he might explode with his desire and knew that if she touched him any further, he would. He snared her hand and rolled her to the bed beside him. He propped himself on his elbow, his arm wrapped around her shoulders, then slid his free hand down the length of her.

He met her gaze as his fingers slid into her slick heat. She gasped and arched against him. Duncan touched her with care, slowly bringing her passion to the boil, the sight of her feeding his own. She writhed against him, she gripped his shoulders, she flushed to her nipples. Her legs twined with his, her hips bucked, she was wet and hot and sweet. She cried his name but he granted her no quarter.

And when she arched off the bed with a scream, he knew he had never felt such satisfaction in any achievement as he did in pleasing Eglantine.

She took but a breath before she smiled mischievously and closed her hand around him once more. Duncan caught his breath and the lady pushed him to his back.

"My turn," she murmured with intent, her fingers driving him to distraction. Duncan found himself heated and writhing. He clutched the linens by the fistful in his desire for control, but Eglantine showed no haste to be done. She knelt above him, the firelight kissing her curves and painting her with gold.

When she urged him within her, Duncan nigh fainted with pleasure of her heat closing around him. But the lady moved with deliberation, echoing his slow pace, drawing out his passion longer than he might have imagined possible. His hands fell to the narrow span of her waist, hers landed upon his chest. And she kissed him with a thoroughness that made his heart clamor.

Eglantine was the one. She was his lady, his woman, his partner. She had his heart and Duncan did not want it back. She had come to him, defying belief and expectation, just like an old tale. 'Twas destiny that brought them together, he was certain of it, and naught would ever tear them apart.

He slipped his thumb between the two of them, wanting to share the rising storm. She gasped then writhed above him, driving him mad with her heat and desire. Duncan strained to hold himself back, he touched her with increasing vigor, he felt a surge of delight when Eglantine cried out once more.

'Twas then and not a moment before that he caught her close and drove deep into her heat, arching high off the bed and roaring as he spilled his seed within her.

And there was naught but Eglantine, her warmth and softness, her scent and her touch. Duncan buried his nose in her hair with a sigh of satisfaction, then kissed her temple as his eyes closed.

"Ah, Eglantine, I do so love you," he managed to murmur before sleep claimed him.

Sleep evaded Eglantine.

Duncan's words echoed in her thoughts throughout that long night. She lay and watched the silk billow above her, savored the heat of his arm around her waist, listened to the lapping of the sea—and wondered.

No man had ever said he loved her. Not even Theobald, with all his charming lies, had ventured so far as this. It had been she who had been so eager to confess tender feelings.

And it had been her confession that had changed all. Aye, Eglantine could mark the change in her relations with Theobald from the very moment she had confessed her love—he had won, he knew it well, and he had begun to exploit her weakness for him from his new position of power.

She had been fool enough to let him.

But Duncan, Duncan was different from Theobald in so many ways. He was spared the other man's cool composure, though, indeed, his impassioned charm was not without allure. And the words had fallen from his lips as if he could not halt them, not as if he would urge her surrender.

Eglantine was shocked how readily she wanted to believe him, even knowing all she did of men, even doubting all she did of Duncan's deeds.

'Twas true that Duncan was a poor liar. She studied him as he slept, seeking the truth in the lines of his features, the sweep of his dark lashes, the unruly tide of his hair. Her gaze fell to his lips time and again, remembering their weight upon hers. He had been uncommonly gentle in his loving this time, and Eglantine realized her previous charge of savagery had stung. She regretted those words and wished she could take them back, but they were said and he would not forget them soon.

But despite her accusation, Duncan was no savage. He was both more gentle than any man with whom she had mated and more passionate. He granted her the choice of whether to welcome him to her bed, whether to consummate what was begun. She knew that if she denied him at the very portal, Duncan would cede to her will. He might rage about her capriciousness, he would have much to say of the matter— but he would not force her, he would not hurt her, he would not take what she did not offer.

'Twas astonishing to realize how fully she trusted him in this matter, at least. But what of the rest? What of Alienor? What of the destroyed foodstuff? What of the missing deed? For the first time in her life, Eglantine's responsibilities warred with her own desires. She had no right to ignore those issues—though in this moment, she was sorely tempted to do so.

'Twas easy to forget responsibility with Duncan in her bed. He made her feel there was naught but they two. Eglantine sighed and brushed the weight of one lock from his brow, knowing she had never felt so treasured in a man's embrace.

Or so warm. Indeed, she was heated from head to toe, cradled against Duncan's strength and warmth, and had no intent to move. So, she lay there sleeplessly, watching him, marveling at the tenderness that welled within her.

She must have dozed, for the weight of a small hand upon her arm made her jump. Eglantine turned toward the touch and met the solemn blue gaze of Esmeraude.

"*Maman?*" she asked, then patted Eglantine's arm as hope lit her eyes. "Up?"

Eglantine smiled, seeing no harm in this indulgence. It had been thoughtful of Célie to ensure that Esmeraude slept elsewhere the night before, but now that they had rediscovered each other, Eglantine did not want to lose this affection with her daughter.

She leaned closer and touched her fingertip to her lips. "Shhh! We must be quiet. Duncan is sleeping."

Esmeraude immediately echoed the gesture, *shhh*ing loud enough to wake the most besotted soul.

Then she grinned. "Duncan will tell me a story?"

Eglantine chuckled beneath her breath and rubbed noses with her daughter. "Everyone does not always want to tell you a story," she teased. "And he is asleep."

"Shhhhhhhh," answered Esmeraude, looking most mischievous as she shook her finger at her mother.

Eglantine laughed as she scooped the toddler up and tucked her beneath the covers. She donned her discarded chemise and settled back in the warm hollow of the mattress, curling around the little girl, who nestled against her happily and sighed contentment.

"Esmeraude?" The worried whisper came from outside the tent, and the child giggled, touching her fingertip to her lips.

"Did you not tell Célie where you had gone?" Eglantine asked. The toddler shook her head, clearly delighted with herself and her game, just as the maid peeked into the tent.

"Esmeraude! You should not be here!" Célie spoke evidently before she realized that Eglantine was awake, then her cheeks pinkened. "My lady, I am most sorry."

"'Tis fine, Célie. there is no harm done."

"But—but 'twas my intent to grant you privacy on this night of nights . . ." Célie's gaze flicked across the bed for the first time and she flushed crimson, clearly having just spied Duncan there. Her voice dropped to a horrified whisper, as she wrung her hands in her apron. "Oh, my lady, oh I have permitted an interruption and I am most apologetic. I shall take Esmeraude immediately—"

"Célie, my mother oft welcomed me to her bed while my father slumbered, particularly after thunderstorms. There is naught amiss in this, and Esmeraude will be fine."

Célie did not look convinced. "But my lord Theobald . . ."

"Is dead." Eglantine smiled. "Do not fret about this, Célie. Indeed, I would think you might welcome some sleep without this busy one beside you."

The maid smiled, though her flush did not fade. "Aye, my lady." She inclined her head, glanced across the bed, and reddened yet more, then ducked out of the tent with such haste that could only indicate relief.

Esmeraude waved her fingertips insouciantly. "Bye-bye, Célie."

Eglantine bit back her smile, knowing that her daughter had achieved precisely what she had sought. "Esmeraude, you can remain only if you are a good girl."

The toddler touched her finger to her lips and *shhhhh*ed again.

"Aye, and more than that." Eglantine gave her a cuddle. "'Tis very early, far too early to be awake. Even Gunther and Gerhard are still sleeping, and so should we. So, close those eyes"—she kissed one eyelid, then the other—"and sleep some more."

Esmeraude spared her mother an impish smile, then nodded and burrowed deeper against Eglantine's warmth. Though she might have preferred to stay awake, the warmth betrayed the toddler and her breathing soon slowed. Eglantine cuddled back against Duncan, intending to sleep herself.

Her eyes flew open when her buttocks encountered what could only be his erection.

Eglantine looked over her shoulder to find Duncan's eyes not only open but twinkling merrily. "Shhhh," he counseled with as much mischief as Esmeraude, one fingertip rising to his lips.

Eglantine laughed quietly. "Don your chemise, for Célie is scandalized enough," she chided. He amiably did her bidding, sparing his cleaned yellow chemise an appreciative sniff. He lay back beside her, wrapping his arm around her waist and looking most pleased.

"How long have you been awake?" she demanded in a whisper.

"Long enough to hear that your maid is surprised to find your spouse in your bed." Duncan sobered. "This Theobald served you poorly, Eglantine. No doubt you fled France because there were those who would compel you to make such a match again."

Eglantine turned, being careful not to disturb the sleeping Esmeraude. "None tried to compel me to wed again."

"I think you gloss the truth, my lady. You could have found spouses of merit for your daughters more readily in France." He smiled and cupped her chin in his hand. "I know you have yet to fully trust me, Eglantine, though I hope that one day you will feel fit to share the truth of this with me."

Duncan turned his brilliant silver gaze upon her and his voice echoed with resolve. "But fear not, Eglantine." He pounded his fist upon his muscled chest and his eyes narrowed. "Any who would demand any toll from you shall have to conquer me first."

Eglantine regarded him in awe. Then she shook her head in bemusement. "You need not fear, either for your hide or for any demanding I wed another."

"Nay?" Duncan nodded approvingly. "'Twould be the manner of sound planning typical of you to ensure that none could follow."

Eglantine could not help but laugh at this not-inaccurate assessment. "I believe, Duncan, that I owe you a story. I swear to you 'tis the truth."

"Theobald is not dead?" Duncan's gaze turned fierce. Eglantine laid a hand upon his arm that he did not rise from the bed and see the deed done without delay.

"He is dead." Eglantine urged a skeptical Duncan back to the pillows and laid her head upon his shoulder.

"You have a champion? Another who will pursue you and demand your hand?" Duncan scowled, and Eglantine silenced him with her fingertips.

"You are worse than Esmeraude! Let me tell the tale." He smiled beneath her touch and Eglantine lay back against his shoulder. "I suppose 'tis simpler to begin at the beginning. I was wed at fourteen to a count, one Robert de Leyrossire. The match was arranged at my birth, and Robert was three decades my senior."

Duncan made a noise that could only signify disgust.

"Alienor was his daughter by a previous match. She was four when Robert and I wed."

"And likely as irksome then as she is now," Duncan muttered. Eglantine chuckled, but he tapped her chin with one finger. "This Robert was the man with the heir who cast you out and did not so much as permit you to attend Robert's funeral?"

Eglantine again was surprised. "Aye. But how did you know?"

"The same way that I know that Alienor made trouble for you from the first." He smiled wryly. "She told the tale differently, but one could read the truth between her words."

Eglantine warmed beneath Duncan's affectionate gaze. Indeed, he took her side with rare tenacity, a trait to which any woman could become accustomed.

"At any rate, I scarcely knew Robert. We met abed and that infrequently, for he was oft away securing and expanding his holdings. He was much concerned with his wealth was Robert." Duncan snorted. "Despite that, I bore Jacqueline to him but ten months after our nuptials." Eglantine fell silent in memory of his anger at the babe's gender. "I thought she was perfect."

Duncan clearly heard what she did not say and anger ran beneath his words. "He did not? She is a gem!"

Eglantine shook her head, liking that Duncan too saw much of merit in her daughter. "He wanted another son and was annoyed that I defied him in this. He spent more time abroad then, but Jacqueline and I were very close. She was my solace in that place."

"Until he died, of a chicken bone he was too proud to have your aid in removing." Duncan nodded at the justice served in this. "He was a fool, Eglantine, and died a fool's death. What did you do when his son cast you out?"

Clearly Alienor had told him much. "I returned to my family home and there encountered a childhood friend of my brother's. Burke de Montvieux is a knight, much accomplished, a very handsome and noble man well known to our family. My brother was teasing him sorely, for Burke had finally fallen prey to a lady's charms and she had spurned him. None believed it, for Burke had much affection for the charms of women and his attentions were always returned."

Duncan harrumphed but said naught.

"So, my brother set out to test his friend's claim. He persuaded women to try to seduce Burke, to win his ardor and prove this so-called love false. Whores and widows took his wager, for Burke would not be a small prize as spouse.

"'Twas a jest such as these two had oft played upon each other, but it made me think. Burke I knew was a man of honor, a man who would treat his lady well. We had been companionable since childhood. Indeed, he might make me a good spouse. So I took my brother Guillaume's dare."

She smiled at a somber Duncan. "And I lost, just as all the other women lost, for Burke's heart was indeed securely held by his lady."

Duncan smiled. "It must have been, for him to decline you."

Eglantine felt herself blush. "But Burke explained to me the power of his love, and I understood immediately that this was how marriage should be. I even dared to believe it might be thus for me, as aged as I am."

He shook his head. "How old *are* you, my Eglantine?"

She lifted her chin, fully expecting him to recoil. "Twenty-eight summers I have seen."

Duncan rolled his eyes and grinned. "If that makes a crone, then I am near dead at thirty and one."

"'Tis not the same for a man."

"You are not so aged that love cannot be yours." Duncan bent and kissed her so soundly that Eglantine nigh lost the thread of her tale. He smiled when he lifted his head, his fingertip tracing the line of her chin. Indeed, she could scarcely catch her breath.

He clucked his tongue. "When one who recounts a tale, Eglantine, the rhythm of the story must be kept, lest one's listeners find other matters of greater interest." He nuzzled her neck and kissed her earlobe with such attention that she decided the tale was not worth the telling.

But Duncan did not share her view. He lifted his head and grinned impishly. "And what happened next?"

Eglantine struggled to recall. "'Twas not long afterward that I was at court, and I met Theobald de Mayneris, a charming knave if ever there was. He made my heart skip and I was certain this was the love of which Burke spoke. I had never had a man court me with such ardor, compliment me with such abandon, grant me such thoughtful gifts." Eglantine frowned. "Theobald charmed me, wed me, and planted Esmeraude in my belly shortly thereafter."

Duncan was silent.

Eglantine grimaced at the memory of her own refusal to heed her good sense and frowned more deeply at the fear that she repeated her mistake. "I knew he gambled, I knew he drank, and I suspected that he was not faithful, but the man had a charm that could not be denied. I erred in trusting him, 'tis true, but there were moments when it seemed worthwhile."

Duncan stiffened beside her, his silence most telling. Did he guess that she drew a parallel between that courtship and this one? Eglantine did not want to look to his eyes and see the truth. She pleated the linens between her fingers instead. "He had naught to his name, of course, so my brother ceded a minor manor to his hand, hoping Theobald would mend his ways and become a fitting spouse."

"He did not," Duncan guessed, his words falling from gritted teeth.

Eglantine shook her head. "Nay, not he. But to his credit, he adored Esmeraude. He could not do too much for her, perhaps because she was his echo in most every way. She has his eyes, his charm, his sense of devilry, his temper, and his lust for his own desire." She brushed the curls back from her sleeping daughter's brow and voiced her deepest doubt. "I fear she may also have his lack of moral fiber."

Duncan caught her shoulders in his grip and gave them an encouraging squeeze. She might have thought this a perfect chance to pledge his support, but he said naught.

Because at the end of their year and a day, Duncan MacLaren would be gone. Eglantine told herself 'twas better to know the truth of it now, even though her chest was tight.

"But matters were amiable enough between us." She continued lightly. "I ran Arnelaine myself and raised the girls, until Alienor came to our door."

"Cheated of her dowry and seeking your aid, despite all she had done against you." Duncan's words were filled with disapproval.

"What choice had I? She had nowhere else to flee and there was a thin link of marriage between us. Indeed, her position could easily have been my own if my own brother had denied me after Robert's death. 'Tis all too readily done. So I took her into my home."

"And she strove to make you regret it every day since."

Eglantine laughed at his well-targeted conclusion, then frowned. "Well, there was another result of her presence, one that I did not anticipate. Theobald was horrified by her circumstances and began to fear for Esmeraude's future. I thought he was merely being protective of his favored one, but in hindsight, it seems he understood even then how dire our situation had become."

"I would wager that he did not ensure Esmeraude's future with cautious choices." Duncan looked most forbidding, though his arm was fast around Eglantine.

"Nay, not he. He gambled with new vigor, seeking to build a dowry beyond renown." She shook her head. "I had no thought that he lost so very much until he died."

"How did he die?"

"I would not disappoint you, but the truth is that he died most mundanely. He caught a chill, he did not cater to it, and it settled into his chest. He was not a vigorous man. He came home to Arnelaine only when his servant carried him there."

"You have been wed to witless men indeed," Duncan said gruffly. "Any man of sense would know that you, of all women, would ensure that those beneath your hand were healed. Never have I seen a woman more sensible or more determined to fulfill her responsibilities, regardless of the expense to herself." He winked at her. "But then, had either of these fools turned to you, they might still draw breath and I would not be so fortunate as to share your bed."

Eglantine was so astonished by this assessment of her character that she took a few moments to continue her tale again.

"A fever had claimed Theobald and he said naught of

sense in the three days it took him to die." Eglantine pursed her lips, feeling no pain at her loss. "'Twas after his funeral mass that I learned he had wagered and lost what was not his to lose. Theobald had gambled the seal of the holding that my brother entrusted to his hand."

"Putting you in debt to your family." Duncan's tone was heavy with scorn. "You should have killed this worm of a man! He deserved no less."

"'Twas worse than that," Eglantine continued as if she had not noted his comment. "He had lost the seal to one Reynaud de Charmonte." She heaved a sigh. "Robert betrothed Jacqueline at birth to his old comrade, Reynaud. He began to visit her a year ago, and Jacqueline dislikes him heartily." She chuckled despite herself. "She calls him 'the old toad,' and I cannot chide her for he is a loathsome man. He is as old as Robert would have been and filled with avarice."

"This reminds you of your own ill-fated nuptials."

Eglantine met Duncan's solemn gaze. "Aye, 'tis a poor measure for Jacqueline, for she is such a sweet and giving child. She deserves a marriage of love, not one of duty." She shook her head. "Matters had strained between us before our departure to this place, since there was little I could do. The betrothal agreement was bound by law and the exchange of coin. My brother refused to fight it, and I had no means of paying a forfeit."

Duncan growled. "Thanks to Theobald and his recklessness."

"Aye. So, I evaded Reynaud's insistence upon setting a date for the nuptials and denied him as many visits as I dared. When Theobald died, Reynaud sent a letter that he would collect Jacqueline shortly. He had arranged that I might join a convent."

"You? Never!"

Eglantine smiled. "Aye, I was not enamored of this course. The title to Kinbeath was a chance, a chance to grant my daughters those marriages, a chance for Jacqueline to make her own choice. 'Twas a chance to ensure that Jacqueline never spoke to me as I spoke to my own mother, so filled with hurt at what I believed to be her betrayal."

"And what of Reynaud and the seal of Arnelaine?"

Eglantine shrugged. "I do not know. Perhaps my brother has purchased it back, though I cannot imagine what price Reynaud would demand. And I have served my only brother with faithlessness, for I fled with all I dared to borrow from his household in his absence."

She shook her head. "Indeed, there is little good in this of me. I lied whenever possible about our course and my identity, I pledged my household to secrecy." She regarded her sleeping child so that she would not have to see the censure in his eyes. "I am no countess, Duncan, and I know of no place called Nemerres. And in the end, I am plagued by doubts. I pray that only Theobald knew of his title to Kinbeath, but have no assurance of the same."

Duncan sighed and rolled to his back, his lips pursing as he stared at the top of the tent. Eglantine feared he would chastise her for her lies, for she knew his regard for honesty.

But he turned a twinkling glance upon her. "With respect, Eglantine, my tale is a finer one. You should have killed Theobald. 'Twould have been fitting and made a better song."

She laughed aloud, uncommonly relieved though she dared not name why, and swatted his shoulder. "I have always admitted that I told a poor tale."

Duncan grinned and caught her close. "But your heart is true, Eglantine, and that is of far greater worth than a good tale. You left all you knew and all you loved to save your daughter from a marriage you guessed would be ill-fated. You defied the odds even in arriving here, and should I be a gambling man, I should put my coin on your making a home at Kinbeath."

Before Eglantine could ask for clarification, Duncan's hand closed over her breast. The admiration in his eyes silenced her questions well before his mouth covered hers.

Though their kiss was not destined to endure. Esmeraude's ears had perked up even in sleep at the utterance of her favorite word. 'Twas not long before she was bouncing on Duncan's chest as the two sang a rollicking ditty together.

Eglantine refused to sing along, citing the poorness of her voice, though she bounced and laughed as well. She felt lighter for having shared the truth with Duncan and much encouraged by his support of her choices.

He had a way of making her feel that she had not compounded error with error, that she had not made a muddle of every choice in her life.

He was a man who could win her heart, without a doubt, or might have won it if Eglantine had not known better than to trust her own instinct in this. Indeed, this past night could have been interpreted as yet another example of her woeful choices when it came to men. She had put aside all the charges held against him, and that to sate her own desire.

'Twas no good sign.

But as she watched Duncan play with Esmeraude, 'twas difficult to believe there was anything wrong with welcoming him in her bed. And that, she well knew, should have troubled her more than it did. Indeed, Eglantine wondered whether Duncan spoke aright, and they might indeed make a good match of this.

'Twould have naught to do with love, of course, for she would not venture to those dangerous lands again. 'Twould merely be an arrangement based upon the good sense of them sharing the land they both desired. And perhaps the desire that flared between them would not fade.

Perhaps Duncan would not leave in a year and a day.

Eglantine told herself 'twas foolish, but the sight of this

man with her child—this man who bedded her so thoroughly, this man who made her breath catch with his powerful tales—awakened a tiny hopeful corner of her heart that had long laid dormant. There was much unresolved between them, but on that morning, Eglantine dared to hope once more.

And this fledgling hope was not for her daughters' futures alone.

Chapter Fifteen

UNCAN WAS HAPPIER THAN EVER HE COULD RE-
call. Eglantine had neither cast him from her bed
nor laid charges of savagery at his feet. She had
not only returned his ardor, but she had confided in him. Her
child pummeled him playfully and the lady watched with an
indulgent eye.

He had found another family. Though this family Duncan
intended not only to keep but to protect with his very life, if
necessary. Dugall would not have his due here.

In the midst of his musings, one of the unpleasant facets
of this family suddenly intruded. Alienor swept into the tent
unannounced and Duncan winced, wondering what manner
of mischief she would make this morn.

His response was evidently shared, for she glared at him
with undisguised hostility. "You should not be in my stepmother's bed!"

Eglantine's clicked her tongue at the girl's rudeness, but
Duncan caught at her waist when she might have risen from
the bed to resolve matters. This was his family, for better or
for worse, and he would see this girl's manner improved.

"Stay warm," he counseled his lady quietly. "There is a
chill in the air this morn." She seemed somewhat surprised at
his words, and he grinned. "'Tis time someone ensured your
welfare." He tucked Esmeraude protectively into the bed

against her astonished mother, then folded his arms across his chest and fixed Alienor with his sternest glance.

He would see Alienor making her way about the camp garbed in more than this sheer chemise if 'twas the last thing he saw done. Truly, the demoiselle had no idea what trouble she might make herself.

Or perhaps she did. Duncan felt his eyes narrow. Either way, Alienor made too much grief for Eglantine.

"Do you not announce yourself at your mother's chamber?" he demanded. "And do you not ever don more than your chemise? There are men about who might take advantage of all you appear to offer."

Though he expected her to lie and retort that he had done as much, Alienor rolled her eyes. She flushed slightly. "I would talk to my stepmother in privacy."

"Why?" Duncan was more than suspicious of the girl's manner, and to his pleasure, Eglantine seemed to share his view.

"Whatever you have to say may be said in Duncan's presence," she said calmly.

Alienor granted them both a glare. "Nay, it cannot!"

Eglantine folded her arms in an echo of Duncan's posture. The way she sat beside him made him proud, for they appeared to face this adversary together. "Aye, it can and it will."

Alienor fumed silently, her hands clenching and unclenching, then shook her head and strode to the bed. "Then here is the truth of it," she declared, her voice shaking. "The King of the Isles, this heathen Dugall, he took my maidenhead last eve and made me his own. You must insist that he wed me, for no less honor will do."

Duncan felt himself smile. "But I thought your maidenhead was already stolen from you."

Eglantine looked similarly unmoved by this speech. "Aye, 'twas not long past that you claimed Duncan had taken it."

Alienor made a little growl in her throat and her eyes glittered. "That was *before* I knew there was a king to be had and before I saw him and before he touched me!" She cast out her hands. "Eglantine, you are impossible as always! You must insist upon this match! 'Tis the least you can do for me."

Duncan began to laugh, but Eglantine dug an elbow into his ribs and he silenced. "What proof have you of his deed?" she asked mildly.

Alienor regarded her in shock. "Eglantine!"

"One cannot accuse a king of such a deed without proof, Alienor." Eglantine was ever practical. "'Tis no small thing to take a bride—nor indeed to lose one's maidenhead."

"No matter how many times it takes," Duncan muttered, and his lady elbowed him again.

"There must be evidence, Alienor," she insisted.

The girl flushed crimson but lifted her chin. Without preamble, she seized the hem of her chemise and hauled it up to her waist, displaying her bloodied thighs. "'Twas you who insisted we not have privacy," she declared defiantly.

Clearly he was not yet ready for the ordeal of this girl. Duncan fell back on the pillows and covered his eyes with a groan, a move that prompted Esmeraude—who was disinterested in Alienor's complaints—to tickle him.

"Such a show of blood is not proof, Alienor," Eglantine said coolly. "It could be naught but your monthly courses."

Duncan grimaced, certain that was more than he wanted to hear. He took refuge in tickling Esmeraude, who was delighted with the return of his attentions.

"You!" Alienor shook a finger at Eglantine. "You have always hated me, you have always denied me my desires, you have always tried to shame me."

"You seem to find shame well enough without assistance," Duncan declared. He braced himself for another jab, but Esmeraude jumped on his chest instead and nigh drove the wind out of him. She giggled at her feat and he hoped heartily that she never grew up.

Aye, Esmeraude was more clever than Alienor, and should she choose to make trouble—as Duncan feared she would— he was certain she would be the death of both himself and Eglantine. Her father's temper, charm, and lack of judgment indeed.

Might the gods have mercy upon them.

"Alienor, you must show some sense in this endeavor." Eglantine spoke more reasonably than Duncan could. "I know that you are impatient to be wed, but a man's affections must be won. And there are many who believe that a woman who is easily bedded is not one to be wed."

"Aye, is that why you couple with *him*, like a common wanton? Heathen vows are so much less binding than those made before a priest, are they not?"

Eglantine straightened, but Duncan sat up and glared at the demoiselle with overmuch to say. "You will not speak to Eglantine thus!"

"Whyever not?" She lifted one shoulder insouciantly. "Because the truth cannot be uttered if it does not suit your favor? You are not wed yet you warm her bed. 'Tis *disgusting*, you are both so old and so filled with lust."

Alienor shuddered, then looked at Eglantine again. "At least you wed Theobald, though he was not worth any maid's trouble. I gather none others would have you. Is that why we flee so far? That you might find another man desperate enough to bed you? And now that you are too old to have much choice, you would show your power in limiting mine?"

"Enough!" Duncan roared and bounded from the bed, no longer content to let his lady manage this discussion. "You will apologize to Eglantine and you will do so immediately!"

"I will not!"

He grabbed Alienor's chin, lifting her to her toes. The girl's eyes widened. "Apologize," he growled, "and I would advise you do it well."

Alienor's lips set mutinously. "I am sorry, Eglantine, that I feel so compelled to speak the truth."

"You feel no such compulsion," Duncan retorted, disliking her audacity. "For you have already admitted this day to a lie that crossed your lips."

Her eyes flashed and she twisted from his grip, rubbing her chin as if she would wipe the stain of his touch away. "I confess naught and I need not do so."

Duncan shrugged and leaned against the bed. "Neither I nor Eglantine need plead your case with King Dugall."

Alienor's lips pinched tightly, then she strode to Eglantine. "He never touched me," she admitted through gritted teeth. "I made to seduce your Duncan MacLaren, but he spurned me." She punctuated this with a glance at Duncan. "Naught happened, which speaks most eloquently of the man's taste."

Eglantine covered her mouth with her hand, though Duncan could not guess whether 'twas horror she hid or laughter. The glint in her eyes, though, made Duncan's heart leap.

Alienor tapped her toe, ever anxious to pursue her own agenda. "Now, what of the king?"

"Did any witness this deflowering?" Duncan demanded. "You cannot blame us for skepticism of your claim."

Alienor opened her mouth and closed it again. Steam fairly rose from her ears. She shook her head and might have spoken, but a man cleared his throat on the outside of the tent.

"Duncan, are you within?"

'Twas Iain, Duncan recognized his voice. So did Alienor, for her lips tightened and she folded her arms about herself. "Aye, Iain, I am here."

"Might I speak with you?"

Duncan shook a heavy finger at the discontented Alienor.

"You will wait here and you will hold your tongue until I am returned. Understand?"

Her eyes narrowed, but she nodded once in agreement, which was more than he had expected. Duncan slipped through the silk, not prepared to receive the entire camp while his lady lay abed.

Iain's expression was strained, though he bowed his head to Duncan in an unexpected display of respect. "I have a request of you this morn."

"Aye?"

Iain frowned, his evidently practiced words falling in haste. "Aye. Last eve I sampled a woman now beneath your care and she, to my dismay, was virginal. I had thought she might be, but she argued otherwise, and in the desire of the moment, I believed her. I took her maidenhead, never guessing from her manner that 'twas intact. Though we parted poorly last eve, I would make matters right in this."

Duncan nodded, not surprised that the ale and the celebration had led to unions unexpected. "Aye, 'tis the mark of a man of honor to finish what he has begun."

Iain nodded gratefully at this encouragement. "My father would expect no less. And so I ask, Duncan, that you put the differences between us aside for the future of this maiden and any bairn I might have planted in her belly." He looked Duncan in the eye, his blue eyes blazing. "I ask you for the hand of the countess's dark-haired daughter in mine."

"I will not have *him*!" Alienor insisted moments after Duncan and Iain came inside the increasingly crowded tent. "He is no one of any merit at all." She cast a glance at Iain that might have daunted the most determined of suitors.

Iain glared back and muttered something in Gael, looking not the least bit swayed from his course.

Duncan sat down heavily beside Eglantine and rubbed his

brow. He had dressed quickly on his return, donning his usual plaid with the yellow chemise beneath, though his feet were yet bare. Eglantine similarly had cast a kirtle over her chemise and fastened back her hair, though she had not troubled with stockings or boots. Esmeraude had been dispatched with Célie to break her fast while this was sorted through.

"He says he took her maidenhead, that she granted it willingly to him," Duncan explained, inviting Eglantine to make what she would of the competing stories.

She did not know what to believe, though any fool could see that there certainly was fire between these two.

"'Twas dark! I thought he was the king!" Alienor cried, then clapped her hand over her mouth in realization of what she had admitted.

Eglantine exchanged a glance with Duncan. "At least 'tis established who took what you offered."

Alienor flushed furiously and wrapped her arms about herself. "'Twas offered and no more. I realized my error and matters halted there."

Duncan translated this for a clearly curious Iain, who denied her claim so hotly that his meaning could not be misconstrued.

"He insists the match was consummated," Duncan murmured in Eglantine's ear.

She nodded. "So I gathered."

"I will not have him," Alienor muttered, evidently sensing that she might lose this battle in the end.

"What of the blood?"

The girl lifted her chin. "'Tis my courses, as you suggested." She flushed, though whether was due to shyness or a bold lie, Eglantine did not know. "I am still a maiden."

"Until the next man snares your eye," Duncan retorted, clearly displeased with the girl's tales.

Eglantine could not blame him. She pursed her lips, deliberately keeping her temper to a simmer. "Consider, Alienor, that if your maidenhead is indeed gone, no man will be pleased to discover as much on the night of his nuptials. 'Tis no small thing that Iain would wed you. You might have the grace to acknowledge the man's sense of honor."

But Alienor sneered. "They have no honor in these parts." She cast her hand at Duncan. "He has none and Iain is no better."

Duncan coughed into his hand. "With respect, Eglantine, I fear she partly speaks aright."

Eglantine turned in surprise. "What is this?"

"Perhaps we should hear from Cormac's son himself." Duncan studied the younger man, whose animosity for Duncan was more than clear.

Duncan frowned. "I would have Iain speak for himself, Eglantine, but he speaks only Gael."

"You might translate."

He flicked her a silvery glance. "If only there were another who could do the task, then you would know no tales were being told."

The admission made no sense to Eglantine, but she was prepared to trust Duncan's judgment. "If you believe it necessary, then we shall summon Louis."

"Louis? He speaks very little Gael."

Eglantine smiled. "He is a better listener than a speaker perhaps, but he does indeed understand nigh all." She dispatched a runner and within a matter of moments, the châtelain joined them, as well. Pleasantries were exchanged, the older man admitted that his cough was much improved, then Duncan cleared his throat. He quickly made Louis familiar with the circumstances facing them and though the châtelain's brows rose, he made no comment.

"My difficulty is that Iain is not without animosity toward Eglantine and her family," Duncan explained, his gaze hard upon the fair man. "And so, 'tis only fitting that I have suspicions of his motives. Would you tell him as much?"

Louis translated smoothly and Eglantine watched Iain's jaw set. He said something hot and fast, and Louis pinched the bridge of his nose.

"Sparing the vulgarities that the ladies might not be offended, Iain says that Duncan has no place charging him with faithlessness of any kind, not when he stole Cormac's legacy. Iain insists the legacy of the chieftainship of Clan MacQuarrie should have fallen to himself, as Cormac's only blood son."

So, 'twas more than Mhairi's death at root. Eglantine watched Duncan smile coldly. "Perhaps his father saw the true nature of his character and did not wish to burden him with unwelcome responsibilities. Or perhaps his father thought Iain's fortune would be better sought in other ways."

Iain caught his breath when this was translated but before he could reply, Duncan continued quickly. "I believe that Iain cannot expect Eglantine to make a decision regarding Alienor without him making a confession. Tell us, Iain MacCormac, of what you have done."

Iain swore. He spat on the floor of the tent and Louis inhaled sharply as he glared at the offending mark. Eglantine swallowed at the animosity in Iain's blue eyes, then at the heat of the words that spilled from his lips.

Louis translated quickly. "He insists he took Alienor's maidenhead, 'tis true, and that none had sampled her before him. He insists that she came to him and that she surrendered willingly and that he would take her for his bride."

Duncan had not lied. Relief nigh took Eglantine to her knees. She slipped her hand through Duncan's elbow and stood straight beside him.

Louis cleared his throat. "Iain further declares that a chieftain of any merit would have already ensured your departure from this holding. He claims that you have no rights here, and he insists that Kinbeath must be held by the clan."

Eglantine felt her brows rise. "Yet he asks to wed my step-daughter? What assurance does he give of her safety wedded to him?"

Iain swore and spoke with heat, though his words did not impress Louis. "He says that they were destined for each other, that she is the blood of his heart, that they would have found each other even if she had not come to Kinbeath. He says that none can keep them apart." Louis looked slightly alarmed. "Even, apparently, you, my lady."

Alienor sneered. "I told you, Eglantine, he is without merit."

Iain glared at her, but Alienor held his gaze unrepentantly. And she was right. Eglantine could not imagine that even Alienor would be well served by a man so filled with bitterness, particularly when that bitterness was directed at their own family.

She spoke crisply. "Alienor, do you swear that he did not take your maidenhead?"

"Aye, I swear it."

Again, Eglantine had a fleeting sense that the girl lied, but she no longer cared. She nodded, pleased that Alienor had finally found some sense. "Then you have spoken aright. You will not wed this man, and further he is not welcome at Kinbeath. Louis, please invite Iain to leave."

When Louis did, Iain stepped forward and shook his fist as he made some threat.

"He says, my lady, that he will steal her."

"I think not!" Alienor retorted with scorn. "You will have naught else from me and you had best understand the truth of it!"

"Aye?" Iain caught at Alienor's shoulders and kissed her so fiercely that she made a little gulp of astonishment. Before any could intervene, he strode out of the tent, sparing one last insult that needed no translation.

Eglantine watched her stepdaughter finger her lips and knew she did not misread the yearning that lit the girl's blue eyes. They were not finished with this matter, that much was certain.

'Twas odd to find that both she and Alienor shared this poor judgment in men when there was no blood between them.

Alienor tossed her hair and stormed out of the tent, no doubt to make trouble for some hapless soul. But Louis did not depart as Eglantine might have expected.

He cleared his throat pointedly and bowed when she glanced his way. "My lady, there is but one thing you should know. Upon my journey to this king's court, I heard much of this man's plans for your future. This handfast was his proposal when the King of the Isles would have removed your vassals with bloodshed."

Eglantine nodded, pleased to have what Duncan had told her confirmed again. Duncan, though, stood stiffly by her side.

Perhaps he did not care to have the tales confirmed by her servant. Surely he would have preferred that she accepted his word on trust alone.

Aye, that would be Duncan's way.

Eglantine smiled, hoping to dispel some of the inexplicable tension between the two men. "Aye, Louis, Duncan has been most honest in this."

Neither man smiled. One of the older man's silver brows rose. "Perhaps not completely honest, my lady. I doubt he admitted that he would have lost the chieftainship of Clan MacQuarrie had he not persuaded you to make this handfast. His objective still is to seize Kinbeath and see you gone—this pledge but grants him more time to see the suzerainty of the King of the Isles assured. If Duncan fails in securing Kinbeath within that year and a day, the chieftainship of Clan

MacQuarrie will indeed fall to Cormac's son Iain, and that by royal decree."

Eglantine's mouth fell open, but Louis bowed low and took his leave. She turned to Duncan, certain she would see a denial in his eyes, but he shook his head slowly. "'Tis not as it appears, Eglantine."

She had been deceived and would not be swayed by his charm! "Were those the terms?"

"Aye, Dugall's terms, but not mine." He caught her hands and compelled her to face him. "I did not lie to you, Eglantine."

"Nay, you did not lie. From the first, you insisted that your desire was only for the title of this land!"

"Nay, Eglantine, no longer." His gaze bored into hers. "I desire you and you alone. I agreed to Dugall's terms to ensure I had the chance to woo you and to win you."

Eglantine shook her head and stepped away. 'Twas all too familiar to her to have a man prove to be less than what she had hoped him to be. "Do not lie to me now."

"Eglantine, I made a pledge to you, a pledge that I would win your heart. You granted me a year and a day, and I mean to put every moment of it to the service of that task." He bent and kissed her hands, folding them together over the heat of his embrace. His eyes glowed with passion when he looked up at her once more. "I swear it to you."

But Eglantine could not summon a reply to her lips. She wanted so much to believe him, but she dared not repeat her error of the past. She shook her head and stepped away, pulling her hands from his.

"Eglantine, do not turn your back upon this."

"'Twas you who counseled me to use the wits I had been granted," she said softly. "And a woman of sense learns from the errors of her past."

Duncan's eyes flashed as he stepped closer. "I am not Theobald!"

"But you are a man and the differences betwixt you two are not clear to me."

He gripped her shoulders and turned her to face him. He stared down at her, his gaze roving her features as if he would read her very thoughts. "The difference, Eglantine," he said softly, "is that I love you, while Theobald loved none but himself. And I have never lied to you, while I suspect he did so frequently."

He took a deep breath, a vulnerability dawning in the depths of his eyes, a fear that Eglantine knew she had put there. She could not look away from him and his voice dropped low. "Perhaps you who forgave Theobald so much might make an effort to find me innocent of his crimes."

With one hard look into her eyes, Duncan turned and left her tent. Eglantine was trembling and she sat once more on the mattress, wondering whether her fears would cost her all she had never hoped to make her own.

But she could not abandon the lessons of the past, however strongly Duncan might desire as much. She feared that he was not the man she hoped he was.

She feared that no man could be the man she hoped Duncan was.

Eglantine could not help but recall how smitten she had been with Theobald. Though that feeling was but a pale shadow of what she felt for Duncan, its memory was a chilling reminder.

She would not make the same mistake she had made before. She could not make the same mistake. Eglantine could not endure another travesty of a marriage, and truly, she did not need to.

But Duncan spoke aright in charging her with unfairness. She would grant him that chance to be judged on his own merit. He might not be intending to leave, Eglantine would not know the truth of it until that year and a day was past, until she knew his decision at the end of their handfast.

Until she knew for certain whether 'twas herself or Kinbeath that he desired most of all.

Should he choose her, she vowed silently, then she would have naught more to fear. A year and a day was a long time, long enough to ensure that she could distinguish between her hope and the truth. It might be long enough to see her tired of Duncan's allure, for the power of Theobald's touch had faded with time.

Though she doubted that would be the case this time, she had doubted that her desire could fade before—and she had been wrong. Eglantine was not a gambler by nature. If she wed again in truth, if she surrendered her heart again, she would be certain beyond doubt that all was as she believed.

This handfast might be long enough for even Eglantine to fall in love. Her instincts told her she had fallen already, but she knew better than to listen to such suspicions. She had a year and a day not only to secure her holding but to learn all of this man, all his hopes and fears and secrets.

He might well destroy her with his departure a year hence, but Eglantine would keep her pride and hide the truth of her own feelings from him, whatever they might be.

A woman had to learn something from a man like Theobald.

Aye, should Duncan choose her over Kinbeath then, Eglantine would pledge to him before the priest and that without regret. And if she came to love him by that fateful day, she would tell him of it when his ring was on her finger and his heart was her own.

She would tell Duncan then and not a moment before.

Dugall left Ceinn-beithe after four days and nights, and though his expression was skeptical, he seemed content to leave Duncan to his fate. Iain, to Duncan's surprise, did not depart with the king's party, though perhaps his lingering was at the king's behest.

Duncan did not care. He had labor to do and his lady's good-will to win. He was wagering upon making his handfast a marriage in a year and making this holding a prize that paid sufficient tithe to Dugall to stay that man's hand. Ceinn-beithe's future had to be secured, and the season of fair weather was too short to waste.

And these new arrivals could benefit from his lifetime in these parts. Duncan suggested final details to Xavier in the construction of the manor, tricks that locals knew from childhood, tricks that ensured the thatch was not snatched by the wind and the rain drained clearly away from the walls.

He labored in the construction of the successive buildings and suggested a plan for clearing the better land for fields while still leaving the beauty of the trees. He organized a woodlot and moved stumps with the other men from the land they chose to till.

He showed Eglantine's vassals how best to work the land they had made their own, where to sow each crop, how to judge the wind and the weather and the drainage, how to outthink the pillaging birds. Part of Dugall's gift for the handfast had been seed—Duncan explained each type to the vassals who were interested, discussing the merits of each grain and its resultant flours with Gunther and Gerhard.

He showed Eglantine's people which woodland plants could be eaten, which made healing potions, which were best for binding a wound, which supplied a substitute for rennet so that cheese might be made of the goat's milk. He found suitable grazing for the livestock, and the boys who aided in the hunt were grateful for Duncan's understanding of what could be found where. Duncan taught several of the boys to fish in the fast-flowing streams, and all appreciated some variety in their fare.

Jacqueline, to Duncan's delight, professed a curiosity for their new home. She might have driven another man mad with all her questions, but Duncan enjoyed discovering the familiar land anew. He began to teach her Gael, at first merely to teach her the names of creatures that he could not name in French, but she loved the language and demanded to know more.

Soon they met each afternoon in the shadow of the great stone when Duncan's labors were completed, and he taught her all he knew. She possessed her mother's clear gaze and intellect and 'twas a joy to watch her progress.

Alienor demanded to join these lessons and though Duncan suspected she would not be patient enough to see results, she showed unexpected tenacity. She had a talent for language and a rare desire to conquer this one. The two girls soon entered a lively competition and learned so quickly that Duncan's head spun. Eglantine came to share in these lessons, and Duncan found himself looking forward to their time together throughout the day.

And, of course, he courted Eglantine with rare vigor. He sang each evening before the company, his songs chosen specifically for her pleasure. He brought her the first flower found in the wood, he sought her out to share the marvels of Ceinn-beithe. He told of legends and customs and tall tales. He played with Esmeraude and imagined that the child would one day run him dry of stories.

Through it all, Duncan was aware of Eglantine's eye upon him. He nigh felt the turmoil in her thoughts, the uncertainty mixed with what could only be hope. Each night he loved her with all the passion and tenderness he possessed, each night he pledged his love—each night she clung to him a little more tightly or held him a little longer.

Each night she came closer to being his own.

Duncan was patient, for he knew that the greatest prizes are not readily won. Aye, he had learned as much in a troubador's tale.

'Twas a month after Dugall's departure that the quiet of the early morning was disturbed by a troubled sound. 'Twas not the first time that Eglantine had heard that distress, but she had been too slow to lend pursuit. Someone was ill and she had best discover who before the illness spread through the camp.

Even if she did not want to rise from bed so soon. She slipped from beneath the weight of Duncan's arm and pushed the softness of the wolf pelt aside. She cast a kirtle over her head, intent on discovering the culprit this time. She darted left and right through the slumbering camp, hampered by the inky haze of the early morning light, guided by naught but the sound.

Eglantine halted when she spied Alienor. The girl was on her knees, vomiting into a pail. Eglantine rolled her eyes in exasperation, guessing that this was no illness readily spread.

Still a maiden indeed. Would she ever have the truth easily from this child?

"Good morning to you," Eglantine said softly, watching her stepdaughter jump. "Are you unwell?"

Alienor started, spat into the pail, then rose shakily to her feet. She was pale and there was sweat upon her brow. "Something I ate, no doubt." She lifted her chin. "Perhaps the fish did not agree."

Eglantine arched a brow. "Three days in a row?"

Alienor's lips thinned. "I have always been sensitive to the least bit of spice."

Eglantine smiled despite herself and crossed the space between them to lay a hand on Alienor's shoulder. "You have always been most hale and you know it as well as I. Whose child takes root in your belly, Alienor?"

"I carry no man's child!"

"You carry a child?" Duncan roared, his approach having been unheard by either woman. Eglantine found him looking more unruly than usual, his expression exasperated as it oft was in Alienor's presence.

"I thought you were asleep."

"You thought wrongly. What is this?" He pushed a hand through his hair impatiently, then glared at the girl as his voice dropped to a growl. "What madness has seized you now, that you would bear a child and tell none of it?" He flung his hands skyward and roared. "Do you imagine none would note the rounding of your belly?"

His protectiveness made Eglantine smile, though Alienor did not share her response.

"I thank you for ensuring that all now know my state," she said tartly.

"There are no secrets in an assembly of this size. Whose babe is it? I will see him treat you with honor, Alienor, of that you can be certain!"

But Alienor lifted her chin high. "I will not wed him. He is worthless and far beneath my favor."

Aha! Eglantine and Duncan exchanged a glance, even as Duncan's lips tightened.

"But Iain offered to wed you," Eglantine reminded her before Duncan could shout. The timing would be right, for she had been a month into her pregnancies herself when her own illness began.

Alienor rounded on her with flashing eyes. "I care not what he desires. 'Tis my babe and my babe alone, and I shall find a father for it more fitting of both of us."

"Alienor, you cannot deny the man his own child," Duncan warned, his words dangerously low. "'Tis not our way—here the father ensures the welfare of the child."

"I can deny him and I will!" She braced her hands on her

hips and tipped back her head, bellowing Iain's name followed by a string of insults in Gael.

Eglantine knew she should not have been surprised by the girl's bold manner, but still she was. Iain appeared with startling speed, his fair hair rumpled and his expression sullen enough to challenge even Alienor's mood.

"Perhaps they are well matched," Duncan mused as he came to stand behind Eglantine.

"'Twas my thought exactly," she admitted. Much of the household had gathered by this point, their eyes lit with curiosity.

"I have something to say to this man," Alienor cried. "And I have learned his own tongue that he might understand me well enough. He has planted his seed in my belly but I will not have him. I intend to tell him why."

"God in heaven," Eglantine murmured to herself, and pinched the bridge of her nose.

Duncan's hand landed on the small of her back, his whisper fanning her ear. "She is bold beyond belief."

"I am embarrassed at her lack of shame." Eglantine shook her head. "Naught good can come of this, but 'tis clear that she will not listen to reason."

"I wondered why she sought to learn Gael." He winked down at her. "Perhaps you might prefer that you had not?"

Eglantine could not help but smile. "I suppose 'tis better to know the worst of it."

He grinned then and bracketed her waist with his hands, pulling her back against his chest. "Aye, Eglantine, 'tis one thing I love about you. You are not one to shirk an ugly proposition."

There was no doubt that that was what they attended here. Alienor spoke with vigor and with anger, jabbing her finger repeatedly at Iain. "This man has taken advantage of my innocence. He has planted his seed in my belly, without remorse or caring for my views on the matter."

Iain replied in kind, his eyes flashing furiously. "'Tis a lie she tells, for she seduced me."

"Not I!"

"Aye, you. Do you think a man would forget a virgin that nigh accosted him? Do you think a man would forget the maiden who nigh singed his soul with the heat of her desire?"

The assembly tittered as Eglantine pressed her temple with her fingertips. Duncan chuckled behind her.

"You shamed me!"

"I offered to wed you." Iain spat. "And you declined me before others."

Opinion clearly shifted in Iain's favor.

But Alienor was not done. "And why should I chain myself to a man of no worth whatsoever? Why should I suffer to see my child live in poverty and starve in the cold of a winter wind? He has naught, he will never have aught but anger to his name." Alienor cupped her belly. "I and this child deserve better."

The assembly fell silent, all eyes upon Iain. He bowed his head, then offered his hand to her. "I love you, Alienor. Betwixt the two of us, we shall make our way."

Alienor spat at his feet, though Eglantine imagined she saw tears glittering in the girl's gaze. "Your love will not keep my babe warm and fed. Your love will not keep the wind from our backs, nor the predators from our door. Your love will not fill my child's belly."

"When poverty comes in the door, love goes out the window," Duncan murmured. Eglantine turned to look at him and his lips curved in a rueful smile. "An old saying hereabouts. I am astounded to find Alienor's argument making sense."

"Aye, I can well understand that," Eglantine agreed.

"No man will wed you with the seed of another in your belly," Iain argued, his expression strained. "What of you and the bairn, then?"

Alienor lifted her chin. "Some man will have me. I am young and fair, and even Eglantine found two men to wed her and warm her bed once her maidenhead was gone." Her eyes narrowed. "You need not fear for the child, Iain. Eglantine has taught me to care for my own."

Eglantine blinked in surprise as Duncan whistled through his teeth. "You said she had a good heart though I confess I doubted it."

Alienor stepped up to Iain to make her final point. "And Eglantine has shown me the value of a poor spouse, in her wedding of Theobald. Do you think I have no eyes in my head? You have naught to your name, no potential for your future, you are lazy, you are surly, you are unworthy of respect, and you have no redeeming virtues whatsoever. I would not be so foolish as to wed a worthless man like you and cast the future of my child to the caprice of the Fates."

"I knew she cared for him," Eglantine said quietly.

"Aye, he cares for her, that much is certain." Duncan shrugged when Eglantine met his gaze, and she smiled at the twinkle in his eyes. "Though 'tis tedious when Alienor does not speak her thoughts clearly."

Eglantine chuckled though she knew she should not.

"I will not have you now," Alienor cried. "I will not have you tomorrow, I will not have you ever, Iain MacCormac. Indeed, I will not so much as teach my child your name."

Eglantine sobered as Iain paled. "That was most cruel."

The fair man said naught, but turned on his heel and stalked away. Alienor shook her fist after him, but Iain did not look back. He strode to the shore, retrieved a boat, and waded out into the sea.

Without so much as a word, he rowed away.

Eglantine's fingers tightened on Duncan's arm with concern. "Duncan, there is naught amusing in this. We must think of the child! Alienor cares for Iain, but he will not return! I fear that this time the girl has said too much."

"Nay," Duncan said, slowly shaking his head. His eyes were narrowed as he watched the younger man and his voice lowered in consideration. "On the contrary, I believe she has said precisely enough."

Eglantine knew her confusion showed, but he would not elaborate. She was left wondering what he knew of Iain that she did not.

Chapter Sixteen

A FORTNIGHT LATER, IAIN CAME OUT OF THE EVENing mist.

It had been raining for several days and the fog hugged the shoreline, though still Duncan looked incessantly for the return of Cormac's son. He had met every tide, certain of what the other man would do, but his conclusion had not been proven aright thus far.

'Twas just as he feared that he had been completely wrong, that Iain was less a man than he had hoped, that the shadow of a boat formed in the mist. Duncan caught his breath.

'Twas Iain. He brought his small forge and Duncan was glad that the sea was as smooth as a bronze mirror. The weight of that forge would have been difficult to manage on uneven waters, particularly as Iain rowed alone.

"You should not have risked the fog," Duncan chided by way of greeting. "You could have become disoriented and lost all." He heard Cormac's gruff protectiveness in his words, then moved to pull the boat farther to shore.

"I could wait no longer," Iain complained. "I had to know! I have been ready four days but the seas were so rough, and truly I paced a trough in the shore." He clutched Duncan's arm, his eyes bright. His manner reminded Duncan of how matters had once stood between them and he dared to hope. "She is well? She is unwed?"

Duncan nodded and clapped the other man on the shoulder, knowing immediately whom he meant. "She is somewhat distraught, though Eglantine says this is typical." He shook his head and smiled ruefully. "In truth, I could not have imagined that Alienor could have been more troublesome, but I have now seen the evidence with mine own eyes."

Iain grinned briefly, then frowned. "She spoke harshly to me, but no less than the truth, Duncan. I truly have naught, and affection will do naught to see her needs fulfilled. Alienor did rightly by me to speak from the heart."

Duncan squeezed the other man's shoulder. "She strove to compel you to make a change."

Iain nodded. "Aye. And I did. Though at first I was so angered with her that I did not trust myself to remain. The woman is so irksome!"

Duncan chuckled under his breath, well aware of that feeling.

"But once alone, I recalled my father's conviction that every man has his own destiny to fill. Alienor was right to criticize my choices, just as my father was right to not place the burden of chieftainship upon my shoulders." He looked up at Duncan, his gaze assessing. "I have blamed you for more than you deserved."

"Cormac should have spoken to you of his intent." Duncan shrugged. "'Twould have been a better thing if he spoke to both of us."

"Nay, 'tis more than that, Duncan." Iain heaved a sigh. "A decade past I made a mistake and have borne its cost overlong. I was vexed at my father, for he refused to grant more coin for my labor of choice. I left for a time."

"Aye, I recall that well. You came back much refreshed."

Iain snorted. "My purse was heavier, of that there is little doubt." Before Duncan could ask his meaning, Iain cleared his throat. "Dugall spoke aright. Had I been chieftain, I would have acted too quickly and my rash choice would have seen Alienor killed."

Iain swallowed. "'Twould have been my own fault that the woman destined for me was not at my side—and I would never have guessed the truth of it." He squared his shoulders. "My father made the right choice, Duncan. He saw the weakness in me and chose you instead."

"Your father wanted you to have the leisure to pursue the labor you loved," Duncan corrected, hoping against hope that he was right. "He wanted you to pursue your own dream and not his."

"Aye. I understand that now. He had no tolerance of my fascination with the forge when I was younger. But I fear I have lost your friendship in these past months of heated words." He glanced up, his expression hopeful. "Might we begin anew?"

Duncan smiled. "Fostership is stronger than blood, Iain. You are my brother, as surely as if we had birthed from the same woman, and I want naught but the best for you." He offered his hand to the younger man. "But if I might have your friendship, as well, that would be an unexpected prize."

Iain clasped Duncan's hand and grinned, the two of them sharing an impulsive and hearty embrace.

"Then as a friend, I would ask your opinion." Iain reached beneath his cloak, and silver flashed as he withdrew his hand. Worry lit his eyes. "What do you think? I feared I would not be able to craft anything of merit any longer, for 'tis practice alone that creates a steady hand."

Duncan took the brooch that Iain offered with something akin to reverence. 'Twas so beautiful that it could not be real.

'Twas a ring brooch, the traditionally shaped pin adorned with a small sword that formed its catch. But this one was a marvel, for a bird of prey wrapped itself around the circumference of the circle, its wing superbly detailed. Every feather was there, distinguished by a careful hand. Its eye glittered red, for a tiny chip of garnet was embedded there, and the silver had been polished to a gleam.

"I thought of the lady's peregrine," Iain explained with a haste born of uncertainty. "I have never seen the like of it. And it seemed that this might be a familiar creature to those nobles of the south." He shrugged and his words fell more quickly in his nervousness. "I have kept the cast for I thought it might be suitable for trade, and I have some silver saved, enough to make a dozen or so, but I do not know their taste in the south, and I do not know . . ."

"Iain, 'tis a beautiful piece," Duncan interrupted, and gave him an encouraging glance. He clasped the younger man's shoulder. "You need not fear any loss of your skills. Indeed, 'tis your finest work to date, and that by a long measure."

"I never felt such joy as when the wing fell exactly right beneath my fingers." Iain smiled sheepishly. "'Twas then I realized that this was the life for me, not that of chieftainship."

Duncan traced the marvel of the work with one fingertip, knowing the delight of which his foster brother spoke. There were times when a song rang from his lips or a word fit to the tune with a precision that made him exultant, that made him yearn to sing thus forever.

Iain took a shaking breath. "I want to wed Alienor. I want to grant her the life she desires. I want to return to the forge, to create works like this." Iain regarded Duncan hopefully. "I recall what you said to Dugall of welcoming artisans to Ceinn-beithe, of making this place a port."

Duncan smiled. "I was thinking of you and how best to fulfill your father's hopes for you."

"But I wondered if I had the skill to see it done. You have traveled south, Duncan. Would a noblewoman desire a pin like this for her cloak?"

Duncan smiled as he marveled that Alienor's sharp tongue could make a change that he with all his good intentions could not.

"Why do we not ask such a noblewoman?" he suggested.

"Eglantine!" Iain nodded quickly. "Aye, I would ask her, if—if she would receive me."

"I assure you that she will."

"Good. There is something I must say to her."

Duncan led a determined Iain through the camp, knowing full well where his lady could be found. He called to her and she glanced up with a smile that made his heart thunder. Ye gods, but the woman would never lose her power to fire his blood!

He hoped for the hundredth time that the way she fairly glowed in his presence was a sign that he came close to winning her. He knew he was close, he was impatient to have her pledge, but he feared to press her too soon.

Duncan was not a particularly patient man—'twas only that the stakes were so high that he steeled himself to wait.

Eglantine halted her discussion with the cooks, clearly surprised to see Iain again. That was naught compared to her astonishment when he bowed low before her in a sign of respect. Her gaze flicked to Duncan in confusion and he smiled, knowing that Iain would appear to her as a changed man.

He was changed—back to the man he once had been.

Then Iain presented Eglantine with the pin and her former astonishment was as naught. Her mouth fell open as she stared at the treasure on her palm. Duncan chuckled.

"Who wrought this marvel?" she demanded, looking from one man to the other. "From whence has it come? I have never seen the like of it!"

Just as Duncan had done, she traced the bird's wing with her fingertip, clearly unable to restrain herself from touching it.

"Iain resumes his craft," Duncan told her, slipping his arm around her waist. "He would build a trade to support Alienor and his child."

"Do you think that the noblewomen of the south would favor such work?" Iain asked urgently. "Do you think they might part with coin to have such adornment on their cloaks?"

Eglantine smiled and grasped Iain's hand in her own, her sincerity more than clear. "Any woman would treasure such a prize," she assured him. "I had no idea you had such skill."

Iain flushed slightly and flicked a glance at Duncan. "I had forgotten it myself."

Eglantine, ever practical, tapped her finger upon the pin. "Have you made a mold that you might cast more of the same? And have you silver enough to do so?"

Iain nodded quickly. "For about a dozen."

"Then you should vary them slightly, perhaps in the hue of the eye or in the way the silver is burnished. Or perhaps you might make a slightly different design. To pay a high price, each person must feel that they have acquired a unique treasure, and 'twill not do to have them confronted with a friend or adversary wearing the same jewel."

Iain nodded at what Duncan thought was sound advice.

Eglantine frowned slightly. "You will fetch the best prices at the hot and cold fairs in Champagne, if you can manage to reach there. They are held in spring and fall."

"I will, I will!"

"There is affluence there and much trade in fine cloth—and the finest cloth demands the finest jewel. This indeed is most fine." She caught her breath and Iain's ears burned red at her evident admiration. "Iain, your skill is considerable. I have never seen such a well-crafted piece." She shook her head, ran a fingertip across it yet again, then made to press the pin back into Iain's hand.

"Nay," that man said, shaking his head. "I would grant it to the Lady Eglantine in compense for what grief I have granted her." He took a deep breath. "I would apologize for my sampling of your maidenly daughter without the solemnity of a pledge between us."

Duncan caught his breath, finding himself fiercely proud of his foster brother in this moment. This was the son of Cormac MacQuarrie!

Eglantine's mouth opened and closed again. Then she shook her head. "All is well that is resolved well, Iain." She tried to give him the pin once more.

But Iain refused to take it. "Then I would grant it as a gift to Lady Eglantine as a mark of my intent to win her daughter's hand." He frowned. "And I would have the lady accept it as apology for all I have cost her."

Eglantine blinked. Duncan fully expected his foster brother to confess to the destruction of the stores, but Iain did no such thing.

He frowned and reached into his chemise once more.

To Duncan's astonishment, Iain offered Eglantine a document of some kind, hung with seals and wrought of heavy vellum. His chest clenched, for he had seen this document once before.

Eglantine paled.

"I stole it from you," Iain admitted. "It seemed most critical that I remove the proof of what I had wrongfully done."

"You? What had you to do with this?" Duncan demanded.

"Years ago I signed this deed, Duncan, at the behest of a Norman lord. He granted me much coin to sign in my father's own name. I cared not what 'twas for—I was irked enough and desirous of my due."

Duncan stared at the younger man in surprise. "But why?"

"You may recall that though I greeted you with joy, matters quickly soured between us." Iain turned to Eglantine. "He came out of the hills and across the sea, singing, filled with tales of far away and prompting laughter all around him. My sister adored Duncan upon sight, my father seemed to see in him something he had never seen in me. We had argued before about my choice of trade, but it seemed to me that my father was more harsh after Duncan came. So I left to seek my fortunes elsewhere."

"And this was how you won that fat purse," Duncan said softly.

"Aye, though that was not the end of it. My father heard the tale after I had returned and we argued viciously. He had planned to grant Ceinn-beithe to another chieftain, one who wanted forfeit from him for some slight. My father would not grant the land after what I had done, for he insisted 'twas no longer his to grant."

Duncan felt his chest tighten. "Do not tell me that this chieftain demanded Mhairi's hand instead." Eglantine's eyes widened.

But Iain hung his head and 'twas all the answer Duncan needed. "I blamed you, Duncan, for 'twas easier than acknowledging my own role, both in her death and in my father's disappointment."

Eglantine shook her head and fingered the deed at the root of it all.

"I never dreamed the tale was not done," Iain admitted. "I never dreamed that I should regret my foolishness as much as I do now."

"He was proud of your skill at the end. He told me that a smith has hands that can conjure magic. He wanted you free of the burden of this chieftainship—though I argued long with him that he should name another to the task."

A tear leaked from Iain's eye.

Duncan gripped the younger man's shoulder, now understanding the bitterness that had filled him. "You should have told me all of this."

"I should have, for you were the only brother I had and the only family left to me now. But I did not. I failed both you and my father, Duncan."

Duncan gripped Iain's shoulder. "'Tis behind us now."

They hugged heartily, and Duncan doubted his were the only eyes glazed with tears. The three stood in silence for a long moment, Eglantine's thumb working ceaselessly over the silver.

"What of the coins in my treasury?" she asked quietly. "Did you grant them to Dugall as tribute?"

Iain blinked, then frowned in sudden comprehension. "'Twas not I who plundered your stores, my lady, nor I who stole your treasury. I found the treasury chest at the perimeter of the camp, hidden in the undergrowth, its lock broken. I did not know what 'twas when I opened it, but I recognized this deed. I took naught else, I swear it to you."

"And this was the morn that you left?"

"Aye. I seized the deed, then I left."

"Was there coin in the trunk?" Duncan demanded.

"I do not think so. It seemed empty but for the deed."

"And where was this?"

Iain granted Duncan directions, clearly disinterested in the matter. He then turned to Eglantine.

"I would put the folly of my youth behind me, Eglantine," Iain confessed with a shaky smile. "I would prove myself a fitting spouse to Alienor and a good father to mine own child. 'Tis the least I might do in my father's memory." He held her gaze steadily as Duncan watched. "I shall even wed Alienor before a priest if 'tis your desire."

"I am not the one you must convince," Eglantine said. She offered the pin again to Iain, her smile ensuring he could not misinterpret. "You may give me another when your trade thrives, if you so choose, and I should be most honored to wear this mark of the talent of the father of my grandchild."

She covered the pin with her hand, pressing it into his palm. "This one, though, would be better plied to win your suit. I fear you will not have an easy time of it, Iain, and the more gifts you bring, the better."

Alienor came to the fire then, her features pale and her expression strained. "She has been most ill with the babe," Duncan informed the frowning man beside him. "Perhaps your plea will be better received in her moment of weakness."

But Iain did not share his smile. "Aye. One must seize whatever advantage can be had with Alienor." He swallowed, his expression as he studied Alienor telling more than enough of his intent. Then he bowed low before them. "I thank you both, for more than I can name."

"And we wish you well," Duncan declared, feeling the man needed a word to bolster his confidence. He held Eglantine tighter, feeling quite parental as Iain made his way to his intended. Delight lit Alienor's features before she summoned a haughty expression.

"He will win her yet, I know he will," Duncan insisted, as if his own force of will would make it so.

"Aye," Eglantine agreed, slanting him a knowing glance that made his heart skip before she indicated the couple again. "Look."

Iain fell on one knee before Alienor whose expression softened. He spoke quickly and urgently, unaware of those who halted to watch. Alienor began to flush, her glance flicking to those who listened, then back to Iain.

Then she reached to take the pin and smiled, ever so slightly.

"Aha!" Duncan murmured.

"Oh, I had not a doubt of his success," Eglantine said softly. "The men in these parts are most tenacious and persuasive." She smiled quickly then, as if she enjoyed a secret jest, and Duncan dared to be encouraged. .

"Are they?" he asked, pulling her into his arms to ensure she did not step away.

"Aye." Her gaze danced over his features and her smile faded. "You believed that he had destroyed the stores?"

"Aye. 'Twas wicked of me, but I did."

"Why did you let me believe you guilty instead?"

Duncan shrugged. "He is my foster brother and Cormac entrusted his welfare to my responsibility. I had hoped that one day he would admit to his error himself." He grinned. "Though it might have served me better if he had done so sooner, 'tis clear why he did not confess."

"He did not do it." Eglantine chewed her bottom lip. "Do you know this place he mentioned?"

"Aye, the tree is distinctive. But if the trunk was empty then . . ."

"It has a false bottom," Eglantine said crisply. "I would find it to be certain that the coin is truly lost."

They slipped around the perimeter of the camp, easily avoiding the notice of others as all gazes were fixed on Alienor and Iain. Duncan seized Eglantine's hand and led her to the tree Iain had described, then bent to rummage through the undergrowth.

His knuckles encountered the cold brass in but a moment. He dragged the chest into the faint light from the fire, grunting at its weight. He and Eglantine stood one to each side so that what little light there was could shine into the box. The wood was damp, though the chest was well made and its lid tightly fitted. The inside was fairly dry.

'Twas empty at first glance, but Eglantine bent and slipped her fingernail into one corner. The bottom was false, as she had said, and its removal revealed the glint of gold.

She looked up at him in confusion. "Why would anyone steal the gold simply to abandon it?"

Duncan shook his head and glanced back toward the

camp. One figure stood straight as a sentinel, watching them. He sighed and strode closer, rubbing his brow with his fingertips.

"I feared this would happen," Louis said quietly. "But I had no chance to move the chest since my return from that heathen court."

Eglantine straightened. "You destroyed the stores."

"Only enough to frighten you. I was certain you would show your father's splendid good sense and return immediately to France, if food was short." The older man half smiled. "You are far more stubborn, my lady, than I guessed."

"But you are sworn in fealty to my house!" Eglantine protested. She was clearly appalled by this breach of faith, and Duncan could understand her disappointment. "How could you in good conscience jeopardize the welfare of so many?"

The older man cleared his throat. "I might ask you the same thing, my lady. This journey was folly, your insistence upon remaining even more so. You jeopardized their welfare. I merely tried to save them."

"You have breached the trust of my father and my family, Louis."

"Nay, my lady. I have kept your father's trust. 'Twas he who so eloquently impressed upon me the import of the greater good."

The two eyed each other, their views as irreconcilable as might be imagined.

Eglantine straightened, showing the poise and dignity of a queen. "You are dismissed from the employ of my household, Louis. I assume that you will return to France, and if you so request it, I shall compose a letter to my brother explaining matters. It is not unlikely that he will find a post for you at Crevy, in deference to my father's commitment to you."

She spoke tonelessly, her manner official even though Duncan could sense her anger. But she had no need of a disloyal man in her household—and Duncan was proud of the grace she showed in this dismissal.

"You may take a palfrey and some few supplies, Louis. Whichever vassals so choose to return to France are welcome to travel with you, provided that their loyalty and explanations are offered first to my brother. Are we understood?"

Louis bowed low. "They should all return with me."

"You may be assured that they will not."

"I shall leave with first light." He surrendered what keys remained in his possession, though truly they were few, then bowed again and returned to the camp. Eglantine watched him go, her fingers slipping over the keys.

"You have known him long?"

"All my life. My father chose him to be my châtelain."

"He served you poorly." Duncan slipped an arm around her waist.

"My father undoubtedly would not agree." They stood in silence for a few moments, then she sighed, clearly dismissing the matter from her thoughts. "Did you know of Iain's role in creating that deed?"

"I learned the truth at the same moment as you."

Eglantine smiled up at him and Duncan's heart thumped. "Aye, you said you had not lied to me." She turned to look after the pair, the firelight gilding her fine features. "Did you know he would do this?"

"I knew he had the skill, and when Alienor spurned him, I hoped he had the desire." Her gaze met his once more. "I did not know, Eglantine, but I hoped with all my heart and soul."

She framed his face in her hands, the glow in her eyes most warm. "Once I called you a barbarian, Duncan MacLaren."

"More than once."

Eglantine chuckled along with him. "Aye, more than once." She regarded him steadily, her smile fading as her eyes darkened with intent. "But I was wrong. You are the most thoughtful and loving man that ever I have known. Truly, you make the king's own courtiers appear vulgar in comparison."

Duncan's heart clenched and he was certain the sweet confession he desired most to hear would now fall from his lady's lips. He could not breathe, he could not look away from the heat in his lady's gaze.

But the clatter of hoofbeats rose from the hills in this most inopportune moment. All turned to strain their eyes against the cloak of the darkness. The hoofbeats grew louder, and despite the fog Duncan discerned that there were three beasts. A man laughed with abandon, then cried something in French.

Eglantine frowned, taking a step away from him. "It cannot be," she whispered, clearly hoping 'twas.

Before Duncan could ask, a knight in full splendor burst into the circle of the firelight. His horse reared at the periphery of the camp, the knight's cloak flared, the firelight glinted off his helm.

He rode a stallion larger and more ebony of hue than any Duncan had ever seen, his trappings were rich, and his garb fairly screamed his high station. Two squires appeared out of the darkness behind them, each wearing more of value upon his back than Duncan had ever had to his name.

The knight doffed his helm and shook out his hair, revealing his handsome features. His beast stamped impatiently and fought the bit, though the knight's gloved hand was tight on the reins.

"Is this the abode of Eglantine, widow of Theobald de Mayneris and sister of Guillaume de Crevy-sur-Seine?" he demanded in French. "Is this the holding of Kinbeath?"

"Burke de Montvieux!" Eglantine cried, the name striking ice into Duncan's heart. "'Tis indeed you!"

With evident delight, she ran toward the new arrival.

Duncan's blood ran cold as the knight smoothly dismounted and caught Eglantine close, kissing her cheeks as they both grinned like fools. This knight not only represented all she had left behind, but he was the one whose affections Eglantine had once tried to win.

And suddenly Eglantine's refusal to confess any tender feelings for Duncan made far more sense. Her heart was already granted, though she had never expected this knight to return her affections.

This knight's riding all the way to Ceinn-beithe could mean only one thing. Duncan would lose all he sought to gain and be compelled to watch victory snatched from his grip.

In his darkest moment, Duncan felt Esmeraude's tiny hand close on his knee. He instinctively took her hand, but still stared after Eglantine like a man struck to stone.

Indeed, his worst nightmare had not only been made flesh but had come to Ceinn-beithe a heartbeat too soon.

◼

Burke did not recognize the woman who raced toward him. She was garbed simply though practically. The wool of her kirtle, though once of fine quality, was worn and the hem was dirtied. Her hair was caught back in a simple braid and she wore no veil. She wore no jewelry, not so much as a circlet or a ring. Her complexion was tanned so gold that she might have been a peasant.

But when she spoke, he knew. Eglantine's voice was unmistakable.

As was her concern for others.

"Burke!" She raced toward him, her expression one of mingled delight and concern. "What news of Brigid? Has she had the child? Is she well, is the babe well? How does Guillaume fare? And is my mother ill this winter?"

Burke dismounted and caught her close, kissing her cheeks to silence her. "Aye, Eglantine, 'tis good to see you, as well."

"Burke!"

"I had never thought to be welcomed solely as a source of news."

"You must tell me immediately."

Burke let his gaze flick over her, content to tease his friend's sister a little bit. Aye, they had tormented her a great deal more when they all were children. "You have changed, Eglantine, though you look well enough. Does this place suit you?"

She gripped his hands and looked as if she would love naught better than to give him a shake. "Burke! You cannot have ridden this far merely to chastise me my poor manners. Tell me the news this moment or I shall make you regret it."

He laughed then and looked deeply into her eyes, urging her to believe him. "All are fine." Her shoulders sagged in relief. "Brigid granted Guillaume a fine son, though the babe was almost too large for her. I fear she waited overlong for her spouse's return."

Though Burke sought to make a jest, Eglantine paled and her grip tightened on his hands. "She is fine, you are certain of it?"

"Aye. Alys and I arrived in time that Alys aided in the birth."

Eglantine exhaled shakily and laid her brow upon his shoulder. "Thank you, Burke. Thank you for this news. I have been so worried for them." She looked up. "And my mother?"

"Seeks to feed the new babe the honeycombs Brigid so favors."

They smiled at each other as relief flooded Eglantine's eyes.

"They miss you, Eglantine. They would know why you fled."

She brushed a suspicious glimmer from her eyes and stepped away. "Guillaume knows the truth of it, for I spoke to him of it oft enough."

"Is that why you took so much from his treasury? Because he denied your will in some matter?"

Eglantine slanted Burke a glance that nigh sliced to his bones. "Is that what you all believe of me?"

"I do not know what to believe." Burke shrugged. "I know only that Guillaume asked me to seek you out, to ensure that you were well. And, Eglantine, I know that you must have had good reason for what you have done."

Eglantine visibly gritted her teeth. "I took what I deemed necessary to survive in this remote place," she said tightly. "For I had not the luxury of failing."

"Jacqueline," Burke guessed.

"Aye. Jacqueline." Eglantine lifted her chin and her eyes glittered with defiance. "Do you come to criticize more than my manners? If you mean to take my daughter back to that wretched Reynaud, I shall fight you and you will lose."

Burke was shocked by this claim, no less by her open display of passion, but Eglantine had always been protective of those she loved.

"Nay, Eglantine." Burke shook his head and touched her chin, knowing he should not have been surprised by what she would sacrifice for her child. "Never that. I but come for news. Guillaume said he would pay the forfeit with but a word of confirmation from you—and assurance that all are well."

"He might have paid it before."

"I do not think he understood how strongly you felt of the matter." But looking at her, Burke could not imagine how any could doubt the truth of it.

Eglantine held his gaze for a long moment, as if assuring herself that there was no censure to be found there, then suddenly her eyes narrowed. "But how did you know where to seek us out?"

Burke grinned. "Your mother."

Eglantine was horrified and her eyes flashed with such vigor that Burke took a step back. "She swore secrecy! She pledged it to me on my father's grave."

Burke hastened to reassure her even as he wondered what had happened to the cool and composed Eglantine he once had known. "The tale was not easily won, Eglantine. She surrendered the truth of it only to Guillaume and myself."

"No others know of it?"

"Nay. I swear it to you."

Wariness dawned in her expression. "But one cannot trust knights not to support each other, particularly when the king's law rests on their side." Eglantine suddenly looked much less welcoming. "Why truly did you come, Burke?"

"I came to lay your family's fears to rest, no more than that." Burke returned her stare with resolve. "And I give you my most solemn pledge that none will hear of this place or its location, not from me or my squires."

"And Guillaume?"

"He sends his pledge that he will pay the forfeit. You have only to give me your word that 'tis your desire."

"'Tis yours, have no doubt of that." Eglantine took a step away. "But where are my manners?" she asked none in particular. "Xavier, might you take the chevalier's steed? And, Gunther, a cup for our guest." She turned and lifted her hands. "Jacqueline! Alienor! You should recall Burke de

Montvieux well enough. Come and give your greetings to our guest."

When the girls did not make an immediate appearance, Burke surveyed the company for the first time. He was surprised by their number. When he looked more closely, many of the faces were familiar, for there were vassals here who had served the Crevy family all their lives. Again, he would not have known them had he not looked carefully, for they all wore the mark of living in the sun and wind.

But they looked oddly contented.

Burke wondered whether they all would return with him to Crevy, now that Eglantine was reassured of her brother's commitment to her cause. As much as he desired to assuage his friend's concerns, such a company would move slowly, too slowly for Burke's purposes.

He wanted to be home with Alys, and that sooner rather than later.

Burke smiled politely as he accepted a chalice brimming with ale of pale gold and doffed his gloves. There was no sign of either girl despite Eglantine's summons, and the lady's cheeks colored. She apologized to Burke and he shrugged off the slight, seeing that she would not forget the matter so readily as that.

"Ah, there is Esmeraude," Eglantine said crisply.

'Twas when Burke followed the lady's gaze that he first saw the savage man glaring at him. The man's anger was so tangible that it could not be directed at a stranger. Burke glanced over his shoulder before he could stop himself.

But no one stood behind him. Even his squires had moved away with the horses, one carrying his helm. He stood alone against the shadows of the distant hills.

Which meant the man glared at *him*.

Burke stared back, uncertain what he could have done in such short order to win such animosity. Indeed, the man looked as if he needed no invitation to rip Burke's hide from his bones.

And truly, he was tall enough and broad enough likely to accomplish the task with ease. He was dressed in the garb of these Scots, dark of hair and silver of eye, a length of wool wound round his hips and cast over his shoulder. His legs were bare and solidly muscled; the knife in his belt looked crude but effective.

"Esmeraude, please come and greet our guest." Eglantine smiled for the child and offered her hand. "You may not recall Burke, but he is a great friend of your uncle Guillaume."

"Nay!" The toddler pouted with a defiance that put Burke in mind of his own young son. He sipped from his cup to hide his smile. Aye, he and Alys had rued the day Bayard learned the word "nay," for the boy employed it in response to all queries.

"Esmeraude! I but ask you to greet a guest, as any young lady of merit should do."

"Nay." The toddler stuck out her tongue at her mother and hid behind the knees of the rough man who had taken such an immediate dislike to Burke.

This indeed was interesting. The child was unafraid of him.

The man offered his index finger to Esmeraude, who clutched it, completely without fear. Indeed, she seemed to expect him to champion her cause against Eglantine. He said something to her, but she shook her head and hovered stubbornly behind him. Eglantine made a low sound of frustration, and Burke was so surprised that she showed any visible signs of emotion that he nearly choked on his ale.

Eglantine, the icy maiden of the court, showed her passions so readily as this? More than the hue of her skin had changed!

He watched in amazement. The man dropped to a crouch beside Esmeraude as if he had all the time in Christendom. He touched the child's chin with surprising gentleness and spoke to her, the low rumble of his voice incomprehensible to Burke at this distance.

Esmeraude huddled beside him, her expression uncertain as she eyed Burke. 'Twas clear this man tried to persuade the child to follow her mother's request—and just as clear that Esmeraude had no interest in the plan.

"They have a rare determination at this age," Burke said to Eglantine. She was probably embarrassed, as Alys tended to be when Bayard did not heed such seemingly simple requests.

Eglantine folded her arms across her chest and watched the child. "If you will forgive me such plain speech, 'tis a relief at least that she no longer embraces every man to cross her path. 'Twould have been troubling indeed for her to hold that habit another decade."

Again Burke feared to choke on his ale, so surprised was he by this blunt conclusion. Eglantine thumped his back with such vigor that he was even more astonished by her familiarity, a fact that did naught to ease his woes.

When he had recovered himself sufficiently to look up, she was laughing at him. "Oh, Burke, you look like a fish cast from the water."

Burke felt his eyes round at this assessment. What had happened to Eglantine in this place? And what had put that twinkle in her eyes?

Of even greater concern, that rough man was striding toward him, a wary Esmeraude holding fast to his shoulder. The little girl was delighted, clearly having won her way in persuading her champion to escort her.

But Burke's tentative smile was wiped away when he noted the murderous gleam still lurking in that man's eyes.

"Eglantine, I beg of you." Burke spoke quickly, while he yet had the chance. "Tell this man I intend no harm to any of you, and that before he chooses to harm me. Tell him I am innocent of whatever crime he would hold me guilty."

The lady laughed, a response that only made this ruffian's countenance darken further. She then turned to the man who carried her child. She introduced Duncan MacLaren with the grace Burke recalled, evidently unaware of the animosity that emanated from the man.

'Twas only when Eglantine hastened away and Duncan's gaze followed her that Burke understood.

Of course. How could he have been so witless? He had pursued Eglantine all the way from France—or so it would appear to one who desired the lady's favor—and this man clearly was smitten with Eglantine.

Fortunately, the misunderstanding could readily be resolved.

Burke smiled and lifted his left hand so that his wedding ring caught the light. "You have naught with which to concern yourself," he said reassuringly. "I am already wed."

Disgust crossed Duncan's features and he set Esmeraude on the ground. "And still you come to court Eglantine?" he demanded, taking a menacing step closer as he scowled. "You noblemen are all the same, seeing naught but your own desires and caring naught for the damage left in your wake!" He flung out his hands and Burke was alarmed at the size of him. "'Tis no wonder the woman cannot imagine a man would treat her well!"

Duncan's voice rose to a bellow that drew the eye of every soul on that holding. "How dare you so dishonor not only the woman whose ring you wear but my lady Eglantine?"

Burke managed to make no defense of himself, however eloquent, before pain exploded in his cheek. He fell backward at the force of the blow and landed most ignobly on his butt.

His squires cried out and drew their blades as they ran toward him. Meanwhile, the cup Burke had held flew skyward. The ale sprinkled down upon the fallen knight even as he stared up at his infuriated assailant. Burke held up a hand to halt his squires, well aware that the entire company watched the proceedings.

Duncan's hands clenched as he glared at Burke, and clearly he longed to finish the task he had begun. Burke knew that one wrong move or word would set the man upon him in truth. He fingered his cheek and considered his choices carefully.

"Boom," said Esmeraude, then clapped her hands and giggled at her own assessment. When no one paid attention to her, she pouted, then lost interest in the two men and toddled away.

Then they both heard the approach of a clearly displeased Eglantine.

Jacqueline was terrified by the knight's arrival.

On, she knew that her uncle Guillaume was opposed to ending her match with Reynaud, for she had listened at the door while her mother argued in favor of breaking that betrothal. And she had heard Guillaume insist upon the sanctity of a contract.

She knew that Burke de Montvieux was her uncle's closest friend, and she guessed immediately why he had come. Who else would her uncle send to collect a wayward niece? Who else but a knight of honor and repute, a friend who could be trusted and a man well known to keep his word?

Who else indeed.

But Jacqueline would not go. Nay, not she. If her mother could break the law, then so could she, and break it she most surely would.

Jacqueline disappeared into the assembly, taking advantage of the long shadows of evening. She ignored her mother's call, knowing that Eglantine could only welcome a family friend. Perhaps her mother even trusted Burke to see her own view. Jacqueline snorted to herself. If so, Eglantine would be glad that Jacqueline had run once she ascertained that knight's mission here.

But Duncan would help her, Jacqueline knew this to be so. He would help her even if her mother could not. Aye, Duncan believed in love and justice beyond that of the king's law, for he sang of such matters all the time.

Jacqueline trusted Duncan, as she could never trust anyone who came from Crevy. She would fetch her heaviest cloak and her sturdiest boots, she would steal some bread from the hearth, she would find Duncan later this evening and request his aid in fleeing Ceinn-beithe. Her mother would applaud her choice once she had confirmed Burke's intent. Her mother would be proud that Jacqueline had been sensible enough to not flee into the wilds alone.

All were gathered near the fire, or in the new hall. Jacqueline ran toward the tents, hopeful that she would not be noticed. She was glad of the shadows between the rustling walls of silk and slipped around the back of her own tent to ensure that she would not be seen. Her heart was hammering with the boldness of what she would do. She strained her ears but heard naught beyond the distant sounds of merriment.

Much relieved, she slipped into her tent and took a deep breath. Her first goal was accomplished and, in a matter of moments, she would be on her way. With shaking fingers Jacqueline struck a flint and lit the smallest lantern, vowing to let it burn as short a time as possible.

When she straightened, her breath caught in fear.

"How charming of you to come to me," Reynaud said with a smirk. He was every bit as old and wrinkled as she recalled, and his eyes were as cold as ever. He stood, his arms folded across his chest, his boots spattered with mud. "Perhaps you were not so reluctant for our match as I had believed."

Jacqueline dropped the lantern and spun to flee. She ran into a hard wall of muscle and a pair of arms closed around her like steel bands. She struggled, to no discernible effect. Reynaud must have picked up the lantern, for she heard it being settled on the small table.

"Very good," he said quietly.

Jacqueline was pushed back into the center of the tent by Reynaud's very large squire. The man grinned stupidly down at her, then gave her a shove that nearly made her lose her footing. Reynaud's gloved hands closed possessively over her shoulders from behind and Jacqueline gasped as he kissed her nape.

"What a delight to finally hold the treasure owed to me for so long."

Revulsion rose in Jacqueline and she twisted against him. His gloved fingers dug more deeply into her skin and the squire smiled, as if he anticipated hurting her, as well.

Knowing she was lost and desperate to make a difference, Jacqueline tipped her head back and screamed. She kicked with vigor, hoping she could somehow escape.

Reynaud swore and clamped his hand over her mouth before the sound had barely left her mouth. He cast her to the bed, and Jacqueline rolled quickly, hoping to flee. But Reynaud was larger and faster than she. He settled his weight atop her, easily holding her wrists in one hand as she fought him.

"Perhaps we shall settle this matter immediately," he said silkily. "So that there can be no question to whom you belong."

Jacqueline's eyes widened in horror at what he meant to

do, but Reynaud's features settled into harsh lines. He flicked a glance at his squire. "See that we are not disturbed, if you please. This will not take long."

The squire bowed and stepped outside the tent, abandoning Jacqueline to Reynaud and a very certain fate.

Chapter Seventeen

DUNCAN MACLAREN, HOW DARE YOU TREAT MY GUEST in this way?"

Could anything else go awry? Both girls were missing, Esmeraude had chosen again to be defiant, there was only simple fare this night and thin ale to be had. Eglantine was embarrassed enough that Burke might find her hospitality lacking.

And that without Duncan blackening the man's eye.

Though Burke seemed to take the incident with his usual grace, Eglantine was not so inclined to let it pass without comment.

"How dare you?" she demanded of Duncan, who merely glowered at her. "How could you greet a guest with your fist?"

"How could he come to court you with another woman's ring upon his hand?" Duncan demanded hotly. "What of the insult to you? If you imagine, Eglantine, that I shall stand aside while another man of Theobald's ilk treats you poorly, you are sadly mistaken."

Though his words clearly were heartfelt, they made no sense to Eglantine. "Burke is wed," she said carefully. "He does not come to court me."

Duncan turned a glare upon Burke, who fingered his cheek and watched them. "He is the one who spurned you before."

"He is the one who counseled me on the merits of love."

"That he might share your charms," Duncan charged heatedly.

"Nay! That I might dare to seek the charms of love."

Duncan studied her carefully. "Then why is he here?"

"My brother sends him to ensure my welfare." Eglantine smiled. "No more than that."

Duncan was not to be so readily persuaded. "You greeted him with affection. You fairly leapt into his embrace!"

"Aye, Duncan." Eglantine slipped her hand through his elbow, touched that he would defend her so ardently. "He is an old friend of our family and I feared for the pregnancy of my brother's bride. Burke brings good news, no more than that."

"Aye?"

"Aye. Perhaps you might trust me in this."

Duncan heaved a sigh. "Then I owe him an apology." He offered his hand to Burke, who hesitated only a moment before accepting aid in rising. "I apologize for my blow, but I thought you of Theobald's ilk."

Burke smiled wryly. "'Tis unfortunate that you had no opportunity to grant him personally what he so roundly deserved."

"Are you sorely injured?" Eglantine asked anxiously.

"'Tis not the first blow I have taken, nor will it be the last." Burke grinned. "With fortune, 'twill heal before my Alys has the chance to comment upon it."

Duncan seemed amused by this. "She will have much to say?"

Burke rolled his eyes. "Oh, indeed." The two men grinned at each other, now in perfect understanding, and Eglantine shook her head.

"Might we show some convention of hospitality?" she asked, disliking the sense that this camaraderie was bought at the expense of herself and Alys. "The meal is hot, if you would do us the honor of joining us at our humble board, Burke."

"I should be delighted," he said, bowing low as if unaware of the hues already blossoming upon his cheek.

Eglantine turned expectantly to Duncan, but he hesitated. His gaze was troubled. "Nay, Eglantine, I will not come without your answer."

"My answer?" Eglantine echoed. She felt Burke halt and turn to watch, but could not look away from the blaze in Duncan's eyes.

"Aye." Duncan frowned, then shoved a hand through his hair before he appealed to her once more. "No obstacles remain between us, Eglantine. You know I am innocent of the crimes you held against me. I have courted your favor these months, I have sought to win you for my own. I have wooed you and I have repeatedly pledged my love." He held her gaze steadily. "And through all of my endeavors, you accepted what I granted yet offered naught in return."

Eglantine swallowed, her fear rising cold within her.

"I would have your answer, Eglantine. I would know whether my labors are wasted. I would know whether your heart is mine to claim."

"I have nigh ten months left to choose," she insisted, her heart pounding fit to burst. "I will answer you when 'tis a year and a day from our handfast."

But Duncan shook his head heavily. "Nay, Eglantine. I cannot endure in this way, uncertain of your favor and our future. I cannot lay abed wondering whether my seed is planted in your belly, wondering what you would do if it took root. I cannot fear that you will leave, that you love another, that all I have to have to offer is not enough.

"You know all of me there is to know." He stepped closer

and cupped her face in his hands. "I ask for only three words, Eglantine, a pledge of three words from the depths of your soul, and never will I ask you for more."

Eglantine stared up at Duncan and her mouth went dry.

She realized that she loved him. Indeed, she loved Duncan as she had never imagined she might love a man. She loved his passion and tenderness, the way he sang and the way he roared, she loved his protectiveness and his laughter and his unpredictability. Eglantine had never imagined that true love might warm her heart, but here 'twas—unsought and unexpected and undeniable all the same.

She wondered what he saw in her eyes, for a fire lit in the depths of his own. He leaned closer, his voice dropping low.

"Tell me, Eglantine," he urged, his thumbs caressing her skin. "Tell me that you love me, or bid me leave. Tell me now and leave no doubts between us."

Eglantine wanted to tell him, she truly did. She parted her lips, but fear stole her voice away. What if all went awry as soon as she uttered those words? What if she confessed her heart's desire and Duncan exploited her weakness, as Theobald had done?

She could not believe it, and her instinct urged her to confess, but Eglantine knew her instincts were faulty.

She dared not trust them, not again.

Eglantine closed her eyes and looked down, away from Duncan's burning gaze. "I cannot," she whispered, fully expecting him to roar in fury.

But he said naught.

She waited, dreading his response, but there was none. Duncan's hands fell from her face, the loss of his touch leaving her shivering with cold. He stepped back and she dared to glance toward him, only to find him looking more defeated than ever she had believed he could.

"Then that is answer enough," he said quietly. "I tried and

I have failed, for whatever I might offer was not sufficient for you." He held her gaze grimly, the flicker of the firelight making him look more remote than ever he had. She was reminded of the cold stones, immovable and alien, that stood in the roads and fields of this land. She was struck as she had been on their first encounter that he was wrought of something different than she.

He touched two fingertips to his lips, flicking a kiss her way. "Farewell, Eglantine."

And against her every expectation, Duncan MacLaren turned and strode into the shadows of the night.

Eglantine looked after him in astonishment, for she had never thought he might leave her. The night swallowed him quickly, as surely as if he had never been. Eglantine heard the sea crashing upon the shore, she heard the wail of the wind, but she could hear Duncan's footfalls no longer.

He was gone.

The first sound to break from the company was Esmeraude's wail of frustration. She ran from the back of the assembly to halt where Duncan had last stood. And she cried his name, stretching out her arms in entreaty. The sound tore at Eglantine's heart, and the household huddled together whispering.

Eglantine stepped forward and lifted Esmeraude, fighting against her own tears. She bounced the child and tried to console her.

"Duncan!" Esmeraude wrapped one hand around her mother's neck, though she stretched one hand after Duncan.

She could not tell the child that Duncan was gone. She could not say the words, for that would make his departure more of a reality than Eglantine desired. So she made nonsense sounds and hummed to her daughter. But no matter how Eglantine turned, Esmeraude looked after the man who had sung to her so many times. Esmeraude buried her face in

Eglantine's neck and wept noisily, finally taking solace from her thumb.

Eglantine glanced up to find Burke's gaze upon her and knew she had shown him a poor welcome this night. "I must apologize, Burke. You find our household in less that ideal circumstance."

"No apology is needed," Burke said with his customary grace. "'Tis sufficient to know that you and yours are well."

"How is Alys?" Eglantine asked belatedly, refusing to look into the darkness behind her, to wonder whether Duncan would return.

Surely he could not be gone for good?

Surely she could not have lost him in truth?

Eglantine hated that she did not know. She would never have anticipated that his conviction to win her had any limit, but his expression before he strode away had been eloquent.

And the dread she had felt of showing her weakness was a mere shadow compared to the consuming fear that she would never see Duncan MacLaren again.

Burke smiled, the expression making him look much younger and less stern. "Alys is well enough, though she will have my hide if I am not home before our second child is due." He did not appear too troubled about this threat, and Eglantine forced a smile in turn.

"Your son must be getting tall," she said, feeling 'twas a hopelessly inane comment but knowing she should make conversation with her guest.

Burke set his chalice aside and leaned forward, propping his elbows upon his knees. "Eglantine, once upon a time, I told you of the power of the love that can blossom between a man and a woman."

"Aye, you told me of Alys."

"Aye, I hoped to inspire you to seek better for yourself than what you had clearly been granted with Robert." Exasperation crossed his features. "You have always been so practical, Eglantine. I could not believe when I heard that you were wedded to Theobald de Mayneris, for all the world knew that he was a worthless knave." Burke's eyes narrowed. "I thought, as many others likely did, that you had reformed him, that you typically had wrought gold from dross."

Eglantine shook her head and hugged Esmeraude closer. "Not I."

"Nay, I know that now." Burke watched her closely. "He used you sorely, Eglantine, and I fear that my counsel led you astray."

"Nay, Burke. 'Twas naught but my own poor judgment at root."

But the knight shook his head and spoke with resolve. "Nay, Eglantine. I have no doubt that Theobald set deliberately to deceive you and, similarly, I would wager that he insisted that you wed quickly. Even he would have discerned that you could not be fooled for long."

Eglantine managed a thin smile. "It matters little, now that he is gone."

Burke shook his head. "Nay, it matters greatly if you measure all men against Theobald's shortfalls."

Eglantine caught her breath. Should she have admitted the truth and told Duncan what he desired to hear?

Would he have stayed by her side if she had? Would he have continued to love her as he had done thus far?

Was he as different from Theobald in this one way as in all others?

Burke reached to wipe the last of Esmeraude's tears, then met Eglantine's gaze steadily. "You have always been a woman of good sense, Eglantine. Never would I have imagined that a child of two summers would show more astute judgment than you."

"I have no good instincts when it comes to men," she argued weakly. "'Twas that at root of my match with Theobald."

Burke arched a brow. "Aye? And what is your instinct in this moment?"

Eglantine looked at her child. She knew with sudden clarity that she could not let Duncan leave her side. She loved him, beyond reason and belief, and could not imagine awakening without him at her side.

"I could lose him," she whispered, the words sending a chill down her spine.

Burke nodded impatiently. "If you have not already. That was a man with tolerance expired, if ever I have seen one. What does your heart tell you to do, Eglantine?"

She swallowed. "To follow Duncan. To persuade him to listen." She smiled uncertainly. "To confess my love."

Burke smiled and lifted Esmeraude from her arms. "As I said, Eglantine, you have always been a woman of splendid good sense."

Esmeraude chose that moment to wail anew, and Eglantine was torn between the new bond forged between they two and her desire to chase Duncan.

But Burke bounced Esmeraude on his knee with the confidence of a man who had soothed toddlers before. "Esmeraude, if your mother goes to fetch Duncan, would you be so kind as to wait with me?"

The little girl considered him in silence, sucking her thumb with rare diligence. Though Eglantine wished the child would hasten her choice, Burke seemed to understand her need for reassurance.

"'Tis the strangest thing, Esmeraude, but I have a son a bit bigger than you. On this journey, I miss him terribly." He leaned closer to confide this, and Eglantine almost laughed to see Esmeraude respond so predictably to his charm.

She preened coyly and Burke smiled. "Indeed, there is a

tale I always tell him in the evening, though I have not re-counted it for over a month. I fear I might forget and oh, he would be sorely disappointed in me." Burke snapped his fingers as though struck by a thought. "Might I tell it to you instead? Would you listen and tell me whether it still seems a good tale?"

Esmeraude's features lit up and she eyed the knight expectantly. "Tell me a story. Now." She did not cuddle close to him as she did with Duncan, but she clearly was contented enough to remain.

"Oh, Burke, I thank you for this." Eglantine's hands rose to her hair and she realized she was in no state to plead with a man to remain forever by her side.

"Go," Burke insisted, then he smiled with a confidence Eglantine was far from feeling. "Duncan will see naught but the stars in your eyes."

Eglantine ran first to the shore where the boats were pulled up and could not discern whether they all were there or not. She scanned the sea, cursing the lack of a moon, but could not tell whether a man had rowed away recently or not.

But this accomplished naught!

She pushed her fingertips to her temples and willed herself to think. Where would Duncan go?

To the great rock of his forebears. No other place would do.

Unless he had left completely. Eglantine's fear lent speed to her steps, and she ran toward the rock. She cursed the mist that hid it from her view. She would cut through the camp and thus save time, though she would have to watch her step. She lunged into the shadows between the tents, praying that she would arrive in time.

Then a woman screamed, the sound cut off too soon.

Jacqueline! Eglantine's footsteps faltered, for only one thing could have prompted her tranquil daughter to scream.

Or more accurately, one person. God in heaven, but Burke had led Reynaud directly here. Again she was torn between duty and desire, but there was no choice. She had to save her daughter, whatever the cost to herself.

Eglantine crept toward the three silken tents, grateful for the sea's waves breaking on the rocks behind her. It would cover the sound of her approach. She hugged the shadows, her heart in her mouth, and eased her way closer, one careful step at a time.

She halted in view of the entry to Jacqueline's tent. A huge man sat there, cleaning his nails with his dagger. His familiar bulk was far from reassuring, for the presence of Reynaud's squire confirmed Reynaud's presence.

There was no doubt that this one's master was inside the tent. Who knew what he had already done, or what Jacqueline had suffered! Eglantine fought her desire to hasten and forced herself to proceed one careful step at a time.

The squire looked bored, a remarkable feat for one so slow of wit as this one. Only at such proximity could Eglantine hear the muted sounds of struggle, and she feared what her daughter endured.

She crouched while she thought, and her hand closed around a rock roughly the shape and size of a goose egg. She gauged the distance to the squire as she weighed the stone in her hand. Eglantine deliberately recalled all the times she had skipped stones with Guillaume at Crevy and bested both him and Burke.

To hesitate was to be lost in such a moment. She stood up and flung the stone at the squire's brow.

It hit him square between the eyes. He made a small grunt at the impact, then fell bonelessly forward.

'Twas enough for Eglantine! She raced toward the tent, stepped hesitantly around the squire, then helped herself to the short dagger he no longer used. She plunged it into the back of her belt, squared her shoulders, and stepped regally into the tent.

"Good evening, Reynaud."

The knight started and turned, his move revealing his grip upon Jacqueline.

To Eglantine's immense relief, Jacqueline's skirts were only about her knees. Her kirtle was torn at the breast but Reynaud was still fully garbed. Her daughter was clearly terrified but as yet unhurt.

Eglantine intended to keep matters that way.

She smiled at the old knight's surprise. "How did you come to be here, Reynaud, without first enjoying the hospitality of our board? Surely you are hungered after your long journey."

Reynaud's smile flashed. "Dame Fortune smiled upon me and delivered my rightful due into my own hands. But three silk tents, three tents for three noblewomen. I had only just entered the first when this little bird flew directly to me." His smile faded. "And where is my squire?"

Eglantine feigned dismay. "He seems to have fallen ill, for he lies in a faint outside the tent."

The knight's eyes narrowed. The pair stared at each other, then Reynaud shrugged. "If you think your presence will persuade me to halt, you are wrong, Eglantine. I have no trouble with an audience."

In a lightning gesture, he folded Jacqueline's arms beneath her, behind her waist, then sat astride her once more. She had time to utter a cry of protest and no more before his hand was once again on her mouth. He now had a free hand, which he used to tear the front of her kirtle open further. Jacqueline's eyes widened in fear when his gloved hand closed over her bare flesh.

Eglantine wanted to wound him for abusing her child thus. She walked farther into the tent, well aware of the weight of the blade hidden from his view. She forced her tone to remain conversational, though 'twas not easily done. "Surely you would not taint your bride before your nuptials?"

"Surely it matters little. And this way I will ensure that you can do naught else with the girl but wed her to me."

"But 'tis not her fault we are here!"

Reynaud glanced up. "What is this?"

Eglantine fabricated the tale as she went, wishing she had half of Duncan's skill. "Jacqueline wanted to wed you, indeed she wanted to wed you even before Theobald fell ill. But she is such a prize that I wagered we could win more coin for her hand. Then I needed funds after Theobald's death, for he left me with naught. My brother would not see fit to demand more coin from you, but I was persuaded another might pay more for Jacqueline's charms."

She held his suspicious gaze, willing him to believe her lie. "I stole her away from you, Reynaud, though the girl desired naught but to do her duty. Your argument is with me alone."

"I will not pay more."

"Nor will any other, as I learned to my distress. All this trouble for naught." Eglantine shrugged. "Of course Jacqueline will wed you, as she desired to do so all along. Do not punish the child for the sins of the mother."

Reynaud shook his head stubbornly. "This cannot be so. She fought me this night, she fights me even now. You lie!"

"Nay, you frighten her. She is virginal, Reynaud, and unaccustomed to the needs of men. She has been sheltered all these years, and I failed to tell her of her marital due as yet. You have startled her, no more than that."

Reynaud's gaze slipped over her and Eglantine had a bold idea. She smiled and lifted one hand to the lace at the neck of her kirtle.

She loosed it slowly. "A virgin suits for a marriage bed and naught else," she said quietly. "Duty and the securing of property is one matter, while pleasure is quite another. I would wager you have been long without a woman, Reynaud, for you must have ridden hard from France's shores."

Eglantine took a step closer and pulled the lace free with a flick of her wrist. "I am no virgin, Reynaud, but I know how a man would be pleasured. You have been sorely inconvenienced, and this at my behest." Eglantine parted her kirtle and untied her chemise, noting how he stared at the shadow of her breasts visible through her chemise. She was but an arm's length away from him, nigh close enough to strike.

"Let me make amends to you. Take the toll for your inconvenience from me, for I alone am responsible for it," she invited huskily. "And leave the taking of Jacqueline for your nuptial bed."

Reynaud slowly smiled. "You always were a temptress, Eglantine. I knew you desired me when you were Robert's bride." He looked down at Jacqueline, his smile broadening. Eglantine had only a moment to believe he truly would fall for her ruse before he proved her wrong.

"Perhaps I shall have both of you this night."

He lunged for Eglantine, but she was prepared for him. She pulled his squire's dagger from the back of her belt and drove it at Reynaud's eyes. He cried out and snatched at her wrists. To her dismay, Eglantine was no match for his strength and skill. The blade fell harmlessly to the ground, but Eglantine stepped back, deliberately drawing him away from her daughter.

She saw the blur of Jacqueline rolling from the bed and knew the girl could not pass them without attracting Reynaud's ire. To her relief, Jacqueline caught up the blade and darted back over the bed. Eglantine heard the silk cut as

Reynaud twisted her arms behind her back. She knew her daughter was safe when his hand closed cruelly over her breast.

And he knew it, as well.

"Bitch!" he muttered in her ear. "Now you shall pay for your deception."

But Eglantine did not care what he did to her. Her every thought was with Jacqueline, urging her daughter to flee as fast and as far as she was able. She had to draw this out as long as possible, to better grant her daughter time to escape.

Eglantine spared Reynaud a knowing glance. "Robert always said you could only take a woman with haste." She sneered. "I see he was not far wrong in that."

Reynaud struck her across the face and she fell. But Eglantine rolled and propped herself up on her hands to survey him.

"A man like Robert, now, he could take a woman over and over until the very dawn." She smiled. "Ah, he had such vigor. For a man his age, 'twas remarkable."

"Robert died a decade my junior."

"Ah, his youth must have been why the memory of his fortitude lingers long." She mused as if she were not afraid. "I believe 'twas twenty times we took our pleasure one night. 'Twas then he told me of your haste. 'Twas true, Reynaud, I always lusted for you, but Robert's tales tempered my desire."

"You lie!" Reynaud stepped over her and gripped her chin, glaring down into her eyes. "But I shall take you twenty-one times all the same. You will remember me, Eglantine, not your dead Robert." He smiled coldly. "Indeed, you may never sit easily again."

Duncan knew he should not have left Eglantine in anger. He sat and glowered out to sea, irked beyond measure at her stubborn refusal to trust him, yet knowing he would return to her side like a moth dazzled by the flame. There was no question of him abandoning her, not before she spurned him in truth.

He should not have lost patience with her. He took a deep breath of the salt-tinged wind. He would walk and let his temper fade completely, then return to the gathering. With luck, she would be waiting for him. Duncan rose, cursing his own tendency to hope beyond expectation, then spun at the echo of running footsteps.

'Twas Jacqueline, her kirtle torn and her eyes wild. "Reynaud, 'tis Reynaud!" she cried, the name all too familiar. Duncan caught her when she might have stumbled, and she gasped for breath. "He attacked me but *Maman* heard him."

"And she offered herself in your stead," Duncan guessed, then swore with vigor when the girl nodded. "Where?"

"In my tent. His squire lies outside the door. I cut the silk at the back and ran and ran and ran." Jacqueline breathed heavily, her terror evident.

"You did well and I am glad you came to me." Duncan drew her kirtle closed and she flushed crimson even as he led her back toward the camp. "Now, go to this Burke and do not leave his side until I return. He will defend you."

"Nay, he brought Reynaud!"

"Nay, he came only to ensure you all were well. I would wager this one followed him." Duncan held the girl's gaze determinedly. "You have naught to fear from him, I swear it to you."

She nodded grimly, looking very much her mother's child. "Then I will go to him." She brandished a blade beneath his nose. "But I shall keep this at hand. He might have lied to you, Duncan. Men oft do."

Duncan escorted her as far as he dared, for time was of the essence. He watched Jacqueline step into the circle of firelight and make her way toward the knight.

He waited no longer than that. Duncan melted into the shadows, his anger rising as he heard Eglantine taunting another. She mocked the man's prowess, and Duncan winced at the sound of a blow falling.

But his Eglantine would do whatever was necessary to save her child. Duncan wished fiercely that one day he too might stand within the circle of his lady's protectiveness, realized 'twas a quest worth any price of pursuit, then took his blade and slashed the silk from top to bottom.

He stepped into the tent, his blade at the ready, and glared at the old knight perched atop Eglantine. "I have come to cut out your heart, Reynaud de Charmonte," he declared coldly, flicking a glance to his lady. A bruise stained her face and her kirtle was torn to her waist. The pleasure that lit her eyes so startled Duncan that 'twas almost his undoing.

But he would have recompense for that bruise.

The older man straightened, his expression turning grim. "Who are you?"

"I am Duncan MacLaren, chieftain of Clan MacQuarrie."

Reynaud sneered, his gaze traveling over Duncan's garb as he smoothed a hand over his own. "A mere savage!"

"A man who takes naught from a woman she does not willingly grant." Duncan smiled thinly. "I fear that you lack not only courtesy but a heart, Reynaud, regardless of your fine attire. Shall we discover the truth of it?"

Reynaud moved with startling speed, bounding to his feet and drawing his sword in a flash. He slashed at Duncan and Eglantine cried out, though Duncan parried in time.

But only just. The man struck again and again with astounding strength. He was agile for his age and driven by fury.

And he was trained, as Duncan was not.

Reynaud struck a trio of times in quick succession, then

paused. He swung unexpectedly from one side then the other. Duncan halted the blow that would have sliced his innards open and cast the blade back upon the older man with a grunt.

They soon were breathing heavily, those blows that went astray slashing the silk tent to ribbons. The lantern flickered as the chill wind from the sea found its way within. Duncan kept his gaze fixed upon the other man and struggled to anticipate his every move. He disliked the sense that he was only defending himself instead of attacking, but the other man's skill far outranked his own.

Which meant perhaps that Reynaud should readily win.

They circled each other, the sweat gathering on Duncan's brow at the boldness of his plan. Reynaud attacked again, his teeth bared, and Duncan took note of precisely where the man's mail tabard ended. Reynaud's throat was bare, which would suit Duncan well enough.

He deliberately moved too slowly and won a nick upon his thigh. Reynaud laughed, and Duncan pretended that the injury was worse than 'twas. He lifted his blade anew, as if 'twas not so readily done, and Reynaud was quick to engage once more.

His sword swung through the air and Duncan ducked, jabbing at the other man's legs. Reynaud darted back and swung his blade low. Duncan winced as it nicked his shoulder. Again he feigned greater injury than he had sustained and fell to one knee.

He groaned and gripped his shoulder as if 'twas sorely wounded. He dropped his knife, ensuring 'twas directly below him, then fell atop it.

And moved no more.

Reynaud laughed, then shoved Duncan with one booted foot. "And whose heart shall we see?" he murmured. Duncan heard the knight sheathe his sword. He peered between his lashes to see Reynaud draw a smaller blade with a jeweled hilt from his belt.

Duncan held his tongue, watching the man carefully. His hand was beneath him, by no accident, and his fingers closed around the hilt of his own blade. Silently he willed Reynaud closer.

"Sadly, you heathens do not fight that well, for all your size and vigor. I had so hoped you would show greater promise than this."

Reynaud raised the knife and bent to drive it into Duncan's chest. Duncan waited until the last moment to strike, but a weight fell suddenly across his back.

"Nay!" Eglantine cried, then she screamed as Reynaud's blade sank home. She must have hidden in the shadows, when Duncan thought she had fled for aid.

"Eglantine!" Duncan bounded to his feet with a roar that astonished the older knight. Reynaud grappled for his sword, but he was not quick enough. Duncan drove his own blade into the other man's throat, grunting as he drove it deeper into the chest.

"Just as I suspected," he muttered, as Reynaud sputtered before him. "There is naught but a stone where your heart should be." He forced the blade deep beneath the mail, then he cast the villain aside, leaving him to die unattended.

But Eglantine. Duncan fell to his knees beside her and turned her pale face to his. He pulled the jeweled blade from her shoulder and the warmth of her blood ran through his fingers. Duncan whispered her name and cradled her close. He could not lose her now! 'Twould be too cruel to be the reason for her demise.

He should not have wished to win her protectiveness; he would never have done so if he had realized this would be the price. Duncan kissed her brow and held her tightly even as he whispered her name once more.

And Eglantine opened her eyes. She smiled at him and raised one hand to touch his face. Her fingers shook and Duncan closed his hand around hers.

"I do not intend to die, Duncan. Not so soon after I have found you." She swallowed and her smile broadened. "'Tis naught but my shoulder that is wounded and 'twill heal. The blow did, though, steal the wind from me."

Relief fed Duncan's anger and he rose to his feet, his lady cradled in his arms. "You should never have taken such a risk! What possesses you to believe that you alone are responsible for solving the woes of all around you?" he demanded, even as he strode toward the company and some aid. "What foolery made you risk your own hide for me?"

Eglantine laughed softly and kicked her feet. Her manner was entirely inappropriate, to Duncan's thinking, though he loved the way she leaned her cheek against his heart.

"He could have killed you! He could have injured you more sorely than this! What then of your daughters and your obligations? Why, if you were not wounded, I should give you a shake fit to rattle your bones!"

"I could not let him kill you, Duncan." Eglantine's voice was low but thrummed with such conviction that Duncan fell silent. He looked into her eyes and found love shining there so brightly that the sight nigh stole his breath away. She raised trembling fingers to his face. "How could I let him kill you when I love you so much as this?"

Duncan caught her close as his vision blurred, the tears streaming down his face as he murmured her name. She had given him the greatest gift of all in those few words alone, and he could not speak for the lump in his throat.

"Do you still love me, Duncan, despite my foolish fears?"

He nodded and his voice was hoarse. "Aye, Eglantine, aye. With all my heart and soul. You need never doubt it."

She smiled and twined her arm around his neck. "Then

kiss me, Duncan, and get us to a priest. I will wait no longer to be wed to you in truth, regardless of how this scratch does bleed."

And Duncan could do naught but comply. He kissed her until they both were breathless, then grinned before he raised his voice and bellowed for Ceinn-beithe's priest.

The lady would have no chance to change her mind.

Epilogue

June 1177
at Château de Villonne

My dear Eglantine—

I sincerely hope that this missive finds you and yours in good health. All is most well here, and I would send my thanks for your speedy dispatch of my spouse last spring. Burke arrived home with naught but a blackened eye to show for his journey. I suspect there is a tale to be told, for he smiles with all the mischief of our son Bayard when asked about it. I similarly suspect that I shall never know the truth of it—but 'tis enough that he was home for the arrival of our second son.

Aye, Amaury entered our lives with a roar this month and thus far has captivated all, including his daunting grandmother. Do you recall Margaux de Montvieux? She is little changed, though she shows a softness of nature in the company of the boys that one might not have expected. She and my father have yet to agree on any matter of import, and, for the sake of peace, we endeavor to ensure that their visits are separately timed.

Your own mother visited us this summer, for she accompanied Brigid and Guillaume from Crevy when they came for the christening of Amaury. 'Twas an event of great boisterousness, for all our blood came to share our celebrations. Bayard along with Rowan and Bronwyn's son, Nicholas, took to tormenting Guillaume and Brigid's young Niall, do-

ing so until the babe wailed. At five summers, Luc and Bri-
anna's Eva is of an age to ignore them all, while her
younger brother Connor watched the older boys with what
might have been awe. God help us when they are all old
enough to run about.

The priest seemed quite relieved when the ceremony was
completed and the chapel was rid of us!

Further to your own family, Guillaume confessed to having found the seal of Arnelaine in his own office, though he
could not understand how it came to be there. He believes
that Theobald did not wager it, after all, though you and I
know well enough that my Burke had it briefly in his possession. How odd that Guillaume found the seal a few days after
Burke's visit to Crevy-sur-Seine!

Arnelaine is now beneath the competent hand of a vassal,
and this season's crops are said to be promising—but Guillaume pledges that the seal is yours, should you wish to return.
Given the tales that Burke shared with me, however, I heartily
doubt you will take advantage of his offer. It sounds as if you
have found happiness finally, Eglantine, and never has a
woman more soundly deserved such happiness than you.

Belated congratulations from me on your nuptials and
every good wish for your continued good fortune. I send you a
gift with this missive and within the care of Alienor's spouse.
It seems he had much fortune at the Champagne fair, though
with such wares I could not have expected much else.

This gift is a most uncommon but undoubtedly useful one.
The companion of Iain is a Gael who has been in my employ
several years—she is both a healer and a midwife and skilled
beyond compare. When Siobhan confessed that she missed
her homeland, I thought of Alienor and the child she carries.
I should not like to think of any woman enduring childbirth
without an experienced hand and fear that in your locale,
skilled midwives may be rare.

And so I dispatch Siobhan to your care, hoping she can be of aid to you and yours. I ask only that you take her beneath your hand as if she were a vassal of your own. She is as loyal as she is gifted.

With every good wish for your harvest and your health—
Your friend,
Alys de Villonne
Lady of Montvieux
& once Alys of Kiltorren

Eglantine folded the missive, knowing she would read it a thousand times again at her leisure. She met the gaze of the redheaded woman before her, noting the freckles across that woman's nose, the lines of laughter fanning from her sparkling eyes, and the solid capability of her hands. Iain was already gone, seeking Alienor, the light of victory bright in his eyes.

"Welcome, Siobhan," Eglantine said in Gael, rolling the name over her tongue as Duncan had labored long to teach her. "Welcome to Ceinn-beithe."

Siobhan smiled. "Aye, 'tis good to hear my mother tongue again. But tell me, Eglantine, if you were born to this land, how do you know Lady Alys? Were you acquainted with her when she lived in Ireland?"

"Nay. I was not born in the land of the Gael."

"Nay? But the language falls so smoothly from your tongue."

"You shall have to tell my husband and teacher that, for he has much to say of my pronunciation."

Siobhan laughed. "Perhaps you should have been born here, for you look as if you belong in these parts."

Eglantine smiled, liking that thought. "Do I then?"

Siobhan's smile broadened. "Aye, it matters naught where one is born, as long as one discovers where one is truly meant to be. Is that not the truth of it?"

A man's cry echoed over the holding, and Eglantine watched Duncan climb the rocks bordering the sea. Esmeraude squealed with laughter as he swung her high, then planted her upon his shoulders. Jacqueline ran alongside laughing, the three of them barefoot, tanned, and wet, no doubt from the sea.

When Duncan's gaze landed upon her, they shared a smile, its heat undiminished by distance. He turned his footsteps immediately toward her and raised his voice in song, her daughters lending their voices to his.

Eglantine watched them stride toward her, her heart filled nigh to bursting. And she knew that Alys's midwife spoke the simple truth.

Eglantine was home because here, at Ceinn-beithe with Duncan by her side, was precisely where she belonged.

"Aye, Siobhan," she murmured, smiling. "That is indeed the truth of it."

Author's Note

For Duncan's song of Mhairi, I heavily reworked a traditional Scottish ballad, bending its words to my (and Duncan's) purposes. The original ballad is called "Annachie Gordon" and has been recorded by Loreena McKennitt with the traditional lyrics. This haunting arrangement is included on her album *Parallel Dreams*.

Happy listening!

Please turn the page for a preview
of the next book in Claire Delacroix's
stunningly romantic Bride Quest series

THE BEAUTY

coming soon from Dell

Chapter One

Ceinn-beithe—April 1183

D
O YOU NOT THINK 'TIS SOMEWHAT HARSH? DUNCAN watched his wife don her veil. She was garbed in somber indigo from head to toe, her fingers devoid of any jewel beyond the simple silver ring he had put upon her left hand.

Eglantine was grimly determined and had he not been so skeptical of the choice she had made, Duncan would have held his tongue while she was in this mood. But they were still in their chamber and, though the assembly waited below, 'twas not too late for Eglantine to change her mind.

"The girl must learn the price of her folly, and better she does so before 'tis too late to change her course." Eglantine anchored the veil to her hair with a heavy circlet, then started to pull the sheer fabric across her face.

Duncan caught her hand in his, stilling her gesture. "'Tis cruel to make your daughter witness her own funeral."

"'Tis our way, Duncan. 'Twas always done thus at Crevy-sur-Seine, by my great-grandfather's decree."

"Not *exactly* thus."

Eglantine sighed. "If we were at Crevy and Jacqueline chose to take the vows of a nun, then such a funeral would be held to mark her departure from the land of the living as surely as if she had died. 'Tis not so appalling to give Jacqueline a taste of what will come of her choice to become a novitiate at Inveresbeinn."

When he said naught, she continued, her eyes glittering. "'Tis no more easy for me, Duncan, than for you to witness this ceremony, but would you not have Jacqueline understand all that she is destined to lose before 'tis said and done?"

"She might find that the life of a novitiate does not suit her, at any rate."

Eglantine frowned, her gaze dropping to their entangled fingers. "She might," she ceded quietly, then met his gaze. "But I cannot rely upon that chance alone, Duncan. I must do *something*! 'Tis my task as her mother to save her from foolish choices."

"'Tis your task as her mother to love her no matter what choices she makes."

Eglantine sighed with exasperation and turned away. "Duncan, you do not understand. I sacrificed all to grant my daughters the chance to wed for love. . . ."

"All?" He endeavored to look indignant, hoping that he might make her smile.

Eglantine did, even if only fleetingly. "And I gained much, 'tis true, but I so wanted to give them the opportunity to find true love. From Alienor, I expected trouble, for she was always willful."

"Marriage seems to suit her well enough."

Now Eglantine smiled in truth. "Not to mention a babe more demanding than she herself. She has no opportunity to be selfish these days." A frown creased Eglantine's brow. "And from Esmeraude, of course, I expect a challenge, for she may be even more willful than Alienor."

"A terrifying thought."

"Indeed." Eglantine shook her head. "But Jacqueline has always been the quiet one who blossomed when given the right opportunity. I was certain that 'twas she who would benefit most from the chance to choose love."

"She has chosen."

"This is no choice! I will not permit her to become a bride of Christ so readily as this."

"But Eglantine, if she has a calling . . ."

She turned away from him, pausing at the portal of their chamber. "Duncan, if she had a calling, I would bless her path, but what Jacqueline has is a fear of men. That demon Reynaud has left a scar upon her that can only be erased by a man wrought of flesh and blood, as well as merit." Eglantine sighed. "She is but twenty years of age, after all."

"Aged for a virgin to remain unwed in any land, Eglantine."

His wife frowned, then appealed to him. "But Duncan, 'tis the mark of Reynaud! Jacqueline is a beauty, she does not lack for suitors. But, because of Reynaud and his crime, she will not even look upon a man. 'Tis wrong!"

"Eglantine . . ."

"I have asked her only to wait two years before becoming a novitiate."

Duncan was taken aback for he did not know this.

"Two years, Duncan! 'Tis naught, but it might well be time enough for her to meet that man of merit who will change her thinking. She is too innocent of the world to make a choice that will govern her life."

"Is that not what marriage is?"

"Duncan! She will not be happy as a cloistered celibate and 'tis her happiness I would ensure, at any cost."

With that, Eglantine swept from the chamber. After a few moments Duncan followed her. He respected his wife's intent, if not her means. His own child, Mhairi, all of four summers of age and blessed with Eglantine's golden hair, took his hand when he reached the hall, her brow puckered in confusion and dismay.

What could he say? Duncan picked her up and kissed her brow, murmuring reassurances to her.

'Twas then he spotted his stepdaughter, standing aside from the proceedings as though she had indeed ceased to draw breath. Noting the resolve in Jacqueline's pale features, Duncan feared that Eglantine's way of bidding her daughter adieu would only erect a barrier between mother and daughter—one that would not be readily removed.

But then, the censers swung, filling the air with heady clouds of incense. Candles were lit and held high, banishing the gloom of an overcast day. The household fell into order, those of higher rank leading the way—first, Eglantine, then her daughters Alienor and Esmeraude. They were followed by Alienor's husband and child, then the closest members of Eglantine's household. The vassals filled the most part of the procession, though 'twould have been otherwise at a great French estate like Crevy. There would have been knights and squires there, visiting nobles and rich relations.

Not so here in the Highlands, and Duncan was reminded once again of what his wife had left behind.

In lieu of more churchmen, the assembly itself began to chant a mournful dirge. The priest began the procession, the empty coffin was hefted to be carried behind him. 'Twas a mock funeral for Jacqueline, she who had left the world of the living to pursue spiritual rewards.

And to serve both God and Christ in the *opus dei*.

Duncan reluctantly stepped to his wife's side, unable to resist a last glance at Jacqueline. She remained to one side, outside the procession. 'Twas as though she had ceased to live on this day. No one spoke to her, none so much as looked at her, by Eglantine's dictate—and indeed, by the custom of their own ritual.

But Jacqueline showed no signs of wavering in her resolve. The girl stood with her mother's straightness of spine, her chin high, her lips set. She was a beautiful young woman, one who usually had roses in her cheeks and stars in her eyes, one whose sweet and giving character was a delight to all in the household. Indeed, in Jacqueline, beauty ran to the core.

She stood there, looking so determined to be brave, to stand steadfast that Duncan's heart nigh broke in half. He watched her catch her breath and blink rapidly when she spied her mother's funereal garb, and he guessed that she was not so certain of her choice as she would have them believe.

Aye, Reynaud had terrified Jacqueline. Duncan wished he could make the matter right. Now he was tempted to lock her up, to compel her to listen to reason, to keep her from tossing her life away.

And that urge showed him that his true feelings were not so different from those of his wife, after all.

"God in heaven," Eglantine muttered through gritted teeth. "I cannot imagine how the girl comes by such a stubborn nature. I do not recall that her father was so obstinate."

Duncan knew better than to suggest the obvious.

The procession wound its way past Jacqueline and out of the hall, into the light patter of rain. The skies hung heavy and gray, threatening a greater downpour. It seemed that even the land mourned his stepdaughter's choice.

And there was naught else Duncan could do.

When they reached the chapel, the family entered first and stood at the front. Even when the chapel seemed full to bursting, still more crowded through the door, the scent of wet wool mingling with the perfume of the censers.

The priest turned and raised his hands, sending a hush through the assembly before he began the funeral mass for the daughter of Ceinn-beithe, Jacqueline.

Ceinn-beithe was behind Jacqueline, only her vows lay ahead. She tried not to think overmuch about it, as her small party rode toward the hills that sheltered Ceinn-beithe on the east. On the far side of these hills and a little farther on, a ways off what might be generously called a main road, lay her destination—the convent of Inveresbeinn.

Her parents had chosen these men to accompany her because they trusted them, but there was not a one among them with whom she might have shared a friendly word. 'Twas a lesson, just as the funeral had been a lesson. This was a lesson in the limited appeal of solitude and silence.

As a novitiate, Jacqueline's world would be one of silence. She knew that, but had not expected 'twould trouble her so much. Even understanding what her mother did and why, did not make the sense of isolation easier to bear. The silence pressed against her ears, making her want to shout, to laugh, to scream.

Jacqueline would persevere at this lesson. She straightened in her saddle, realized 'twould be two days' ride to the convent, and began to murmur the rosary.

But there was more than silence lurking in the hills.

With lightning speed, two men on massive stallions erupted from behind a curve in the road, swinging their swords as they raced toward them. The little party froze in shock as the bandits bore down upon them.

Jacqueline halted her steed, startled by their appearance and ferocity. One of her escorts slapped the buttocks of her horse, sending it fleeing from the fray. Jacqueline could not help but look back.

The attacking knight in the lead struck down two of her escorts before those men even had time to draw their blades. A knight? One heard of knights turning to banditry in France, but not here. Fear rippled down her spine—Jacqueline had learned to expect ill of knights from abroad.

The third of her party had drawn his sword but was no

match for the knight's prowess. He fell to the ground and moved no more.

Then the attacker's course was unobstructed.

He rode like an avenging angel, as if he were determined to smote those who defied him. He was tall and broad of shoulder. His red cloak flared behind him, his tabard was white with a cross of red on the shoulder. His mail gleamed, even though the day was overcast. His ebony stallion was caparisoned in white and red, that fine beast fairly snorting fire.

And when he fixed his gaze upon her, Jacqueline thought her heart might stop. The knight bore down upon her, and she did not hesitate.

Jacqueline dug her heels into her palfrey's sides. It needed little urging to run at full gallop across the peat, but was no match for the long strides of the black stallion.

Looking over her shoulder, she saw the stallion drawing closer, the steam of its breath almost touching her. Jacqueline gave a little cry and tried to urge her horse to go even faster.

But the knight snatched her from her own saddle, so quickly that her breath was stolen away. He cast her across his saddle, so she lay on her belly before him. The sight of the rollicking ground beneath her made her dizzy. He was strong, wrought of muscle and steel. Jacqueline screamed and fought him all the same.

He swore and caught her against him in a tight grip, his arm locked around her chest and arms. He pulled her up so that she sat before him now, though she was no less free to move. Indeed, she could feel every relentless increment of him, his chain mail digging into her back.

"Let me go!" she demanded. She gave a powerful wrench that only rubbed her wool kirtle so hard against his mail that she was sure the wool left a burn on her flesh.

"Nay." He spoke grimly, his French as fluent as her own,

his words tight and hot. "Be still or you will frighten the steed."

"I should think naught would frighten this monster," Jacqueline snapped. A French knight holding her captive was no reassurance at all—she could not help but think of Reynaud, holding her down, heaving himself atop her.

The knight laughed under his breath, though 'twas a mirthless sound. He reined the steed in to a canter and turned back toward his companion. Jacqueline squirmed, though she made no progress in escaping her captor.

Just as she had made none against Reynaud.

Indeed, this knight doffed his helm, easily holding her captive with one arm. When he cast his helm toward a saddlebag, Jacqueline could not restrain her curiosity.

She turned to look and caught her breath, certain she looked into the face of a dark angel. Her captor's lips were drawn to a tight line, his eyes were narrowed to hostile slits. He would have been a handsome man—had it not been for his ferocious expression and the scar upon his cheek.

And the patch over one eye.

Then he smiled, as though anticipating a hearty meal, and Jacqueline panicked. She managed to punch his nose, then kicked the stallion hard. The beast shied and Jacqueline took advantage of the moment of surprise to jump from its back.

She turned her ankle on impact, but ran all the same.

The knight swore with savagery behind her, but Jacqueline did not waste a moment in looking back. She leapt into the scree of rocks, knowing that the stallion could not follow her, and ran as though the devil himself pursued her.

She was not entirely certain he did not.

The knight did pursue her, though, punctuating his progress with oaths. Jacqueline would not consider how he would hurt her if she was caught. She simply ran.

But he gained upon her, for he was much taller and more

agile than she. Jacqueline glanced back when his footfalls grew loud, her own steps faltering at his proximity and his fury. She stumbled, then fell, and he was upon her.

He was quick with the braided leather he carried, but to her astonishment, he was not harsh. He bound her knees loosely, though she was sufficiently hobbled that she could not have fled. He tied her wrists behind her back, moving with such speed that Jacqueline had no hope of a second escape.

She writhed on the ground, seeking a weakness in the knots that she did not find. He stared down at her from his considerable height. He tore a length of cloth from his tabard, exposing more of his chain mail, then crouched before her.

Fearing the worst, Jacqueline flinched but he glared at her. "You are worth more to me whole," he snapped, then reached for her injured ankle.

Jacqueline cried out and squirmed away. She would not suffer his touching her.

He glared at her, snatching at her foot and catching her all too easily. Jacqueline felt the heat of a blush stain her cheeks at his familiarity.

He removed her shoe and stocking with surprising care.

She rolled and tried to crawl away from him, though 'twas not easily done with hands and knees bound. He caught her foot and chuckled. "A fine view, but you cannot imagine you would get far."

"I will not lie meekly while I am raped!"

He laughed then, the sound so surprising that Jacqueline rolled to her back once more. He crouched before her and held her ankle in one hand, his grip resolute but gentle. He had doffed his gloves and his hand was warm.

His smile was nigh mirthless but there was a heat in his gaze that made her tremble. "If touching a woman's foot is akin to rape, then there are far more lawless men in this world than even I imagined." His eyes narrowed as he watched her.

"Or are you so innocent of men that you do not know the nature of intimacy?"

There was a look about him that warned Jacqueline he had thoughts of contributing to her education. "My innocence is not of issue here," she retorted, and tried to draw her ankle away.

He moved his thumb smoothly across her instep, the deliberate caress making her tremble with something that was not entirely fear.

"I should say 'tis. And the preservation of your innocence shall be a considerable concern . . . at least for others." He flicked her a hot glance that made a lump of dread rise in Jacqueline's throat. He did not wait for an answer, but checked the way her ankle had already begun to swell, the heat of his fingers moving deftly across her bare flesh.

Jacqueline did not know quite what to make of him. She had expected him to strike her, but truly, she had little experience of strange men. Let alone such treacherous circumstances. She deliberately kept her expression impassive, hoping she could hide both her terror and the curious sensations his touch awakened within her.

"'Tis not broken," he informed her, bound it, then sat back on his heels. He donned his gloves once more and watched her. She nigh fidgeted beneath the intensity of his gaze and felt she should confess something, anything, whatever would make him look away from her. "'Twill heal quickly enough, Mhairi."

Jacqueline blinked. "Mhairi? I am not Mhairi!"

His eyes narrowed to hostile slits. "You lie."

"Nay. I *never* lie!" Jacqueline bristled. "And I would not lie about my own name. Mhairi is my younger sister, she is but four summers of age." 'Twas a golden opportunity to pretend she did not fear him. "Most can tell us apart."

This seemed to amuse him, however fleetingly. "The Mhairi I seek would be of an age with you."

"Then she is not me." Jacqueline spoke firmly, determined

to save herself with her wits and the truth. None else could aid her here.

"Nay?" His gaze flicked over her ample curves and she saw that his eyes were a startlingly dark green. "Then who are you?"

She answered honestly, certain her identity would prove his error and win her freedom. "I am Jacqueline of Ceinn-beithe."

Something flickered in his gaze, though Jacqueline would not have gone so far as to call it doubt. His words, though, were even more terse. "Who holds Ceinn-beithe in these days?"

"Duncan MacLaren, my stepfather. And my mother, Eglantine. Who are you?"

The knight shook his head, ignoring her question. "I do not know that name. You lie."

"I do not!"

"Then how did he come to wrest Ceinn-beithe from Cormac MacQuarrie's grip?"

"Duncan is Cormac's chosen heir. He is the chieftain of Clan MacQuarrie."

"Nay, in this you clearly lie." His lips tightened to a harsh line again. "Cormac is the chieftain of Clan MacQuarrie."

"Not since he died, some ten years past. Duncan is his heir."

The knight studied her in silence, as though assessing her honesty. Jacqueline could not guess his conclusion.

"And what of Cormac's daughter Mhairi?" He eyed her distrustfully.

Understanding swept through Jacqueline. "Oh, you seek *that* Mhairi! She is long dead, for she killed herself upon her father's insistence that she wed a man she did not love. 'Twas her loss that killed Cormac, to hear Duncan tell it."

"That I can well imagine," he said. He glanced back at his

companion. To Jacqueline's relief the men who had accompanied her were not fatally injured, for they were being marshalled toward her. Their hands had been trussed behind their backs and the other attacker urged them forward at the point of his sword.

"Well?" the knight's comrade called.

"She claims she is not Mhairi, that Mhairi is dead." The knight pushed to his feet. "She claims to be the stepdaughter of the new chieftain of Clan MacQuarrie."

He then smiled down at Jacqueline. 'Twas not an encouraging smile and Jacqueline suddenly doubted that he would free her. He bent and picked her up in his arms, cradling her against his chest.

"Either way," he said silkily, "she will do very well."

"You cannot do this!"

That smile reappeared, no less disconcerting from such close proximity. "Can I not?"

"But you have not even told me who you are, or what you want. I have tried to help, I have told you everything!"

He chuckled then, a low dark sound. "Your mistake, my beauty. Now you have naught with which to bargain." His teeth flashed in a wolfish smile, and he suddenly looked both wicked and dashing. "And I, for once in all my days, hold every advantage."

Jacqueline's heart stopped cold. "Nay!" Jacqueline screamed but made little sound before the knight clamped one gloved hand over her mouth. She struggled, but to no avail. The man kept her silent and powerless with disconcerting ease.

She was helpless in a man's grip once more, prey to his every whim, and his intent was naught good. Fear rose to choke Jacqueline with the taste of that leather, her memory of being captive beneath Reynaud too similar to be denied. She fought to stay aware, knowing that if she fainted she could not aid herself.

But the terror of that memory and the similarity of her circumstances was too strong to be denied. Jacqueline's last glimpse was of the resolute lines of the knight's visage, the flicker of desire in his eyes.

God in heaven, but she could not change the truth. She had fallen prey to a demon on her way to the Lord.